John Preston is the
Touching the Moon, al
Moon in Uganda. He
Sunday Telegraph. Gho

'One of the funniest travel books to come out of Africa'
– *Sunday Times*

'The most entertaining travel book since Bill Bryson's *The Lost Continent*'
– *Time Out*

GHOSTING

John Preston

BLACK SWAN

GHOSTING
A BLACK SWAN BOOK : 0 552 99667 X

First published in Great Britain

PRINTING HISTORY
Black Swan edition published 1996

Set in 11/12pt Linotype Melior by
Phoenix Typesetting, Ilkley, West Yorkshire

Black Swan Books are published by Transworld Publishers Ltd,
61–63 Uxbridge Road, London W5 5SA,
in Australia by Transworld Publishers (Australia) Pty Ltd,
15–25 Helles Avenue, Moorebank, NSW 2170
and in New Zealand by Transworld Publishers (NZ) Ltd,
3 William Pickering Drive, Albany, Auckland.

Reproduced, printed and bound in Great Britain by
Cox & Wyman Ltd, Reading, Berks.

For Maria

'I never learned life was for living' – Lord Reith

'And beyond the Wild Wood again,' he asked: 'where it's all blue and dim, and one sees what may be hills or perhaps they mayn't, and something like the smoke of towns, or is it only cloud-drift?'

'Beyond the Wild Wood comes the Wide World,' said the Rat. 'And that's something that doesn't matter, either to you or me. I've never been there, and I'm never going, nor you either if you've got any sense at all. Don't ever refer to it again, please.'
– Kenneth Grahame, *The Wind in the Willows*

'Ghost: A faint secondary image on a television screen, formed by reflection of the transmitting waves or by a defect in the receiver.'
– *Collins English Dictionary*

PART ONE

Chapter One

As the lights grew dim I started to come alive. People were running about, cameras being trundled into place, microphones swinging overhead like short, stubby cranes. I could hear anxious whispers coming from off to my left, see hands arcing through the gloom. Dark shapes signalling frantically to one another. And there I sat, still and impassive. Dusted with powder, luxuriantly coiffed, my hair set into one sculpted mass.

Trisha was on my left in a sludge green dress with earrings the size of golf balls dangling just above her shoulders. I have been tempted to say something about this. Such things could easily prove a distraction. In earlier days I might well have made a scene. Not a full-scale loss of temper, but still a quick run up the hump, stopping someway short of my confrontational top gear: ramming speed. So far though I have kept quiet. I can't afford to be thought difficult. Not anymore. And anyway, I can always make my points in other ways.

We are a team, Trisha and I — at least in the eyes of the people upstairs who have detected some kind of spark between us, some natural rapport that they think makes us well matched. I am baffled as to what this could be. As far as I can tell we have nothing in common at all. We hardly ever talk to one another when we're not at work, beyond the occasional invigorating exchange.

'Have you seen the hanging baskets on level three?'
'Yes, aren't they delightful.'

She's another of those dauntingly self-assured women. Nothing pliable about her, possessed of a certain professional winsomeness that is nowhere near as alluring as she believes. A thin vein of charm, no humour, make-up put on with a wallpapering brush. A common enough type. Once, towards the beginning of our partnership, about a year ago now, I was invited to dinner at her house. The plan, presumably, was for us to get to know one another better, cement the relationship. She had seen the flash of silver in my coattails – still something for her to hang on to, even now.

I realize that I cannot remember a single thing about the dinner – who was there, what we talked about, even where her house was – apart from the fact we had hake to eat. Nothing particularly unusual about that, I know, but somehow it struck me as odd. Served with considerable ceremony too, as if it was a great delicacy we had long been denied. Grey wedges of it lolling about in a watery sauce.

'Not hake?' cried one of my fellow guests excitedly.

Trisha was bashful but proud.

'Yes,' she confessed. 'Hake it is.'

I suppose I've always been rather traditionally minded about what I eat. Fussy too. Fussy in most things probably. I have hedged myself about with familiarity, in fish and in other areas. I pushed my food around the plate until it threatened to develop some momentum of its own. The invitation was never repeated. Nor, of course, returned.

As a result of our being reckoned to be on the same wavelength, Trisha and I are encouraged to indulge in some brief bits of chat together – to add to the atmosphere of apparent informality. Even this can be a strain. Trisha is a lot more adept at it than I am, always lighting on some tiny topic that will carry across from one item to the next. Coming from an older, more reserved school, this sort of thing does not come naturally to me. Departures from the script, badinage, little bits of off-the-cuff

12

nonsense – while I acquit myself perfectly well, I can always feel the sweat start to creep round the back of my neck. The fear is always there: what if I run out of things to say? Where on earth would I be then?

But tonight, in the light of her foolery with the earrings – there have been other similar instances: brooches, scarves, even some kind of headband – I have presented her with a well-nigh unavoidable subject of conversation. Already I had felt her gaze drift downwards to my collar and could sense a remark brewing behind those charcoal eyes. It didn't take long.

'That really is a marvellous tie you have on tonight, Dickie,' she said, in a voice only minutely underscored by irritation.

And so it is, a real flamethrower of a thing, a riot of different colours and shapes, crammed onto the same piece of material. I was sent it by an admirer. Appalled at first, I'd already thrown it in the bin when I realized it might have its uses. Well, she needs to be shown who she's playing with – a master.

I inclined my head to one side. 'Thank you, Trisha. How kind you are.' It is this kind of old-style civility that has become a hallmark of mine. I never even had to work at it. Came quite naturally, although I've never known where from.

Out beyond our puddle of light people were clustered round, peering in. High above my head hung row upon row of lamps, like long black crows roosting in the rafters. On the far wall I could just make out the bulging gleam of the clock, its second hand bouncing silently round the dial. It was twenty-two minutes to seven. We had been on the air for almost half an hour. Our audience was returning from work, settling down to watch us work our way through the lighter items of the day's news. As is customary on such occasions, I was on what's known as open-line, hooked up to the studio control room from where chatter poured constantly into my ear. Mostly the talk is to do with timings: take it a little more slowly, skip an item, turn and smile winningly at Trisha. On interviews, of course, instructions will be given down the earpiece on what line of questioning to adopt. I, however, need little guidance. Only the faintest nudging is needed to keep me on course, as well as on schedule. I know my stuff.

Not many of us can cope with being on open-line. It means that you can hear everything that's going on in the control room. Every aside, joke, crackle of plastic cups. Most people have to manage on half-line so that they hear only those instructions aimed specifically at them. Trisha, for instance, despite her glazed imperturbability, her perfect timing and her fake sex appeal is still on half-line, and I suspect will stay there.

We are an exclusive crowd, we open-liners. There is a technique to it, I suppose, but like my old-style civility it seems to have stolen in from elsewhere. Principally, you have to make a gap between what's going on on the outside and what, if anything – preferably not much – is going on inside. External and internal activity kept as far apart as possible.

There I was then, the picture of unhurried calm, my public voice as rich and measured as always, while all the time people were shouting, laughing and colliding with one another in my ear. Trisha finished her piece and I read the introduction to the next bit of film about a waterskier, training hard for some forthcoming championships, but hampered by a shortage of volunteers to drive her boat. The film had been shot in one of the old gravel pits alongside the M4, now flooded and used for watersports. The girl – Dawn? Doreen? Everything goes right through me – was explaining her predicament while the wind kept blowing her hair across her face.

Then she was out on the lake, the tow bar in one hand, throwing up a great wall of water as she swept past towards the ramp. Up she went and span round, passing the bar from one hand to another, behind her back, through her legs, twisting round and round before landing back down again and kicking up a further sheet of water. Cut to some spirited clapping by two large women in anoraks – family presumably – in front of the clubhouse. Back to me for some more complimentary things about Dawn or Doreen's prowess.

It was at this point that I heard something in my ear. Something that made me start to falter – at least that's how it seemed – and sent my attention wandering upstairs. I kept right on going, reciting the script, doing my job, but I had slipped away, gone elsewhere. All I heard at first though was the usual chatter, some indistinct mumbling, and a snatch from what must have been an earlier recipe programme being replayed through one of the monitors, 'Mmm. A lovely kebabby sort of smell.'

But that wasn't all. There was something else. Another sound that seemed to lie behind the chatter. A thin, mechanical sort of whine threading its way between the words. To begin with I was inclined to put it down to some fault in the equipment. But the more I listened, the less sure I was. The more I listened, the more it sounded like a baby crying. It seemed to be coming from a long way off; faint, plaintive, yet swelling. Getting steadily louder. I was more surprised than anything else. Not normally prey to distractions, I couldn't work out what was going on. I looked across at Trisha but she, of course, had noticed nothing.

Afterwards, as soon as we had finished, I went to see Tony, the floor manager, a tall, meek man who regards me with such awe that I'm almost apt to find it embarrassing. And as I moved noiselessly across the floor on my composition soles, I was aware of cutting a stately figure. I could sense a certain thrill as I passed by. Everyone knew all about me. Who I was, what I've done. Although I am not really old, I seem to have been around for so long, been through so much, survived such setbacks, I am practically a monument. Perhaps it's only natural that I create ripples.

Tony was talking to an electrician who stood with a length of black cable draped round his neck. He had his chin stuck out as he tried to be more assertive. The man with the cable round his neck shifted from one foot to the other looking faintly contrite. Neither of them had heard me coming. I cleared my throat, or rather gave a little 'Ahem' behind a half-raised hand. Here again, the effect was gratifying. The man with the cable jumped as if it had just given him a shock while Tony, too, hopped back in surprise.

'Ah, hello, Dickie.'

They took a while to settle down again. There was a longish pause. Something – nerves presumably – made Tony take the quite inappropriate step of effecting introductions.

'You know Dickie Chambers, of course.'

The electrician, whose own name passed me by, muttered under his breath and gave a short, ducking bow.

'Yes. Now is there anything I can do for you, Dickie?'

I swung my eyes left. Tony, though hardly quick on the uptake, got the message after a further few moments of uncertainty. The electrician was asked to come back when we'd finished. He laid the cable down on the floor and walked away.

'I am sorry to be a nuisance.'

'Not at all, Dickie. Not at all. Always a pleasure. A most attractive tie, incidentally.'

'Thank you. I just wondered if you noticed anything unusual about the show tonight?'

'Unusual?' The question had completely floored him. 'Unusual?' He rolled his eyes around helplessly. 'How do you mean exactly?'

'Oh, I don't know. I didn't think I was entirely up to scratch.' I have a reputation for being the consummate professional. 'Something not quite right.'

'Not quite right? I can't say I noticed anything. No.

I must say I thought you were every bit as good as always. Perhaps better – yes, if such a thing were possible . . .'

We were moving onto unproductive ground here. Tony, even more confused now, seemed to think I was in need of reassurance. It was not a role he took to comfortably. Nor one I saw any need to encourage.

'. . . an example to us all . . .' He was still going.

I waited until he had finished and asked if I might have a look at a tape of the show, just to see for myself.

'Of course, Dickie. No problem.' He was so very eager to please.

We went up the stairs to the box together. Me in front, Tony two steps behind.

'By the way,' I said, as we got to the top. 'Did we have visitors in here tonight? It's not that I mind, of course. Just that I do like to be told in advance.'

'Visitors? Visitors? I don't think so, Dickie,' he said, joining me on the top step – it was rather cramped. 'No, I'm sure we didn't.'

Although the door handle was nearest to me, I made no effort to reach for it. Tony looked unsure whether to stretch across and open the door for me, but there wasn't enough room.

'No babies then?' I asked.

He laughed thinking that I had made a joke – rare but not unheard of. Then something told him, a slight tremor in the air perhaps, that I was being serious.

'Babies, Dickie?'

He seemed lost for words, before plumping hard for exactitude. 'There were no babies of any kind in here, Dickie. I can promise you that.'

'You're sure about that?'

'Absolutely one hundred per cent.'

'Good. Just making sure.'

I opened the door. The video monitors were stacked up to one side of the control desk. Tony rewound the tape while I took a seat. On screen the first wall of water was gathered in and pulled back down into the lake.

'A bit further. There. Let's start there.'

This time I noticed several things that had made no impression on me before. The way the trees came down almost to the water, the pennants flapping on the clubhouse roof, the shadows of the clouds on the light brown water.

I listened to my voice reciting the script, stopping as the girl turned to start her approach to the ramp, then picking up again as she landed in a cleft of spray and swept back to the shore. I pulled my chair in closer as the film finished and the picture switched back to me.

This was the point I had heard something, I was sure of it. But there was no sign of anything at all. My voice didn't stumble. My eyes gave nothing away. There was nothing to suggest my attention had strayed.

'Looks fine to me, Dickie,' said Tony, still sounding wary after our exchange on the stairs.

He was right. I thanked him for his patience. After further inquiries as to whether there was anything else he could do – 'Oh no,' I said, 'I mustn't take up any more of your valuable time' – he turned and went back downstairs, leaving me alone in the control room. For a while I toyed with the idea of running the film again, but there was no point. I knew there was nothing. The certainty only made it worse. Before I had been curious. Now I was mystified.

I could have sworn I had heard a baby crying out. This, though, wasn't an ordinary cry. It was like nothing I had ever heard before. A shriek, first of surprise, then of pain mixed with entreaty, rising higher and higher until it tapered off altogether; like a length of wire, very thin wire, being pushed sharply through the middle of my ear.

Chapter Two

Driving home that night the mist was even thicker than usual. It drifted off the river in great folds and seemed to sit above the road, trapped between the verges. Occasionally cars went by in the opposite direction, dark, apparently driverless vehicles travelling as slowly and uncertainly as I was, tyres hissing on the wet tarmac.

I sat quite upright behind the steering wheel, head twisting nervously from side to side as I tried to work out where I was. On either side of the road it was just possible to make out the shapes of houses, hidden down mist-choked lanes. Lighted windows glowing yellow through the gloom. I even stopped for a while trying to get my bearings. As I got out of the car – the heavy door swung open as if someone was pulling it – the mist seemed to press up against me, damp white air swirling all round. It streamed through my fingers and ran up my sleeves. Stationary, things were no clearer than they had been before. All I could see were the faint trunks of trees crowding the lay-by, their tops hanging poised somewhere over my head. Drips falling on my shoulders. I got back in and drove off.

Then, half a mile or so later, I swung the car first left, then right through a long S-bend. There must have been something familiar about the angle of the turn. All at once I realized just where I was. I felt hugely relieved, as if I had rejoined the map after veering off altogether for a while. But no, it was all right. Everything was fine. In fact, I was practically home.

This stretch of the river is noted for the wealth of its residents – some of us are really rolling – and for the quaint nature of its architecture. English cottage style predominates, with some grander, more eccentric houses down by the water. It's like a little slice of something generally thought to have disappeared, a careful recreation of English village life that few of us can ever have experienced at first hand. We picked it up – appropriately enough – from television. Almost all of us around here work in television. Some don't work in television as much as they would like. Others who started off there have been brought low by old age, madness, drink or disgrace. But scarcely anyone hasn't been in television at some stage. It's made us suspicious, careful about our privacy. Behind our high hedges we tend to lead isolated lives, as far removed as possible from the lives of our viewing public.

I turned into my driveway and stopped. Ahead of me were a pair of large metal gates. These are electronically controlled and were installed recently at considerable expense. I have a weakness for gadgets, and at the time I was guarding my privacy with particular care. I had become, I suppose, something of a recluse. They were the latest thing, I was told, for those who wished to shut themselves away from the world, to insulate themselves from unwelcome surprises. A special device, built into the gatepost, would only open the gates upon recognition of my voice. No-one else could get in unless the system had also been programmed to recognize them.

Unfortunately they have caused nothing but trouble. The procedure should be simple enough. I sit in my car, open the window and announce myself to the gatepost. The gates then swing magisterially open to admit me. In two years this can't have happened properly more than half a dozen times. They are, it seems, peculiarly sensitive to atmospheric conditions. Once, three weeks after installation I returned home late one night, not feeling at all well, fearful that I might even have been pursued. I opened the car window, said who I was and waited impatiently to be admitted. Nothing happened. I tried again. The same thing. The gatepost – my own gatepost – was refusing to recognize me. I pleaded with it, implored it to see sense, but to no avail. It was having none of it. I had to spend the night curled up in the back of the car until the repair men came out in the morning.

Had I been using my normal voice, they wanted to know? Of course I had, I answered angrily. Did they think I'd been doing impersonations? They couldn't understand what had gone wrong. And try as I might, I couldn't help feeling that the gates had subjected me to some sort of moral judgement.

The mist had thinned out, but there was still enough of it about to cause the usual problems. Only after a number of attempts did the gates start to swing back on their hinges. They are supposed to open together of course, to create the right, suitably grand effect. For reasons that the repair men have been unable to work out, this always fails to happen. While the right gate is vigorous enough and almost bursts open with excitement at my arrival, the left is rather different, a pathetic halting affair that lags far behind like a dog dragging a wounded leg. I veer between irritation and finding this a strangely moving sight as the left hand gate struggles to perform the one task it has been designed for.

My headlights picked out a brief assortment of scenes from the garden as I made my way up the drive. The garden needs attention, there is no doubt about that. I have done almost nothing since the gardener stormed off. I had never imagined he would be so sensitive. For a while I tried out a few boys from the village without much success. It's not as if the vegetation is running amok or anything like that, but the grass is a lot longer than it should be and there are molehills dotting the lawn.

I had a run-in over the garden with my neighbours, the Pinkertons, in the summer. We share a fence. They complained that some fruit trees of mine were spilling over onto their side. I offered them as much of the fruit – plums – as they wanted but they were having none of it. They disapproved of me, didn't want my plums or anything else. I invited them over to inspect the problem from my side of the fence. They came, a tiny, fragile, elderly couple, shooting distrustful glances at me as we walked around the grounds. To break the ice I asked them if their union had been blessed with children – or indeed grandchildren.

No, they said, very sharply and almost in unison, they did not have any children. Sensing some common ground, I launched into my own feelings about the inadvisability of procreation: population explosion, Earth toppling off its axis, time for responsible people – ourselves – to speak out, and so on. Throughout all this the Pinkertons began to look more and more agitated, whispering to one another and shuffling their feet about in a way that I should have known signalled trouble. But I paid no heed and pressed blithely on. As soon as I had finished they explained, in taut, unhappy voices, that their not having children had nothing to do with my arguments – none of which, incidentally, they felt able to agree with. It was due to the fact that they were brother and sister.

Momentarily put out, but soon rallying gamely, I said the first thing that came into my mind. 'All the more sensible then to exercise restraint.'

They both stared at me in astonishment and soon afterwards, as if already fired up, began to make veiled threats about a formal complaint to the council. Clearly they thought that I would do anything to avoid yet more unfavourable publicity. I wanted to tell them that they could hardly be more wrong. I was beyond all that now. So far beyond – or so I imagined – as to be well-nigh invulnerable.

We had a look at the trees – the branches were heavy with rotting fruit, the grass round about stained and spattered with purple juice. I made suitably conciliatory noises. Then, by way of a diversion, I asked them if they would like to see the spinney. Further glances of suspicion – what was I trying to lure them into? – and then curiosity got the better of them. Keen gardeners, they couldn't resist it. Yes, they said with cautious enthusiasm, they would like to see the spinney. A rash offer on my part, as it turned out. I hadn't been in this part of the garden for months, and we found our way blocked by a wall of knotted tendrils that rose up almost sheer before us.

'Here we are,' I said merrily. 'Let's see if we can find a way in.'

At that moment there were sounds of breaking branches from the other side of the wall. Bursting out of the greenery came a small child, covered in mud, twigs stuck in her hair.

It took me a while to recognize her as the grand-daughter of Mrs Potter, my cleaning lady – I hadn't seen her that often before, and besides, the child really was filthy.

'Why,' I said, 'it's little Zena.'

There was no response. Leaning forward, I tried again, as stilted as ever in my dealings with children.

'Hello to you, little Zena.'

I had no idea what she was doing in the spinney, and no opportunity to find out either. The child stopped in her tracks, turned to face the Pinkertons, and began to hiss with such ferocity that all three of us shied back in fright. Then she turned and ran back towards the house. The Pinkertons, I saw, were greatly shocked by this. They were holding on to one another for support and evidently thought that I had staged all this to discomfit them still further. The walk round the garden was at an end. I promised to do something about the trees. The Pinkertons looked as if they didn't believe me – quite rightly – and issued further threats about what would happen if I didn't. We said goodbye. That was several months ago. Since then the growth has continued unchecked.

My house is sizeable, but not particularly grand compared to a number of others round here. Nor does it have any of the more ridiculous touches – castellations, flamingos – favoured by some of my neighbours. I bought it when I was first married and all seemed well with me. When it ceased being well I stayed here, mainly through lack of initiative, but also through obstinacy. For a while I became an embarrassment, someone to be avoided. It was odd. I had embarrassed myself, of course, but part of me couldn't help finding a strange sort of satisfaction in it. I felt more solid than I had ever done before, trailing my disgrace round the district with something akin to pride. But soon afterwards I developed my obsession with privacy, and before long I stopped going out at all. Seldom spotted, rumoured to have gone very strange – hair down below shoulders, bearded, torn clothes, etc., I was believed to have 'let myself go'.

I suppose I had, sitting alone at home surrounded by my poison-pen letters. I received hundreds of them, piled so thick they wouldn't fit through the letter box. They came as a big surprise. I, who excited no feelings at all within my own breast, seemed to do so quite readily within the breasts of others. Perhaps it was my infuriating air of self-possession that prompted these outpourings of rage. Perhaps people just felt let down. I found it oddly comforting. I liked to think of my correspondents with their scissors and their old newspapers, carefully cutting out words and letters and sticking them in place. Beforehand, I would never have believed that this kind of thing still went on – the wrinkled paper, the jumble of typefaces. Surely the effort alone would take the edge off their anger. But not at all, they're at it all the time. It's a thriving little cottage industry. I felt a strange sense of kinship with my poison pen-pals, thinking of them frothing up into hysteria over their pots of glue. Such anger, such passion – and all directed at me.

Now I am back, rehabilitated. When I walk through the front door and pick up the mail that Mrs Potter will have left inconveniently stacked on the banisters – it always blows onto the floor when I come in; Mrs Potter leaves by the back door – I can pretty well guarantee that there won't be one single letter of abuse. Not one. Instead my postbag will be bulging with invitations to open church fêtes, head up charity appeals, sit on school governing boards. All those things designed specifically for those of high moral character. Or in my case, those who have atoned sufficiently for a brief lapse in behaviour while under considerable stress.

I drew up by the front door, turned off the engine and sat for a while. Quite often I find myself reluctant to go back inside the house. I have this idea that I will come back one night and discover that everything has changed. The furnishings are different, the garden has been tidied up and there is someone inside waiting for me. I have no idea who. Not my wife. Certainly not my wife. More like someone I have never met before. At least no-one I can remember. It's so vivid I can almost believe it.

But when I do get back in, of course, everything is exactly the same. Just the way I left it. I have never been that bothered by my surroundings. A certain degree of comfort, an imposing exterior, that's all I ask. When we first moved in I gave my new wife a free hand with the furnishings. I'd never seen her so enthusiastic about anything before. At the time I found this charming. How my heart swelled as she unwrapped each new purchase. I grew used to sitting docilely by as a steady stream of delivery men unloaded the results of yet another day's shopping.

'Where do you want the ottoman, Dickie?' they would ask.

'Ah, over there, I think. By the bar stools.'

Once a magazine came to do a feature on us, to catch a flavour of our harmonious home life. I watched as the photographer and his assistant gazed speechless round our living-room. They'd never seen anything like it before – the astonishing jumble of styles, the absence of any restraining hand.

'Now then,' I asked them, 'where would you like us to pose?'

They went into a huddle. There was a lot of shaking of heads. Eventually we were set against some boxes that my wife hadn't got round to opening, with the French windows behind opening out onto the lawn, then in perfect trim.

As expected, the mail blew from the bannisters as soon as I opened the door. Before I turned the light on I could see a number of white envelopes fluttering slowly to the floor. I stooped to pick them up and felt a twinge of something in my back – sciatica probably; my mother had problems with her joints. These little signs of ageing always take me by surprise. Partly this is to do with my being a mythical figure and feeling resentful – I think quite understandably – that death should creep up on me at the same rate as it does on everyone else. And partly it's a personal thing: I just can't believe it. How can I be slowing up when I haven't got properly started yet? Naturally I'm reluctant to take responsibility for my life. How can I be sure it's really mine, if I haven't picked up someone else's by mistake? Once I thought there was something welling up inside me – an inner tap had been turned on, and it was this that had brought me to the edge of disaster. Now I'm not so sure. I have my doubts. The more I think about it – and I've been thinking about it a good deal lately – the less certain I am.

All this and back pain too. It's really no fun living alone. I straightened myself up and went into the living-room. There weren't that many letters – a small postbag compared to what I'm used to. Most were local appeals of one kind or another. Would I allow a new scout hut to be named after me? Well, I might. I might. I shall have to do whatever's best for the welfare of the children.

For some reason, I was restless. I tried sitting down but I fidgeted so much that in the end I got up and paced around. I don't know why I was like this. Afterwards I wondered if this might have been prior warning of a kind – I clung on to the idea for a while – but I doubt it. I'd eaten earlier at work. It was more likely to be indigestion. And yet, however hard I tried, I couldn't shake off this mounting sense of anxiety. The more I cast about for an explanation, the more this dread seemed to thicken about me; to steal up and hang across my shoulders like a damp cloak. A feeling too – and this came all in a rush – that I was being watched. That I was no longer alone.

I even turned to check, spinning around. But the room was empty. As empty as always. The feeling, however, persisted. It wouldn't go away. I wasn't sure what to do. Although all my instincts were to keep moving about, I tried to keep as still as possible, as if I might be somehow less conspicuous that way. So I stayed where I was, standing by the french windows, staring out across the lawn, as this fearfulness lapped all around.

Hoping that it might distract me, might help to calm me down, I made an effort to concentrate on what I was looking at. There was nothing much to see – a dark sweep of lawn sloping down to a line of silhouetted tall trees beyond. I kept staring though, and after a while I did begin to feel a little calmer. I really must learn to take things easier, I told myself sternly. I owed it to myself. And to so many others.

I must have looked down, briefly switched my gaze elsewhere. The next time I looked up, something caught my eye. At least that's how it appeared. I couldn't be sure. I just had this fleeting sense of something tall and swaying. Faintly luminescent. It seemed to flicker, almost to brush across the corner of my vision. At first I wondered if it might be a tree branch. A silver birch perhaps that had sprouted on the grass and shot up. Strange though that I hadn't noticed it before. I may be neglectful, but I'm not normally that unobservant. I went over to the door to turn on the garden lights. When I got back there was nothing there. I moved closer to the window to make sure. The same sweep of lawn, the same darker smudge beyond. But no silver birch. Nothing. Amid my disquiet I felt rather annoyed, as if I was the butt of some practical joke.

Several minutes went by. Slowly something dawned on me. The longer I kept staring through the window, the more obvious it became. I must have imagined it. What other explanation could there be? And once again I began to give myself a good talking to. Overwork had clearly made me jittery, prey to these tiny delusions. Though of no great consequence in themselves, they were clearly pointers to a measure of strain. Hardly surprising under the circumstances: I drove myself very hard. Everyone knew that.

At that moment a figure appeared on the other side of the glass. No more than a few feet away. It was turned away from me. Head bent, shoulders hunched in this pitiful aspect. Strands of hair plastered down. Clothes grey like the mist; torn, almost in shreds. An impression of utter wretchedness. I must have cried out; to have whimpered or wailed in some way. Alerted to my presence, it began to turn round. Arms jutting forward beseechingly, thin and crooked. Wheeling slowly about.

I lunged for the curtain pull. The curtains yawned open like a mouth, almost spilling off the ends of the rail. I heaved on the other drawstring. Just before the curtains closed, I caught a glimpse of the face outside. I couldn't help it – even though all my instincts were to look away. As I sank to the floor I shut my eyes tight, hoping to shut it out. But it rose before me, sweeping in and rearing up on the insides of my eyelids. And with it came a memory – not clear, but distant, from long ago – of seeing photographs of bodies cut from the Arctic ice years after they had died. Many years later. The flesh preserved, but shrunken and yet slack. Almost jellified.

For a long time I did nothing. Just sat there, bunched up, rocking myself back and forth. I couldn't believe it. I wouldn't allow myself to believe it. I wanted to make it all go away. It was as if the more I rocked back and forth, the more chance I had of detaching it from my mind. Once again I had the feeling – familiar enough – that this must all be a mistake. I was picking up the wrong signals. Things would correct themselves in a moment. They had to. If I waited long enough everything would return to normal. A mistake, that was all. Simply a mistake.

So I stayed there, arms clasped round my knees, head buried in my thighs. Rocking, rocking. All rolled up tight so that no-one could get in. I hadn't drawn the other curtains. Outside it was quite dark, any stars too faint to show through the remains of the mist. I felt exposed, alone. Also terribly weak, as if my limbs had turned to lead. For a long while I did nothing. Then finally I crawled over to the other windows and managed to pull the curtains, without looking through the glass, reaching blindly up to tug at the drawstring.

After that I couldn't think what to do, so I turned on the television. A show hosted by one of my less immediate neighbours: glistening black hair, shining like pitch, sloppy grin, conspiratorial winks. The audience beside themselves. I watched it through to the end. Then the next programme. And the next, right until closedown, and the white dot shrank away into the depths of my set. All the while I kept spinning round to make sure I was alone, thinking I could hear footfalls in the hall, tapping on the glass. Desperate for distraction I could find nothing that held my concentration for more than a few seconds. In the end I just stayed put, listening to the clock chime its way into the small hours. By the time I finally crept up to bed it was almost two o'clock.

I woke shortly after four, pulse racing, pyjamas soaked in sweat. Not at all myself. As I struggled back to consciousness I wondered if I had called out in my sleep. For an instant it seemed as if the echo of my voice still hung about the room, disappearing off under the pelmets.

'Hello,' I called out. 'Is anybody there?'

I could hardly recognize my own voice. Tremulous and squawky, it threw itself around the room like a trapped bird before settling back in my throat.

'Hello?'

Still nothing.

There was a faint grey light in the bedroom, not bright enough to see by, more like a worn patch in the darkness. I had the impression it had turned very cold outside. My hand reached for the switch and turned on the bedside lamp. I took a mouthful of water – there was a thin film of dust on the surface. The water tasted old, almost peppery, as if it had been standing there for weeks. I could hardly bring myself to swallow it.

Something had disturbed me, roused me from a sleep normally marked only by dreams of extraordinary wholesomeness: green sloping meadows, snowy crags, gingham dresses, lambs a'leaping. My nocturnal world was like a kind of clockwork Switzerland. But this felt more solid, more immediate than that; almost like a visitation. It was like staring down a long tunnel where someone was hurrying forward to meet me, eager to renew acquaintance.

A shape was materializing out of the darkness, bearing down. Something cloaked, elusive – to me anyhow. Had I lived in an earlier century and been possessed of a more excitable nature, I might have flailed my arms about and shouted 'Begone' in my still quavering voice. As it was, I simply drew back, turned my head aside and did my best to switch my attention elsewhere.

I could hear the wind whistling through the trees. Downstairs, out on the gravel, the swing seat was rocking on its chains. I lay there for some time, propped high on the pillows. Finally my heart started to slow down. I even read for a while. All the time though I couldn't shake off this sensation, not so much of being observed – I was quite sure by now that no-one else was there – but of acting in a way that covered the possibility of my being observed. Thus, when I turned down the page of my book, leaving the hero mired in seemingly endless boyhood, and put it down on the bedside table, I was acting with all my customary contrivance, behaving as I felt someone should behave after reading in bed and having shrugged off – bravely – an unpleasant shock to the system.

Here I am, I thought, acting quite naturally. And then: There He Is, as if viewed from quite a different perspective. Dabbing at his nose, a persistent cold not quite shaken off, reaching for the light, and settling himself down once again. But then this was hardly new. Quite the contrary. I'd been living with it off and on for more than fifty years, this sense of somehow hovering above myself in varying stages of disbelief. And really I preferred it that way. There were things I had no desire to be reunited with. Besides, it was the middle of the night, far too late to be worrying about such things. Especially when I could be somewhere else: up near the snowline, leaning on my shepherd's crook.

I straightened the sheets and took one last sip of the peppery water. Amid the relief as I started to sink into sleep I felt a familiar sense of abdication, of bidding adieu. I couldn't help thinking of a burial at sea, preferably also at night – a dim shape sliding from under a brightly coloured shroud, one hand poking out from the coverlet waving to the crowd. 'Goodbye everyone. My dear friends, goodbye.'

Then just before the waters closed above my head, I stopped quite abruptly. My feet had jarred against something; they could slide no further. It was as if some carefully planned assault on my composure was underway, an attempt to undermine my very being. But hadn't I suffered enough already? Been subjected to my proper quota of indignities – and plenty more? I thought that was over, finished with. After all, it wasn't as if I was asking for much. Quite the reverse. I only wanted to be left alone.

Chapter Three

Sometime during my middle period – post-youthful celebrity, pre-national disgrace – I hosted a gameshow series in which families were required to compete against one another for prizes so undesirable that a number of people didn't even bother to take them home. But still they kept coming, as if the prizes were of no great consequence. It was appearing on television that mattered. I used to wonder, privately, if they might not be in it for reasons not so far removed from mine; confirming their own existence, both to themselves, of course, and to as many other people as possible.

The idea behind the show was perfectly simple. I gave one member of each family – preferably the oldest – a word. Another, usually the youngest, got another word. With the aid of visual clues helpfully provided by me as and when I felt moved to do so – 'For God's sake, go a little easier on them, Dickie,' the producer would moan in my ear – for I could be an exacting host – everyone had to guess the chain of connection that led from one word to the other.

Somehow the fact that each team consisted of a family gave the game a special tension. It was as if each family hoped, indeed expected, some natural understanding would come to their rescue; clues passed down the bloodline from parent to child helping them on to victory. It never happened. Sitting up in my Quizmaster's chair, in my hard oval of light, I used to watch the contestants writhe in agonies of incomprehension, beating their brows and groaning with frustration.

'Is it something to do with fir trees, Dickie? Or at least forestry of some sort?'

'Oh, dear me. No, I'm afraid not. You're completely on the wrong track there. Would it be of any help if I was to say the words, Grand Canyon?'

So it was now as I sat slumped on the sofa while dawn broke all around me, the sky above the river foamed with orange and white. I forced myself to steer my mind down channels, twisted, sclerosed, searching for some chain of connection.

It was no good. I was as hopeless at it as the others – and some of them, believe me, could barely count.

'Flower. Nursery. Rattle, Mr Palmer.' I would cry, waving around pictures of babies and market gardens. 'Can't you see? It's so easy.'

Now I too was lost among the fir trees, desperate for guidance. For a long time there was nothing. The sky righted itself, the clouds rolled in. And then what came next could hardly have been less welcome. Another hi-tone assault on my inner ear, thankfully not as acute as last time, nor as disturbing. Just this dry, tuneless tinkling that seemed to rise up from all around like an orchestra of triangle players stirring into life.

Phone? I thought at first. Old-fashioned bell telephone ringing somewhere nearby? Stop me if I'm getting close. It was too irregular for that though. Visual clue perhaps? Surely a little assistance . . . But I was doing myself no favours. What then?

It came at me in a rush. Not phone at all. No, no. Not phone. Oh no. Something quite different.

When I was young, every Christmas and birthday my mother would give me a metal puzzle – shiny interconnected metal shapes you were supposed to take apart and put together again. They were almost the only concessions she made to my being a child. Twice a year, the same rectangular box with instructions printed

34

on the underside in a language I couldn't understand. Contents wrapped in tissue paper tinkling away lightly within. To begin with I was inclined to put this down to vagueness on my mother's part. Vagueness and a certain lack of imagination. As time went by though I started to see it in a less sympathetic light. Worst of all were my efforts to solve the puzzles while my parents – my mother took a keen interest, my father less so – looked on. I had no aptitude for this sort of thing, could hardly disentangle two of the rings, let alone a chain of them. I remember how cold they were, how the metal never seemed to warm up despite repeated handling.

I must have been about eight when I started wearing the greaseproof paper. I had caught a particularly severe form of eczema. It broke out all over my hands, deep crevasses in my skin where tiny red rivers threaded their course. There was some discussion as to whether the eczema might have been brought on by handling the metal puzzles. The doctor favoured the idea; my mother was having none of it. My father, characteristically, played no part. Whatever the cause, I was, the doctor warned, highly infectious. Human contact of the most innocent, casual kind could prove disastrous – a lesson that I was to take to heart with far greater eagerness than anyone could have foreseen. For the first time I felt a sense of potency shift briefly within me. My hands were like great raw instruments of contagion. I had only to advance, arms outstretched, fingers spread wide, for people in my path to run frantically for cover.

After a while, to cut down on the risk of my infecting anyone else, my mother encased my hands in bags made from greaseproof paper. When I swung my arms about the bags fluttered and cracked like sails in the wind. Through the greaseproof paper my hands looked unrecognizable: grey and swollen, as if they were swimming around on their own in old, soapy water.

It was around this time that I realized that I was the product of an unhappy marriage. Only rarely, I think, does one come across a couple with less in common than my mother and father. Whatever brought them together in the first place has always remained a mystery to me. After the briefest of courtships they had married during the early days of the last war. This in itself was not unusual; thousands of other ill-matched couples did the same. But there was something about the scale of their incompatability, their inability to relate to one another on any level, that set them apart from everyone else. It's possible that my mother thought my father had a lot more money than he in fact possessed. Some years before he had invented a type of propeller, widely adopted by the manufacturers of pleasure steamers. But he had been swindled out of any profits by his partner, also his oldest friend, who vanished one day and left my father well nigh bankrupt.

I see now that my father must have presented an almost irresistible target to any swindler. He was an odd mixture of abstraction and precision. Much of the time he appeared to be entirely disengaged from anything going on around him. Often literally so. He slept a great deal in the day, always in the same position: sprawled in his armchair, mouth open, head thrown back over his right shoulder, as if one ear was always cocked, listening for anyone creeping up behind. When awakened, he would start suddenly with a gasp of surprise, looking blankly around him. I could see the lack of recognition in his eyes as he stared at me, struggling to remember who I was. Even awake, he gave the impression of having mislaid a vital part of himself somewhere, a lost key which if retrieved would bring order and sense back into his life. Until then he remained floating helplessly in suspension. At night, I would often lie in bed hearing him pacing back and forth along the landing, often for hours, his tread soft and even on the linoleum. I thought at first that he must be sleepwalking. But once when I opened my bedroom door, expecting to see him pass by with arms extended and eyes glazed, I found he was wide awake – rather more so in fact that he usually was during the day. He stopped, asked me in a whisper if I was feeling all right, nodded a lot; then fetched some water from the bathroom – I remember he over-filled the glass – and helped me back into bed. Afterwards, I liked to think – though not with any measure of confidence – that he had been standing guard over me.

Alongside this, he had an extraordinary memory for the dates on which things – almost inevitably quite insignificant things – had happened to him. The first time he had eaten a certain dish – olives, tinned pears, oxtail – or what he had been wearing on a particular occasion. Complete outfits would be recalled, even down to his socks. They were like little reminders he'd latched on to, to convince himself that he'd really been there at all.

My mother too was thwarted, though in more obvious ways. She was a tall, thin, angular woman with a beautiful curved neck which held out the promise of a better-looking face than she actually possessed. Her life had not come up to expectations. The prime offender here of course was my father. Closely followed by the one unavoidable proof of their union: myself. My mother's attitude towards me swung about wildly. At times she was warm, attentive, kindly. But it never lasted long. It was as if she were trying these things on for size to see if they fitted – they did not – or how long she could carry them off before her resolve gave out. Bidden onto her knee – it was like sitting on a gear stick – she would bounce me up and down for a while, going through the motions of motherhood, before growing impatient and setting me down. Then the distance would yawn between us once again, more unbroachable than ever.

We lived in a small detached house in North London, dwarfed on either side by its larger neighbours. There were few visitors; my parents scarcely knew anyone. I seldom went out. Occasionally I would meet other children and try to strike up a friendship. I might even go round to their homes and meet their parents.

But my efforts would always founder soon afterwards when the time came for me to invite them back to our house. I was ashamed of what they might find: my father sprawled asleep in his chair, my mother grimly dismembering something in the kitchen, while all the time the radio shook and rattled.

My mother listened to the radio all the time – plays, comedy shows, church services. And at a far louder volume than seemed necessary. It was like an aural blanket she had hung up between herself and the outside world. The noise of the radio ran through our house as if it were part of the foundations. I grew to loathe it. I saw it as an intruder, almost like another child, sitting there squat and black on the dresser and upsetting what little harmony existed. I wanted to hurl it to the floor and watch it explode in a shower of sparks and bursting valves. The radio and I seemed locked in competition, both of us vying greedily for my mother's attention. It didn't take long before I realized that I could never hope to match its attractions, however hard I tried.

But slowly my attitude changed. I began to recognize the different radio voices, even to adopt them as my own; and to welcome the steadiness, the authority they represented. Their faultless, measured tones, their air of unhurried calm, the richness of their delivery. I knew their names, the way they sounded, their peculiar inflections. These men became heroes to me – Royston Vaughan, Derek Winstanley, Godfrey Teale. Of course, I'm going back a long way now. They seemed to come from somewhere quite free of any doubt or uncertainty. For a while, at least, I felt that nothing could go wrong as long as they rumbled away.

I also realized around this time that my mother was colour-blind. One day we went to buy a new school uniform. My mother was her usual peremptory self with the shop assistant. The issue of a blazer came up. She waved away the first one he brought over without even having me try it on. The same thing happened with the second. I assumed that this had something to do with the fact that I had my hands encased in the greaseproof paper; perhaps my mother wished to spare me any unnecessary fiddling with buttons. But then I saw that she was getting more and more irritated. A wardrobe was open, full of various sizes and colours of blazers. She pulled one out, draped it across my chest and said, 'There. Now what's wrong with this?'

The assistant looked surprised. 'I thought Madam said that the blazer was to be scarlet.'

'Yes,' said my mother, 'that's quite right.'

'I . . . I beg your pardon, but this blazer is green.'

My mother seemed at first not to have noticed what he'd said. Either that, or she was so unaccustomed to being contradicted that it took a while for it to sink in.

'Green? What are you talking about? Of course it's not green. It's scarlet. Purple at a pinch. Can't you see that?'

Having sensed weakness, she was not about to back off now. 'Can't you tell what colour it is?'

The man didn't know what to say. He opened and shut his mouth a few times. I began to feel sorry for him.

'I imagine you must be here on some sort of special placement scheme,' she went on. 'All very commendable, no doubt. None the less it does seem unfortunate. Someone in your position. The potential for confusion can hardly be overstated. I suppose we should at least be grateful that you haven't become a bus driver.'

'What do you mean?' he asked unhappily.

'Why, your being colour-blind, of course.'

'But I'm not colour-blind,' he said.

My mother put on her most tolerant voice. 'I'm afraid it's my sad duty to tell you that you are.'

'I'm not colour-blind,' the man repeated in a quiet, dogged sort of way. 'I'm not.'

'You must be.'

'No . . . Perhaps . . .'

'Yes?'

'Perhaps you are . . .' He tailed off.

My mother sighed. She did it in such a way as to suggest she was limbering up for a swift victory. 'There's only one way to sort this out. Richard, what colour is this blazer?'

They were both waiting for my answer. My gaze switched from one to the other. A sense of dread soaked through me.

'I don't know,' I said.

'Don't be absurd. You must know. What colour is it?'

When I didn't say anything, I was led, dragged really, over to the front of the shop, where my mother held the blazer up against the window.

'Tell me.'

I looked up at her. My eyes were already filling up with tears. I didn't want to have to say anything. Above all, I wanted to be back home; up in my room, with only the voices blaring through the brickwork for company.

'Well, come on.'

Colours flooded in and out of the blazer as it was held there, awaiting my verdict. I couldn't be sure what I was seeing anymore. Not for the first time I doubted my perception. Nothing was fixed; everything shifted about. Colours, shapes, they all rearranged themselves at will. As soon as you thought you'd got something pinned down, it slid away and altered again. In the end my decision seemed to have as much to do with loyalty or the lack of it, as with anything else.

'I'm afraid it's green,' I said.

My mother drew her other arm back. For a moment I thought she might hit me. Instead, she thrust the blazer into the hands of the assistant, grabbed my arm and marched out of the shop. She didn't let go until we'd walked all the way home.

The incident was never mentioned. Two weeks later she called me into the kitchen and explained that she was giving me the money to go and buy a new uniform. She had to raise her voice over the sound of the radio.

'Aren't you coming too?' I asked. But she gave no sign of having heard me.

Chapter Four

The only break in our routine came once a year when we went on holiday. This was principally for my benefit – I was left in no doubt about that. My father showed little interest in his surroundings, least of all in any change in them. My mother made it clear that it would take a lot more than a holiday to transform her life into something acceptable. Not that I cared. I didn't mind where we went. I just wanted to get away.

On this occasion we caught a train down to the South Coast, and then a chartered bus collected us from the station and took us round the bay to our hotel. In the harbour yachts were moored in neat lines either side of long pontoons. Around the front, seats made from old oil drums and painted yellow had been set out in rows facing the sea. Old people – some of them older than I'd ever seen before – sat there staring out at the sun glinting weakly on the horizon. An avenue of windblown palm trees led up to the hotel, a huge mauve building blotched with brown where the sea air had eaten through the paint. Small drifts of sand blew through the front door and piled up around the reception desk.

The hotel had a special facility, much prized by its guests. There was a room where parents could abandon their children in the care of trained staff, all of them brimming with jollity and keen to please. Perhaps, it was suggested, I can't remember who by – either by my mother, or else by the moon-faced receptionist who put his head down very close to mine when he talked – I might enjoy playing there, along with the other children.

I very much doubt it, I thought. But I went anyway; looked round the door, saw the cluster of preoccupied faces and heard the gusts of laughter. I shrank back in horror, hung there on the threshold. I couldn't go in. All that joining in, that participation. I knew it wasn't for me. A few heads turned my way, one of the jolly women started towards the door, a welcoming look in her eye. But I was gone, back to the long, cold arms of my mother. She wasn't getting rid of me that easily.

Our days on holiday soon fell into as familiar a pattern as our days at home. We would take packed lunches down to the beach and spread out a blanket in the lee of one of the breakwaters. Bales of seaweed lay across the wooden beams, like horses' manes hung out to dry. There was more sand in the lobby of the hotel than there was on the beach. Large flat stones creaked and slid under our feet. The water was a dull green colour. All day a chain ferry made its way back and forth across the mouth of the bay to the spit of land on the other side. Lying with my ear to the stones I could hear the chain booming away in the depths. Everything sounded hollow, as if the beach itself was just the thinnest of crusts across a huge empty cavern below.

My parents seldom argued; they didn't feel strongly enough about one another for that. On this particular occasion though they had exchanged words before we even got down to the beach. There had been a disagreement over the packed lunches. My father wanted crab sandwiches – not unreasonably, I thought, considering we were by the sea. My mother refused, saying she would have nothing to do with any creature that let its young cling to its unarmoured parts. She got her way. But the atmosphere was even more strained than usual as we spread out our blanket.

While it was not unheard of for my father to show enthusiasm for anything, such occasions were certainly rare. There were, however, times when a tremendous struggle seemed to be going on inside him; he would cast off his usual torpor, becoming instead almost childlike in his eagerness to pursue some particular whim. We had not been sitting on the blanket for more than a few minutes when he announced that he wished to go swimming. The news did not provoke much of a reaction. My mother ignored it, probably thinking it was a deliberate attempt to irritate her still further. Swimming was hardly an unusual thing to want to do; it was just that we had been on holiday for more than a week without my father showing any desire to go near the water. Once he had made his announcement he seemed suddenly to be overcome with doubts, as if it might not be such a good idea after all. I saw him looking at me uncertainly. He wanted guidance. What could I do? It wasn't my place to get involved. I looked away. Now he had no choice; he had to go through with it.

He got undressed beneath a towel. First he removed his shorts. I was happy to see them go. They were enormous baggy things, stretching down to just above his knees, and almost as wide as they were long. My father's legs stuck out beneath, thin and bowed. I was embarrassed to be seen with him dressed like that. I'd tried to tell him he looked absurd, but nothing I said made any impression. He wasn't bothered about his appearance. Instead, I'd taken to pretending he was nothing to do with me, doing my best to share in the general merriment as he flapped past.

With some difficulty he slipped on his swimming trunks, before making his way unsteadily across the stones down towards the sea. At the water's edge he turned and waved. My mother didn't notice; she was reading a magazine. I suppose I must have waved back, lifting one of my inflamed hands, still encased in its greaseproof paper. My father strode into the sea until the water reached his chest, and then, launching himself gingerly forward, he started to swim. I saw his head bobbing up and down in the water, rising to the top of one wave and then disappearing over the other side.

I lay back, gazing at the clouds sweeping across the sky. As I did so I was aware, if only dimly, of the particular nature of my outward self. Yes, I thought, here is the air moving over my distinctive profile, somehow moulding itself to my outline, helping to form the almost-Mount Rushmore cast of my features. On the inside, of course, it was a different story. There everything seemed both fluid and brittle; sloshing about but apt to break at any moment. Even at this stage I found myself pining for a measure of solidity that I suspected I lacked. Nothing too specific as yet – that came later. Little more than this nagging sense of insufficiency.

I must have drifted off to sleep. I woke to the sounds of a commotion close by. There was a lot of shouting. It took me a few moments to make any sense of what I was seeing. A man was being carried up the beach. Someone was supporting his shoulders, trying to get a grip on his slick, slippery skin. Another man had him by his ankles. A third was endeavouring to pull up the swimming trunks that had slipped down over his hips. I got to my feet. My mother looked up to see what was happening. I found that I couldn't speak. The words refused to come. I could only point across the beach to where my father was being lowered gently onto the stones.

We had to run round the tops of the breakwaters, feet sliding about, to where my father lay stretched out on his back. One of the men was crouched beside him giving him the kiss of life. My mother must have explained who we were. Someone put their arm around me. I remember how it hung like a dead weight over my shoulders. The man giving my father the kiss of life was growing redder and redder as he blew into his mouth. There was no reaction. After a while he stopped. The skin on my father's face already had a strange pallor to it. His lips jutted forward, as if seeking something to fasten on to. His eyes were open but turned upwards, the pupils had almost disappeared, as if he were thoroughly exasperated by the whole business.

Soon two other men arrived, running down the beach, their long coats blowing out behind them. One of them introduced himself as a doctor. He looked at my father and started whispering to the man with him. He then ran back up the promenade. We stood around for a while, no-one saying anything. Finally an ambulance came. My father was lifted onto a stretcher, strapped in and driven away.

I can't be sure what happened next. Presumably I was taken back to the hotel. I don't remember my mother being there; perhaps she went to the hospital with my father. One of the women from the nursery was deputed to look after me, but they were short-staffed that day and she kept having to rush off and check on the other children. I was quite sure my father was dead. No-one, though, would break the news to me. It was not until the afternoon that I overheard two people talking by the reception desk as I was coming down the stairs.

'It's hard to believe,' said a woman's voice. 'Not here. I mean, really.' She sounded affronted, as though someone had behaved inconsiderately and spoiled things for everybody else.

'I know,' said another voice, also female. 'Isn't it extraordinary? I can hardly believe it myself.'

There followed some further discussion about how we were all at the mercy of the elements. Fire, in particular, but water too; the great bringer of life, but also an effective instrument of its removal. I made my way past them. They didn't notice me.

Down in the basement was what the hotel advertised as a games room. A table tennis table, warped and rickety, stood at one end of the room. A darts board, bulbous with mould, was fixed to the wall at the other.

The room smelled of damp, a special salty kind of damp as if the sea were just waiting to reclaim it. There were no windows. What light there was came from a single bulb set up high in the ceiling that cast faint watery patterns on the walls. My father and I had come down here once for a game of table tennis, but had given up after a few minutes. It was hopeless, like two people fixing on the one thing they had the least aptitude for. I couldn't hold the bat properly. My father was so uncoordinated that even hitting the ball back and forth three times to play for service proved beyond him.

Now I picked up the ball and threw it against the wall. The noise, an empty tock, reverberated round the room, spreading out to meet the waves on the walls. I fetched the ball and tried again, this time just catching the echo of the first throw with the noise of the second. Then I did it again, and again, and for a moment it seemed that the room was filled with the sound of table tennis balls bouncing about in some kind of perpetual motion. I stood there feeling as if I was trapped inside these patterns of noise, that they were pulling tighter and tighter like slip knots. I had not yet begun to feel grief for my father, that came later. But more than ever I felt I had no control over anything that happened to me. The ground could give way at any moment, I saw that only too clearly. There was a balance to things – somehow I saw that as well. A balance that I couldn't possibly understand, but would have to tread very carefully in future for fear of upsetting.

They found me later that afternoon, apparently after instigating a full-scale search of the hotel. Several people arrived all at once, a number of guests and various hotel staff, smart in their maroon uniforms. Everybody seemed very pleased. 'We've found him, we've found the bereaved boy,' I could hear someone shouting up the stairs outside.

They advanced awkwardly across the floor to where

I sat against the wall, crouched in a pale green glow.

What was I doing here? they all wanted to know. What had happened? Was I all right?

'He looks all right,' said someone.

I hardly had a chance to say anything.

Had I been here long?

I couldn't answer this; I had no idea how long I'd been there.

Had I got lost?

'Yes,' I said, obligingly turning my face up to theirs, 'Yes. That's it. I got lost.'

Chapter Five

My father's funeral was a poorly attended affair: some cousins, one or two neighbours observing the proprieties. A few days beforehand my eczema cleared up. It vanished almost overnight. One morning I woke up, my hands clasped over my chest, fingers interlocked. When I got them apart there was nothing to be seen, apart from a few faint pink patches. I turned them over and over, unable to believe my eyes. The next day even the pink patches had gone. It seemed so unfair that in some strange way my father's death should have led to this. I couldn't shake off the idea that he had given his life in order for me to have clear skin.

My mother and I were given clods of earth to drop into the open grave. My mother threw hers in with an angry backhand flip. There was a sharp crack as it hit the coffin. I let mine drop from my hand. It bounced on the strips of turf that had been laid all round the grave and rolled slowly in. Afterwards the other mourners were invited back for tea. They all made excuses. In the end my mother and I went home on our own.

I never realized I would miss my father so much. At night I lay awake listening for his familiar tread in the corridor. Although he had hardly been much of a pillar of strength to me, I still felt his absence keenly. The house seemed empty without him around, the air even thinner than before. And I too felt emptier. Somewhere inside me a plug had been pulled. Never strong, my self-belief ebbed away. So too did what little faith I had in my ability to change or affect anything around me. At first I wondered if I hadn't simply inherited my father's deficiencies, his sense of being in some way detached from life. But as time went by I grew to believe that his death had signalled a halt in my development, had left me with an absence where some vital part of myself should have been. Without anyone else to do it for me, I did my best to sustain myself, and, in failing, only grew to doubt myself the more.

Naturally, I kept this all to myself. On the outside I couldn't be faulted. Impeccably behaved in public, I had always attracted admiring comments from strangers, much to my mother's annoyance. See how his hair – flaxen – falls across one eye. Exquisite! Such a shame about his poor hands, but you know he never seems to complain. So brave! We felt a glow just being near him. And so on. But these surface flatteries brought me little by way of reassurance. Increasingly, a gap was opening up between the way I was perceived and the way I felt. On the inside I knew that I could be undone at any moment, that I needed what few resources I possessed to keep myself from falling apart. The slightest thing might set me off, betray my helplessness. I had to be constantly on my guard. Perhaps it was the strain of doing so that led to this mounting conviction that I was quite unqualified to be living my life. That it was too big a burden for me to carry. I wanted to surrender it, thrust it away from me. Let someone else take the strain. But who? There was nobody I could think of. No-one at all.

Least of all my mother. After my father's death my relationship with my mother changed in several important ways, none of them welcome. Although I was only twelve years old she compensated for the loss of my father by treating me as a replacement adult. In the evenings we would sit uneasily together while she would try and start up conversations about the important topics of the day: the National Health

Service, the new housing estates being built everywhere you looked, the Beveridge Report.

'Steady on,' I wanted to say, 'these are big questions. How can I possibly answer them? I can barely dress myself unaided.' In the end, of course, I said nothing. And indeed, nothing I might have said would have made any difference. She wasn't really looking for contributions; she was practically talking to herself.

What I couldn't understand was that she'd never discussed such things with my father when he was around. Presumably this was how she imagined her life might have unfolded had everything gone according to plan: lively debates on important issues of the day. All I was doing was filling a role. At the time though I was acutely aware of not being able to match up to her expectations. It was as if I found myself caught in limbo between childhood – where I never felt I really belonged – and this pretend adulthood, for which I was equally unsuited. Before long, grief at my father's death had turned into confusion, and then resentment at his having left me to face all this on my own.

This sense of isolation followed me to my new school. Every morning I would make my way down the hill with the thin white sweep of the stadium roof in the distance. The streets fanned out all round and the dark gulleys through which the trains ran back and forth to still more distant suburbs. A bus took me the mile or so to the gates of the local Secondary Modern. There I would join the crocodile of pupils making their way up the short drive to the main entrance, swinging their satchels and scuffing their feet along the sides of the kerbstones. Except that all my efforts to become part of that throng ended in failure. No-one wanted to know; they were all too preoccupied to pay me any attention. And so I hung back, envying them their assurance, their solidity, the way they never seemed at the mercy of these sudden gusts of grief or loneliness that threatened to send me sprawling. What few friendships I made – and I'm using the word in its loosest possible sense here – never lasted long. Always they got swept away and I would start again with a new cast of faces and the same great unbroken circles of mistrust. I expected too much from people – I see that now. Above all, I wanted their trust, their unwavering loyalty. Anything that fell short hurt me much more than I cared to admit; I became unduly sensitive to slights, always on the lookout for any signs of betrayal. And yet I couldn't lose this yearning for intimacy, this desire to batten onto someone else and let some of their assurance rub off on me. However much I tried to push it down it soon sprang right up again.

It drove me to make a confession to one of the other boys. He must have been a few months older than me – at least he was in the class above, and this was enough to confer on him a wisdom, a depth of experience that I couldn't help but admire. Even among his fellows he stood out as appearing quite untroubled by any doubts or uncertainties. I remember how he walked, with his hands thrust in his jacket pockets and his toes turned inwards, and somehow this served to lend him added distinction. I came across him one afternoon by the chapel, not doing anything in particular, just hanging about, as if waiting for some approach. It was one of the first days of summer. Above the high iron crags on the schoolhouse roof the sky was turquoise blue. I asked if I might have a word. If he was surprised he didn't show it. Instead he simply turned and began to walk. We made our way through the red brick cloister, past the clock tower and out between the Nissen huts, left over from the war and now turned into classrooms. We didn't stop until we got to the vegetable garden. Rows of greenhouses stretched off into the distance and alongside them, down at ground level, long rectangular flower beds covered with glass frames.

We stopped by one of these. The flowers within were all twisted and tangled and pressed against the underside of the glass. The sun was as hot as I could remember it, beating down on the greenhouse roofs and sending the glare bouncing about from one to another. I started to explain that I had no real friends, that I craved a degree of human warmth that never seemed to be forthcoming. Again, he didn't show any surprise, but bent his head attentively enough to mine. There were twin red patches on the tops of each of his cheeks and his thick black hair curled over the fold of his collar. Whatever fears I'd had quickly disappeared. Instead I had the sense that I had made the right decision, that he was just the sort of person to confide in, and the sense of relief this brought caused me to talk for rather longer than I had intended.

'It must be difficult for you,' he said when I had finished.

'Oh, it is difficult, yes,' I agreed. 'It's awfully difficult.'

'Vexing . . .'

'That's it exactly.'

Although he offered no advice as such, or did little more than listen as I talked, I was left with a feeling that an understanding had been established. Nothing too close as yet, but still something to build on. That night I went to bed feeling more heartened than I had done in a long time.

The next morning I was crossing in front of one of the classroom blocks on my way to a lesson when I saw him, standing by a bench with a number of other boys. As I got closer they began to chant. Still I kept walking. It took me a while to make out the words.

'No friends,' they chanted. 'No friends. He's got no friends.'

They were laughing so hard that they almost lost their rhythm. It was too late to go back. I had no alternative but to walk past them. My confessor stood watching me, quite unabashed, the same attentive, benign expression on his face as he'd had the day before. Laughter swelled, stretched out and started to recede behind me. I turned the corner beyond the bench, stopped and lent against a wall. For a while I thought I wouldn't be able to move any further, that if I tried my knees would give way and I would sink, like empty trousers, to the ground. Then I heard voices coming closer. My tormentors were following me. I forced myself to start moving again, keeping close to the wall, before sinking into an open doorway.

Laughing all the time, they walked past without noticing me.

I was not a bright boy at school. Things went through me; nothing much stuck. Just about the only thing I had any aptitude for was singing. I discovered this quite by chance. At the age of eleven all pupils were auditioned for the school choir. The music master, a wizened, white-haired man called Baines, would play a hymn on the piano while each boy attempted to sing along. A hideous series of squawks and grunts invariably resulted. Expressions of pain creased up Mr Baines's face. It was as much as he could do to carry on playing.

When it came to my turn something quite unexpected happened. I opened my mouth and there issued forth a clear piping treble. I was so surprised I stopped. I looked round in case anyone was throwing their voice, using me as they might a ventriloquist's dummy. But no, they all looked as surprised as I did. We started again, Mr Baines frowning at me, as if I wouldn't be able to pull off the same trick twice. A number of the other children tittered in anticipation. He started to play. The same thing happened. Up, up I went, racing up the scale. Higher and higher, leaving the others far behind, hoisting myself into a new golden land of opportunity. '*Will your anchor hold in the storm of life?*' I piped.

> '*Will the clouds unfold their wings of strife?*
> *When the stray tides lift and the cables strain*
> *Will your anchor drift, or firm remain?*'

*   *   *

54

When I finished Mr Baines started to clap, encouraging everyone else to do the same. Making it quite clear they were being coerced, the other boys began to join in. Slow, reluctant applause rang around the classroom. As someone whose anchor subsequently drifted much further than anyone could have envisaged – if indeed it ever touched bottom – I can only acknowledge the aptness of the hymn. Here though was the first evidence of those lilting cadences that have stood me in such good stead. A musicality of tone that has given my speaking voice its own special timbre. When people have tried to dissect my peculiar appeal they always come back to my voice, attractive, easy on the ear, but somehow more than that, as if there's a tune going on somewhere under my tongue. As time has passed the melody may have faded – I sang no more – but the melodiousness has lingered on.

And so I joined the choir. We practised after lessons during the week and sang at matins every morning. Before long I was singing solo. There was a steady turnover of choir members. Older boys were constantly dropping out when their voices began to break. First they would become hoarse, and then, a few days later, they'd emerge croaking and grunting with pride.

My own voice, though, showed no sign of breaking. I grew concerned, tugging away at my testicles to try and speed things up. I thought I did this unobtrusively enough, until one day when my mother remarked, 'You're clutching yourself again, Richard.' She said this in the sort of offhand way that suggested she wasn't shocked, or anything like that – she just didn't want me to think she hadn't spotted it. Eventually, long after my contemporaries had all left the choir, my voice did slip down an octave or so. It found its own level and stayed there. I stopped singing, although Mr Baines claimed he could hardly tell the difference and implored me to carry on.

By now I was of an age where I could be left alone. My mother took to going on long solitary walks. To begin with I had no idea where she went. I never asked; no information was volunteered. And then one day she returned home with someone else. Visitors were sufficiently unusual for me to pay special attention. I walked into the kitchen to see a man in a check shirt and trousers, hitched high up over his waist, holding a spirit level to the wall. The man's name was Tom, my mother said, and he would be doing some repairwork around the house. There was plenty of scope for this. Due to subsidence, those houses on either side of us had begun to lean in opposite directions; so much so that our house was being slowly lifted out of the ground, uprooted like a tooth.

We shook hands. Tom had brown, weatherbeaten skin, stretched so tightly over his face that when he smiled – a broad but narrow grin that showed more of his bottom teeth than his top – his ears bent forward. It gave him a look of being rapt with attention at everything that was said to him. At first I found this reassuring. He looked as if he was not only transfixed, but also deeply concerned; as if he held your best interests at heart. But after a while I began to wonder if Tom really took in anything. If indeed he wasn't perhaps a bit simple.

Certainly he was the most literal-minded man I think I have ever met, never abandoning a subject until he had exhausted it completely. He would latch on to a particular topic – the fluctuating price of butter, I remember, was one such example – and become almost physically stuck there, unable to move until jolted on to something else. There was mention of an accident, it seemed he had been knocked down at some stage by an earth-moving vehicle. But there was no way of telling if he had been any different beforehand.

It was clear he doted on my mother, following her round with a look of blind adoration on his face. I assumed she wouldn't care for this, that Tom's days would be numbered as a result. After all, she hadn't taken kindly to it when I'd tried much the same thing.

On the contrary, though, she seemed to like it. I couldn't understand why – it was impossible to imagine Tom talking about the Beveridge Report with any greater fluency than I had done. Before long he came almost every afternoon around five o'clock and often stayed for supper, seldom saying anything during the meal, but always lowering his face towards the table when he'd finished so that the light caught his plate and he could see if it was completely clean.

Slowly I began to be aware that my mother's mood brightened whenever Tom was around. She was more agreeable, warmer, even girlish – though this last involved what seemed an extraordinary degree of contrivance. Towards me, Tom behaved with unfailing courtesy and good humour. I responded with deep suspicion. For a long time I wasn't even sure what I suspected him of, or at least couldn't bring myself to believe it. But gradually I began to see. He had stolen my mother's heart. Not exactly stolen it, no. He didn't have enough initiative for that. She had picked him out, apparently at random, and thrust it into his hands. But why? I could see that he was a blank slate on which she could inscribe her will, along with anything else she wanted. But wasn't I blank enough already? Surely she didn't have to go to these lengths.

All this time I still didn't know what Tom did for a living. I only found out quite by chance. About a mile away from our house there was a park. A grim, joyless place, thickly wooded on one side, sloping sharply downwards on the other. Local residents came there to drag their dogs round the narrow pathways. What few flowers there were seemed to die just as they were on the point of coming into bloom. The pond was choked with rubbish. A few ducks struggled to stay upright on the brown muddy banks.

I went there one day to try and work out what to do with my life. I was now close to school-leaving age. My teachers could detect no sign of any skill or talent, even aptitude, in me and had been unable to advise on a particular career. There was some suggestion that I might set my sights on becoming a steward on an ocean liner. I tried to delude myself that they'd recognized something in me, some hidden ability, that made me suitable for such work. Was this to be my destiny then? Bent low in a starched white jacket, proffering trays of sandwiches? Maybe it was. I had no idea what to do. The thought of having to fend for myself filled me with horror. While there had never been much in the way of comfort or reassurance at home, the outside world still seemed a much colder, more daunting place.

I looked up from all this uncertainty to see Tom. He was pushing a wheelbarrow in his half-running, half-walking way round the inner circuit of the park. He must have gone right past without noticing me. Although he was already some way away I could hear him loudly greeting the regular visitors as he trotted by. And there too, sitting on another bench, wearing an orange headscarf and staring out at the rows of houses that stretched all the way to Mill Hill, I saw my mother. She was sitting by herself, apparently lost in thought. If Tom kept going – he showed no sign of stopping – he would shortly pass her. I felt a mounting sense of anxiety. It was as if Tom was embarked on some blind orbit round our lives. An orbit which, if completed, was going to leave us all fused indissolubly together, bound into the same shapeless mass. It was like being back in the table tennis room at the hotel with the invisible slip knots tightening around me. I knew that my life was not properly my own – by now I was quite sure about this. And yet, I was suddenly aware too that if I was to be at the mercy of outside forces, I wanted them to be bigger ones than these.

Was it at that moment that I saw myself towering spectrally over people's lives? Spun between their aerials, disappearing down their chimneys? I can't say so with any certainty; things were a good deal vaguer than that. Whatever impulse had me then, I can hardly call it initiative, or even ambition. It felt more like self-preservation. The choice was all mine. If I stayed where I was and did nothing, then that would be compliance. If not, I would be breaking these bonds. My legs felt very heavy. When I got to my feet I felt as if I was wearing a suit of armour. I could hardly walk. Gathering up my things as quickly as I could, I lumbered off out of the park. Down the hill Tom ran on regardless.

Chapter Six

Thanks to Tom's attentions our house was in better condition than it had been for years. There was hardly a thing he hadn't touched. He had fixed it back onto the foundations, repointed the brickwork and recently embarked on rewiring the entire place. Clusters of wires hung dangling from the ceilings and brushed the tops of our heads as we walked below. My mother had entered into the spirit of all this with unusual gusto. Furniture had been replaced, crockery too. Carpets had been beaten and shampooed. A certain amount of redecoration had already taken place. Tom had encouraged my mother to take a free hand over the choice of colours – not that she'd needed much prompting. I can scarcely bring myself to describe what had gone on, the assault upon the eye that our living-room now represented.

Partly as a result, I took to spending more and more time up in my room. With the radio as my guide – it still thundered through the walls whenever Tom wasn't around – I began to read aloud, trying to measure my voice to that of the announcer. I felt that with practice it was possible that I too might develop the same consistency of tone, the right note of gravity. In the evenings I would take myself upstairs and lie on my bed, book in hand, and try to force some authority into the way I sounded. It was slow going. For a long while

I thought I wasn't getting anywhere. But at last all the hours of practice started to pay off.

One night I picked a passage, started to read, and suddenly it was as if this voice drifted out of me like ectoplasm, not mine as such, yet fully formed and independent, carrying its own weight:

'So things passed until, the day after the funeral and about three o'clock of a bitter, foggy, frosty afternoon, I was standing at the door for a moment, full of sad thoughts about my father, when I saw someone drawing slowly near along the road. He was plainly blind, for he tapped before him with a stick, and wore a great green shade over his eyes and nose; and he was hunched, as if with age or weakness, and wore a huge old tattered sea-cloak with a hood, that made him appear positively deformed. I never saw in my life a more dreadful looking figure.'

Tom took to bringing my mother presents. Small things at first – a pair of secateurs, some piano wire – which became bigger as his confidence grew. One day he arrived with a television. It must have been one of the first sets ever made. Tom never said where he had got it from. The television was the size of a fridge, he had to lower it off the back of a van and bring it into the house on a trolley. None of our neighbours had one; they crowded around the front door and asked if they could come in and have a look. My mother said there wasn't room for them all – they'd have to go back home and wait for an invitation.

She didn't know whether to be excited or dis-approving. Once Tom had got the television into the living room she walked round it, opening the sliding doors and then shutting them again quickly, as if she didn't dare to look inside. He fixed a plug onto the end of the wire and connected it up. After a few minutes a fuzzy black and white picture swam onto the screen, and what sounded like a hailstorm came through the speaker. Tom turned the set first this way and that, heaving it onto its corners, trying to improve the reception. It made little difference. Not that they seemed to care. The television was manoevered back onto the trolley and over into a corner where a glass table had been.

Before long they would sit and watch it every evening, faces rapt, with this monochrome reflection flickering across Tom's stretched, shiny face. They never noticed me as I stole away upstairs to practise my reading.

It was the day after my eighteenth birthday – characteristically I had opted for the minimum of fuss – when my mother announced that there was something she wished to tell me. It had been a long time, she said, since she had taken a holiday. The last occasion, I may remember, had been cruelly interrupted by the death of my father. She paused, I assumed in deference to his memory. When she started again I saw that she was nervous, strangely unsure of herself. She pushed a strand of hair back over her ear. It kept falling forward. Her hair, I noticed for the first time, was going grey. I realized that my mother was getting old. Her face was lined. She wore no make-up other than a thin line of pale blue eye shadow across her eyelids, and this was a recent addition. She walked now with a faintly rollicking gait and complained of pains in her hips. I felt a sudden stab of tenderness for her. It couldn't have been easy, bringing up a child on her own. In future, I resolved, I would make more of an effort to help, try to make myself a more worthy son.

I was so preoccupied with this resolution I hardly heard what my mother was saying. Now I began to pay more attention. She wished to go away, she said. I nodded encouragingly, completely failing to see what was coming. Preoccupation with her welfare had blinded me to my own. She wished to go away, she repeated. But not with me. It had all been arranged. I could remain at the house by myself if I wished, or go and stay with my cousins nearby.

And there was one further piece of information. Just one other thing she wanted to add. My mother was going to be accompanied on this holiday – destination never specified – by Tom. This was announced in a faintly defiant sort of way, as if she expected some exclamation of surprise from me. I don't think I let her down here.

'With Tom?' I cried. 'With Tom? But why?'

My mother shrugged, gave some brief outline of Tom's sterling qualities – reliability, constancy, immense aptitude for handiwork of almost any kind.

I felt a huge wave was about to break under my heart. 'Not Tom,' I wanted to say. 'Mother, please. The man's an imbecile. He should be the one who's staying behind. You and I could be so much happier by ourselves.' If it was stimulating conversation she was looking for, I was the one. I had been selling myself short. Not giving of my best. The force of my feelings took me aback. There were primitive things heaving away here, things I had hardly glimpsed in myself before. It was as if I had received a direct hit amidships. Everything was being swept from its appointed place. I felt I might burst, great torrents of water cascading all around, washing me away.

In the event I said nothing. Not a thing. Did nothing either, gave no sign of what was going on. So much had rushed to the surface that I didn't know where to begin. That was part of it; I wasn't sure if I any longer had the right vocabulary to express what I felt. My mother, evidently thinking this silence signified indifference, maybe even approval, left me where I was and made her way stiffly along the veranda – a recent innovation – and out onto the sun deck – yet another.

I went upstairs to lie down. I needed to think things over. Due to the rebuilding work I had been moved temporarily from my usual room to the spare bedroom across the landing from my mother. As far as I could remember no-one had ever used it before. The door was stiff on its hinges, there was dust on top of the skirting boards. On the wall by the bed hung a painting of a couple sitting in a gazebo on a moonlit night. The man, some sort of cavalryman by the look of his uniform, was staring devotedly into the girl's eyes, a hand resting lightly on the sleeve of her ballgown. She looked to be more divided in her attentions, one eye on her admirer, the other taking in the stillness of the scene, as if weighing up just where her loyalties lay.

I lay there wondering what to do. A major decision looked imminent. My presence here was no longer required, that at least was obvious. I would have to light out on my own. But I wasn't substantial enough for that, not by a long way. What else could I do then? Abandon myself to circumstance? But where was I to start? If only there could be some sign, an indication of which way to go. Towards the top of the picture on the horizon was what the artist had apparently intended to be a tree, its branches spread out against the night sky. Lack of technique, however, had given the tree the look of a lone figure signalling wildly to the couple in the gazebo, waving long, telescopic arms in a bid to attract attention, but getting nowhere.

That night I had a dream. It had been years since I'd remembered a dream, or even been aware of having had one. Once or twice I'd woken up with a dim sense of having just chased something out of my head, but this was much clearer than anything like that. I dreamed I got out of bed and went downstairs, out to the back door. I had no idea what I was supposed to be doing there; it was as if I had surrendered even more control of myself than usual. I drew the bolts on the door and pulled it towards me.

There waiting on the mat outside was my father. I hadn't been expecting to see him − I hadn't been expecting to see anyone − but somehow the fact that he was there didn't take me greatly by surprise. To begin with I thought he looked quite normal. He was wearing a dark suit and a shirt without a collar. His hair was cut shorter than usual at the sides, but it seemed to suit him, making his face look longer, more composed than I remembered. What struck me more than anything else was that he appeared to have grown. Then, as I looked down, I saw that his feet were suspended some six inches above the ground. They were like the feet of a medieval saint in a painting, as white as alabaster, and pointing vertically down at the ground.

'Thank God you've come,' he said. 'I'm freezing. I couldn't get in. I couldn't even be sure I'd got the right house.'

His voice sounded much the same. A little chesty perhaps, as though he was just getting over a cold, but otherwise no different. Even so, I felt I should be asking for some proof of identity. I needed to be quite sure this really was my father; that it wasn't a trick, some ruse to gain admission. But all the time I couldn't take my eyes off his feet as they hung poised and useless in the air, swinging slightly from side to side.

He gazed over my shoulder into the kitchen. 'Aren't you going to invite me in?'

I held open the door. Somehow my father made his way past me. He didn't walk in, obviously enough, but at the same time it was hard to work out just how he did manage to propel himself. He seemed to glide about, like a curtain swishing on a rail. He stood in the middle of the kitchen looking around. Neither of us said anything for a while. I saw that he was deeply shocked by all of Tom's home improvements. He picked up a cup and saucer and then put them back down again on the table, hurriedly and yet as carefully as he could. That cowed, bewildered expression had come back into his eyes.

'What's been going on?' he asked.

It was difficult to know where to start. 'All sorts of things.'

'Have you missed me?'

'Yes,' I said truthfully. 'I have. I've missed you a lot.'

He shook his head. 'I've missed you too. I can't tell you how lonely I've been. Most of the time I can't remember a thing. Then just occasionally there are these glimpses, I think I know where I am, but I can't be sure . . .'

He broke off. I saw that he was close to tears. More than anything else I wanted to go over and put my arm around his shoulder, to tell my father that I loved him. But something held me back. I wasn't used to feeling protective of anyone, apart from myself.

'The worst of it is that I don't know how old I am anymore. Sometimes everything is quite normal, I'm as old as I feel I should be. But then it can all change. Suddenly I'm a small boy again. You can't imagine how awful that is. I have these memories, but I'm not sure if they're mine or not . . .' Again he broke off and swished back and forth, his fist pushed against his mouth, more distressed than ever.

'It's very difficult when you feel upset about something but you can't be sure what it is,' he said. 'All I can remember is being by myself in this big house. It was shuttered up. I don't know where my parents had gone, whoever they were, but everyone had moved out. I even had to cook for myself, although I was far too young to know the drill. But I was sure that if I waited there for long enough my parents would come back and everything would be all right.

'Then one day I heard this car pull into the drive. I went outside and there standing on the gravel was the biggest car I had ever seen. It had great wide running boards and a spare wheel mounted along the side. But what struck me most of all was that instead of being painted, it had been stripped down to the grey metal. The whole car looked as if it was made out of pewter.

'A man got out dressed in a navy blue chauffeur's uniform and held the door open for me. I got in and we drove for a long way, four or five hours at least. The further we drove the more the scenery flattened out and the fewer houses there were. After a while there was no sign of anyone else at all, no other cars, no trees, no houses – just grass stretching away on every side as far as I could see. The grass was this bright emerald green, like a carpet. It was so bright it hurt my eyes, I had to look away.

'Finally we pulled into the side of the road and the chauffeur turned off the engine.

' "This is where you should get out," he said.

' "Here?" I said. "Here? There's nothing for me here. What am I supposed to do?"

'But it was as though he hadn't heard me. He got out and opened the door. I didn't move. There I was sitting in the back seat putting on a little show of resistance. But both of us knew it couldn't last for long. He stood and waited for the moment to pass. I got out of the car and stood on the verge. "I'm not a foundling, you know," I said. "I'll be missed."

' "Don't worry," said the chauffeur. "You'll be home again before you can turn round."

'He climbed back inside the car and drove off. I stood and watched as the car grew smaller and smaller. And then, quite suddenly, it had gone. I was all alone. For a while I stood by the side of the road, hoping that another car might come by, but there was nothing. I had no idea what to do. I sat down on the grass and tried to remember some details about my life, just how I'd got here, what might have happened before. But it was hopeless, I couldn't remember a thing.

'After a while I did the only thing I could think of doing. I got up and began to turn around. Very slowly at first, but then picking up speed. I whirled around and around, getting faster and faster, until everything became this blur of green and I could hardly stay on my feet.

'But still I kept on turning. I didn't dare stop in case things were still exactly the same. So I carried on. Around and around. And gradually I became aware that something was happening. I had to make a few more rotations before I could be sure. But I seemed to be getting lighter. The faster I turned, the lighter I was becoming. There could be no doubt about it. I was disappearing, growing fainter and fainter. Evaporating away. My arms went first, and then my feet. Before long I had vanished. After that I can't remember much. It was as if I was blown about on breezes; no control over anything. Swept around, hither and thither. I've no idea how I ended up here tonight. Just a stroke of luck, I suppose.'

He looked at me and I saw his top lip was trembling. 'I don't know why this is happening,' he said. 'I wish we could all be together again. I can't pretend it was much fun, but it was better than this.'

I made a move towards him without being sure just what I had in mind. To put my arm around his shoulder, I suppose. But as soon as he saw me coming he drew back, startled.

'No,' he said. 'You mustn't get too close.'

'Why not?'

'You don't understand. Warmth. Any sign of it and I have to be off.'

'Surely just . . .'

'No, no. Keep away.'

But somehow I couldn't stop myself. Again I started moving across the floor. Now my hands were thrust out, clasped together. Beseeching.

'What are you doing?' asked my father. His voice had got shriller, more fearful.

'Please,' I said. 'Take it. Take it off me, please.'

'I don't know what you mean.'

'My life, take it away. It doesn't belong to me.'

'I don't want it. Don't you think I haven't got enough problems. Give it to someone else. There are people who make a specialty of that sort of thing.'

But still I came forward, my arms extended. As I got closer, almost close enough to reach out and touch him, he turned away. At first I thought he was just trying to ignore me. But having started to turn, he kept right on turning. Once, twice. And then round and round, as if there were a spindle running through him, spinning away.

And as he turned, I could see him starting to disappear – blurring at the edges, and then seeming to melt into the background, until there was nothing left of him but his head and a thin trail of neck. I could see his face, turned up towards the ceiling, but looking more frightened than I'd ever seen him look before. I heard him trying to shout something, but his words seemed to fly apart before they reached me, as if thrown out of a centrifuge. Until, at last, there was nothing left except this faint patch of light and this sound that clung to it for a few moments like the furthest ripples of an echo. Then they too were gone.

For a long time afterwards I just stood there in the kitchen. I felt that things should somehow have become clearer to me, that a way ahead would have been revealed, but I was more churned up than ever. Eventually, I bolted the door, turned off the light, and went back upstairs to rejoin my sleeping self.

Soon after two o'clock I woke up. I could smell burning. A pleasant, autumnal, woodcutter's cottage sort of smell. Not long afterwards wisps of smoke started curling under the bedroom door. Once again I got out of bed – this was turning into a busy night for me – and put on my dressing gown. On the landing the smoke was a lot thicker. I could still see clearly enough but it was getting more difficult all the time. There was a noise too. It took me a few moments to realize what it was – I was still half-asleep. Coming from my mother's room I could hear the sound of screaming, a high, warbling screech that seemed to weave its way in and out of the smoke. I ran towards her bedroom door. At first I thought she must have locked herself in. I had to put my shoulder to it before it gave way and I fell forward into the room.

From the ceiling above my mother's bed a cluster of

cables was throwing out a stream of sparks, bucking and twisting wildly as it did so. Piles of clothing had caught fire, and what looked like they might have been cushions. A line of small blue flames was making its way slowly up the wardrobe door. I got across to the bed. Fireflies seemed to be darting around in front of my eyes. My mother was huddled in the middle of her bed, bedclothes drawn up in front of her. I grabbed hold of her arm. Seeing me, she began to scream all the louder. Then, as I tried to pull her to the edge of the bed, she started banging against my chest with her fists.

'Don't worry, Mother,' I said. 'It's all right. I'm here' – thinking as I spoke that these were words that had long been there inside me, half-formed, waiting for a suitable occasion. And what could be more suitable than this? Wasn't this what every boy secretly dreamed of, rescuing his mother from an electrified bed? But the more I tried to drag her off the bed the harder she kept hitting me. At first I imagined I was dealing with a simple case of hysteria. Her nerves had gone. Self-control too. But as I wrestled with my mother on the burning eiderdown I realized I was wrong. She wasn't just lashing out in all directions. As she pummelled away, her eyes were fixed firmly on mine. She knew exactly who I was. That was the trouble: It came to me all at once that I was the wrong rescuer. Not the one she'd been hoping for – even expecting. Yet again I had found myself caught up in a situation where I had no set role to play.

What was I to do? I couldn't just leave her there – although at this point the temptation was almost overwhelming. Instead I resolved to be less chivalrous, altogether firmer. The way back to the door was already blocked. Even the walls were ablaze. The woodchips in the wallpaper were igniting like matchheads. In places it was falling away in long, flaming strips. I managed to get one of my mother's arms in some kind of lock and dragged her, remaining limbs still flailing about, off the bed and across to the bay window. It had got a good deal hotter. Above us the curtain rail had sprung off its mountings and had begun to quiver and glow. The wardrobe was roaring like an oven. I felt that I was about to melt, to shrivel away. If it should come to that, I thought, at least it wouldn't take long. Bone-dry, I would go up like tinder, vanish in an instant, no vital sap inside me to hold the flames at bay.

My mother, as if exhausted by our exertions, or else varying her tactics, had slumped in my arms, all fight apparently gone out of her. I couldn't get the window open. The frame had warped in the heat. There was a jewellery box on the dressing table close by, a heavy dark brown thing with cracked veneer. It was one of the few heirlooms my mother possessed and much prized by her as a result. I threw it against the glass. It broke two of the panes and I managed to push out another two with my arm. The cold air seemed to suck the flames around me, drawing them out over my arms and shoulders.

I brushed away as much of the glass as possible and propped my mother up against the wall. Through the open window I could hear the sound of a fire engine bell a long way off. Coming from below and rather louder were shouts of alarm. People were standing in the flower bed among the roses and chrysanthemums looking up at me in a vacant sort of way. They were calling out, although I couldn't make out what they were saying. A number of others were busy unfolding a large white sheet. It kept snagging on the rose bushes. Finally they spread it out, each of them digging their heels in the grass and leaning backwards, bracing themselves for any impact.

I tried to swing my mother out onto the windowsill. As I lifted her legs round, she suddenly came back to life and started struggling as violently as before. She was also screaming again. This time, though, there was a strangely exultant note in her voice. Despite the heat a shiver went through me; she sounded as if she was crowing with delight.

'Mother, please. Be reasonable,' I pleaded to no avail. I felt terribly tired, as if this was all too much for me. I simply wanted to go back to bed. To forget about everything. It was as much as I could do to summon the energy for one last try. I pulled my mother's face round to mine, holding her chin tight between my fingers.

'We're going to jump,' I shouted.

She tried to shake her head.

'It's the only way.'

She didn't say anything, just tried to shake her head again, as though to comply with anything I said was more than she could bear. I twisted her round once more and somehow got her feet over the edge. She was already trying to claw her way back into the room. As hard as I could, I pushed her in the small of her back. In that instant before she fell I could feel the affront, the rage, pulsing through my fingers.

As soon as she had gone I climbed out onto the sill. By now I had lost all sense of being in any discomfort. There was no pain, just this terrible tiredness. Everything was burning now. It all seemed to be liquefying before my eyes. Everything I remembered from my childhood just dissolving in this molten tide of flame. I took one last look and launched myself out into the air.

I felt as if I was falling for a long time, wheeling slowly round and round, my pyjamas billowing out above me, air caught in the folds. I could see further than I had ever seen before. I could see the roads stretching out for miles in all directions and the lines of yellow street lights disappearing off into the distance. I even thought I could see where London ended and the dark roll of the countryside began. And as I fell, for the first time in my life I had this tremendous sense of release. It was as if everything had been siphoned out of me; a great sluice had swept me clean. I looked at the white patch of sheet held taut over the flower bed below, and wondered if I would ever touch the ground again.

PART TWO

Chapter Seven

Down along this stretch of the riverbank there are some complex social distinctions. My more excitable neighbours – excluding the Pinkertons, who are in a class of their own – I mean those who turned their backs when I was having my difficulties and are now all over me again, believe that we are under threat of invasion. 'Surely not,' I say, counselling my now customary restraint.

'Oh yes,' they insist, and not just under threat. It's worse than that. It's already happening. There are interlopers about.

My neighbours are worried by their neighbours, at least by their more recent ones. Due to lax planning laws a number of new houses have appeared on the opposite bank of the river, houses which we do not consider altogether becoming to the area. Prefabricated boxes have sprung up, often literally overnight. One day there is an expanse of virgin watermeadow with waving bullrushes and unusual marsh grasses. The next, a cluster of mobile homes with elderly couples dozing away in their porches, looking as if they've been there all their lives.

At first they came in ones and twos, but now they're all over the place, spreading out in concentric circles like wagons round a campfire. What are we to do? Our corner of Olde England may never be the same. No wonder we're upset. So far there have been meetings, petitions, even calls to arms. Out of our chateaux we spill forth, to do battle among the chalets.

We think they're vulgar. And so they are. What complicates everything, of course, is that so are we. Florid but spindly, we've sprung up fast, without proper roots in our money. Not that anyone cares to admit it – except me, oddly enough. Never having been able to subscribe to the view that one's personality is reflected in one's possessions – or even in one's conduct – the idea of anyone getting defensive about such things strikes me as absurd. But I'm very much in the minority on this one. Elsewhere, there is a good deal of touchiness on all questions of taste and sophistication. We don't quite know how to behave. How could we? We're vulgar.

At one of our recent meetings, where public spirited- ness and self-interest mingle quite effortlessly, someone stood up to ask what we should do if we bumped into one of the new arrivals while out shopping, or on a walk. Should we make any effort to acknowledge them, or should we simply pretend they don't exist? A lengthy debate ensued. A number of other people were similarly troubled. This whole question of riverside etiquette is an awkward one. Living as we do some thirty-five miles away from London, we are right on the junction of two different codes of behaviour. In London no-one would dream of greeting total strangers; at least, to do so would signal either desperation or religious mania, possibly both. In the country, though, quite the reverse is true. People greet one another the whole time, usually in a dauntingly hale manner. 'Isn't life marvellous,' they manage to imply. 'And aren't we so very lucky to be able to share it.'

Being stuck between the two it's difficult to know what to do. Some people make no effort at all, while others boom cheerily at everyone in sight. Then there are those who try to combine the two and give out faint, incoherent mumbles that can be taken up or ignored according to taste. The situation is made particularly difficult by the fact that so many of us are well known. Questions of public obligation arise. In my case I can hardly fail to acknowledge people, particularly if they've given some sign of recognition. They could go away feeling slighted, with quite the wrong idea of me.

I seldom encounter anyone while shopping because I don't do much; Mrs Potter does it instead. Occasionally, though, I go out for a walk, strolling around the lanes to check on life outside my own overgrown acre. I have a set procedure at the ready in case I spot any strangers bearing down on me. It goes as follows: adopt my faintly patrician air, incline my unmistakeable head, and inquire just what it is that brings them to our neck of the wild wood.

It never fails. After a moment or two of disbelief, they realize who I am – assuming they don't live in a burrow – and are duly rendered speechless, flushing and stuttering and generally forgetting themselves. Often they look at me as if they're unsure I'm there – even reaching out to touch me and check that I have really been made flesh. This can go on for a while, the shock not so much wearing off but deepening, until I decide that enough is enough. A few last words, and then I'm off, vanishing as quickly as I came, leaving nothing behind but a memory already beginning to be clouded by doubt.

Latterly, though, I have been less than my hearty pre-emptive self, saying nothing out on my rambles, but anxiously scanning any passers-by in case I might recognize them. I can hardly blame this on the chalet dwellers, all of whom seem so harmless that it's probably churlish to kick up a fuss about them. They have, however, lent substance to this sense I have of being increasingly hemmed in, if not actually besieged.

Even in my moments of deepest disgrace I set my face defiantly at the world, and on those few occasions I ventured out did so in a way that could hardly fail to prompt a twinge of admiration. But this is different. I feel as if there's something lying in wait for me. Something bent on spooking me, doing me harm. Why should I, an apparition to so many, be troubled by apparitions myself? Is it revenge, some calling to account? But I'm getting no answers at all.

I don't know what to do. I am so concerned not to give any hint that I might be on the slide once more that I don't dare vary my routine in any way. I must behave quite normally. Having already atoned for one lapse, I know I may not be so lucky next time; it would be taken as evidence of serious character deficiency. The strain, though, is getting to me. I feel some sort of confrontation is inevitable, no matter what steps I take. In the meantime it seems the only thing I can do is wait.

Chapter Eight

For a while I thought that things were as bad as they could possibly be. My own injuries were comparatively slight: some minor burns on my back and arms and a spread of deep purple bruises across my chest. There were, however, a number of other problems. The house, at least the bottom storey of it, had been saved. The top half had gone completely, burnt clean away. As for Tom, there was no sign of him. He had left his job in the park, as well as his lodgings, on the morning after the fire and vanished. In the weeks that followed there were reports that he had been sighted at Southampton docks, clutching his toolbox and boarding a boat for Australia, but nothing was ever confirmed.

My mother had suffered the worst of all. Instead of landing in the middle of the sheet as I had done she had hit the edge and fallen into the flower bed, breaking two of her ribs and dislocating a shoulder. But it slowly became clear that the damage was not just physical. At first she refused to talk. This went on for some time; indeed I had to assure the doctors that she was not actually dumb.

Then when she did start to speak she made no sense. She complained that at night Chinamen in grey serge coolie suits and hats were climbing up the creeper on the outside of the hospital and breaking into the wards. There they would carouse with those patients they liked the look of and pick on those they didn't. An awkward situation to begin with was exacerbated by the language difficulties. Dreadful things were going on under cover of darkness, she said. People taken advantage of in the most disgraceful ways. The staff paid no attention at all. And the noise too; quite impossible to sleep through.

There could be no question of her being sent home: she had no home to go to for a start – and besides, she needed professional help. After a few weeks during which there was no improvement to her condition – the Chinamen had begun making free with the patients right around the clock – she was transferred to another hospital to see if she would respond to further treatment.

In the meantime I had been sent to stay with my father's cousins, the Aylwyns. Although they didn't live that far away we had never been close. In fact, it wasn't until I went to stay with them that I realized they were my father's cousins and not my mother's, as I had thought. A childless couple in late middle age, they took considerable pains to play up their own unsuitability for such an arrangement, pretending to be much more frail than they actually were – I was sure they exercised in secret. They would whisper anxiously to one another when they thought I couldn't hear. Guarded when I first arrived, they soon became more and more worried and secretive. It wasn't hard to see why. There was a stranger in their house. What if I liked it and decided to stay? They might never get rid of me. In a way I could even sympathize. I was going through a difficult time; I could be sullen, uncommunicative. The fire hadn't just taken it out of my mother. We'd both shrivelled in the heat.

The Aylwyns never tried to pretend that having me around was anything other than an inconvenience. I did my best to make myself as passive as possible; I didn't say much, I kept out of their way. For their part, any signs of my presence were eradicated as quickly as possible. Everything I touched was whisked away to be cleaned; the place was spotless, like an operating theatre. While I couldn't be sure – the atmosphere encouraged a certain suspicion – the portions of food I was given at mealtimes seemed to become steadily smaller. In the evenings I would go to my room immediately after supper, lie on my bed and carry on with my reading aloud. It was my only solace. I took refuge in that part of myself which I least understood, that which least belonged to me. My voice gurgled out from some invisible source and lapped against the walls. I tried to keep the volume down; I didn't want to create a disturbance.

I had not been at the Aylwyns long, however, when this led to an awkward misunderstanding. I was about halfway through my appointed passage one night when I heard a knock on the door. I was pacing myself, seeing how far I could get on a lungful of air. Having just started a long sentence, I decided to carry on until the end.

> 'I pictured them to myself, the many generations, old men and children, man and maid, all bones now, each afloat in his little box of rotting wood; and Blackbeard himself in a great coffin bigger than all the rest, coming crashing into the weaker ones, as a ship in a heavy sea comes crashing down sometimes in the trough, on a small boat that is trying to board her.'

There was another knock on the door, more insistent this time. I put down my book and went to answer it. Mr Aylwyn was standing there in his pyjamas. He looked at me oddly. 'We heard you,' he said.

'I'm sorry.'

'No, no. It's all right.' He smiled in a curdled sort of way. 'We know what you were doing.'

'You do?'

'Yes, we guessed.'

He reached out and put his hand on my forearm. 'We wondered if you might like to join us.'

'Join you? What do you mean?'

'The three of us.'

He held open the door. There was something about his expression – about his bearing generally – that made it hard for me to refuse. I got up from the bed. Mr Aylwyn led the way through to the living room. The curtains were drawn, a single candle burned in the corner. Mrs Aylwyn was kneeling on the carpet, her hands pressed together out in front of her. Mr Aylwyn knelt down beside her. He indicated that I should do the same. I must have held back because Mrs Aylwyn turned around and pulled at my trousers.

When all three of us were kneeling Mr Aylwyn began to pray in a thin monotone voice. He offered thanks to the Lord and apologies that, until now, our prayers had not come from one single source, but had been scattered, fragmentary things. A series of responses followed. Mr and Mrs Aylwyn fed each other their lines with well-practised ease. Finally he announced that we should each pray in silence. I closed my eyes, held up my hands and prayed for my release, uncomfortably aware that Mr and Mrs Aylwyn were almost certainly doing the same. After we had finished they both wished me good night with more warmth than usual. When she got to her feet Mrs Aylwyn's pink dressing gown stood out stiffly all round her, like a tepee.

It was on the following evening that the question of my future arose. Over dessert they began quizzing me. What exactly were my plans, they wanted to know.

I had none, I said.

None at all? They exchanged glances. But surely I must have a few ideas?

No, no, I said. Not one.

They were appalled. Mr Aylwyn had a habit when under stress of very deliberately smoothing his hair back over his forehead with the flat of his hand. He did so now. His wife, less able to keep herself under control, fidgeted convulsively. Together, they ran through various possible job ideas. Engineering, perhaps? Soon dismissed – I was almost innumerate.

Something with animals? Too highly strung. Carto-graphy? No sense of direction. Pipe-laying? Alas, I shrugged, my eczema. All kinds of options were entertained. Mrs Aylwyn, listing to one side on the sofa in a posture apparently designed to convey deep concern, asked me if I'd ever considered some sort of ancillary work in the merchant navy.

There had to be something. They weren't going to give up. Had I ever felt touched by ambition, they wanted to know? Had there ever been a moment, just one, when I had envisaged myself in a particular setting, perhaps even enjoying a degree of fulfilment?

And still I said nothing, at least nothing that could in any way be construed as denoting enthusiasm, or a willingness to play ball. It wasn't as though I had never fantasized about what might become of me. On the contrary I did little else. The trouble was that all my dreams seemed quite unrealizable. I wanted one of those big empty public lives, as rich on the outside as it was barren within. Something expressly tailored to my own deficiencies. That I felt would suit me fine. But how was I to go about getting one? There was no set path, and even if there had been, what chance did I stand?

How about school, they wanted to know? Had I shown any ability for anything there?

'Well,' I said, thinking hard. 'Not really. No, I don't think so.'

'Nothing?' they chorused.

'No. I'm afraid not . . . apart from singing.'

The relief this news prompted was all too evident. However, it began to fade as they tried to work out how my thin glimmer of talent could have any practical application. Mrs Aylwyn had turned to her husband and seized him by the wrist.

'Singing,' she repeated a number of times, an edge of desperation coming into her voice. 'Singing . . .'

Did I want to sing professionally, she wondered? Give recitals, join a glee club, toy with operetta?

'I don't know.'

I had never considered it. Principally because I was nowhere near good enough. But it wasn't just that. I knew I wanted something to issue forth from my mouth; not song though. Talk was quite sufficient. I wanted to talk. Not to say anything in particular, just to let my voice run on unimpeded, skipping down dark-wooded pathways, tumbling over stiles. I saw myself chattering inconsequentially away, a vehicle for all kinds of imported sentiments. By articulating them I could make them mine. They would shape me, make me, round me off.

I tried to explain this as best I could. Even so I had a strong sense of losing my audience. How could the Aylwyns possibly understand any of this? It didn't even make that much sense to me. When I had finished no-one said anything. Mr Aylwyn got to his feet and went into the kitchen, leaving his wife alone on the sofa, staring fixedly at the wall. After a while he came back in. He had lit himself a pipe and was waving the match about to extinguish it. It wouldn't go out. Every time he was about to speak it kept flaring up.

'Now I can't promise anything,' he said, shaking it again. 'But it is just possible I might be able to help.'

It was hard to know who was the more surprised, me or Mrs Aylwyn.

'You?' she exclaimed in amazement. 'How?'

But Mr Aylwyn didn't want to say; at least he had no intention of starting until we were both suitably attentive. Even then it was a long drawn-out story, much savoured in the telling. During the war it turned out that he had served with a special service unit, set up to help entertain the troops overseas. The unit was designed to boost morale, to take the men's minds off the fighting. He had, he confessed, always wanted to become a conjurer, an ambition that looked to have been thwarted by the outbreak of hostilities. But the formation of the unit provided an unexpected opportunity for him to display his skills.

For a while he had worked in the Far East with another conjurer; together they formed a double act. The arrangement hadn't lasted long – the other man had come down with dysentery and been sent home. Left on his own, Mr Aylwyn soon found his popularity waning. His confidence suffered, the troops grew restless, they started to laugh at his tricks. In the end he decided to re-apply for enlistment as a regular soldier – he had originally been turned down on the grounds of health. This time he was accepted.

After the war he and his former partner had kept in touch. The other man had also given up conjuring. Neither of them, he realized with hindsight, had ever had any real flair for it. Now his partner was the general manager of a repertory theatre in the Midlands. Assuming I was agreeable, said Mr Aylwyn, waving another burning match with a flourish, he could write to him and ask if there was a job there.

I couldn't remember ever having been to a theatre. There wasn't one near where we lived, and even if there had been we wouldn't have gone to it; my mother liked to take her distractions in private, my father had plenty of his own. None the less, the idea did appeal. At least it was a move in the right direction; a step away from reality rather than towards it.

'Yes,' I said. 'Thank you. I would like that very much.'

'Good,' said Mr Aylwyn. 'Then I will write tomorrow morning.'

'Tomorrow?' cried Mrs Aylwyn. 'Why wait until tomorrow? You can write tonight.'

The next few days passed anxiously as we waited for a reply. On the seventh day after Mr Aylwyn had sent his letter, I came down to breakfast to find an envelope propped up against my cup and both the Aylwyns craning forward in anticipation. I slit open the envelope. The letter was written on lined notepaper, although no attempt had been made to follow the lines.

Instead the writing veered at a sharp angle upwards from left to right.

It just happened that a job had fallen vacant, the letter said. Indeed, it had done so only two days before Mr Aylwyn's letter had arrived. An accident, although no details were given. The timing therefore could hardly have been better. The job involved various backstage duties, along with almost anything else that needed doing. The hours were long, the wages small, but I was welcome to come for a three-month trial. I should present myself in two days' time at the theatre and ask for Mr Gardner. More information would be forthcoming on my arrival. If I wanted accommodation then that too could be arranged without any trouble. Crammed between the bottom line and the end of the page, the signature looked as if it were trying to curl itself up like a snail.

The Aylwyns could hardly contain themselves. I had never seen them in such good humour before. There was never any question of my not taking the job. The whole thing was effectively sealed. All I had to do was pack up my things and get ready.

'Haven't you forgotten something?' asked Mrs Aylwyn, in one of our last days together.

'Forgotten something? No, I don't believe so.'

'Think carefully, Richard.'

I did my best. I'd already cleared the drawers and checked under the bed.

'I can't think of anything.'

She lowered her voice. 'Your mother, Richard. Don't you think you should go and see your mother?'

My previous attempts to see my mother had all been rebuffed by her doctors. They'd advised against it. Not while she was in such a sensitive state – best to wait a few more weeks. I had written to her twice, telling her what I'd been up to. I found it heavy-going; this kind of expression didn't come easily to me. You could have squeezed more feeling into a chain letter. She hadn't replied. When I told the doctors I was going away, possibly for some time, they said they needed to have a talk first about my visiting her before they could come to a decision. The man who called back sounded unsure of himself. He said it was all right for me to come and see her – but not for long. Half an hour would be ample. He also warned me that I mustn't say anything that might disturb her; after all, she had suffered a great deal. Progress was understandably slow.

She had been moved again, this time to a smaller hospital right on the northern edges of London, away from the Chinamens' immediate circle of influence. I caught a bus through the outer suburbs to where the streets began to tail off into countryside. The gaps between the houses grew bigger, gardens giving way to fields. The hospital was a broad, gabled building hung with red scalloped tiles. Above the porch, black beams set into the pebble-dash splayed out upwards towards the roof. A drive led up through an avenue of cedar trees. It had rained earlier in the day and the gravel was dotted with brown puddles. On the lawn a number of men were playing bowls.

At the reception desk I pressed the bell. There was a muffled ringing that brought out a nurse from an office behind. I asked for my mother. She consulted the register, looked at a note that was pinned to one of the pages and then back at me. My mother, she said, was in the garden. We set off down a corridor covered in polished tiles. I couldn't remember ever having been anywhere so quiet in my life. It was as if a giant muffler had been wrapped around the place. There was no sound at all apart from the squeak of our shoes and the distant rattle of cutlery. We passed groups of people sitting around tables, looking as if they were all on the verge of conversation. But no-one said a thing. They just sat slumped in their chairs and looked silently at one another.

We went outside and down a path that led up to a small grass-covered mound. On top of the mound there were two chairs and a pair of crescent shaped flower beds. These were full of tulips in bloom, stiff yellow flowers that jutted up in neat rows. On one of the chairs, facing away from me, was a figure sitting with her hands clasped in her lap. The nurse stopped and pointed at the figure on the bench. She wasn't coming any closer. I remembered the time in the park near our old house when I had watched my mother gazing out across the rooftops, while Tom embarked on his blind, lolloping circuit round our lives. I stepped forward.

'Hello, Mother,' I said.

She twisted her head round to look at me. I saw her eyes narrow as she began to squint.

'Who's there?'

'It's me,' I said, 'Dick.'

I walked round to the front of the bench. My mother continued staring up at me, not saying anything. And then, abruptly, she thrust her hands out towards me, while at the same time turning her head away. I took her hands, expecting them to be rough, abrasive to the touch. Instead, they were quite smooth, as soft as anything I had ever held. I couldn't get over it. I wondered if they'd been giving out handcreams in the hospital. My mother's skin was like a child's.

And it wasn't just her hands that were in good shape. She was less gaunt, less bony than I remembered. Her cheeks had filled out and her hair had been dyed a deep chestnut colour. The effect had been to soften her features, to make her look younger, more sympathetic. I had always thought of my mother as possessing many of the same qualities as slate – the obduracy in particular, as well as the brittleness. But now it no longer seemed so appropriate. I could hardly believe this was the same person.

'How nice of you to come and see me,' she said, gently pulling her hands away. 'Do come and sit down.'

The nurse had gone. I caught a glimpse of her white uniform as she walked towards the house. I sat down on the edge of the bench, for some reason not wanting to allow myself to lean back.

'You're looking well,' said my mother. 'Very well. I can't get over it. How would you describe yourself now?'

'How do you mean?'

'You're not a boy any more. I suppose you must be a man.'

'Yes,' I said. 'I suppose so. A young man anyway.'

'That's a start though, isn't it? I do like your breeches, that lovely canary colour.'

'No, Mother,' I said. 'Actually, it's the tulips that are yellow. My trousers are brown.'

'Oh well,' said my mother indulgently, 'have it your own way.'

'And you, Mother. Tell me how you are.'

'I'm fine,' she said. 'I haven't felt better in years. Of course my nerves are very delicate. I'm not robust. I have to be shielded from any sort of unpleasantness. My doctor says he's never come across anyone quite so highly strung. Do you know where the nurse has gone?'

'I think the nurse has gone back inside.'

'Never mind about that. It's so nice just to see you.'

'Yes,' I said, 'it's nice to see you too.'

I waited for my mother to ask me what I'd been doing, but she showed no signs of wanting to know. I asked if she had got my letters.

'You wrote to me too?' she exclaimed in apparent astonishment. 'My, you have been good. I'm sure I must have got them. The service here is first class. I don't read much anymore though. I hardly ever pick up a book. I'm not much good at following stories; the characters never seem to engage me.'

I started telling my mother that I was going away, that I had a job, but it was obvious she wasn't taking a lot of it in. After a while I stopped and together we sat on the bench and stared at the tulips and the lawns beyond. The men were still playing bowls. I could see the arcs of spray as the bowls rolled across the wet grass. I thought that I had never felt so separated from anyone in my life.

'How are your hands?' she asked.

'My hands? What about them?'

'Didn't you used to suffer from terrible eczema? You had to wear greaseproof paper bags tied around your wrists. Perhaps you've forgotten. It was a long time ago. All cleared up now, has it?'

'Yes,' I said. 'All cleared up.'

'Thank goodness.'

She lapsed back into silence. I sat there for a few minutes longer and was about to get up and say goodbye when I saw that my mother's shoulders were shaking. At first I thought she was sobbing, that our reunion had proved too much for her.

'Are you all right, Mother? Shall I fetch someone?'

But then I saw that my mother was laughing. She took out a handkerchief and began wiping her eyes. 'You must excuse me. The shock. It must be the shock. You see, I wasn't sure if I'd ever see you again.'

'Not see me again? But I'm your son,' I said. 'Did you think I was going to abandon you? Forget all about you? Surely you knew I would never do that.'

At this my mother started shaking again, dabbing at her cheeks with the handkerchief as if it were a powder puff.

'Oh dear. I don't know what's got into me.'

'We belong together. We share the same blood.'

She shrugged. 'Perhaps. I haven't been a very good mother though, have I?'

'I'm sure you did your best . . . it can't have been easy.'

'I tried to love you. I really did. Occasionally I thought I'd managed it. But you weren't exactly a lovable child, that was the trouble.'

'What do you mean?'

I could see my mother preparing to get expansive. She settled herself back on the bench and undid the top button of her coat. I noticed that she was wearing a necklace made up of what looked to be large moonstones; they gleamed, a milky blue, against the long sweep of her throat.

'You were a very forgettable boy. I think that's the best way to describe it. It's a terrible thing for a mother to say, I know, but sometimes you just used to slip my mind. You seemed so insubstantial, so easy to ignore. It was hard to believe you were really a proper person at all. I used to look at you and wonder where you could have come from. And you only made it worse in a way; you seemed as unsure about yourself as I was. There was your lack of initiative for a start. But also the way you used to cling to me, as if you couldn't stand up by yourself. I'd see other children in our street, they all seemed so boisterous, always rushing about and getting into mischief. But you hardly ever uttered, let alone raised your voice. I tried to talk to your father about it, but that was hopeless. He said there was nothing wrong with you. What did he know? Most of the time he was fast asleep.

'After he died I made a special effort. I tried to encourage you, talk to you, interest you in the outside world. But I never felt I was getting anywhere. That kind of thing is very diminishing. It wears you down. Eventually, I admit, I rather gave up.

'What's the matter? Why are you looking at me like that? It's best for you to know these things.'

'No, it isn't,' I said. 'I don't want to know anything.'

'You're a man now,' said my mother. 'You shouldn't be getting upset.'

'I think you're very unkind.'

My mother looked at me and I saw a flicker of something, possibly nerves, pass across the lower half of her face. 'Not really,' she said. 'I wouldn't say that.'

'I would,' I went on. 'You don't think of anyone else but yourself.' I could hear my voice starting to break free of its adult moorings. 'You never thought about me, how I was feeling. You never even cared.'

She held up one of her new pink hands, palm facing me. 'I don't like to interrupt you. But I do think you should remember where you are. There are a lot of very sick, unhappy people here, and I'm one of them. The slightest shock could set me back months. Under the circumstances, I don't think this is the place to start airing personal grievances.'

I kept quiet. The effort made me shake.

'Are you going to come and see me again?' said my mother. 'I do hope so, now you know where to find me. But I must warn you that I can't see anyone for too long. It's not allowed. Where are you going? We've got plenty of time left.'

'I don't think I want to stay here,' I said. 'And I don't know if I ever want to come back either.'

'Obviously I can't force you. But I'll always be here if you want to drop by. I'm not planning to go anywhere for a while. In future, though, do try and make an appointment beforehand, it's so much easier for the staff.'

I stood over my mother. She sat gazing ahead of her. Several nurses had come out onto the lawn and were calling the men in for their tea. None of them took any notice to begin with. They carried on playing bowls. Then one of the nurses simply picked up the jack, put it in her coat pocket and walked back inside. With nothing left to aim at, the men soon fell into step in a meek line behind her.

'I'm going.'

She twisted her head towards me, as she had done when I'd arrived, this time giving me an even longer look of appraisal. 'Dickie,' she said, nodding slightly.

'Yes,' I said. 'Dickie. Or Dick. I answer to either.'

'Thank you so much for coming. Goodbye now.'

'Goodbye, Mother.'

I walked down the slope back onto the path. In the hospital tea was being served, but still no-one seemed to be talking. Large urns sat steaming on trolleys. People collected their mugs of tea from the nurse and then filed silently away again, holding them out from their bodies in case they spilt any. I hurried back through the front door and away down the drive. With every step I struggled to bring myself under control. I forced my mind onto other things: cloud formations, the state of the flower beds, anything I could think of. Anything at all. And by the time I reached the gate I had already begun to purge the whole episode from my system. I could feel my heels stretching and the air circulating beneath my feet. I had also made a resolution. That was it, I swore to myself. I was never going back. Never. I could be clear about one thing, at least: whatever happened, that was the last time I would ever see my mother.

And so, in a way, it was.

Chapter Nine

On the day I left the Aylwyns made great and unconvincing play about what a wrench this was going to be for them – how their lives would seem so dull without me around. They insisted on driving me to the station and even offered to help with my bags, until they remembered how sickly they were supposed to be. On the platform we wished each other goodbye. I shook Mr Aylwyn's hand. His wife presented her taut cheek for me to brush with my lips. As the train pulled out from under the huge glass canopy I watched them turn and hurry past the ticket barrier.

It was early autumn. The sun emerged briefly to cast a thin light across the rooftops and then disappeared. We steamed out into the country. I realized it had been years since I'd been out of London – not since my father's death. The fields had been freshly ploughed. As we went on, the earth changed from brown to a dull red colour. I sat back watching the wires as they rose and fell from one telegraph pole to the next. There were pylons everywhere, a tracery of cable marching across the land.

I found it hard to believe that I hadn't stepped through yet another window and into a different world. At one point I saw a flock of white birds, some way off, but flying at what seemed to be the same speed as the train. Perhaps it was the light, or the lack of it, but they seemed to shine in the gloom, the flash of their wings like metal strips, as, locked briefly together, we sped our way through the afternoon.

Not long afterwards it began to rain, a steady drizzle that left strings of droplets across the glass. A couple of hours later the train began to slow. On either side of the tracks were long low factories. Most looked to be deserted, but just occasionally crouched figures in overalls could be glimpsed through lighted windows, streams of sparks shooting over their heads. After the factories came rows of white painted houses with wrought-iron balconies and arched windows. Smart, manicured gardens stretched right to the foot of the embankment.

We pulled into the station, carriages cannoning into one another. I picked up my suitcase and stepped down onto the platform. I asked the ticket collector if he could give me directions to the theatre. He took me into his booth and pointed out the way on a map all but obliterated by inky fingerprints. Outside a few shoppers leant forward into the wind. The rain had become heavier. A long wide street led up from the station to the centre of town. There were bench seats every few yards for those who got short of breath. Later I learned that the town had a higher percentage of old age pensioners than anywhere else in the country; specially ridged paving slabs had recently been laid to make sure they didn't lose their footing.

I couldn't get over the size of everything. Growing up in London, I had got used to buildings towering overhead, crowding in on every side. Here it was as if the scenery had been lowered, scaled down to my sort of size. I didn't even have to lean back to see where the roofs stopped and the sky took over. I felt as if I could reach up and touch the chimneypots set squat on the dark grey tiles. Already, it seemed, I was bigger. I had been stretched, pulled upwards and out of myself. I really felt quite light-headed. Walking tall then, if uncertainly, I tottered across the non-slip paving stones and down towards the town centre.

The theatre was on one side of a car park. It looked like an enormous grey ship that had accidentally moored there and been left to decay. Above a low awning, the building rose in a series of tiers with little rounded balconies and windows scarcely bigger than portholes. Several of the windows, especially nearer the top, had been boarded over. On either side of the doors there were glass cases containing playbills. But there was condensation on the inside of the glass and it was impossible to see anything apart from a few blurred faces hidden behind the mist. I asked at the box office where I might find Mr Gardner. A woman told me to go round to the stage door and ask again.

At the back of the theatre a doorway opened directly onto the car park. The door was already open. Inside, two corridors led off in opposite directions. Both were unlit. No-one came by. Thinking I could hear voices down the left-hand corridor, I put down my bag and went to see if I could find anybody. Tiny windowless rooms opened out on either side. Soon I could hardly see where I was going. The voices got louder. I heard a man asking over and over again, 'Are you quite sure it wasn't loaded, Margery?' and the sound of a woman crying in a soft mechanical sort of way.

I felt my way forward. In front of me I could make out something small and rounded at about hip height. It shone dully in the gloom. I put my hand out. A door knob. The voices were coming from the other side. I tried to knock on the door but it made no sound. I tried again. Nothing. I waited, wondering what to do. I'd come this far; there didn't seem any point in going back. I twisted the knob and pushed. The door swung away from me. It hardly weighed a thing.

For a while I couldn't see anything. When my eyes got used to the light I saw that a number of people were staring at me. The woman who was crying had her back to the door. She carried on for a while, a handkerchief pressed to her face, her shoulders rising and falling, until a man holding a gun nudged her and she too turned around. From far away in the darkness a man's voice called out, 'What is this? What on earth's going on?'

There was an old man sitting off to one side in a wheelchair, his legs covered with a blanket. Sounding very unsure of himself, he said, 'Emil?'

No-one replied.

'Emil?' he said again. 'Is it really you?'

'No, of course it's not,' said the man with the gun.

'Who is it then?'

'I don't know. Who are you?' he asked me.

'I've come to work here,' I said. 'I'm looking for Mr Gardner.'

My words seemed to fall uselessly at my feet. I wasn't sure if anyone could hear what I was saying.

'Who is it?' shouted the voice from the darkness.

'He says he's come to work here.'

'Work here? What as?'

'I think it must be poor Jerry's replacement.'

'Is it? Oh . . . Even so, he shouldn't be here,' said the voice.

And then, to me, 'You shouldn't be here.'

'I don't know where else to go,' I said.

'You should be with Roy. Does anyone know where Roy's got to? He must be around. Roy, are you there?'

'Yes,' said a voice from just behind me.

'Ah, good. You are there. Can you look after this young man? He says he's come to start work. I'm sure you can find him something to do.'

I felt a hand on my left arm. We went out through the door I'd come in by. I saw that it was made of canvas stretched across a wooden frame. In the corridor I tried to turn round and introduce myself, but the hand had moved between my shoulders and was still pushing me along. We stopped by the stage door where I had left my suitcase.

'So you managed to find us then?'

The man standing behind me must have been in his late fifties. His skin, however, was quite unlined, as if it had never really been touched by age. He was very fat and I remember being struck by the contrast between his physical bulk and the way his eyes constantly slid about, never seeming to focus on anything. He didn't bother to introduce himself. Instead he asked after Mr Aylwyn and recalled, rather improbably I thought, what fun they had had when they had worked together. All the time his gaze played over me like a hosepipe.

'Perhaps I had better show you round first,' he said. 'Then you won't lose your way again.'

We set off down the other corridor, away from the stage. There were more doors on either side, all closed. The corridor led into a workshop. Lengths of timber were stacked up round the walls, along with rolls of white canvas. There were several buckets full of wallpapering paste. A half-built wooden fireplace stood in the middle of the floor. Upstairs from a kind of makeshift loft came the sound of sawing. Sawdust dropped onto a pile of boxes below.

'Arthur,' he called out, 'where are you?'

The sawing stopped but there was no reply.

'I've brought someone to see you, Arthur.'

A man climbed down a ladder that was fixed to the wall. He had an apron tied round his waist, wore half-framed glasses and had a cigarette in his mouth. His hair, greying round the temples but black everywhere else, was plastered down with pomade. He came over looking nervous, took no notice of me, and immediately started talking about a consignment of timber that had failed to arrive. Roy seemed quite unconcerned, telling the man not to get so worked up, to relax and enjoy himself.

'Arthur worries so,' he said to me. 'It eats him up.'

Arthur smiled weakly and continued to look worried. He had a hunted air, as if he might be tripped up at any moment, robbed of what little composure he had.

'You must learn to look on the bright side,' said Roy.

'I suppose so,' he agreed.

'Do you know, I think it's going to be a lovely day.'

'Do you?' he said suspiciously. 'Why?'

'I heard it on the radio. Showers in the morning, but then sunshine breaking through.'

The sun was already coming out. There was a skylight in the roof that cast a bright rectangle of light onto the floor in front of us. As we talked the rectangle slowly inched its way across the floor towards my feet.

'See what I mean?' said Roy.

'Yes,' said Arthur. 'Yes, it has turned out nice.'

Accommodation had been arranged for me in a house nearby, just on the other side of the car park. The landlady, a small irritable woman with badly dyed red hair, rented out a couple of rooms. The larger one was already let to two apprentice electricians – the local Electricity Board ran a training centre in the town. I was to have the other.

The room was like a shoebox turned on its end. There was a narrow bed and a wooden chair wedged alongside it. By spreadeagling myself on the square of carpet I could almost touch all four corners of the room at the same time. The ceiling though was very high. The one light hung from a ceiling rose so far above the bed that any illumination had all but faded away by the time it got down to head height. To reach the window I had to stand on the bed. There was a view out across picket fences to where a ridge of hills ran along the horizon.

Often clouds sat on top of the hills, as if resting there in mid-flight. I never had anything to do with the electricians. They left before I got up in the mornings and never stayed out late. At weekends they went fishing. I would see their rods in long canvas cases leaning up against the bannisters. Occasionally on my way to the bathroom I'd glance into their bedroom – they always left the door ajar. The walls were covered with wiring diagrams.

I took to the work more readily than I'd ever imagined. During the day I would be sent out to run errands. Either that or I would sit in rehearsals and take a note of anything that might be needed. Every evening before the show began I went round lighting the gas lamps. While there was electric light everywhere else in the theatre, the original gas lamps had been left in the auditorium. The lamps hissed and cast a deep orange light through their frosted bowls. When they were all lit – it took almost an hour – I would stand on stage and look out across the faded plush at the dim horseshoe rings of light reaching up, one on top of another. The air crinkled and vibrated in the heat.

Once the show started I had to help shift the scenery and make sure the actors were ready, waiting in the wings for their cues. Sometimes I would be sent up to where the painted backcloths were lowered down onto the stage. There was a long wooden balcony running just under the slope of the roof. Coils of rope were wound around iron cleats bolted to the wall. It took two of us to lower one of the backcloths, paying out the rope hand over hand until it was in position. Hauling them up was harder still, with someone having to stand on the balcony rail, leaning out to get as good a grip on the rope as possible. When they hung out of sight, tied off on their cleats, the cloths swayed about in the slightest breeze and the ropes creaked like the rigging of a sailing ship.

Within a couple of weeks I had been put in charge of pulling the curtain up and down. By the side of the stage there were two ropes side by side, stretching high up into the darkness. The left-hand rope brought the curtain down, the right-hand one pulled it back up. At the end of each show I would do the curtain calls. This entailed pulling hard on the downward rope, waiting until the curtain was about to hit the ground – I could just see the edge of the stage out of the corner of my eye – and then grabbing hold of the right-hand rope which was speeding upwards on its ascent. The momentum would carry me some ten feet up into the air, before I leapt back onto the left-hand rope to bring the curtain in again.

I couldn't remember ever enjoying anything so much in my life. The more I did it, the more agile I became, jumping across from one rope to the other, kicking myself off from the wall, flipping through the air like an acrobat. The volume of applause hardly ever warranted anything more than the briefest of bows. But I was determined to keep it going for as long as possible. Every night I rode my way up and down the ropes until the final hand clap had died away and the seats had all tipped back.

There were evenings when so few people came to the theatre that the actors onstage outnumbered the audience. On such occasions everyone would gather beforehand in one of the dressing rooms and take a vote on whether to carry on with the show. The mood at these meetings was very solemn. The decision though was always unanimous – they would continue; it was their duty, a matter of professional pride. They wouldn't be able to live with themselves otherwise. Theories abounded as to why audiences had declined so drastically. Mortality certainly had something to do with it. Regular visitors were dying off – a flu epidemic the year before had carried off close on a hundred – while others had become so infirm that they could no longer get out. Almost everyone agreed, however, that there was another factor here that couldn't be ignored – the choice of plays.

In the past the plays put on had hardly changed from year to year – a constant succession of old West End farces and thrillers. Attendances stayed consistently high. But lately there had been a number of innovations. Some months before the theatre's director, Malcolm Forley, had gone up to London, ostensibly to see his sister and to visit the sales. He had returned a changed man. There he had fallen – disastrously – under the influence of naturalism.

In London naturalism had become very popular. It was all the rage. An entirely new type of theatre had come into fashion; one that dispensed with escapism and artifice and concentrated instead on reality – preferably pared down to its starkest essentials. Along with this, there had been a big change in the approach to acting. It was no longer enough to concentrate simply on the words. Now as much attention had to be paid to whatever emotions lay behind them, in order to create a clear unimpeded line between feeling and speech.

The effect of all this on Malcolm had been considerable; he had undergone a conversion. It was evident in the way he looked. Slightly stooped with a very full lower lip, he had previously been rather a fey man. He dressed in purple, he had a neat beard trimmed in a squarish Scandinavian style. All that had gone. Now he wore a kind of siren suit in olive green the wardrobe department had made up for him. Hair straggled over his cheeks. His cuffs were unbuttoned and frayed.

And there were other, less obvious, signs. In the past he'd been known as something of a soft touch, always fussing over people if they were feeling out of sorts. Prone to hypochondria himself, he would ensure that the heating backstage was turned up to its maximum setting, even providing hot water bottles and blankets for the older actors during cold weather. Lately though he had insisted that the heating be turned off and all external doors left open. Several people had complained that they were in danger of catching pneumonia, but it made no difference. He was quite inflexible.

I watched all this from the sidelines, not sure what to think. This was my first introduction to a 'creative temperament' – the enormous self-regard, the complete lack of any sense of personal absurdity, that strange combination of limpness and ego. I must say I was hugely impressed; I even like to think that some of it rubbed off on me for use in later life.

The plays too had changed. Audiences now found themselves faced with unrelenting portrayals of the sorts of things they had come to the theatre to avoid. Not surprisingly, they didn't care for it. They had no wish to be reminded of the world outside, let alone to have its more harrowing events played out in front of them. Even those plays which had comprised the stock fare of the theatre – which Malcolm, at Roy's insistence, had reluctantly agreed to carry on directing – were presented in radically different style. Everything now had to be played as realistically as possible. All frivolity was ruthlessly excised, any comic content kept to a bare minimum.

Audiences were confused. So too were the actors. A good many of them had been there for a long time. They did not take easily to change. Few of them ever left the theatre and moved on anywhere else. There was nowhere left for them to go. Mr Cheeseman, the man who thought I was Emil when I first arrived, had been there for more than sixty years. For much of the time he was confined to a wheelchair. Most of the other actors had once entertained hopes of stardom, or some sort of prominence. Now they had lapsed into varying stages of disenchantment, their lack of ability covered only by brittle layers of conceit.

It must have been in the second or third week I was there that I became aware of just how deep divisions were between Malcolm and the rest of the company. By then my life had settled into a routine. I swung between my customary loneliness and an uneasy bumptiousness as I tried to keep up with everyone else. There were times at rehearsals when one of the actors or actresses was away and I was asked to read for them. Here, as with the singing at school, I acquitted myself rather well, showing, I thought, an unusual dexterity in tackling both male and female parts.

On this occasion though all the actors were present, and I was sitting off to one side of the stage taking notes. Malcolm was by himself in the middle of the stalls – he had a special desk with a built-in light which rested on top of the seats in front of him. At one point Henry Travis, the man who had kept asking if the gun was loaded, had to lose his temper. Once, before the war, Henry had looked set for a promising career; a film studio put him under contract, his picture appeared in a number of magazines. But the films had all been flops. He had been criticized for being impossibly wooden – and this at a time when immobility was held in high regard. His contract had not been renewed. Instead he had ended up here. Now in his early sixties he was one of the company's leading men, usually playing characters a good deal younger than himself.

After his first attempt Malcolm stopped him – he simply held up his hand and waited for it to be noticed – and asked him to try again. Henry repeated his lines. Once again Malcolm stopped him and asked him to have another go. He did so. This time after Henry had finished, Malcolm got out from behind his desk and came forward towards the stage. He was smiling in a mirthless, bemused sort of way and shaking his head slightly from side to side.

'Tell me, Henry,' he said, 'what exactly are you feeling?'

Henry was clearly surprised by the question. 'What do you mean?'

'What are you supposed to be doing?'

'I'm being angry,' he said. 'That's what you wanted, isn't it?'

'And how do you show your anger.'

'You know how . . . I raise my voice.'

'You raise your voice. Anything else?'

'Let me see.' He thought for a few moments. 'No, I don't think so. Is there something wrong? I can make it louder if you like.'

'You're missing the point, I'm afraid. I want to know what you're feeling.'

104

'Feeling?' said Henry. 'Well, I'm rather cold. I think we all are.'

'No, no. I want you to tell me about your emotions.'

Henry had closed his eyes. I realized for the first time how striking-looking he was: long straight nose, sharp jutting chin, peculiarly flat cheeks. He was like a fish; his face seemed to lose all definition when it wasn't in profile. As if aware of this, he had a habit of turning away from whoever he was talking to, so they saw only his lifting jaw, his head tilted back to catch the light.

'You know,' he said, 'I don't mean to be difficult, but isn't that rather prying?'

Malcolm smiled again. His teeth looked very white. 'I just want to know what feelings are going on inside you when you're losing your temper.'

By now everyone was paying close attention. Even those actors who normally disappeared into a fog of self-absorption whenever anyone else was talking had emerged from their cocoons to see what was going on.

'Nothing,' said Henry at last.

'Nothing?'

'That's right.'

'Nothing at all?'

'No,' said Henry triumphantly. 'I'm a complete blank.'

Whatever Malcolm had been expecting, it wasn't this. For a while he seemed unable to speak, merely shaking his head about more vigorously than before. Once he had himself under control he began to talk about the importance of acting from the inside, about letting feelings flow through from the heart to the outward self. He went on for some time. I could see the other actors making faces at one another and looking unhappy. As if seeking solidarity, they started drifting towards one another. When Malcolm had finished he turned to them and said, 'I'm sure I don't need to explain any of this to you.'

No-one said anything.

'You do all understand what I'm talking about?' he asked.

After a few moments one man was nudged forward. When he spoke he sounded shocked. 'Do you mean that when we say something on stage we should be going through the same feelings as the character we're playing?'

'Yes, of course I'm saying that. Surely it's obvious.'

A ripple of surprise ran through everyone.

'That doesn't seem right somehow,' he said.

There was a general murmur of agreement.

For a moment it looked as if Malcolm was about to carry on, to explain himself further, but just as he was about to open his mouth, he seemed to think better of it. Instead he walked slowly back to his seat in the stalls. He spent the rest of rehearsals bent forward, almost kneeling, his head propped up on his hands, scarcely saying a word.

While much of this made as little sense to me as it did to everyone else, I found myself instinctively siding with Henry, coming down on the side of contrivance. This was the path for me. It had to be. Although the mechanics were still far from clear, the desire to dissemble, to hide myself wherever possible, was already taking root. The more I thought about naturalism, the less I liked the sound of it. It certainly didn't sound like my sort of thing. Even then, all my instincts ran in quite the opposite direction.

There were eight shows a week: every evening apart from Sundays, and matinees on Thursdays and Saturdays. After showing me round on my first day I'd had little to do with Roy. Twice he had walked past me with only the briefest of nods. But then in the middle of my fourth week I was sweeping the floor backstage, eyes fixed on the ground, when I narrowly missed a pair of brown shoes standing quite still in the path of the broom.

'There you are,' said Roy. 'I've been looking for you. Are you busy on Sunday?'

No, I said. I wasn't busy.

'Good.' He nodded, satisfied. 'Come to lunch.'

And he strode off through the pile of dust I'd been sweeping up.

On the Sunday morning I arrived early and waited outside until the neighbourhood church clocks had struck one. Roy lived in a street of tall sandstone houses, ten minutes walk from the centre of town. I walked down some steps to the basement flat and pressed the bell. I could hear shuffling from the other side of the door. It opened a few inches, not wide enough for me to see who was inside.

'Yes?'

'Does Mr Gardner live here?'

'Yes.'

'I've been invited to lunch.'

The door was opened slowly, with obvious reluctance. A figure stood there frowning, glasses crooked on his nose.

'Hello, Arthur. I didn't know you were going to be here.'

Without saying anything, he turned and walked back through the hallway. The flat was airless. The walls were covered with hundreds of framed photographs. All of them, I saw, were of Roy, looking out beyond the camera with that same slow, unfocused gaze. He called out from the kitchen that he'd be with us in a minute. In the meantime we were to go through to the living-room and make ourselves at home.

Arthur sat on the sofa and picked up a newspaper. For a long time he couldn't bring himself to say anything. He held on to both edges of the paper. It stretched between his hands as if it were about to split apart. After a while he put it down.

'I may smell of creosote,' he said.

'I can't smell anything.'

'Maybe you're just saying that.'

'No,' I said. 'I'm not. I promise you.'

'I've been creosoting a shed,' said Arthur.

'Where?'

107

'I beg your pardon?'

'Where is the shed?'

'Where?' he repeated incredulously. 'In my garden.'

He picked up the paper again and began to read. Eventually Roy came in. He had an apron hung round his neck and tied over his stomach in a long loose bow. His hands were clasped out in front of him.

'Have you been having a nice chat?' he asked.

'I suppose so,' said Arthur.

'Good. And what have you been talking about?'

Arthur cleared his throat. 'About my shed,' he said.

'Well, well, well. I don't like to break things up, but it is time to eat.'

In the dining-room Arthur and I sat opposite one another while Roy did the carving. He jabbed the fork into the joint and left it there, standing upright, while he sharpened the knife. Arthur had picked up his napkin ring and kept turning it over in his hands. He took no notice when Roy put a plate of meat down in front of him, and didn't make any effort to help himself to vegetables.

'Do you like your napkin ring, Arthur?' asked Roy.

'It's all right,' he said, putting it down hurriedly. 'Where's it from?'

'From Sheffield,' said Roy. 'It says so on the inside.'

The vegetables were passed over to me, and then back to Arthur, who roused himself and took two boiled potatoes and a spoonful of carrots.

'You don't want any more carrots, Arthur?' said Roy. He shook his head.

Roy had several spoonfuls of everything. 'I can't tell you how pleased we both were that you were able to come today,' he said to me.

I started to say that it was very kind of him to invite me, but I didn't get very far. He waved my words away. 'The pleasure is ours. I know Arthur has been particularly looking forward to it.'

Arthur's head shot up, his mouth half-open.

'We get so out of touch, you see,' Roy continued.

'The young, they live in a world of their own. We do our best, although we can only guess at what goes on. But if we don't find out, how are we to stay young ourselves? It's not easy, I assure you. Besides, you may not realize, Arthur, that I feel a great responsibility for young Dick here.'

'You do?' said Arthur.

'I do indeed. I don't know if you're aware that Dick has no father of his own. And his mother is, temporarily we hope, detained in an institution. A good deal of weight therefore falls on my shoulders.'

Arthur grunted.

'I should be failing in my duty if I was not to tell him . . . well, how the land lies. There are certain things I feel he should know about. Certain habits. Inclinations some may call them, that he hasn't come across before.'

Arthur, I saw, had turned very pale.

'I'm sorry,' said Roy, his hand cupped behind his ear. 'Did you say something? I didn't quite catch it.'

Arthur addressed his plate. He was holding his knife and fork, crossed like divining rods, above one of his potatoes. 'I don't think we should talk about that,' he said. 'Not here.'

'Why ever not,' said Roy. 'We're all men of the world, aren't we?'

'Oh yes,' I said, my mouth full, 'we are.'

'There you are, you see. It's pointless to pretend otherwise. Anyway, I'm sure it wouldn't surprise Dick to learn that there are a number of these poor fellows in the theatre. Some rather more overt than others. But a disproportionate amount, in any case.'

'What sort of men?' I asked.

'Why, men who enjoy one another's company to a far greater degree than nature intended. I think that's the best way of putting it, don't you? Brrr, the things they get up to. I can hardly bear to think about it.'

'No,' said Arthur. 'Nor can I.'

'Fair chills the blood. The most unlikely people too.

109

One could name names, of course. But there probably isn't much point. What is important though is that Dick should not feel pressurized into doing anything that he might not feel drawn to doing. Isn't that right?'

Arthur said nothing.

'I daresay you've heard about the club. Perhaps even been there already.'

'No,' I said. 'What club is that?'

'Well, go there if you wish,' continued Roy without answering my question. 'But be careful. I think that's all I would want to say. And if anything happens that upsets you in any way I hope you will feel able to come and tell either myself about it – or Arthur, if he's not too busy. You wouldn't mind that, would you, Arthur?'

Arthur agreed that he wouldn't mind, albeit in a scarcely audible voice.

I listened to all this in a state of some confusion. Any mention of sex, however oblique, always unsettled me. The truth was that I had yet to have any sexual experience. Not a thing. I'd had stirrings, of course, but they were all turned inwards, away from everyone else. By way of compensation, I'd tried to cultivate the world-weariness of the uninitiated – I even carried it off fairly well. I tended to take a tolerant view of such things, while seeing myself as above all that; rather too self-contained for it to be really necessary.

But there were still times when I couldn't help wondering if I was quite normal. If my development hadn't got stuck at some crucial stage, or stopped altogether. At night sometimes, after the electricians had gone to sleep, I would stand in front of the bathroom mirror and stare at myself, always beset by the same doubts. There could be no doubt that this was me. Whenever I moved my reflection moved right along with me; we were a carefully coordinated pair. And yet, I felt no sense of kinship with my outer form, no confidence that it was really mine. Sometimes I would stand there for hours, hardly moving, just reflecting on this sense of separation, while all around me fanning out on every side, bodies lay stretched out, dead to the world, their owner/occupiers slumbering peacefully away within.

'As a matter of fact, I am particularly busy right now,' said Arthur.

Roy looked at me, a smile tugging at the sides of his mouth.

'Poor Arthur,' he said. 'He does worry so.'

After the show finished each night I would go round extinguishing the gas lamps. By the time I was through everyone else had usually gone. But a few days after I'd been at Roy's, I came back to find a group of actors still hanging around the stage door. They stood aside to let me go by. I was almost out of the door when one of them asked if I might care to join them.

'Where are you going?' I asked.

'Oh,' he said. 'We're not exactly spoiled for choice, are we? Just the club, I suppose. It's the only place where you can get a drink at this time of night. But you're welcome to come along.'

It didn't take long for me to make up my mind. I said yes, as much out of a desire to escape my own company as anything else. In the event, the place could hardly have been less threatening. A plain black door next to the chemists in the High Street led into a long dark room with a jukebox and dance floor at one end. At the other end was a bar. Above it, several Chianti bottles hung suspended under a narrow strip of thatch.

A cluster of men stood by the bar, four or five of them huddled together. They stopped talking when we walked in, swung round to look at us, and then turned hurriedly back to resume their conversation. Everyone seemed strangely cowed and unsure of themselves – as if they were just getting used to company again after suffering some crushing personal loss. There was an air of injured innocence about the place, people circling one another warily, all aware that they bruised far too easily for their own good.

111

We went to sit down. Two men were dancing. Clinging grimly to one another, faces buried in each other's shoulders, they inched their way round the tiny dance floor. We hadn't been there long when I heard someone cough apologetically behind me. It was followed by a tap on my shoulder. I turned round to see a man standing there, small, wiry, middle-aged. His legs were bowed. He looked like he might once have been a jockey.

'I wonder if I might have this dance,' he said.

I was so taken aback I said nothing. Silence was taken as assent. No-one else at the table spoke. I stood up. The man's head barely reached my chest. We walked over to the dance floor.

'I'll lead, if you don't mind,' he said. 'You follow.'

We moved off around the floor. I found it surprisingly easy. He danced well with tight, economical little movements. Even the difference in our heights wasn't a problem. We held one another out with stiff, angled arms. I looked down, seeing his flat, iron-grey hair and his face staring intently at my shirt front. Towards the end of the dance he began to move closer, bending his head in as if preparing to put it on my chest. I thrust him away in time to the music. We continued without missing a step.

The record ended. The other two couples stopped dancing but stayed clutching one another, waiting for the moment when they could resume. We disengaged. He thanked me and walked away over to the jukebox. I went back to the table feeling rather pleased with myself without being quite sure why; perhaps it was to do with giving pleasure at no personal cost.

When I sat down no-one said anything much. Although there were one or two jokes, they sounded thin, half-hearted. On the whole everyone was rather quiet, as if they had witnessed something unsettling but didn't care to dwell on it.

Chapter Ten

As the weeks went by I began to feel that I belonged.
It was the first time in my life I'd ever felt this way.
Of course, I couldn't be sure how long it would last
– I couldn't shake this suspicion that it might all be
whisked away in an instant. Even so, I was determined
to savour it to the full. At work I went about my
allotted tasks as efficiently and cheerily as I could.
It paid off. People now recognized me; they knew
who I was. They remembered my name – and used
it with an ease and intimacy that I'd never been able
to muster. 'Look, there's Dick,' they would call out, the
more observant ones, while I'd oblige with some happy
inanity in return.

Outside work, my horizons continued to broaden
in unexpected ways. The barman in the club took to
greeting me with a long yodel of delight. I let myself
be piloted around the dance floor by a succession of
tongue-tied, broken men. They shuffled forward for the
privilege. I don't recall anyone ever saying anything, as
chins out, shoulders back, we swept through our steps.
It seemed the least I could do. In return I found myself
on the receiving end of small displays of consideration,
often from people I'd hardly met. A balance appeared to
be establishing itself here, to do with kindness as well
as trust. I wasn't sure how it worked yet – its precise
reciprocal nature – but I'd grasped enough to want to
pursue it further.

Each morning before I went off to work I would lie in bed, staring out of the window, and reflect on my good fortune. Outside the town, on top of the crest of hills, there was a racing stable. Usually the hills were covered in mist. But occasionally, when the weather was clear, I could make out horses up on the gallops, a cluster of brown dots speeding along the skyline. Soon I was to see the horses at closer quarters. One afternoon I was summoned to see Malcolm in his office. This was at the top of the theatre, up a series of narrowing flights of stairs. The office itself was small: a square of ragged carpet, a desk and a tiny, low chair – it might have been a child's – on which visitors were expected to sit. Malcolm sat on the other side of the desk, his hands crossed over his chest.

He had something of my father's vagueness about him; the way in which he'd suddenly come to, as if disturbed from some deep reverie of his own. But while my father never did it consciously – he couldn't help himself, poor man – with Malcolm it appeared a good deal more deliberate. So it was now as I stood waiting by the door while he affected not to notice me. After a few moments there was the usual start of surprise, and then an invitation to sit down. He smiled his humourless smile.

I'd settled in all right? he wanted to know.

Oh yes, I assured him. I'd settled in surprisingly well.

'Good.'

He had, he said, been impressed with me in the short time I had been there. Yes, I was a little gauche, it was true. Impressionable too. Furthermore, I was, was I not – and here he lent forward to look at me more closely – someone who liked the sound of his own voice?

I hung my head, could not deny it.

'Just as I thought.'

He had gathered as much from my varied readings at rehearsals. It was indeed the reason he'd asked to see me. What he had in mind was this: he was planning to do a play. A Russian play – something never seen in this theatre before. A play set in times not so very different from our own, about the collapse of the old order, dwelling on the moral malaise that had hastened its end, the tragi-comedy of lives pledged to a moribund cause. The almost physical paralysis that resulted from such widespread inertia. A play encompassing all aspects of society – he drew great circles in the air – from the most lofty offices of state, down – a hand swooped below the desk – to the lowliest ostler. Was I with him so far?

Yes, I said, I thought so.

Then he would continue. Among the multitude of parts that the play had to offer, there was, he said, one that he felt might suit me – if I felt up to it.

I was so astonished I couldn't speak.

It was not a large part, he said. In fact, I did not come on until the very final scene of the play; it was, however, a crucial one. My presence was, in many ways, the final proof that dissolution was at hand, that an era was coming to pass. I was to be Old Gregor, the coachman. Old Gregor, symbol of decay, and yet harbinger of hope for a brighter tomorrow.

Was I still there? Malcolm asked.

'Yes,' I said . . . I believed I was.

'Excellent.'

There was a pause while I tried to digest this. After a while something occurred to me. 'May I ask a question?'

He held up one of his hands. 'I think I know what you're going to say.' He had his eyes half-closed, and his other hand was pinching the bridge of his nose. When he spoke he did so very deliberately, as if making an effort to keep himself under control. 'You want to know how such a play could have any chance of success in a place like this.' He sighed. 'Do you think you're the first person to point this out? I would have thought a young man such as yourself, an idealist, I hope, would have been the first to brush aside such objections. These people are ripe for change, don't you see? They may not recognize it themselves, they may try to pretend otherwise. But the only way they can ever come to terms with their own worthlessness is to see it laid out in front of them.'

'No, actually it wasn't that.'

He looked up. 'What was it then?'

'I wondered just how old would Old Gregor be?'

'How old would Old Gregor be? I see Old Gregor as being extremely old,' said Malcolm. 'Certainly in his seventies. Perhaps older still. Getting a little unsteady on his feet. Bent low by age and infirmity. But a lot of those Russian servants had tremendous stamina, you know, they were like little pack horses. Why, is there something wrong?'

'No no, not wrong. But . . . well, wouldn't it be more appropriate if I was to play someone younger?'

Malcolm laughed and shook his head. There was, he explained, a tradition in the theatre that small parts such as this should be played by someone in my position. To have cast someone older would have been a break with normal practice, as well as proving more expensive. 'Anyway,' he said, 'it's largely a matter of attitude. There's probably some part of you that's already wizened up, bloodless, perhaps just undeveloped. All you have to do is let that come to the fore. Besides,' he added, 'you'll be heavily made up.'

He gave me a copy of the script and told me to study it carefully. That night, in my room, I went through it searching for any mentions of Old Gregor. There were two. At the end of the second act he appeared carrying an armful of logs for the fire – they failed to light in Act Three – but said nothing. Then as the curtain was about to fall Gregor came on again, and announced to the surviving members of the family that the carriage had arrived. It was the only means of escape for those whose spirits remained intact and were still fit to travel. He exited, stumping off into the driveway, completely unaware of the anguish he had left behind.

We started rehearsals a week later. I did my best to give Gregor a distinctive air of decrepitude. On the third day Malcolm took me aside and warned me against making him too old – my log carrying was taking an eternity. People had begun to complain. It was important that I should try and inject at least some faint signs of life into him. There was, he said, no need for me to mutter so much either.

Although horses played no direct part in the action, and could only be heard at key moments jangling their harnesses offstage, Malcolm decided it would be useful for some of us to get a better idea of how they behaved. A visit to the racing stables was arranged for those whose parts required some knowledge of grooming and tack. Several of the actors cried off at the last moment. On the day only two of us turned up as arranged: Henry and myself. Just as I was far too young for my part, so he was far too old for his – a foppish, melancholy medical student much given to moping round the out-buildings, reflecting on lost opportunities.

Together we caught the bus up the long hill through the outskirts and into the country. We walked the last mile along the road to the stables, and then out to where the horses were being exercised. The grass on the gallops was still covered with beads of dew; it felt like sponge underfoot. Larks rose all around, whirring and trilling overhead. The race horses thudded by, slinging divots out behind them. From where we were I could see the town laid out before us, the threads of streets, the grey roofs glinting in the sun. I could even make out roughly where my house was. For some reason I found it oddly disconcerting. I felt I had no business being up here; as if it meant I'd lost touch with whatever thin string tethered me to the ground down there.

Looking back through my tin telescope, I can only liken it to that uncomfortable feeling I still get whenever

I walk into a strange room and see myself chattering away in the corner. What can I possibly be doing here, I wonder? My reassuring tones spill forth in the strangest of places – places I wouldn't be seen dead in. Of course, these channels only open one way. But what if it were different? What if things changed and my curved glass visor was suddenly pulled up, wrenched away? Where would I be then? I know just where. In terrible trouble: shrieking and trembling, buffeted about all over the place, like a genie parted from his bottle.

Back then though I had no idea. It seemed that I had learned almost nothing and absorbed still less. We walked down the length of one of the gallops and then turned to retrace our steps. Henry walked purposefully enough, his arms clasped behind him, but he had taken hardly any notice of either me or the horses. He had an austere, remote sort of bearing which his appearance – that nose, those cheeks – did much to complement. His face seldom registered anything; the mask of impassivity stayed in place, as if set in stone. He gave the impression that any activity, any seismic upheavals, happened far below the surface, safe from the risk of detection. I was, I realized, rather in awe of him.

But all the time there was something nagging away at me. I couldn't be sure what it was. It felt as though I had been here before, or at least somewhere very like it. The great expanse of grass seemed familiar. All at once it came back to me – my father's dream. I closed my eyes and had a momentary glimpse of him spinning around and around in the kitchen, blurring away like egg white, and then disappearing off into nothing.

Whenever I thought about my father – and I tried not to – I found he had turned into a figure like Henry; his uncertainty, his abstraction, had gone and been replaced by something more solid, more stately. This, I decided, was the sort of late father I wanted. That way I could convince myself that I wasn't so much trying on Henry's mannerisms – his air of detachment looked

118

as if it might fit me very well – so much as inheriting things that were rightfully mine.

Off to one side of the gallops, not far from the stables, a ring had been marked out in the turf and fenced off with wooden palings. Several of the horses were being led round the ring by their jockeys. Without saying anything to me, Henry veered off and strode across the grass. By the time I caught up he was leaning over the fence. The horses had all been exercised. Their coats shone with sweat and there was steam rising off their backs. They were walking about in their own heat-haze. One horse in particular was playing up. Whenever any of the others got too close it would threaten to rear up. Ripples of alarm ran across its flanks, its breath came in short, juddering whinnies. A couple of the stable boys had taken hold of its reins and were trying to pull the horse across to the side of the ring. Henry, I saw, was following this keenly.

As I looked more closely at him, I became aware that something odd was going on. It took me a while to be sure. But there could be no doubt about it: Henry was matching his own movements to those of the horse. They seemed to be locked together. When the horse tossed its head, Henry's head would jerk back at the same angle. When it lowered its shoulders he did the same, as if shifting about under an invisible bridle. The horse, it was true, put a lot more into it – Henry's movements probably wouldn't have been noticeable if I hadn't been standing next to him – but still it looked as if he was being powered by a weaker version of the same nervous system.

For no apparent reason the horse suddenly calmed down, all resistance vanished. The stable boys gave it some oats from a bucket and then led it off towards the stables. It ambled obediently behind them. As soon as the horse was out of the ring Henry returned to normal, only a glance in my direction betraying the fact he felt he might have given himself away. 'Lovely animals,' he conceded flatly.

'Oh yes.'

There was a pause in which his features stayed as immobile as ever. But while I didn't meet his gaze I was aware that he had twisted round and was looking at me more searchingly than usual. Whenever I saw Henry full face I had the odd sense that something unnatural was going on; I wanted him to turn back into profile where he belonged. I felt myself shrinking under his scrutiny, wanting to bunch myself up and roll away. Behind us another group of horses galloped by. The ground shook with the pounding of their hooves.

'Majestic beasts,' he went on, gazing at me all the while. 'Very proud, wouldn't you say?'

'I would.'

'Mmm. A great deal to be said for pride, of course.'

'I suppose so.'

'No doubt about it.' He started walking back along the gallops. I followed, my feet sliding about, scrambling to get a grip. Henry walked on ahead, hands in his pockets. Then he slowed and called back over his shoulder, 'How would you describe me, for instance?'

I didn't know what to say. Some sort of frankness seemed called for, and yet I didn't feel we were on anything like those sort of terms.

'Come on. What would you say I was like?'

'I'm not sure . . . proud, I suppose.'

'Good. Yes. Proud. Anything else?'

'It's difficult . . .' We were walking side by side now, in step across the damp grass. 'Aloof?' I ventured.

'Quite right. Proud and aloof. And I hope if we were going to pursue this you might also say that you find me faintly forbidding.'

'Yes,' I said. 'And that.'

He nodded. 'Now ask yourself this question. Why am I like that?'

This was more difficult still. 'How do you mean?'

'Well, do you think I was made like this? Or have I sought to improve on nature by adding a few little contrivances of my own – some airs as well as graces?'

I needed time to think. 'The latter?'

'The latter. Well spotted.'

He had his head tilted as we walked along, his nose lifting into the breeze. Although no more than average height he managed to give the impression of looking down on everyone around him, watching as more aggravated, less composed types hurried about below.

'All right then, ask yourself something else. Why am I telling you this?'

My immediate reaction was to say I had no idea. But, despite my unease at the way our conversation was going, I still felt a peculiar affinity with Henry. I had a dim sense of something shared, an overlap between us; as if we might be linked by the same sort of deficiencies. Not that I would ever have dreamed of telling him so. I did find him forbidding, that was quite true; but at the same time I couldn't help being drawn to him, like a pupil seeking out instruction.

'Look at yourself,' said Henry, before I could speak. 'When you open your inner eye and look around, what do you see?'

'Not very much,' I confessed.

'Practically nothing, I suspect. You're far too insubstantial for your own good. There's nothing there really, is there?'

'No,' I said, and this time my mouth seemed full of air – it was almost stoppering my throat. 'Not really.'

He shook his head. 'That won't do. You're unformed, that's the trouble. Everyone starts off unformed, of course. But most people find themselves hardening into personalities. It happens of its own accord. Some people though have to do the job themselves. You can't go through life the way you are, you'll fall apart in no time. What you need are some mannerisms, some outward devices. Do you understand what I'm saying?'

'Yes,' I said, 'I believe I do.'

'Pick on something you think might suit you. What about me? Is there anything there you like the look of?'

It wasn't a particularly windy day, the larks rose and fell as if they were on plumb lines, but still my reply got blown away.

'I'm sorry,' said Henry. 'I didn't hear what you said.'

'Your assurance,' I said, more loudly this time.

'My assurance. You like that?'

I indicated as much.

'A lot of that has to do with posture. Posture, and poise, and unconcern too. Unconcern is all very well, but it's no good by itself. Otherwise people will simply treat you with the same indifference as you treat them. And that won't do at all. What you need is another layer, further concealment. Again, look at me. What do you see?'

'You can be very touchy,' I said, admiringly.

'I can be very touchy,' agreed Henry. 'Almost anything can set me off. And what a temper I have. Volcanic. Sometimes I frighten myself. One moment I'm equable, even-handed, the soul of moderation. And then, Boom! I've jumped straight out of one skin and into another. People don't know how to react. I must warn you though that this all takes time. A lot depends on what you can get away with. Build up slowly, and keep your eyes open; there are lessons to be learned in the most unlikely places. Above all, practise; cloak yourself with little quirks. Learn to let yourself be governed by contrivance.'

'That's what I'm after,' I said.

We walked the rest of the way back to the bus stop in silence. I needed time to digest all this. A lot of things which had previously appeared both incomprehensible and beyond my grasp had suddenly become clear. I looked into the future and I could see all kinds of doors swinging open. For some reason I saw them as brown, translucent flimsy things, slippery to the touch. Beyond – the actual geography was hard to piece together – lay the biggest wardrobe I had ever seen. It stretched far over the gallops and off into the distance on specially contoured rails. Row upon row of different clothes just hanging there. A whole range of fancy apparel. Anything I liked I could take down and try on. Everything could be made to fit. I saw that I didn't have to be held back by the same sort of uncertainties that had plagued my father. Quite the reverse, in fact. Nothing need hold me back at all.

'Just one other thing,' said Henry as we reached the bus stop. 'You won't go telling anyone else about this, will you?'

'About what?'

'About what we've been talking about?'

I was offended he'd even thought it necessary to ask. For a moment I saw myself taking umbrage, rearing back on a high horse of my own making. It seemed an encouraging sign, something to build on.

'No,' I said, 'of course not.'

'Good. Take in what I've said . . .'

'I will . . .'

'Think about it . . .'

'Yes.'

'. . . and then pretend our conversation never happened.'

Almost immediately a bus came by. We were the only two passengers. We sat in separate seats, Henry in front, me behind. The bus drew away, gathering speed. I gazed out at the manicured fields, the white paling fences, the houses bunching together as we neared town. In truth though I hardly saw a thing.

Chapter Eleven

It was partly as a result of Henry's advice that I threw myself into the play even more keenly than before. After two weeks of rehearsals I felt that I had ironed out any inconsistencies in my portrayal: Old Gregor was in my blood. I'd never known such excitement. And I wasn't the only one. Nobody could remember seeing Malcolm in such a good mood. His enthusiasm had even affected the actors – at least they cast off some of their listlessness and made more effort than usual to remember their lines.

At night I would fall asleep as soon as I got home, jumping out of bed the next morning before the sun was up and walking the streets until it was time for me to start work. Sometimes I walked the streets as Old Gregor, practising the odd hobbling gait I had devised for him. There was scarcely anyone else about at that time of day. Those that were tended to walk in much the same way, so I attracted little attention as I staggered from one street corner to the next.

Above all, I had a sense of accelerating destiny. I thought – and here I was making what proved to be a terrible mistake – that instead of being tossed haplessly from one stray circumstance to the next, I was able to exert some control over my life. That I was able to make things happen. As for my manner, I was trying out various new characteristics, not simply plumping for any one thing, as Henry had suggested, but varying the mix until I found a suitable combination. To my fledgling haughtiness, I added a certain airiness, a nonchalance that I felt might prove useful in extricating me from any embarrassing jams. I was taking on more than I could handle, I knew that. But still the lure of dissembling carried me on.

Throughout the rehearsal period I had seen little of either Roy or Arthur. Then one morning I ran into Arthur standing on the stage, gazing up into the darkness above. He was holding a half-extended tape measure that trailed from his hand and snaked across the floor. He started when he saw me and, as usual, needed time to collect himself.

'What have you been up to?' he asked.

'Oh, let me see. This and that.'

Arthur took off his glasses, polished them on his apron, and put them back on again. 'This and that,' he repeated.

'As I say.'

'You've changed,' he said.

'What do you mean?'

'What I said. You've changed.'

'Oh fiddle-dee-dee. Surely not.'

'Yes,' he said sadly. 'I can't quite put my finger on it, but there's something different about you.'

'I don't know what you're talking about.'

A group of actors were standing nearby, laughing shrilly. One of them held his hand over his heart, his fingers splayed out across his chest.

'I'm growing up,' I said, 'becoming more my own man.'

'Yes,' he said doubtfully, 'I suppose that might be it.'

He began to reel in the tape measure, hunched forward over the winder. The metal tab at the end of the tape smacked against the casing.

'You're not the same though,' he said.

'Arthur' – I had to cast around for a suitable, explanatory tone – 'we all change. None of us stays the same for ever, you see. It's part of the process of life.'

'Is it?' said Arthur. 'I don't change. I stay the same.'

'Perhaps you're holding yourself back.'

'No. Not me.' I was aware of an almost mournful look in his eyes – as if I'd been guilty of some cruel betrayal he was struggling to come to terms with.

'Not me,' he said again.

I excused myself; explained that I couldn't hang around, I had things to do. Arthur nodded, he turned away. At the time I thought no more of our meeting. It passed right out of my mind until a few days later when a number of things fell abruptly into place.

On the day of the opening I woke even earlier than usual, and this time lay in bed waiting for the dawn chorus to start and the sky outside to lighten. But the birds took their time and the sky outside stayed a darker shade of grey, with only a few splashes of white to send the day on its way. I looked at the clock and then at the sky, and wondered if the two had somehow fallen out of alignment.

At the theatre all was bustle and industry. I helped paint some trellis work, and checked that my logs were in place for the evening. At six o'clock I went into my dressing-room, shared with several of the other minor roles, and began to change. It had been decided that I should wear a brown jerkin and green leggings on stage, and moreover that my face should be almost entirely obscured by white whiskers. Both the jerkin and the leggings were much too small for me, but since I was going to be bent almost double anyway I was told that it made no difference. Gluing on my beard proved especially difficult. The glue stuck to my fingers more than it did to the long hanks of hair. I had to use so much of it that the fumes made me dizzy.

I can't pretend that I was untroubled by nerves. I was word perfect, my movements too were as carefully rehearsed as I dared. But still I couldn't be sure that everything would go just as it should. Fortunately I wasn't the only one. Everyone else seemed equally

on edge. Everyone, that is, except Henry, who I saw outside in the corridor. He was already dressed in his blazer and riding boots, leaning against the wall smoking a cigarette. He stepped back into a doorway to allow Mr Cheeseman to be pushed past in his bathchair.

'Is that really you?' he asked.

'Yes. At least I think so.'

'I hardly recognized you. It's awfully good. I do like the yellow streaks.'

'That's the glue. Do you think it matters?'

'Quite the reverse. How do you feel?'

I confessed that I was feeling very churned up.

Henry waved one of his hands. 'There's nothing to worry about. All this fuss, it's quite unnecessary. How do I seem to you?'

'Calm,' I said, 'unnaturally calm.'

'Exactly. Well, there you are.'

Half an hour before the curtain was due to go up Malcolm came backstage for a final inspection. He nodded approvingly and made a few minor adjustments, brushing lapels and straightening collars. I stayed crouched in my jerkin. He passed by without comment.

Although officially a member of the cast, I still had to carry on with all my old duties. I pulled the curtain up and then stood, costumed, in the wings, making sure everyone was ready for their entrances. The play went well, far better than anyone had anticipated, the human drama being played out on stage striking some unexpected chords among the audience. It wasn't clear whether they spotted any of their own deficiencies, but they showed every sign of enjoying themselves. There was laughter, scattered applause, then gasps as the scale of the tragi-comedy began to reveal itself. I managed my log-carrying without mishap – and even prompted a murmur of sympathy that such an old man should be so cruelly laden. During the interval there was talk – cautious but excited – to the effect that this could prove the theatre's biggest success for some time.

The second act only seemed to build on the success of the first. The time had almost come for my second entrance. In order to pass from the left-hand side of the stage to the right I had to walk down a narrow passage that ran under the stage. One faint bulb, a nightlight, was there to light the way. There was a room off to one side of the passageway, more of a cupboard than a room, where shoes were kept. They were stacked on shelves from floor to ceiling. As I made my way down the passage I heard the sound of rustling. I wondered momentarily if it might be mice, but I had too much on my mind to give it any more thought.

I was level with the entrance to the shoe store when a voice from within whispered, 'Hello, Dickie.'

I didn't recognize the voice at first. My eyes weren't properly adjusted to the gloom, so that all I could see was a dark shape standing there, quite motionless.

'Who's that?' I whispered back.

'It's just me.'

'Oh. What are you doing in there?'

'Nothing in particular. This and that, as you would say.'

Above me I could hear the actors quite clearly – could even see the soles of their feet through the slits in the floorboards and the tread on one of Mr Cheeseman's wheels. As my eyes got used to the dark I could see Arthur's outline start to take shape more clearly. His spectacles gleamed faintly whenever he moved.

'It's going very well, don't you think?'

He shrugged. 'Not really my sort of thing. Actually, it's a stroke of luck bumping into you like this. There was something I wanted to have a word about.'

'It's going to have to wait if you don't mind, Arthur. It's time for my entrance.'

But Arthur gave no sign of having heard me.

'I've been thinking about what you said the other day,' he continued. 'Been thinking about it a lot, as a matter of fact. You were right . . .'

I had no idea what he was talking about.

'. . . I have been holding myself back.'

Nerves made me impatient. 'Not now, Arthur, please,' I hissed. 'I really must get on.'

Again, my words made no impression at all.

'Things build up and sooner or later they have to come out. They have to, you see,' he said.

'What do?'

'My feelings.'

'Feelings? What feelings?'

'I know what some people would call them. But they'd be wrong. I want you to realize that.'

Due to the size of the shoe store and the fact that we had to whisper I'd moved closer to Arthur. We were standing only a foot or so apart. Without my noticing he'd managed to manoeuvre himself around, so that he now had his back to the door.

There was a squeak as he pushed it shut.

'What are you doing?'

But even as I asked I started to see this was far worse than anything I'd ever imagined. I took a step towards the door hoping that Arthur might move aside. Instead he flattened himself against it, barring my way.

'Arthur, please,' I said. 'You can't.'

'I can,' said Arthur.

'But the play . . . I must go on.'

I could see him shake his head. 'You don't need to worry about that. It doesn't matter.'

'But it does matter. It matters a lot.'

'No. Much more important things. What matters are people. Lives draining away. Loneliness . . . a chance to be happy. That's what's important.'

'Not now, though. Please.'

From above came the sound of horses hooves – they were being brought round to await my entrance. I started to sob, silently. It was as if tears were being forced out through my skin. What was I to do? There was only one thing for it . . . I launched myself at Arthur, hoping to knock him aside. I felt my elbow connect with his chest.

For a moment I thought I'd made it. But then I found myself being picked up and set down again. Arthur held me by the shoulders, stiff-armed and formal, like one of my dancing partners. He sighed, then wiped the back of his hand across his brow.

'There's no point you trying anything like that,' he said. He sounded disappointed.

I heard the cue for my entrance. This was the moment – my moment – when I was to stump blithely through all that devastation towards the glow of a new dawn. But nothing happened. There was a pause while everyone waited for me. The silence opened up like a pit all around. I could feel the alarm take hold as the actors realized that I wasn't there.

'I wonder if Old Gregor heard me the first time,' said Henry. 'He's getting a bit deaf.'

'Old Gregor,' he called out. 'Are you there?'

There was another pause and a few smothered coughs from the audience.

'Perhaps he's still outside with the horses,' he said. 'I don't know where he could have got to.'

What happened next isn't easy to describe. I have often wondered since exactly what options were open to me. I could have done nothing. That might have been better. But this was something I'd been preparing for for weeks – perhaps unconsciously for a good deal longer than that. I couldn't bear to see it all slip away. What is certain is that I gave little thought to the consequences of my actions.

'I'm here,' I cried. 'Down here.'

No-one said anything for a while. The pit of silence grew deeper than ever. Then Henry, standing right over my head, said quietly. 'What are you doing down there?'

There was a note in his voice that I had never heard before. It sounded as if all his poise had fallen clean away.

Even at this stage there seemed some faint chance of averting disaster.

130

'I'm detained in the harness room,' I said. 'I'm having trouble.'

'Trouble? What sort of trouble?'

'It's difficult to explain. May I make a suggestion?'

'I wish you would.'

'Perhaps we could all meet up out on the driveway and commence our journey there.'

But at this point an awkward situation was made a good deal worse. From where I was it was difficult to work out what had happened. To my surprise, I heard a breathless voice from above announce that the horses were now ready. Someone else was speaking my lines. It took me a few moments to realize that it was Malcolm. He must have taken it upon himself to try and salvage things. However, this news, far from resolving the confusion, only served to complicate it.

'Who are you?' I heard Mr Cheeseman ask.

'I am Old Gregor,' announced Malcolm, 'the coachman.'

'No you're not.'

'Yes I am,' said Malcolm.

'He's not.'

'He is now,' said someone else.

Mr Cheeseman sounded bewildered. 'How many Old Gregors are there?'

'I *am* Old Gregor,' said Malcolm, more loudly this time. 'And the coach is now ready.'

I could hear more whispering, and then finally slow footfalls as the actors left the stage. There was a hum of conversation from the audience. People were talking openly to one another, looking for guidance. A single shot rang out from the wings. The hum of conversation died and then started up again, louder than ever. It continued as the curtain fell. There was scattered applause, followed almost immediately by the sound of people getting to their feet.

My memories of what happened next are unclear. I remember being in the shoe room, staring at the floor – I couldn't bring myself to look up. I heard

131

the door open and then squeak shut again. It took me a while to realize I was alone. Whoever found me there escorted me upstairs. Accusing faces looked out of open doorways as we walked along. I was shown into Roy's office. He was standing in the middle of the room. I thought that I had never seen anyone so angry before. His eyes had hardened into fierce little points. His skin was red and there was a thin line of sweat across his forehead like a hatband. Most noticeably of all though he seemed to have swollen with rage, to have blown himself up so that his normal bulk was distended still further. I had almost to mould myself to his curves, to squeeze myself into what little space there was between his body and the wall.

'Why did you miss your entrance?' he demanded.

I didn't want to say anything. I knew from the start that nothing would make any difference. And just as he seemed puffed out with anger, so I shrank to be on the receiving end of it. It sapped me, eroded me. My loose nonchalance was nowhere to be seen.

'Malcolm has had to go home. I've never seen him so upset. What were you doing under the stage?'

'I couldn't get out.'

'What do you mean? Were you locked in?'

'Not . . . no.'

'Was there someone else down there with you?'

Once again I had a sense of invisible slip knots tightening all around me, of being at the mercy of forces way beyond my control. It was hard to work out what was going on. There was no doubt that Roy was furious. At the same time though I couldn't shake this suspicion that somewhere beneath his anger he was relishing all this, indeed that he had secretly willed it to happen.

'You were all alone?' he asked.

'Yes,' I said, 'I was all alone.'

'Was it nerves?'

'No. Not nerves.'

'What then?'

But I wasn't saying. It had nothing to do with trying to protect Arthur. Rather, I saw that any explanation would only have spoiled the sport. I'd have been exceeding my role in all this. I realized – without being sure why – that Arthur was sacrosanct. He could do what he liked. Whereas I . . . I was just the plaything.

'This is a very awkward situation,' said Roy.

'Yes.'

'Of course, there's no way you can be allowed to stay here.'

'No?' I was unable to prise the question mark off the end of it.

'After tonight? Certainly not.'

'When would you like me to go?'

'No point in prolonging things.'

'You . . . you mean now?'

'Better like this.'

I was much too close to tears to do anything but nod. Through blurring vision I was aware of something pale, with a faint gloss to it, being extended towards me. Roy was holding out his hand for me to shake. I took it, at least laid my hand across his to be pressed, and then released. I made my way back downstairs. Everyone had disappeared. The dressing-room doors were closed. I wondered if they were all hiding themselves until I'd gone. I changed out of my costume, collected what possessions I had accumulated and stepped outside.

It was raining, a thin slanting shower that sent the few pedestrians scurrying along the pavements. I walked home as quickly as I could. Not because of the rain – I hardly noticed it. I had this horror that I might soil myself. There was a smell of cooking in the hallway. I was halfway up the stairs when I saw that the electricians were coming down, carrying their fishing rods. They had to hold them out over the bannisters to let me get past.

In my room I packed my case, climbed into bed and hoped that sleep would come soon. I must have dozed, then woken, then fallen into a state where I was suspended somewhere between the two. It seemed as though I was floating down some watery channel, foliage brushing across my face, ripples lapping at my sides. Already I had grown used, on the point of sleep, to this sense of imminent separation; of somehow dividing myself up into handy component parts. Now I saw more clearly than ever that there were things I couldn't possibly continue with on my water-borne safari. Things that my life was just too puny to accommodate. They would weigh me down, get in the way. All those things that hurt too much, that threatened to betray me, those mewling, ungovernable feelings. I couldn't allow them to remain part of me and survive. They would have to go, be wrapped up and cast off.

And it was as if I twisted in my sodden bed and pushed this weakling bundle into the reeds, thrust it away from me, down into the darkness. All at once I was a good deal lighter – I bobbed up like cork. In this state then, half asleep, half awake, borne along that dividing line between my old unsatisfactory life and some distant prospect of the next, I drifted on through the night.

Chapter Twelve

I don't think I have ever seen a more crestfallen couple than the Aylwyns when I knocked at their door, suitcase in hand. They couldn't believe it. What little blood that circulated around Mrs Aylwyn drained away as soon as she saw me, while her husband bent slowly forward into his old stoop like a burning match. I believe they must have seriously toyed with the idea of turning me away. I could sense the reluctance strung between them as they stood there appalled, either side of the hallway. But in the end their consciences got the better of them. They stepped aside and invited me back in. There was no actual invitation as such. Rather they stood aside and made defeated little waving motions with their hands to beckon me inside.

On the surface, at least, life continued much as before. There were, however, a number of small, but telling changes. I was no longer asked to join them for evening prayers. I thought at first they had given them up – perhaps lost their faith altogether as a result of my reappearance. But they were still at it, only on their own. I saw them one night as I made my way from the bedroom to the bathroom. They were kneeling as before in the living-room, arms extended, hands pressed together. Mr Aylwyn's entreaties ran together in one long aggrieved-sounding slur. They had also bought a television in my absence. It sat in the corner of the living-room, covered with a tablecloth when not in use. A good deal of discussion went on about what programmes were suitable for them. They were worried about being corrupted. Little escaped their censure – only religious broadcasts and the occasional quiz show if the questions were of a high enough calibre. I never stayed to watch, disappearing off to my room to unroll my voice, however briefly, and ponder my future.

My main priority – we were all agreed on this – was for me to find another job. But Mr Aylwyn had exhausted his one contact and a number of visits to different employment agencies only ended in disappointment. Devoid of any personal initiative I waited for a sign, some reassurance that I hadn't been entirely forgotten. Nothing came. A month went by. The Aylwyns' patience was on the point of giving out. Mealtimes were an embarrassment for us all; what food I was given came dotted about the plate in tiny piles. Every day I would scan the situations vacant column. I went for various interviews, all without success. Things were getting desperate.

And then one morning I went into the kitchen to find a newspaper folded and propped up alongside the sliver of toast that now passed for my breakfast. An advertisement had been circled in black ink, so heavily that the paper had been perforated in places. It was for a junior filing clerk at the BBC. The job would suit a school-leaver, it said. There was no mention of any educational qualifications, although applicants were expected to have an interest in broadcasting, basic numeracy skills and a cheerful disposition.

Mrs Aylwyn's head looked as if it was on a wire; when she stared up at me her shoulders came too in one lunging movement. What did I think, she wanted to know? I read the announcement again, cleared my throat and contrived to regain some of my loose nonchalance. I agreed that it was certainly worth applying for.

She then glanced away and said something else – at least her mouth moved, but very little sound emerged.

'I'm sorry,' I said. 'I didn't quite catch that.'

Mrs Aylwyn appeared strangely embarrassed, as if she'd been caught out. 'I . . . I wasn't talking to you.'

'But there's no-one else here,' I felt obliged to inform her, Mr Aylwyn having already eaten and exited on some mission of his own.

Now it was Mrs Aylwyn's turn to clear her throat. 'I wasn't talking to you,' she said again, even more hesitantly than before.

I gazed about, to make quite sure. We were definitely alone. 'I don't know who else you could have been talking to,' I said.

There was a pause, her eyes stayed cast down. She gave the impression of digging deep within herself, summoning an admission. 'To God,' said Mrs Aylwyn quietly.

Ten days later I was invited for an interview. I turned up outside an ivy-clad building by the side of the Great West Road, gave my name to the receptionist, and was shown into a room where I was asked to wait. The room was empty. A few minutes later a man came in and asked where everyone else was.

'I don't know,' I said. 'I haven't seen anybody else.'

He looked surprised, went outside and came back in with a sheaf of papers. He sat down beside me and took out a pen and my letter of application.

'Have you ever done this sort of work before?'

'No.'

'Or had any experience of filing?'

I shook my head.

His pen hovered over the paper.

'But you are interested in broadcasting?'

'Oh yes,' I said and started to give him a brief outline of my listening habits: farming programmes, variety shows, plays, talks, concerts, quizzes, children's hour.

After a while he said, 'You're not making any of this up, are you?'

'No,' I assured him. 'It's all true.'

We talked for a little longer. And then he put his papers away, rose to his feet and thanked me for coming in. He would, he said, let me know one way or the other as soon as possible.

A few days afterwards a letter arrived to tell me that my interview had been successful. I passed it across the breakfast table to the Aylwyns. Mr Aylwyn read it first and then showed it to his wife. I saw them exchange a glance and Mrs Aylwyn's eyes seemed to drift briefly upwards. Neither of them spoke. I too was lost for words. I had often rehearsed the moment when I would announce that the time had come for me to leave. Now that it had arrived though there wasn't much point in saying anything. We all just took it as read.

That same day I found a room south of the river in a house set on the junction of three roads. One large road split into two narrower ones and the house had been built on the wedge of land where the main road divided. My room was on the top floor at the back of the house, under the eaves. One round window looked down into a yard below. There was a bed, a hard-backed chair, a wash-stand and a chest of drawers. The landlord was a melancholy divorcé with an eleven-year-old daughter, a pale, listless girl with sums written on her legs in crayon. I had nothing to do with them, apart from sharing a bathroom and lavatory. The lavatory was outside with only a stable door to shield the occupant. There was no electricity, but a torch hanging on a nail beside the cistern. At night the landlord would often go out there in his dressing gown and pyjamas. The torchlight within threw the shadow of giant feet across the yard.

On my first day at work, Mr Menzies, the man who had interviewed me, took me down to the basement. Metal shelves stretched away as far as I could see. The shelves were crammed with buff-coloured cardboard boxes, each one numbered down the side. At the far end of the room was a door. He unlocked it, and then had difficulty finding the light switch on the other side. This room appeared smaller but it was hard to tell. It was piled high with more boxes. A number of them had recording tape spilling out of them. Some of the tapes had no boxes and were simply stacked up on their spools in great teetering columns, unravelling onto the floor. Whenever either of us moved, the tape rustled and shimmered in the gloom.

My job, he said, was to sort out these tapes. I should box up those without boxes and sort the others into numerical order, according to the labels stuck on the spools. These were to be taken outside and filed on the shelves. There was a step ladder to enable me to get to the top of the piles and a luggage trolley to help move the tapes about. If I had any queries, he said, I should call him on the internal telephone beside the door.

And so I set to, climbing the step ladder, lifting down the tapes and trying to put them in order. I hardly saw anyone from one day to the next. By the end of the first week I couldn't see any sign of progress. If anything, things were in even more of a mess than before. There was tape everywhere, spreading out across the floor. It appeared to have a life of its own, ebbing and flowing like a dry brown sea. When I walked it wrapped itself round my ankles, sliding and crackling underfoot. At times I would hold up handfuls of tape over my head and let it fall over my face and shoulders, millions of dried words cascading over me. As soon as I'd cleared one pile, several more were revealed. There were whole chambers hidden away behind the columns of shimmering spools. Mr Menzies came down, grimaced and told me not to lose heart.

It took a month before my efforts began to pay off. Slowly the room was emptying, the shelves next door filling up. I can't pretend that this didn't give me satisfaction. I had imposed order where before there had been only chaos. Six weeks later the room was almost clear. I was down to the last few piles. But the closer I was to completion, the more the work began to depress me. Once the room had been full of lost voices, pressed together in this silent throng. Now there was nothing. Nothing except bare walls and these few last cries being chased into their boxes. I began to yearn for something different – for company, and the occasional glimpse of daylight.

I was leaving to go home one evening when I saw an announcement on the noticeboard at the top of the stairs. There were a number of vacancies for temporary announcers, it said. Several regular members of staff were on annual leave. Vacancies therefore existed in several departments, with the possibility of full employment for those who particularly distinguished themselves. Previous broadcasting experience was not essential. However, some theatrical background was, along with a personable nature and a good clear voice.

That evening I wrote asking for the relevant application form. A week or so later I was invited for an audition.

I bought myself a new set of clothes for the occasion – suit, shirt, tie and shoes. The shirt collar rubbed my neck, the jacket was too narrow across my shoulders, the shoes pinched my toes. I caught the Tube to Oxford Circus and walked up Regent Street, stopping every few yards to collect myself and ease the chafing. Despite the discomfort, I still felt as if I were being blown along, steered by some protective breeze. My steps hurried or slowed according to the wind speed.

Broadcasting House rose before me, as vast and grey as a battleship. Before I went in through the main doors I stood for a moment, staring up in awe. I marvelled at the sweep of the walls, at the great curved terraces stacked up in tiers, the stone porch like a prow above my head. And I thought of that multitude of radio signals, speeding down invisible wires, stretching off to the furthest reaches of the country, all emanating from here, spreading out in long, filigree ripples. Everything that had shaped me, bolstered me, made me what I was, this was the source of it all.

High up on the roof a pylon jutted into the sky. It seemed to be scraping the underside of the clouds, snagging each one and trying to hold it back. But the clouds swept on, and so did I. At the front desk I was told to take a seat; someone would be down to collect me shortly. I sat as still as I could and watched people streaming by, joking, clutching piles of folders, milling around the lifts. It was like a railway station, everyone bustling, resolute, set on their destinations. I thought how assured they all looked, how self-possessed. How they seemed to fit quite comfortably into themselves, with no great effort of will. And I found myself thinking about being back at the seaside with my parents at the mauve and brown hotel, looking into the nursery, seeing the other children there, playing, laughing, equally at ease among the throng. I had known then that I could never join in, that such things were denied me for ever. In a way there was no reason to suppose anything would be different here. Except that I couldn't quite believe that this was the real world, it all seemed satisfactorily remote and unreal. Vaporous, too, with disembodied voices flying down invisible wires, and inaudible chatter behind sound-proofed doors. I felt this was the place for me. It had to be. There was nowhere else.

A woman lent over me, holding a clipboard against her chest – Would I come this way?

We set off past the reception desk, down corridors interspersed with swing doors. Up flights of stairs, down again, along more corridors. My guide walked, pumping her elbows up and down, brisk and business-like, pulling doors open, standing aside, and then striding on ahead. The doors flew back against the walls and banged in our wake. Soon I lost any sense of direction. Eventually we stopped. She checked that the number outside tallied with that on her clipboard and knocked – less certainly than I might have expected. Her fingers hit the door, then seemed to bounce off, making a little involuntary flourish in the air before she brought them back to her side. There was no reply.

She pushed open the door and beckoned me in. We were in a small room with a table covered in green baize and two chairs. A microphone stuck up through a hole in the table on the end of a short metal stalk. One of the walls was made of glass. Behind it a number of people sat talking to one another. I could see they were talking, but there was no sound. A number of them had stopwatches hanging around their necks. On either side of the glass wall were two speakers.

There were some papers on the table in front of one of the chairs. I should study them carefully, said the woman. I would have five minutes to look them over and then I would be asked to read one of the passages aloud. Did I understand?

I nodded. The door swung shut behind her. I sat down, picked up the papers and began to read. The print swam about uselessly in front of me. It made no sense at all. Occasional sentences formed themselves in front of my eyes. The words knotted together momentarily and drifted apart. I wondered if it might be any better if I picked another passage. But it was exactly the same. As I stared at the letters they seemed to uncurl themselves, flattening out into long featureless black lines that ran from one side of the page to the other. I wanted to squeeze them back into some sort of shape. However, they just lay there, lolling about, all the bounce gone out of them.

A man's voice came through the speakers saying that they were ready for me to start. I should turn to the last of the three passages. I did so. It was as bad as the first two. The type had melted like tar. I needed to tell them that something had gone wrong. Badly wrong. I held up my hand. But the voice from the speaker carried on regardless. If I looked above the door, it said, I would see two lights alongside one another. The one on the left was red, the other green.

The voice chuckled in a relaxing sort of way. I wasn't, was I, by any chance colour blind?

No, I wanted to say. No, not me, that was my mother. I've got different problems entirely. But again there was no opportunity. When the green light came on, the voice continued, I should begin to read. Perhaps I might like to have a drink of water before I started? There was a jug and two glasses on the table in front of me. No? I'd made no response. In which case I should simply wait for the signal.

So I sat there, staring up at the wall, holding the papers, the words stretching out lifeless before me. I didn't know what to do. When the green light came on it seemed to do so slowly. Not like a normal bulb, more like a candle as the flame starts to take hold, the filament glowing, then getting steadily brighter. I opened my mouth – and began to speak.

I had no idea what I was saying. Yet it was as if the lines on the paper were somehow being pulled through me, and words were being drawn forth, as if on lengths of string. They unfurled like bunting. To my astonishment I could hear my voice ringing out from some secret cavity, clear and confident. It rose and fell, paused for effect, laid its stresses in appropriate places. But all the while the sense of what I was saying passed me right by – the nature of the words, the way they ran one into another, even the subject matter – it meant nothing. So much so that I couldn't be sure where to stop. I feared that I might carry straight on, from one piece into another without noticing. But even here something was governing my actions. I slowed automatically, summoned a last authoritative flourish, and brought myself up, flushed but hardly even breathless, at the last full stop.

When I lifted my head, it was to see the air thick with glistening threads, the walls hung with streamers. I put down the sheets of paper and held onto the edge of the table with both hands. I thought it might float upwards and take me with it. How did I feel? Not triumphant exactly – I wouldn't allow myself that. But somehow both quite empty and at the same time fulfilled. Not wanting for anything.

Behind the plate glass people were leaning forward, talking to one another, their stopwatches dangling. After a while a different voice came through the speakers, thanking me for my reading. That would be all for the time being. I should wait where I was. Someone would be along shortly to escort me back downstairs.

A minute or so later the same woman who had shown me in opened the door and said I was to follow her. We walked back down the endless corridors, with their shining floors and narrow numbered doorways. Down the stairs. Along more corridors. She stumped much as before. But I glided.

Chapter Thirteen

A week later I got a letter to tell me that my audition
had been successful. My initial contract would be for
three months with an assessment at the end to work out
how I'd done. I should report back to the front desk on
the following Monday: from there I'd be assigned to a
particular department. Mr Menzies couldn't hide his
disappointment at my departure. He sounded baffled
that I should want to go. 'It seems a shame to leave,'
he said, 'when you've made such a good start.' But he
wished me well and said that I could always return
at the end of my trial period.

The next Monday I reported back to the front desk.
Again, there were people streaming back and forth
across the floor, looking busy. This time though
something had changed. Now I felt I had almost as
much right to be striding about as they did. Seldom
before had I been quite so aware of a desire to belong.
I found myself craning forward in my chair, eager to
take my place among them. I could hardly wait.

The same woman who had escorted me up to my
audition came down to meet me again. She was even
more eager than I remembered; it threatened to run
away with her and leave her breathless. The other
thing I noticed was her fingers. They were surprisingly
broad, splayed towards the tips, her nails clipped into
shallow crescents. We shook hands easily enough, then
had some difficulty in separating them.

There had, she explained, been a mix-up. After the first letter had gone out, a second one had been sent asking everyone to come in an hour earlier. 'Had I not received it?' I told her that the second letter had never arrived. Either that or my landlord had forgotten to pass it on – he wasn't used to my getting mail. She smiled unhappily. What it meant was that everyone else had already turned up and been assigned to specific duties. There was only one unoccupied slot left – the final shift of the day, the closedown announcements. Was I familiar with these?

Indeed I was, I said. I knew them well.

And I did, of course. For years they had been the last thing I heard at night. A rundown of the following day's programmes, a short, comforting religious homily or reading, and then – always preceded by some distant roar like shingle on a beach – the national anthem. I would turn off my radio as the final chords died around me. I couldn't bear the empty hissing that came next. I'd come to look upon the closedown announcements as models of constancy, as well as reassurance. Surely the world couldn't be so cruel after all? Not with such warmth, such concern being expressed every night? They sent me off to sleep buoyant with expectation and gave me fresh heart for the day ahead. Admittedly, the reassurance they dispensed never lasted long. Usually it was gone by morning. That, however, I suspected, had more to do with my own failings than with anything else.

Now, it seemed, I was to join them. But only as an observer. I would spend a week there, watching the announcers at work. After that my future would be determined by the holiday roster. Once again we set forth, a shorter walk this time, and stopped outside a door with a small cross made out of a bullrush pinned to it.

When the door opened I saw that the room was full of people. Everybody turned to look at us. I was introduced. No-one said anything. Then I was left on my own. There was nowhere to sit. All the chairs were taken. Some people were sitting on tops of tables. Others were perched on a window-sill. With obvious reluctance they shifted along until there was just room for me to fit on the end. It took a while for everyone to settle back down again. When they'd done so one of the men began talking. Just before he started he looked around to make sure there weren't going to be any more interruptions. He seemed to be in the middle of running through some sort of schedule. A number of late changes had been made to the published programmes, he said. These would affect the length of the introductory announcements. Wordings would have to be altered, timings checked, in some cases whole passages rewritten. It wasn't easy to follow. A number of the terms were new to me. People listened and wrote things down on pads of paper. I tried to look at my neighbour's notes, but these too meant nothing.

Afterwards the man moved on to another list, this time of passages of the Bible chosen for readings. Here again there had been changes. It all took a long time. There was no room to move about, we were sitting so tightly packed together. I could feel my feet going to sleep, a tingling paralysis creeping steadily up each of my legs. I tried to restore circulation by rotating first one foot, then the other. But I didn't want to make a spectacle of myself. In the end there wasn't much I could do except sit there and wait.

By the time we broke for lunch I'd lost all sensation below both knees. As I lowered myself down from the window-sill, the floor swam about below, distant and strange. Trying to walk, I had to kick one leg forward at a time, as if I were wearing diving boots. By the time I got out of the room everyone had already gone. A last few were disappearing down the corridor. I stumbled after them, slowly picking up speed, trying to keep them in view.

Eventually I found myself in the canteen. I pushed open a last set of swing doors, and there opening out in front of me was an enormous, low-ceilinged room. The noise was overwhelming, the din of conversation matched by the banging of cutlery. On my right was a pile of trays and a queue snaking away along a self-service counter. I picked up a tray and joined the queue. The people I'd been following were just ahead of me, helping themselves to food. They were busy opening the glass hatches, having a look at what was inside, either taking it or pushing it back. I wasn't in the least hungry – I didn't feel I could hold anything down. On the other hand, I felt I might have more resilience with something in my stomach. I took some biscuits, an apple and a piece of cheese. Bunched together – more people had joined the end of the queue – we made our way up to the till. I paid for my food. The others were looking for a table. They'd stopped in the middle of the room and were turning about, heads swivelling, seeing if anywhere was free.

There was an empty table, back near the entrance. They set off towards it. As I followed them I was attempting an awkward manoeuvre; both hanging back and hurrying along, not wanting to appear too eager, and yet hoping I wouldn't be left behind. At the same time I had one eye on the vacant table, counting the chairs to see if there was enough room for me. There looked to be a couple of spare places. They were all taking their seats now, lifting their plates off their trays, still talking. I reached the table and stood by one of the empty chairs, hoping I would be asked to sit down. I could feel myself silently imploring them to take notice. Again, no-one said anything. I might as well have been invisible. I've no idea how long I was standing there – probably no more than a few seconds. But they kept their heads down, never even glanced my way. And so I moved on, forced my still semi-detached feet into motion. Saw a spare chair – at the next door table, in fact – and sat there, unwrapping my biscuits, spreading the knife back and forth, trying to work up sufficient saliva to swallow.

At one point, one of the men caught my eye. I don't think it was anything other than accidental. There was no sign of recognition on his part. Still, I looked away before he had the chance to do the same; my chin swung round as if I'd been slapped. How could I not help but feel slighted? For so long I'd invested these people with my aspirations, had entrusted my nightly welfare to them and seen them as embodiments of all I held true. They'd meant everything to me. Now I was among them – at least trying to be. But they wanted none of it.

When they finished their lunch, stacked their plates and got up to go I stayed where I was. I gave them a couple of minutes start before I followed. I felt less sick than before, but still light-headed, untethered to the floor – everything around was zig-zagging into herringbone patterns. I took my tray over to a hatch in the wall as I'd seen others do. Behind, the air was thick with steam, clouds billowing around me. A pair of hands reached out and took the tray away.

There was no-one back in the room except for a man stretched out on a chair, a newspaper folded in his lap. He looked up in surprise when he saw me. What was I doing there, he asked. I explained how I was the new trainee – I'd understood that we were supposed to carry on after lunch. He shook his head. There was nothing for me to do now. Not for several hours, in fact. The best thing would be if I was to come back in the evening. Even then, he said, I shouldn't hurry. He must have seen me hesitate, unsure of what to do, because he made as if to shoo me away.

I walked down to the reception, out of the main entrance and into the street. Outside I felt even more uneasy. So many people, hurrying along, glazed with indifference. Wrapped tight within their own skins, that great tide of life, pressing up on every side, pulsing

149

away, as I strove to match my faint flicker to theirs. I thought of how diminished people are in numbers, how cheapened. How they seemed to forget about each other so quickly. With me, it was hard enough to make any impression in the first place. I started to walk, with no idea of where I was going. For hours, I wandered about as the light faded and people headed home from work. I kept on going, hardly daring to stop – as if everything might close around me even more oppressively if I lingered in any one place. Soon it was dark. The streetlights were switched on. Under their orange glare I felt not so much the illusion of warmth, but more its absence. What if I didn't go back? What if I just surrendered myself to fate and carried on walking, just to see where I might end up? What then? These and other questions jostled unanswered in my mind. I was still pondering them when I realized I was back where I had started from, right outside the main entrance.

The room was full again. A discussion was underway. One of the men who'd been sitting at the next door table in the canteen was talking about predestination. He kept wiping his nose with the back of his hand. 'I'm not saying there is no such thing as free will,' he said, sounding defensive. 'I'm not saying that. What I am saying is that it only goes so far. Ultimately, there is a set pattern to anyone's life, one which they can do little to alter. That is my point.'

'Now hold on,' said someone else. 'Let me be quite clear on this. What you're saying then is that our lives are already mapped out from the very beginning?'

'Yes, I believe so.'

'And that nothing anyone ever does can change that?'

'They can alter things a bit, but not very much,' said the first man. 'Only within certain bounds.'

'I think that's absolute nonsense,' replied the second. He looked around, seeking support. People seemed unsure how to react; they didn't want to commit themselves. 'If that were true then we might as well switch off now and just let ourselves be carried along – by destiny, or whatever you care to call it. Your theory, such as it is, takes no account of human volition.'

'Give him his due,' said a third. 'Would we really be here if we all had free will?'

There was a thin ripple of laughter. Both men were now showing signs of annoyance. 'Call it what you like,' said the first man. 'I don't care. My point is simply this – our lives follow an appointed course. We like to believe that we're all in control, that we are the ones who can set that course. But we're not. We're quite wrong – it's all been worked out in advance.'

'Who by though?'

'By God, presumably,' said someone from the other side of the room.

The first man shrugged. He didn't claim to be sure. 'Not necessarily by God. But I think with God's assistance.'

'What?' said the second man. '*What?* Oh really.'

'So does this apply to everybody?' he asked. 'Are we all controlled from on high?'

'No, not everyone. Maybe only a select few. Certain favoured people marked out for special attention.'

'Certain people? What sort of people? Are you talking about saints now?'

'I don't think they need be saints. Emissaries might be a better word.'

'No,' said the second man. 'No, no.' He shook his head. 'I won't have that.'

Throughout this exchange I had been aware of something unusual going on. No-one had said anything, or done anything to signal any change of attitude. All I can say is that I felt less apart, less isolated than before. As if I were being drawn in, included in things. It may have been that they were simply too engrossed in their conversation to bother to exclude me. But I couldn't help hoping, even thinking, otherwise. Not that I said anything, of course. The grounds for misunderstanding were still far too great. I suppose I wanted a measure of proof before I could be sure.

The door burst open. A man was standing there, leaning forward, fighting for breath. His face was red and he had one hand clutching his throat.

'Godfrey. What is it?'

But the man didn't answer. He sat down heavily on a stool.

'What's the matter, Godfrey?'

People were crowding around. A glass of water was held out to him. He took a sip, then another. His shoulders were heaving up and down. He was struggling to say something. It took a few attempts before he got there. 'Most odd,' he said at last. His voice was hardly above a whisper.

'Can you tell us?'

'I was walking up Regent Street . . .'

'Walking up Regent Street. Yes?'

'And something flew down my throat.'

'What sort of thing?'

'I can't be sure. An insect of some kind . . . Possibly a locust.' He sounded embarrassed.

'A locust? A locust flew down your throat, Godfrey?'

'I don't know. A big insect, at any rate. I . . . I think it's still there.'

'What do you mean?'

'It's still there inside. I can feel it.'

He began touching his throat, his fingers feeling gingerly around his Adam's apple.

'Can you breathe all right, Godfrey?'

'I can breathe.'

'And you say it's still in there?'

'It feels like it.'

Someone brought a torch. The man on the stool opened his mouth and tilted his head back. Various people pointed the torch inside his mouth, but were unable to see anything.

'We need something to hold his tongue down.'

'But what?'

'Something long and flat.'

'A knife?'

'No, not a knife.'

'I've got an idea.'

Someone went outside and came back with the cross that had been pinned to the other side of the door. He stuck the long end in Godfrey's mouth and pressed on his tongue while someone else held the torch. This too though was unsuccessful. They couldn't see anything.

'It could be that you've actually swallowed the insect, Godfrey, but it's scratched the inside of your throat on the way down, and that's what you can feel.'

'I suppose so. Maybe that is what's happened. I don't know.'

'Wait. Sshh.'

Everyone fell silent.

'What was that?'

'What was what?'

'That noise.'

'What noise?'

'Say something, Godfrey.'

'What do you want me to say?'

'Anything. It doesn't matter. Just talk.'

'I was walking up Regent Street,' he began again, glancing fearfully from side to side, 'I was on my way into work. Not really paying much attention to anything . . .'

'There. Can you hear it?'

'Hear what?'

'It's like a whirring of wings.'

'I don't hear it.'

'I did. Take my word for it. There's something in there.'

'How can we be sure?'

'I know a way. Godfrey, are you able to come into the studio for a moment?'

'I think I may have been wrong,' said Godfrey. 'I think I probably did swallow it, and it's just the

scratching, like you said. On the inside of my throat.'
He looked around. 'I think that's it.'

'Possibly. It's possible. But we need to be quite sure.
How do you feel about walking?'

He didn't know. In the end, he was lifted to his
feet and supported as we all made our way down
the corridor to the studio. Once inside, Godfrey was
positioned in front of the microphone while the rest of
us went into the sound booth next door.

'Take your time, Godfrey. There's no need to worry.
Just start when you're ready.'

I saw his hands shake as he picked up the paper in
front of him. He read from the passage that had been
chosen for that night's epilogue. He got to the bottom
of the first page and was told he could stop. The tape
was rewound and played through the speakers. I could
hear nothing at first. Then, faintly – as if it were running
both beneath and alongside his voice – I heard a dry
rustling sound: wings beating in feeble little flurries.
Dying down, then starting up again. It was impossible
to miss now. There was no need for anyone to point it
out.

'Godfrey. Can you hear me?'

'Yes,' he said, and even this now seemed to bear
the faint flutter of a wing-beat.

'Just stay there. Keep as still as you can. We're
fetching the nurse right away.'

'What is it? Do tell me. Please.'

'Don't say anything, Godfrey. It's better not.'

The nurse arrived almost immediately. Several of the
men from the office helped Godfrey away while she
held his head upright, one hand gripping the back of
his neck. When they'd gone everyone was quiet for a
while. Then the man who kept wiping his nose said,
'What are we going to do?'

'What about?'

'About tonight, of course.'

'I don't know.'

'Well, we'll have to decide soon. There's only an

hour to go.'

'We'll have to find someone else.'

'There isn't anybody. What are we going to do?'

'We'll have to find someone else,' he said again.

'Don't just keep saying that. Who?'

And then something quite unexpected happened.

Chapter Fourteen

'And suddenly there came a sound from heaven as of a rushing mighty wind, and it filled all the house where they were sitting. And there appeared unto them cloven tongues like as of fire, and it sat upon each of them. And they were all filled with the Holy Ghost, and began to speak with other tongues as the spirit gave them utterance.

And there were dwelling at Jerusalem Jews, devout men, out of every nation under heaven. Now when this was noised abroad, the multitude came together, and were confounded, because that every man heard them speak in his own language. And they were all amazed and marvelled, saying one to another, Behold, are not all these which speak Galileans? And how hear we every man in our own tongue, wherein we were born? Parthians, and Medes, and Elamites, and the dwellers in Mesopotamia, and in Judaea, and Cappadocia, in Pontus, and Asia. Phrygia, and Pamphylia, in Egypt, and in the parts of Libya about Cyrene, and strangers of Rome, Jews and proselytes, Cretes and Arabians, we do hear them speak in our tongues the wonderful words of God.

And they were all amazed, and were in doubt, saying one to another, What meaneth this? Others mocking said, These men are full of new wine. But Peter, standing up with the eleven, lifted up his voice, and said unto them. Ye men of Judaea, and all ye that dwell at Jerusalem, be this known unto you, and harken unto my words:

For these are not drunken, as ye suppose, seeing it is but the third hour of the day. But this is what was spoken by the prophet Joel; And it shall come to pass in the last days, saith God, I will pour out of my spirit upon all flesh: and your sons and your daughters shall prophesy, and your young men shall see visions, and your old men shall dream dreams. And on my servants and on my handmaidens I will pour out in those days of my Spirit; and they shall prophesy: And I will shew wonders in heaven above, and signs in the earth beneath; blood and fire, and vapours of smoke: the sun shall be turned into darkness, and the moon into blood, before that great and notable day of the Lord come:

And it shall come to pass, that whosoever shall call on the name of the Lord shall be saved.'

And then I leaned in a little closer to the microphone and wished everyone a very good night.

Chapter Fifteen

In the months that followed my life changed out of all recognition. Or so I thought at the time. In retrospect, I can see that although a great deal changed, one or two things did stay the same, at least for a while. I was asked to continue reading the Closedown announcements. A decision over what would happen in the long run had been postponed, pending medical bulletins and further discussion. Upon being examined in hospital, a large insect was indeed found to have lodged itself in Godfrey's throat. It had been removed easily enough, but he was taking a lot longer to recover than anticipated. There had been complications; he had not responded well to treatment. In the meantime I was to carry on.

A number of my colleagues were unhappy about this; they thought I was far too inexperienced to shoulder such a responsibility. Others, however, felt I was worth persevering with. They got their way. At first I was closely supervised. Someone would stand over me counting down on their fingers so that I got the timings right, conducting me like an orchestra to make sure I didn't stray off-key. But it wasn't long before they realized I didn't need such careful cosseting. There was nothing to worry about: I was a natural.

Every night then I would run through the next morning's programmes, read out my set passage, wish everyone good night and wait while the national anthem broke, crashing all around me. I saw it disappearing off into the night, bringing comfort and sleep. I imagined my audience preparing for bed: parched, elderly types, peeling back the blankets and sliding between the sheets, slipping towards their rest. It was like sitting at the centre of the universe.

The renewal of my contract was never in any doubt. As time went by I began to add small personalized touches to the script, amending it here and there to suit my delivery. Everyone was agreed that my voice possessed certain unusual characteristics — a warmth and colour that other presenters seemed unable to match. Their voices were dull, monochrome things in comparison. Most of the time they sounded as if they were intoning the names of the war dead. But mine was different. It allowed listeners to exercise their own imaginations; it set off these little pictorial explosions in their heads. At least, so everyone assured me. I struggled to believe them, to find some internal equivalent for all this balm I was dispensing. But nothing ever went off in my head, no comfort ever came my way. I can only think that in straining to kick my own imagination into life I must inadvertently have activated theirs.

As my life changed, so I struggled to keep up with it. It wasn't easy. However much I tried to layer myself, to follow Henry's instructions, these feelings of disbelief threatened to rush in and pull me apart. There were times — it all depended on the booking arrangements — when my closedown talks would be recorded an hour or two in advance. On these occasions I'd catch the bus home, climb into bed and listen to myself on the radio as the outside world pitched and turned around me and the giant feet spread their shadow across the yard below.

But I persevered and slowly I too began to change. I grew used to people recognizing my voice, in shops, on the street; grew to recognize that look of confusion as they tried to place me and sought to match how I looked to the way I sounded. Was I who they thought I was, they would ask embarrassedly? And I was, that was the extraordinary thing. It didn't happen often, but even a few times was enough to puff me out with pride. Although I hadn't yet become pompous, already I was trying out a few lofty airs to see which one suited me best. Had the circumstances arisen – they never did – I knew I could refer to myself as a person of some renown and be assured that my imaginary audience would get confused. Was this wry self-deprecation on my part, they might wonder, or simply an acknowledgement of fact?

It was springtime. The air was thick with renewal, my own included. I was still young, a coming man who had almost arrived. The more I thought about myself, the better I felt. I took driving lessons and bought a car. Soon afterwards I left my room south of the river and rented a flat down the hill from Paddington Station on a road lined with cherry trees. For most of the year these trees were a disgrace. Their bark was splashed with arcs of dog urine, their trunks piled high with bottles and cans. But for three weeks or so they came into their own. Every morning another one had burst into life. The pavements were strewn with petals. They blew in pink drifts across the road. I was trying out some small changes to my appearance to go with my new station in life. I had become, I suppose, something of a peacock. One day you might see me in brown, the next I might be in blue. I'd even taken to wearing a large handkerchief stuffed loosely into the breast pocket of my jacket, partly to add my own dash of colour to the general picture, and partly to ensure that I didn't get obscured by all this natural profusion.

The flat was in one of those large white stuccoed buildings with a long glass-covered porch that ran down to the street. I'd moved in thinking that it had just what I was looking for; a prestigious address, a touch of grandeur – to go with my new personal hauteur – and two bedrooms in the unlikely event of anyone coming to stay. But it soon turned out that I had been deceived. My good will had been abused; the place was not what it was cracked up to be. The stucco was held on with chicken wire to stop it falling off. The landlord had run off to the Isle of Man and been declared bankrupt in his absence, the new owners were trying to repossess the house in order to knock it down. During the first winter I was there the heating failed nine times: the boiler for the building was down in the basement, a small black thing like a liquor-still mounted on spindly metal legs. Several of the flats had already been vacated, their owners leaving hurriedly overnight, sometimes with piles of belongings still stacked outside their doors. A time switch was installed in the hall to control the lighting. It went off after a few seconds. Climbing the stairs was an hazardous business, conducted for the most part in total darkness.

A number of flats had been reoccupied, though not by people who had undergone the same rigorous vetting to do with income and character as I had. It was not unusual to find men standing on the landings in the darkness; seldom talking, just hanging around, blowing long streams of smoke out into the stairwell. I would feel my way up the bannisters towards the orange tips of their cigarettes, doing some prolonged throat clearing to alert them to my presence. It never made any difference. I might as well have been invisible. Occasionally matches would be struck and I would see the dim outline of faces; shining skin and eyes whose whites were blotched with brown. Outside I was someone, a soothing presence easing the godly towards their rest. Inside I was nobody. No-one at all.

There were parties, comings and goings at all hours of the night, girls' voices squealing with excitement. Everything seemed to revolve around the flat directly below mine. The music never stopped, a dull thump that sent the dust rising in horizontal clouds from my carpet.

One night, coming home late from work, I fell over a body lying in the hall. As my eyes got used to the gloom, I saw that this was Mrs Montague who lived in one of the downstairs flats. Her windowsills were covered with boxes of geraniums. A Spanish widow – her late husband had been English – she was very religious and wore a large wooden crucifix around her neck, even a veil on Sundays.

Now she was lying on her side, breathing heavily, with great hoarse intakes of air. When I put my face close to hers there was a strong smell of alcohol. Things were really falling apart. When a woman of Mrs Montague's respectability passed out cold on the hall floor, it suggested that the moral fabric of the house was in as bad a shape as the rest of it. I shook her gently by the shoulder. 'Mrs Montague . . . Mrs Montague . . . Excuse me.'

There was no response. If anything, her breathing got even more laboured. I couldn't think what to do. I didn't want to leave her. On the other hand, she was much too heavy to move. I got my hands under her arms – comfortingly warm but not damp – and tried to lift, but I barely succeeded in getting her back off the floor. After a while I just sat there. Soon I felt her breathing begin to dictate mine in the way that a dominant partner, even if unconscious, can pull everything round to their will. Now I too was taking my breaths in huge shuddering gasps. I don't know how long I was there. It seemed as if time had ballooned out around us; as if the air itself had turned black and spherical and was holding Mrs Montague and me trapped in this ridiculous tableau.

I had my hand resting on her stomach below the clasp of a large belt that had twisted round to one side. It's hard to identify precisely my own part in what happened next. True, no-one else was involved

162

and Mrs Montague continued to take a purely passive role, but still I find it hard to claim responsibility for my actions. Personal volition hardly played any part at all. It was as though I simply sat and watched as my hand walked its way up the front of Mrs Montague's dress, stopping when it got to her chest. Ah yes, I thought in a detached sort of way, checking the heartbeat, probably prudent in a case like this. My hand stopped, hovered for a while, and then began inexpertly to rub in a large circle. I suppose there must have been sexual motives somewhere here. I can acknowledge that now, although it's hard to imagine anything less coloured by eroticism. I really didn't know what I was doing. Mrs Montague did not stir. I could feel her heartbeat coursing up my arm, as strong and vigorous as the thump of the music that came up through my floor.

. But my hand also registered something else. Beyond the sound of our breathing, locked in unison, and the creaking of corsetry – also audible – there was a faint rustling sound. I applied a little more pressure to Mrs Montague. The sound got louder. It is important to remember the circumstances here. It was late. I was already tired. Perhaps it was not so odd then that at this point I was gripped by what started as a suspicion, but grew rapidly into something stronger. It was as if deep inside my head a bush caught fire. Mrs Montague, I thought with a force that made me draw back my hand in alarm, was not the flesh and blood creature I had taken her to be. No, far from it. She was, in fact, made principally of straw. Of course this was nonsense. I think I even realized it at the time, but somehow that just made it worse, to be so rattled by such a stupid notion.

And I was rattled. I was still sitting there with my hand drawn back when the front door swung open and the light went on. I saw a girl in a green coat, a handbag hooked over one arm. I recognized her. She lived in the flat that all the men hung around outside. She was young, barely out of her teens by the look of it, her hair so blond it stood out round her head as the light went out, a shock of white bobbing about in the darkness.

'Hello,' I called out.

There was a pause. 'Who's there?' She had traces of a Scottish accent, her voice tinny, unnaturally high.

'We haven't met. I live upstairs.'

'What are you doing?'

'I'm on the floor with Mrs Montague.'

Again there was a pause, longer this time. Some further explanation seemed necessary. 'I came in to find her lying here. I'm not sure what to do.'

I could hear the sound of her footsteps on the tiled floor and smell the gusts of perfume as she got closer.

'Where is she?'

'She's down here with me.'

The girl knelt beside us. All at once, I felt as though our stock of experience had just jumped tenfold. Mrs Montague had temporarily mislaid her own stock of experience, while I had yet to acquire one. But this girl, who knew what she got up to? Not me. I couldn't even begin to guess. I might have been almost famous, but in certain vital respects I had yet to embark on anything that could properly be called a life. It's difficult to explain at this stage; all I can say is that I saw her as having been shaped and enriched by experience, while I remained pretty well untouched by it. Everything went through me. It scarcely touched the sides.

'She's drunk.'

'I know. What do you think we should do?'

The girl coughed. She'd done it when she first came in, before she was aware of anyone else being there. Now she did it again. It was a hard, dry, nervous sort of cough.

'Not much we can do. Has she got any jewellery on her?'

'I've no idea.'

'At least we can keep her things for her, so she doesn't get robbed.'

We set to examining Mrs Montague. I felt back on familiar ground. She groaned as we tried to pull off her rings, without success. Her joints were swollen, the rings wouldn't move. I ran my fingers over her ears looking for earrings and felt the smooth, fat little catkins of her earlobes. There was nothing. Her neck too was bare. There was no sign of the cross that she normally wore. It looked as if Mrs Montague had come out unadorned, already stripped for action. Either that, or someone else had got to her first.

'We can't just leave her on the floor though.'

'Why not? There's nothing else we can do.'

There was something in this. Perhaps the girl had been in this sort of situation before. For me, of course, it was all utterly novel. I did my best to compose Mrs Montague for the night, trying to fold her arms across her chest as if laying her out for inspection. But she was having none of it. Her arms kept flopping back onto the floor and attempts to roll her over onto her side – I had this fear that she might choke – proved equally unsuccessful.

'Come on. She'll be fine.'

We left Mrs Montague behind in the hall, the prostrate bulk of her slipping away into darkness. Ahead of me I could make out the girl's outline quite clearly as we climbed the stairs, see the metallic sheen of her stockings in front of my eyes. Unusually, there was no-one else waiting in the stairwell that night. When we got to the landing she got out her keys, unlocked the door of her flat and turned on the light.

She was smaller than I had thought downstairs, thinner, her face more pinched. Her hair stood up above her ears like the wings on a helmet. I found myself wondering what she'd grow into: shrewish, bad-tempered perhaps. There was something about the set of her mouth that suggested petulance. She might even have been a little knock-kneed; that would probably become more pronounced. But still I was captivated. It must have been her air of soiled innocence. My own innocence at the time was as white as could be. I found myself staring in admiration.

She gave her dry cough. 'Do you want to come in? I could make some coffee.'

I should give some idea of the tone in which this invitation was delivered. There was nothing suggestive about it. Perhaps she was being polite. Her voice had a dreamy, disengaged quality to it, as if she wasn't really sure I was there. Perhaps she just wanted company, however spectral. I only know that I couldn't think what to do, and that the scale of my indecision was far greater than the situation warranted.

For reasons I still cannot properly explain, this represented an important moment of choice for me. There are doors one can go through or not go through in life, of course – although things are rarely as simple as that. There's a lot of rubbish talked about how one comes to a fork in the forest, a parting of the ways in the wood. Either you're lost anyway, or else one of the paths is grown over. Most of the time you find you're not even in the right wood. But still, I couldn't shake the idea that this was a big moment, something I needed to think carefully about.

I looked through into the girl's flat. I could see a pair of red curtains and an airline poster stuck on the wall, a photograph of a plane hanging motionless in a brilliant blue sky. It felt as if I were poised between some prospect of the real world and somewhere else a good deal less real, where nothing was tethered to the ground – least of all the people – and where straw did indeed pass for substance.

I remember I was mainly in blue that day. I looked down the front of my jacket trying to decide what to do. The girl gave no signs of impatience, didn't seem bothered one way or the other. We stood on the stairs in the half-darkness, waiting. Still I hung back. And in the end the decision seemed to be made for me, unharnessed to any emotion or impulse that I could recognize as my own.

'No thank you,' I heard myself saying – voice echoing round the stairwell. 'It's already late. I have to be up early.'

The girl nodded. That was the end of it. I wished her goodnight. If she said anything in reply I didn't hear it. I climbed up the remaining stairs to my flat and let myself in.

The next morning there was no sign of Mrs Montague in the hall. I didn't see her again until a few days later. Crucifix back in place, laden with seedboxes, she was walking briskly down the hill towards the shops at the bottom. I wished her good morning. She passed by without any sign of recognition.

Chapter Sixteen

There were times at work, especially at weekends, when I would be left completely unsupervised. The procedure was straightforward enough. I'd pick up a key from the front desk, walk down the deserted corridors, unlock the studio and let myself in. Someone was always in the sound booth, of course, operating the recording equipment. But we only ever spoke through our respective microphones. Other than that I saw no-one.

In order to save electricity, the lights were always kept on low – the corridors illuminated only by a line of flickering beacons stretching off into the distance. One night I had come out of the studio and was setting off back down to the main entrance when I heard someone calling my name.

'Who's there?' I said, perhaps more loudly than necessary.

'I'm sorry. I hope I didn't give you a shock,' said a man's voice.

'I just didn't see anyone there, that's all.'

'I wanted to tell you how much I've been admiring your broadcasts.'

'Oh,' I said, 'why, thank you.'

'Tonight, for instance, I don't think I've ever been so moved by the Parable of the Sower – those unhappy people without any roots in themselves. You brought out the meaning for me in an entirely new way.'

'That's very kind.'

'I must admit, I was curious to see what you looked like. It's odd, I'd never have pictured you the way you are.'

'Well,' I said, 'perhaps I don't add up.'

'Excuse me for asking, but are you by any chance a little cross-eyed?'

'I don't believe so.'

'I notice that you don't look at me directly when you speak.'

'I can't see you very clearly.'

'Is that better?'

It was better, in a way. He'd moved out into the light. But at the same time – and I think this must have had to do with his having peculiarly colourless skin – he seemed to soak up whatever light was around. So that while his features were clearer, the whole remained somehow indistinct. He introduced himself. His name was Ralph Harding, he said. He was an announcer too, one of the previous year's intake of trainees. I asked what he was doing now.

He shrugged. 'Whatever comes along. You know the sort of thing.'

'This and that?'

'I can see you do.'

There was a pause while I tried to think of something to say.

'Anyway,' he said, 'I mustn't keep you.'

'You're not keeping me.'

But he was already moving off.

'We . . . we might have a drink together sometime.'

'Yes,' he said. 'We might. I should enjoy that. I'm so pleased to have met you.'

'Goodbye then.'

'Goodbye.'

And he disappeared back off into the darkness.

On the floor where I worked there was a short length of corridor divided by two pairs of swing doors. You walked through one pair, and there almost immediately were two more doors. The effect was disorientating; it was like being in an airlock. A few days later I was halfway through the first set of doors when I saw Ralph coming towards me. In daylight his skin had an almost lemony hue to it. I checked my pace, prepared to greet him. But as he got closer I realized that, instead of slowing down, he seemed to be quickening his pace.

'Ralph,' my voice looped out to catch him. 'Hello.'

He only stopped when we drew level.

'We met the other night,' I said. 'You remember?'

'Of course I do. Hello, Dickie. How nice to see you.'

'How are you keeping?'

'Oh fine. I expect you're very busy.'

'Keeping busy,' I agreed. 'And you too, I suppose?'

A tip of his head suggested this was the case.

'We must have that drink sometime,' I said.

'What drink would that be?'

'The other night. We talked about meeting up for a drink.'

'Did we? Well then, we must.'

'When would be a good time for you?'

'Ah. Let's not make a specific arrangement now, if you don't mind.'

'Of course. As you wish.'

'Why don't I get in touch when things are less hectic?'

'Yes,' I said, 'you get in touch.'

Once again he had begun to move off. He let one long wrist trail out behind him by way of farewell. I stood and watched as he made his way through the second set of doors. And despite everything – my layers of contrivance and new lofty airs – there was a sudden lurching and stabbing in my stomach. An aching loneliness that twisted up my gut. These isolation pains; they made me want to clutch myself, to lean against something for support. I felt as if I were pulling something from inside me, digging into myself to bring forth my weakling bundle, holding it out, damp and dripping. But there was no-one there to take it away. No-one at all. It took as big an effort of will as I'd ever mustered for me to straighten up, set my features back into impassivity and continue on my watchful, stately way.

Three weeks later a notice was posted in the office announcing that Godfrey would not be returning to work. Further complications had set in. He was close to retirement age anyway, and it was felt that a lengthy period of recuperation would offer the best chance of a full recovery. To mark his leaving there was to be a party. Contributions were invited for a present.

A room had been reserved in the basement, chairs pushed against the walls, trestle tables covered with cloths. Waitresses in pinafore dresses handed round trays of wrinkled sandwiches. By the time I arrived the room was already crowded. I hung about on the sidelines. A group of secretaries stood in a huddle nearby. They nodded at me. I half-raised a hand in acknowledgement, and put it down again. Some of the men in the office had been talking about them a few days earlier – talking and laughing and swopping vulgar stories. I'd listened astonished. I thought I knew these women they mentioned, some of those they said were so energetic, so dextrous, so easily carried away with passion. I had seen them, tight, pinched women in pencil skirts, as far away from any idea of abandonment as it seemed possible to be. I wanted to believe they were lying. It would have made everything so much easier. But I was worn down by their attention to detail, and by their faint air of puzzlement, as if they couldn't quite believe it either. It made me realize that there must be a whole side to these women, to women generally, I had never considered. They were like huge grey icebergs concealing a good two thirds of their bulk beneath the surface; their natures, strange sundered things, with the outside bearing no resemblance to what was within.

171

I felt a hand on my sleeve. 'Hello, Dickie.'

I spun round. 'Oh, hello.'

'I always seem to be making you jump. Are you alone?'

I made as if to check. 'I am, yes.'

'Good. You've met Helen before.'

There was a woman standing beside Ralph, half-concealed, unsure just when to come forward. I couldn't help thinking that he seemed to have produced her from behind his back.

'I have,' I said. It was the woman who'd accompanied me to my audition. Her hair had been cut. I wondered if she'd done it herself. It looked like a sou'wester. Her eyelids were edged with a thin line of blue, much in the style my mother had adopted after the arrival of Tom. Her manner though was much the same as before – that eagerness undermined by uncertainty, those cheery bursts that gave out abruptly as she wondered if she was overdoing it. We began to talk – at least she said something to me and I said something back. This in itself was unusual. Such unscripted fluency was normally beyond me. But to my surprise I found that I seemed to have been imbued with some of Ralph's assurance, fortified by his example. One of the waitresses came round with a jug of fruit punch. Helen held her hand over her glass. Again I noted her broad fingers and crescent nails. I wondered how old she was. It was hard to tell. There was something both overripe and spinsterish about her; as if she hadn't yet given up hope, but had already tried to hedge herself against disappointment.

And still we were chattering away. These imported sentiments fell out of me, bridging gaps and eliciting confidences.

'I've never felt at ease in crowds,' she was admitting.

'No?' I said, hearty and incredulous. 'Now why ever is that?'

We were interrupted by Godfrey's farewell speech. He talked now as if he was using only one vocal chord;

his voice, thin and hesitant, seemed to bend out of one side of his mouth like a coathanger. It was clearly an effort for him to speak for long. He said how much he'd enjoyed his work and how much he was going to miss us all, and then he turned away to shield his face during the applause that followed.

Someone put on a record. People began to dance. We stood and watched them. After a while I said, 'Shall we?'

Helen was about to say no. It was her natural reaction to things. But then she changed her mind. 'If you like.'

I could see that she was as taken aback by her own boldness as I was with mine. Neither of us knew where it had come from. We moved onto the floor. We'd only gone a few steps when she said, 'Do you mind if we stop.'

'What's the matter?'

'It's just . . . well, shouldn't you be leading?'

'I beg your pardon?'

'I think you should be leading,' she repeated. 'You're the man. It is the normal way.'

'Oh,' I said, 'forgive me.'

We set off again. If anything, progress was even slower and more jerky than before. Either way, we were a singularly uncoordinated pair. I could see other couples getting out of the way whenever we came close. But we finished one dance, and then another. By this time there were some signs that we were getting the hang of it, and so we carried on. We didn't stop until the waitresses started clearing up the plates and glasses.

'I wonder where Ralph is,' said Helen.

We looked around.

'I can't see him anywhere.'

'He must have gone,' I said. 'A number of people already have.'

Indeed, the room was almost empty. Helen went and got her coat. She came back with it already on. There was a glove sticking out of each of the pockets.

'Where do you think everyone has got to?'

'They just seem to have melted away.'

'They do, don't they? I've never known anything like it.'

Together we went outside. The sky was deep orange above the car park, the clouds bulging and bright.

'Can I give you a lift?' I asked.

'No, thank you all the same.'

But I persisted. 'Are you sure?'

And again she wavered. 'Which way are you going?'

Something – some magnetic stirring I could neither comprehend nor identify – told me I would be better off plumping for south.

'I'm heading south,' I said.

'Oh. Are you by any chance going anywhere near –?'

'Near—?' I exclaimed. 'Near—? It just so happens I have to go right past it.'

'No,' she said, standing there, irresolute. 'I couldn't . . .'

'It's no trouble. Please.' I held the passenger door open while Helen got in, tucking her skirt under her knees. She sat upright, her hands folded in her lap. Neither of us said anything for a while. Then, as I pulled out to overtake another car, she gave a gasp, quickly stifled. A gloved hand swung over her mouth.

'I'm sorry,' she said, 'I'm rather a nervous passenger.'

'Am I driving too fast?'

'Not at all. You drive very smoothly.'

We drove on in silence.

'Have you ever thought . . . ?' she began, and stopped.

'Yes?'

'Have you ever thought, well, how easy it would be to have some sort of device which prevented people from being thrown forward if a car had to come to a sudden halt?'

'A harness, do you mean?'

'A harness might impede the driver's movement too much, don't you think? Perhaps a belt of some kind.'

'Strapping us into our seats.'

'With a release mechanism, of course . . .'

'. . . In case of emergencies.'

'That's right.'

'It's odd that you should say that. Once or twice I've found my own thoughts straying along similar lines. I believe such an idea has recently been put forward in Germany.'

'The Germans can be very clever like that,' said Helen.

'Yes, they certainly can.'

In this agreeable manner we passed the rest of the journey. I had the strange sense of doing everything correctly – and having no idea why I was doing it. Again, I had surrendered all control. A wind gusted through me. Following Helen's directions, and insisting on taking her to her front door, we pulled up beside a row of houses. Each had a little garden outside surrounded by miniature picket fencing, hardly more than a foot high. A dog was barking away inside.

'That's Rags,' said Helen. 'He always knows when I'm home.' She reached for the door lever.

'Goodnight then.'

'Thank you for a lovely evening,' she said. 'I haven't enjoyed myself so much in a long time.'

She sounded suddenly flustered, getting out of the car and slamming the door behind her. I sat and waited as she unlatched the gate and walked up the path to the porch. A lantern hung inside, suspended from a hook.

Chapter Seventeen

Two days later I was back. Why? I was obeying instincts. I saw that clearly enough. Whose instincts though? I couldn't be sure they were mine. I couldn't be sure of anything. I needed guidance. But there was no-one to turn to. And so I let myself be tugged along, neither having the volition to go anywhere else, nor the resistance to stop.

When I arrived, only a few minutes late. Helen was already standing in the porch, a headscarf tied under her chin. Inside the dog was crying. We walked to an Italian restaurant nearby. She had never been there herself, she said, although she had heard nothing but good things about it from her neighbours. There were only two other customers. Before we were shown to our table Helen's gestural vigour got the better of her. She was opening her arms to allow her coat to be removed when she caught a hatstand with the back of her hand. The hatstand toppled, but didn't fall. No damage was done. None the less, I saw that the incident had upset her. She needed time to regain her equilibrium. As if in recognition of this, the waiter treated her like an old woman, bending attentively to make sure she was comfortable, chair the right distance from the table, napkin not causing her any difficulties, and so forth. We were given menus. Helen studied hers closely, having obvious difficulty making up her mind.

'So much to choose from. I hope I'm not holding you up.'

'No, no,' I said reassuringly, 'we have all the time in the world.'

'What is this?' she asked, pointing at one of the dishes.

'A pizza? It's a thin layer of dough covered with tomato paste and topped with a special kind of Italian cheese.'

'What shape would that dough be?'

'It would be circular. Round.'

'You know all the latest dishes.'

'Well,' I said, 'I'm largely self-taught.'

Finally she decided. I ordered wine. Helen drank in appreciative little sips, not lifting her glass too far from the table. Over dinner, conversation turned to her family. She told me how she had lost one parent, her mother, when she was just a child, and her father, who had never been robust, followed a few years later. That left just her and her older sister, now a nurse in the West Country. As she did so, she relaxed. The gap between her inner caution and her outward liability narrowed. And I too was relaxing, albeit in a confused sort of way. I'd never had anyone talk to me so honestly before, laying their history out so openly. This lack of restraint, I couldn't get over it. I wasn't sure how to react. In this I was helped by the fact that more than ever I seemed governed by received behaviour; picking up stray signals from elsewhere and pressing them into service. One moment I found myself preying on Helen, the next apparently throwing myself on her mercy. It made for an uneasy combination. Yet from the outside I hardly faltered. I signalled the waiter for more wine. Helen's hand hovered over the top of the glass as he made to pour it, and then moved away.

'What about you?' she said.

'How do you mean?'

'Here I am, going on all this time about myself. And you've hardly said anything about your own family.'

'There isn't much to say.'

She laughed. 'There must be something.'

'No, not really.'

'But what about your parents, your upbringing?'

Slowly, reluctantly, I let slip a few details. For the sake of convenience I decided to orphan myself at the same time – making no mention of my mother, except to wipe her out with the same freak wave that had done for my father. It neatened things up all round. When I had finished Helen sighed sadly and said, 'What a pair we are.'

We both reflected on this.

'Life can be very unkind sometimes.'

'Yes,' she said. 'It certainly can.'

When I called for the bill Helen offered to pay her share. I wouldn't hear of it. One of the waiters helped her into her coat, while another stood by to lend assistance. Outside it had started to rain, a light drizzle that blew into our faces and spattered our coats as we walked back.

'Would you care to come in for coffee?' she said, stooping to unfasten the gate.

'If it's not too much trouble.'

As she turned the key in the front door she said, 'You won't expect anything too grand, will you?'

We stepped into a hallway so narrow that there was barely room for the two of us. Beyond it was a frosted glass door. Through the glass I could see something brown jumping up and down. When this door was opened a dog ran between my legs, skidded on the wooden floor, then turned and started to bark.

'You mustn't mind Rags,' said Helen. 'He's not used to strangers.'

We walked into the living room.

'I did warn you it was a small house.'

'No, no,' I said. 'It's charming. So . . . compact.'

'Would you like a look round? It won't take long.'

We went through another door.

'This is the kitchen.'

178

'Where?'

'You're in it.'

'So I am.'

'Why don't you go back and sit on the sofa and I'll make the coffee. I'm afraid I can't offer you a drink. I don't normally keep alcohol in the house.'

A few minutes later she came back with a tray and put it on the table. She poured out two mugs of coffee and sat down on the floor.

'You can probably fit here,' I said, indicating the other end of the sofa.

'Actually I'm quite happy on the floor.' She had her hands cradled round the mug and was blowing over the top of it.

A homely sort of quiet descended.

'Would you mind if I asked you something?'

'Ask away,' I said, as hale as could be.

'You're a very private person, aren't you?' said Helen.

'I . . . Am I?'

'I think so.'

'I suppose I am.'

'I'm a private person too, you see. It's just that I can't stop asking questions. I don't know when to stop.'

She sounded as if she had grown used to telling herself off. Helen, I saw, was keen on establishing a kindred link, some more common ground we could call our own. I couldn't help but be touched. At least, I assume that was what made me stretch out my hand towards her shoulder – she was half-turned away from me on the floor. But it was like watching a fish swim away from me in an aquarium. I had no idea of what I intended to do. Unseen forces were at work, swarming into me. When I next spoke I found my voice had thickened, become almost hoarse. 'Helen.'

She looked up. 'Are you all right?'

'I'm . . . not sure.'

'You've gone very pale.'

I retrieved my hand and put it up to my forehead.

179

'I do feel rather faint.'

Helen had already got to her feet and was standing over me.

'Would it help to lie down?'

'It might,' I said. 'I don't know.'

I twisted round on the sofa and started lifting my legs over one of the arms.

'No, not here. There isn't room. Do you think you can make it upstairs?'

There was a briskness about Helen, a capacity to cope, that I had only seen at work. It was as if I was bringing out the best in her. Nodding now, a shambling mute, I was helped up the staircase. A bend in the middle, I remember, with a bathroom on the half-landing and then up another flight to the top floor. Helen behind me on the stairs to catch me in case I fell. I was steered into a room with a dressing table by the window and a stool alongside it. Along the opposite wall was what appeared to be the bottom half of a child's bunk. She sat me down. I was sweating. It must have been the climb.

'Do you think it was something you ate?' she asked.

I wasn't able to say.

'You poor thing.'

She pulled the curtains shut and asked if I would be happier lying in darkness. I indicated that the light was not troubling me. A damp face flannel was laid across my forehead. Helen stood over me, looking concerned.

'I am sorry to be such a nuisance,' I said.

'Don't worry about me. How wretched for you.'

'I'm sure if I lie down for a few minutes I'll feel well enough to drive.'

But here Helen was quite firm.

'You'll do no such thing. Not in that state. I think you should stay the night.'

'I couldn't possibly. Besides, this must be your bed.'

'Never mind about that. I told you I was quite happy on the floor.'

I heard Helen go downstairs. Noises in the bathroom,

taps, the soft flush of the lavatory – and then she was back in the room.

'Is there anything I can get you?' she asked.

'I don't think so.'

'A pan, anything like that?'

I assured her it wasn't necessary.

'Nothing at all?'

'Actually,' I said, 'there is something.'

'What would you like?'

'I wonder if you would think it very wrong if I was to ask you to sleep in here with me.'

There was a pause, and then Helen said, much more quietly, 'In here?'

'Yes.'

'Do . . . do you think it would make you feel more restful?'

'I think it might.'

I shut my eyes while she made up her mind. A few moments later she went back downstairs. There were shushing sounds – to the dog presumably. She came back up and started laying cushions on the floor and unfolding blankets. I could hear her climbing into her makeshift bed.

'You will wake me up in the night if you need anything,' she said.

'All right.'

There was a click as the light was turned off.

'Good night.'

I don't know how long I slept for – two hours, maybe three. When I woke up the room was bathed in blue light. It seemed to seep in around the curtains. Everything looked watery, and yet at the same time hard, sharply defined, as if it had been cut out in silhouette.

'Helen?'

She was standing by the window, her back towards the bed. Her white nightdress reached down to the floor. 'How are you feeling?' she asked.

181

'A little better.'

'That's good.'

'Are you all right?'

'I couldn't sleep,' she said. She turned back towards the window. After a while I got out of the bed and went to join her.

'You're shivering.'

'No I'm not.'

I fetched a blanket and tried to drape it across her shoulders. But she shrugged it off and stepped away.

'What's the matter?'

She shook her head. Her left hand was held out, as if fending me off.

'Helen.'

'What is it?'

'Would you like me to hold you?'

She turned around slowly.

'Is that what you want?'

I placed my hand flat against hers. After a moment – a tremor of shock – her fingers slowly curled, locked with mine. We stood there, arms straightened, hands clasped. I could smell her flat powdery smell and see how her head was tilted back and her eyes half-closed.

'Helen.'

'Yes.'

'Will you show yourself to me?'

She unclasped my hand. We could see one another quite clearly now. The light had diluted like ink. Her eyes were open and fixed on mine. For a bashful person she could muster a disconcertingly direct gaze. 'How much of myself?'

'Everything.'

'Are you sure?'

Was it hoarseness or irresolution that took my voice away? Either way, I did nothing, just stood there. She took hold of the hem of her nightdress and pulled it up to her thighs. Her knees were slightly bent. She looked as if she were about to launch herself forward like a parachutist. For a while she stayed like that, with a bunch of material in each hand. Then she straightened up and pulled the nightdress over her head.

I had never seen a naked woman before. My first reaction was one of surprise. I had expected . . . I'm not sure what. All I can say is that I hadn't expected everything to add up so simply, to look as if it all belonged together. I'd had a feeling – although I was loathe to admit it to myself – that under Helen's clothes there would be, not just skin, limbs and so forth, but a whole series of detachable lumps and extras before one got down to anything more solid. Even then the details eluded me. But no, I was quite wrong. It couldn't be more plain. For there she was, all of a piece.

She was still holding the nightdress against her side. She let it fall. I was still peering forward, scarcely able to believe my eyes. Helen took a step towards me. With a dry chink, like broken crockery being fitted together, she put her lips on mine.

Sometime later I unglued my eyes to see Helen above me, arching backwards. Her skin was translucent, her veins stood out so clearly it was like looking at a diagram. And as I was cantered across the sheets, I realized I had unleashed far more than I could handle. There came from her throat a sound I had never heard before. It seemed to emerge from deep inside her, dredged up from her most private insides, like a sea lion's bellow.

The house shook, little Rags snapped awake, the neighbours cursed and clutched their valuables. Underneath, all I could do was look up, shocked by this frenzy, aware that I could do nothing to match it. Any noise I made, and I tended to stay quiet at moments of crisis, were as nothing. Tiny bird calls of alarm came from up near the roof of my mouth. But while I chirruped away, I felt deeper, more ominous feelings starting to shift within me. Things I couldn't easily control. All at once, I had this fear that I might split open. I caught glimpses of that rawness, those red rivulets still running beneath.

183

It was as if whatever fine thread united us was being pulled to breaking point. Already I could feel my seams stretching, starting to tear apart. It hurt so badly I could hardly manage to hold myself in. The pain made me cry out. From above there came an answering roar. On and on we went then, juddering through the small hours.

Chapter Eighteen

At work I was increasingly in demand. As well as continuing to read the Closedown announcements, I grew used to being shuttled around different departments, filling in wherever needed. But it didn't take long before people started asking specially for me. So it was that I came to introduce Down on the Riverbank, a weekly programme for anglers and all those who enjoyed the gentle rhythm of the river. I confessed that I had never fished in my life. It didn't matter. No-one was remotely concerned.

Every Tuesday afternoon I would go along to the Effects Studio to record that week's programme. It was a large room filled with every conceivable device for creating sound effects: tin baths, boxes of crockery, panes of glass, coconut shells, cymbals, gongs, dustbins, piles of roller skates, cupboards, free-standing doors. A huge thunder sheet hung on the far wall. Various electric motors were mounted on benches beneath. Alongside was a long bank of turn-tables. Propped up against another wall was a big drum with a pound of potatoes inside to simulate avalanches. On the floor were all sorts of different surfaces – paving slabs, parquet, carpet, tarmac, gravel, even a short grass path.

Off to one side was a sound booth were I sat up on a stool, script in hand, a microphone suspended above my head. I'd always try and conjure the scene in my mind beforehand; the dripping trees and muddy banks, a lingering dampness in the air, dragonflies heaving themselves into the air, rats and voles peering out of their burrows, anglers dotted about half-hidden beneath their umbrellas. Meanwhile all around me people fussed about with jugs and buckets to suggest I was standing beside some teeming pond. A man wearing gumboots waited in a paddling pool ready to move his feet about and produce the appropriate eddies and gurgles. A voice in my ear asked if everything was all right. Ready whenever you like, I replied.

All is quiet. In front of my face the green light comes on. Theme music plays and fades away. The man in the pool starts to tread water as I come sloshing through the shallows. The reel unwinds, the line sings out as my imaginary fly is cast upon the waters.

'Good evening, ladies and gentlemen. Tonight we bait our hooks for the elusive pike.'

Down in the depths something stirs.

Only in front of the microphone did I come alive. Only there was I able to lose myself entirely as my voice tripped and tumbled away. It rang out of this hidden chamber and raced ahead while the rest of me lumbered behind. Elsewhere, I aimed to put as much distance between myself and the world as possible. During the day I tended to keep apart, my inability to join in being taken for haughtiness as my reputation grew. Gradually, my bearing took on a more starchy, tightly-buttoned quality, my shirt grew steadily more stuffed. To carry this off entailed contrivance on a bigger scale than anything I'd tried before. It was hard-going; once again I was feeling my way forward in the dark, unsure of what lay ahead.

Still, I managed it well enough. Others seemed convinced anyway, and their belief helped fuel my confidence. Yet despite my surface gloss and new-found fluency there were times when I felt the need to retreat, to check on my composure and ensure that everything had stayed in place. I took to spending more time than was strictly necessary in the lavatory. I came to look upon it as a kind of refuge. Always when I closed and locked the door behind me I would have a sense of enormous relief. Everything shut out, time held in suspension. Retreating from my outer life. Most of the time I simply sat there. Here too though things didn't come easily; it wasn't so different to sex. These natural functions, I just couldn't seem to get the hang of them. Everyone else took them in their stride. They let themselves go with such ease, such lack of self-consciousness. They didn't care. Meanwhile I stayed crouched alongside, holding myself in for as long as I could.

But however hard I tried, it proved impossible to escape a measure of intrusion. I was there late one afternoon when I became aware of movement in the cubicle to my left. I can't put it any more definitely than that. There was a gap of around six inches between the bottom of the partition wall and the floor. The tiled floor was highly polished. Likewise, the partition was made of some material, plastic presumably, that had a pale milky sheen to it. Directly beneath the partition wall was a pool of light shading off towards the edges. In the pool of light I could see the reflection of a pair of shoes. I thought at first they must be mine. They looked the same, as far as I could tell – the reflection was necessarily dim.

I moved my feet to make sure. There was no corresponding movement from the shoes. They stayed stuck in their reflective glow, toes angling towards me. I lent forward to look at them more closely. They appeared to be a similar style to mine, possibly even the same size. But it was hard to be sure. I wondered where the reflection was coming from. It might, I thought, have been projected off the curve of the bowl next door. At any rate, the effect was disconcerting, as if the feet were inching into my cubicle, violating my own lavatorial space.

And there was something else – a smell – I don't

really like to mention it. But this was so strong it seemed to fill the cubicle. A richly agricultural sort of smell that drove out any weak odours that I may have mustered and flattened them against the walls. I stood up and pulled my trousers over my knees, hurriedly putting myself back together after this brief respite of calm. I'd already been in there quite long enough. But as I did so I was aware of similar sounds coming from my left. Again I craned forward, checking for any signs of movement. The feet, however, remained where they were.

I tore a length of lavatory paper off the roll, then another. The same sounds, as if in unison, came from next door. But whereas my own movements were hurried, even flustered, I had the impression that whoever was in the adjoining cubicle remained quite unconcerned – possibly unaware – that my movements appeared in some way matched to his.

I pulled the chain. The two flushes went off together in a single cascade. I straightened up, made sure my outer layers were properly adjusted and once more checked the floor to see what had happened to the feet. There was no sign of them. The pool of light was empty. I looked round the rest of the cubicle to make sure they weren't there. No, they had disappeared. I drew back the lock and stepped outside. To my left, the door was also swinging open.

'Why, how nice to see you, Dickie.'

'Ah,' I said, 'hello.'

'This is a pleasant coincidence.'

'Yes. I suppose it must be.'

In step we made our way across to the basins and began to wash our hands. I found myself paying far more attention than usual to the application of the soap, making sure it got right between my fingers and up my wrists. Ralph, I noticed, lathered himself up like a surgeon. He unbuttoned his cuffs and held his hands up in front of him when he had finished. We went over to the roller towel. It hung there damp and twisted.

'You go first, Dickie.'

'No, no. After you.'

Ralph had to pull the towel a few times before he found a section that was suitably dry. When he had finished he tried to pull it again for me. The metal casing clanked as the towel gave out and the end came away.

'I am sorry.'

I dried myself as best I could. My hands felt oddly large and unwieldy, almost as they'd done when I used to wear the greaseproof paper bags. Ralph stood alongside watching. Afterwards he said, 'Are you by any chance doing anything this evening, Dickie?'

'This evening?' I parroted. 'No, I don't think so.'

'Might you be free for a drink?'

'I believe I might.'

'Good. Would seven-thirty suit?'

We arranged to meet later by the main entrance. Ralph moved off down the corridor. As we went our separate ways I was aware that my shoes were squeaking slightly on the grey linoleum.

The pub was crowded. People were clustered around the long brass-topped bar. Ralph, however, made his way through without any trouble. He got served straightaway. We collected our drinks and took them over to a corner. There were only two seats free. One was a chair, the other a bar stool. Ralph took the stool. I sat below on the chair. Due to the difference in our seat heights, it was almost as if I were sitting on his knee.

'Now then,' said Ralph. He waited, half-smiling, for me to think of something to say. But I couldn't. Sipping away at my beer, I became more and more uncomfortable. In the meantime Ralph sat there, patiently enough, watching my efforts to fix on a suitable topic come to nothing.

After a while he said, 'This is fun. I don't know why we've never done it before.' And there we rested for another few minutes. I found myself contrasting

Ralph's demeanour – self-possessed, perfectly relaxed – with my own, in which such things were only held onto by an immense effort of will. Of course, I tried to convince myself they belonged there quite naturally. But it was at times like this that the full extent of my contrivance became clear.

'Tell me about yourself, Dickie.'

'Oh,' I began, 'there really isn't that much to tell.'

'Nonsense,' he said.

And so I did. I found myself telling him about my mother and father. About my father's uncertainty and my mother's impatience. About our lack of contact with our neighbours, about our house – even about Tom and the fire. I couldn't help it. All those hedges and restraints, those timely white lies that I'd employed so successfully with Helen had disappeared. Instead I felt as if an enormous magnet had been trained on me, tugging everything I would have preferred to keep hidden to the surface. Ralph nodded, chivvying me gently on whenever I tried to come to a halt.

As he sat there, he made several small adjustments to his posture. I noticed how he had crossed one leg over the other, revealing a band of flesh between the tops of his socks and the bottoms of his turn-ups. There was nothing unduly odd about this – my own lower legs would not, I thought, have looked so very different in the same circumstances. And yet, I found myself staring at this thin shank of leg – unable to suppress the feeling that there was something almost brazen about the displaying of it. As for his shoes, they turned out to bear little resemblance to my own, except in colour – black – and general style. They were, however, highly polished. Looking at both ends of Ralph, as it were – at his face, which tonight looked paler than ever, his nose with its slightly whittled tip and at his shoes which caught the light whenever he moved, I couldn't help thinking that all the radiance within him had drained away to his feet. As if – I never meant to go this far – he might not necessarily even be the right way up. But I strugggled to banish such thoughts from my mind as my slim history came spilling forth.

When I got to the end he said, 'Fascinating. Simply fascinating.'

I shrugged, shook my head. As always I was aware that my past didn't add up to much, being pretty much free of incident or, at least, of anything I would willingly mark down as experience. For the first time I was aware too how very distant it all seemed. So much had happened to me since then, of course, and in such a short time. But still I felt as though everything had slipped away, ceased to be mine.

'Such a sad story. Your hands have healed up awfully well. But I can't help feeling that you're being unfair on your mother. She sounds like an exceptional woman, doing her best in very trying circumstances. Perhaps you should try to be more forgiving towards her.'

'Perhaps,' I said dully.

'Sometimes a friend can see these things more clearly by virtue of being detached.'

'Detached?'

'That's right.'

Ralph was holding his empty glass tilted towards me. It took me a few moments to get the message. I asked him if he wanted the same again.

'Why not something a bit stronger this time,' he said. 'I'm sure we could both do with it.'

I got up to go to the bar. It wasn't easy. People stayed bunched together, not taking any notice as I tried to squeeze between them. There was a moistness in the air that made everything look slightly spangled. Lights hanging on long braided flexes cast a damp glare on the heads of those below. Getting back from the bar proved even more awkward. The ice in our glasses had almost melted by the time I made it.

'There you are,' said Ralph.

'Sorry.'

'I was beginning to get concerned.'

Again I struggled for something to say. I'd often been

conscious before of this sense of existing on the edge of the tolerance of others, aware that it could give out at any moment. Talking about my mother had brought it all back. After I left home there'd been a period when I'd become chirpy, even rather full of myself. Then there was my loose nonchalance. But now that had changed. Given the right circumstances – these were not the right circumstances – I could be puffed up easily enough; at times I could be little else. But the chirpiness had gone. The trouble was that however hard I tried to cloak myself with conceits, there always seemed some part that was left exposed. As soon as you'd covered up one bit, another came unstuck.

I was just pondering the implications of this when Ralph said, 'I hope you won't take it amiss, Dickie, when I say how very much I've come to admire you in these last few months –

'Oh dear, shall I thump you on the back?'

I tried to indicate that it wasn't necessary.

'Something must have gone down the wrong way. Are you better now?'

'Yes. Think so.'

'Why don't you try taking another drink? That might help.'

I did as he suggested. The whisky burned my throat. I wasn't sure if I'd be able to keep it down.

'It's not just the way that you present yourself,' Ralph continued. 'You have a lovely speaking voice, of course, I don't think anyone could deny that. But what use you make of it! How it rings out with such authority. And warmth. It's like a beacon.'

'It is?'

'Oh yes. Throwing light into darkened places.'

A few moments later I asked. 'These darkened places, where exactly would they be?'

'Wherever ignorance and greed hold sway. Wherever men lose the light within themselves. Wherever they give up charge of their lives . . . Is that dark enough for you, Dickie?'

'Yes,' I said. 'Yes, I would have thought so.'

We both drank.

'You have a very nice voice,' I said.

He shook his head. 'Not like you.'

It was true. Ralph's voice was curiously colourless. There was a hollow ring to it, a rattle, like loose hoops on a barrel. It seemed to go with his complexion. I couldn't help thinking how unfair it was, that I should hold such advantages and have so little idea of what to do with them. All at once I wanted to explain how I was looking for something to articulate me, to round me off. Another confessional urge began to make its way, unbidden, up my throat.

'I don't know where my voice comes from,' I said.

'I'm sorry, I didn't quite catch that.'

'My voice, it doesn't feel as if it belongs to me. It never has.'

'Whose is it then?'

'I don't know. These shapes just land on my tongue.'

Ralph was staring down at me.

'Poor Dickie. It must be difficult for you.'

'Oh, it is difficult,' I agreed. 'It really is.'

'Mmm. Vexing.'

'I beg your pardon?'

'I said it must be vexing for you.'

I lifted my head to meet Ralph's gaze. For a moment I thought I saw some dimly remembered shadow flit across, and beneath, his face. Then it was gone, chased away.

'Is everything all right?' he asked.

'I don't know.'

'I expect you'd like another drink.'

'I'm not sure if I should have anything else. I've already drunk more than I'm used to. I have rather a weak head, you see.'

'I can't say I've noticed. Surely you can manage something?' Ralph sounded shocked, even a little affronted.

'I don't want to be rude.'

'That's a relief.'

'All right, I'll have whatever you're having.'

I waited while Ralph went to the bar. I was, I realized, looking forward to a few minutes in which to steady myself, set myself back in order. But he was back in no time at all, carrying two more glasses.

'Here's to you, Dickie.'

For the sake of decorum I wet my lips, no more. I put the glass down on the table, resolving to leave it there. Then, almost immediately, I picked it up again. This time I did take a drink. Followed by another. And then one more. It was hard to believe that I was responsible for such actions; that if I didn't keep a firm grip the whisky would slop out and make a mess. The more I thought about it, the odder it seemed. I looked at my hand holding the glass. It didn't feel like my hand at all. Or my arm either, come to that. I wanted to try and trace it along my sleeve to where it joined my shoulder, to see how I connected up. But it proved more difficult than I'd anticipated. I got stuck halfway. A closer inspection was required; I needed to bend forward to see what had gone wrong.

'Careful, Dickie,' said Ralph.

'What's the matter?'

'You seemed about to topple over.'

'Did I?'

'I daresay you were only adjusting yourself.'

He had reached out to steady me. I sank back in my chair, grateful for Ralph's concern, and found myself looking admiringly at him, any flaws quite forgotten. Not only at his ankles, but at the way he fitted together so neatly. They'd made an even better job of him than Helen; how he seemed not simply at ease, but actually to revel in himself. I, on the other hand, felt that I could come apart at any moment. It wouldn't take much to set me off.

'I do hope I'm not keeping you,' said Ralph.

'In what way?'

'I'm not stopping you from going anywhere?'

'But I have nowhere else to go.'

He lowered his glass. 'Helen's not expecting you then?'

'Helen?' I said. 'Not as far as I know.'

'Good. I wouldn't want to disrupt anything.' He settled on his stool and recrossed his legs. I was reminded of going to see my mother in the hospital, standing there waiting by the tulip beds as she prepared to enlarge upon my deficiencies.

'Helen's very special, don't you think?'

'If you say so.'

'Such a lovely shy smile. And always beautifully turned out.'

'She's an unwieldy sort of beast.'

'Well,' said Ralph, looking at me oddly, 'that's one way of putting it. Here's to you both, anyway. May I ask a personal question, Dickie?'

'Another one?'

He laughed. 'Tell me, how do you see your career progressing?'

It wasn't something I had ever asked myself; I'd had so little hand in what had happened this far that it seemed unfair to start interfering now. All I wanted was to be shut in a sound-proofed room and let my voice resound across the nation; this unbroken line of speech unreeling constantly away.

I said that I had little in the way of plans.

'You must have some idea?'

'No, not really.'

Ralph shook his head. He seemed about to say something and then changed his mind. 'One could easily get the wrong idea about you, Dickie,' he said. 'But you have an innocence about you, an air of being almost untouched by life.'

'That's the way I am,' I admitted.

'Like a child.'

'Yes, more or less.'

At this point one of us got some more drinks, although I can't be sure who it was. All I know is that when I looked down at my glass again it was full.

'So you haven't thought about going into television?'

'Television?' I said scornfully. 'Do you really think it'll ever catch on?'

'Dickie, it already has. Where have you been? It's the future, you know. There's no doubt about that.'

'Not for me.'

'I wouldn't be so dismissive. You'd do well on television. You have a very personable nature. It's a gift, you shouldn't squander it.'

I remembered the television flickering away noiselessly in the corner of our living-room, my mother and Tom sitting watching it as I stole away unnoticed to practise my reading. Up in my room I'd listened to all those disembodied voices on the radio, without faces to call their own, or to get in the way. How I'd dreamed of taking my place among them. Now I was there. What possible reason could there be for changing anything?

'They're crying out for people like us. No accents, no hint of any antecedents. We might have been made for it.'

Still I stood fast. 'I don't think so.'

But the subject made me uneasy. How could I be sure what I should be doing? Sometimes such things were vouchsafed, but mostly not. When in doubt I tended to stay put until fate swept me up again. On the other hand, it was hard to tell where these prevailing winds might come from. They could blow in from the most unlikely places, from far away, or from right under my nose.

Ralph bent forward so that he was staring down at me. 'Don't hide yourself away, Dickie. As you said the other night, "Let your light so shine before men, that they may see your good works, and glorify your Father which is in heaven."'

'Did I say that? Are you sure? I never take much notice. I do hope my father is in heaven though.'

'Take my word for it.'

'All these lights,' I said. 'It's hard to keep track.'

I found myself thinking of Henry, of being up on the gallops with the horses thudding by, and

Henry lifting his unreadable face into the breeze; of the contoured rails that stretched off into the distance, bearing all those opportunities for further dissembling and concealment. Remaking myself in whatever image I chose, presenting myself as all of a piece, just like Ralph or Helen.

'Trust me,' said Ralph.

How readily I went along with anything that looked like being the proper way ahead, bearing some promise of official sanction. Of all my dreads, the one in which I blundered off course and towards disaster was the worst. It was all a matter of latching onto the right beacon. Besides, I was drunk. My level of suggestibility, always way too high, could take off altogether at times.

'I'll have to think about it,' I said.

'Why don't you do that? But not for too long. They're holding special auditions soon. You have to put your name down first. Is there something interesting going on under your chair, Dickie?'

'What makes you ask?'

'Never mind. Perhaps we should be going.'

'Another drink?' I said, perking up and taking us both by surprise.

'Haven't we both had enough? Besides, I'm sure Helen is expecting you. She's probably cooked one of her delicious meals.'

'It can wait.'

'Now Dickie. That's not very nice.'

'Not very nice! Not very nice!'

Ralph was getting to his feet. His overcoat was over his arm. When I looked for mine it had disappeared.

'What have you lost, Dickie?'

'Coat.'

'But you've got it on.'

'So I have.'

We walked between the tables and towards the door. I found it harder than I'd expected. It was all a matter of trying to thread myself through the gaps, and at the same time keep up sufficient speed to stop myself from

197

falling over. I grasped the door handle and pushed.

'Other way, I think.'

I pulled the door and got it open far enough for us both to slip through. The surprise of being outside again hit me as much as the cold air. It was a cloudless night. The moon hung above us, thin as a scythe. Already the puddles had frozen over.

'How do you feel?' Ralph was asking.

'A great deal better,' I said. 'It was very hot in there, didn't you think? Uncomfortably so.'

'You shouldn't have kept your coat on.'

'No, I shouldn't,' I agreed.

'I have enjoyed our evening.'

'So have I.'

'I hope I haven't led you astray.'

'Why would you want to do that?'

Ralph was looking at me. I shifted out of his eye line and tried to assure him that I was perfectly all right.

'I was feeling a bit unsteady for a while,' I confessed. 'In fact, at one stage I even wondered if you were the right way up.'

'I am the right way up,' said Ralph.

'Of course you are.'

'Are you all right to drive, Dickie?'

'All right to drive Dickie. All right to drive anybody.'

'Good. Where have you left your car?'

'It must be round here somewhere. Can I offer you a lift?'

'No, thank you very much. Well, this is where we part company.'

Ralph clasped me above the elbows. I did the same to him and we stayed like that until I felt him pulling away. He walked off without looking back. Behind me I heard the noise from the pub, bursts of laughter, the clink of glasses. Once or twice I thought I might head off in search of my car. But each time I tried the signals seemed to get lost before they reached my feet. Nothing happened. My feet stayed where they were. By the time I was able to walk again the streets were deserted.

Chapter Nineteen

How quickly Helen and I had settled into a routine. I now spent roughly half of each week at her house. Occasionally we'd go out. But for much of the time we'd stay in, sit by the fireside and make our own entertainment. Rags curled up by the hearth, Helen repairing an old cushion cover and watching while I finished off whatever evening meal she had prepared.

'Did you enjoy your chops?'

'Delicious.'

'Yes,' she said contentedly. 'You're a simple feeder.'

Afterwards she would often suggest that we played a board game. There was a stack of long flat cardboard boxes piled up on top of one of the cupboards. I had as little aptitude for any of this as I'd had for disentangling the metal puzzles of my childhood. Helen, however, took it all very seriously, plotting her moves with enormous care. Her eyes would follow the perimeter squares and her lips would shape her calculations. But any pleasure that winning brought her was soon clouded by doubt.

'You were being kind, weren't you?'

'Kind? How do you mean?'

'You weren't really trying.'

'Of course I was. You outfoxed me.'

She never looked convinced though and took to examining me closely during play to make sure I wasn't cheating on her behalf.

The two of us would take Rags out for his final walk of the day. We'd make our way along the ribbon of path, through the gate and out into the darkened streets. Rags ran on ahead while Helen and I strode arm in arm along the narrow pavement.

And then it would be time for bed.

'Shall we go upstairs?' The suggestion was always Helen's, never mine.

'You go first. I'll be up in a minute.'

More than a minute later her voice would call down the stairs, 'Are you still down there?'

'I'm on my way.'

Up I'd go. Helen would be waiting by the bedroom door, already changed into her nightdress, an odd expression on her face – half bashful, half expectant, as if she couldn't quite believe what she would soon become. I did my best to encourage this bashfulness, I felt more at home there, and to push aside the expectancy. But it only ever worked for so long.

For some reason she always liked me to lead the way into the bedroom. The curtains would already be drawn, the bed turned down. A single light burned alongside. What followed had also settled into a pattern. Nothing was ever said. Helen stood at the head of the bed while I stayed near the foot. There would be a pause as the silence thickened and set around us. Then Helen would lean over, take hold of the hem of her nightdress and draw it up over her head.

There she stood, quite naked. Not moving. It was almost as if she was inviting me to criticize her nakedness; to see her for herself, unadorned and sadly flawed. Except the flaws didn't seem so bad to me – admittedly I had nothing to compare her with. Or maybe it was that I found something reassuring about the extent of her imperfections. At any rate I had no difficulty drawing back behind my lazy scrutinizing eye. I noted the dimples on her thighs, the long bow of muscle running up each calf, the way in which the waistband of her skirt had left an imprint around her stomach. I noted too the way in which her breasts were disproportionately small to the width of her shoulders – they jutted up as if braced from the back – the dark tracery of her pubic hair, the hollow at her throat. I noted all this. Above all, I noted her bearing, that air of openness with its faint shade of defiance.

I could have gone on like this all night, carried away on a long inventory of appraisal. But some response was required on my part. I knew that. The source of my own desire remained a complete mystery to me. How could I trust it, be sure it was really mine? Or confident that there was enough of it to go round? I had this fear it might disappear at any moment, and leave me blank, featureless, all gender gone. Then I would be left, somehow more naked than naked, with nothing to cover myself up with. I dreaded that more than anything else – and for this reason our nightly couplings were especially hazardous. What might be left of me by the time we were finished? It was like the level in a glass; sinking, always sinking, never getting refilled. If the level fell too far there was no telling what might happen.

Against this I had to contend with Helen's attitude, which proved different in every way. Far from operating with diminishing resources, she gave every impression that she found it all hugely invigorating, as if it recharged her, made her into the person she always wanted to be but couldn't normally sustain. Her clumsiness disappeared. Instead, she appeared quite assured. Not taking the lead, of course, but not prepared to hang about indefinitely either.

And so I would close in and try my best, always fearful that I would fail to match up to expectations. Always astonished to find myself doing whatever seemed required. How we clung to one another – Helen lost in some outer sphere beyond focus or speech, and me hanging on gamely, banging back and forth, like a diner repeatedly thrusting away some elasticated dish he'd never ordered in the first place. I couldn't lose this sense of splitting open. I wanted to draw myself about me, keep myself concealed. But all the time it was as if there were this pressure bursting away, threatening to tear me apart – as if all my efforts to keep from disintegrating were being undone from within.

Afterwards came the relief that I had made it through. We both needed time to adjust. Helen to rejoin her old self – she settled back down with such an air of disappointment. I meanwhile would check myself over for any signs of surface damage. There we lay, locked in our post-coital gloom. The bed was so narrow we couldn't help but stay embraced. A piece of wood running down the outer edge to keep the mattress from sliding off dug into my back. Helen sighed away. It took a few minutes for her breathing to steady, to regain its measured rise and fall. Although we were pressed together I'd learned with practise to distance myself; it was almost possible to believe I was on my own – or, at least, that there was a big enough gap between us to prevent anything getting through.

The most difficult thing was working out when Helen had gone to sleep. Several times I would think she'd made it, and then there would be sudden signs of life: a cough, another sigh, reaching over me for a drink of water. After which the whole process would start again, with my waiting, trying to gauge if she'd at last dropped off. Somehow I never seemed to get it right.

'Are you awake?'

'What?'

'So am I,' she would whisper, taking no notice of my simulated drowsiness. 'What are you thinking about?'

'I'm not thinking about anything.'

'You must be thinking about something.'

'No,' I said. 'No, I'm not.'

'Oh.'

'I've been thinking . . .' she said.

'Have you?'

'Yes.'

'What have you been thinking about?'

'We are happy, aren't we?'

'Why do you ask?'

'I don't know . . . Sometimes I wonder if you really care for me.'

'Of course I care. Of course I do. You know that. I've just got an unusual way of showing it.'

'Yes, that's what Ralph said.'

'Ralph? When have you seen Ralph?'

'He's been very good to me.'

'In what way?'

But she didn't answer.

'Ralph thinks that I should go into television,' I said.

'Television? Do you think it will catch on?'

'I think it might. People are desperate for distraction. They'll try anything.'

'You'd be good on television.'

'What makes you say that?'

'You never show your real feelings. There's nothing to get in the way.'

The blue light swam about us. 'Is that what you think?'

'Yes.'

'I'm going to turn over now, if you don't mind.'

'All right,' said Helen. 'Then I'll hold onto the blankets.'

Chapter Twenty

A number of wooden easels had been set up around the room, a few feet apart. We had been told to pretend they were cameras, to use them as practice for the real thing before being called in for our auditions. Other than that there had been little guidance. Only a few words at the beginning to welcome us and explain that this business of appearing natural might involve more artifice than we had imagined. Then we'd each been given a clipboard and a page of script and left to go through our paces.

Over on the other side of the room I could see Ralph addressing his easel, quite at ease, chatting to it confidentially. But the rest of us were finding it a lot harder. Everybody stumbling, whirring, springing apart. Struggling to keep hold of ourselves – those selves we wished to put forward as our own. Rolling our perfect English around our tongues. Arms flailing helplessly about, windmilling this way and that. My neck seemed to have grown as long and wavy as my mother's, barely able to keep my head balanced on my shoulders. Whenever I tried to move everything threatened to come unstuck. Meanwhile people passed among us, checking on our progress. All around voices were being raised, mannerisms adjusted. Shreds of inflection flew past like ectoplasm. Mine, I would cry. That's mine, and I would lunge forward and cram it back into my mouth, only to find it wasn't mine at all but someone else's. Some of them tasted disgusting. Then I'd be left where I started, trying to flag down another passing quirk, to see if it could be made to fit. It was like the sales: elbows going, tempers fraying. You couldn't hear yourself think.

All the time I kept talking, trying to make an impression. Aiming my words at a point just below the top of my easel. Hand half in pocket, half out, the interrogatory stoop, the sympathetic ear, the ready chuckle. Mastering the moves. Poise without stiffness, authority without swagger – that was the theory anyway. I tried to remember what I'd read earlier; how it was important not to be frightened of the camera. How it would home in on the smallest tremor of unease and pump it up into full-scale dementia. Every so often someone's name would be called and they'd break off and be taken to the studio next door, there to be dusted down and have their airs more closely scrutinized.

Those remaining would stop, then slowly pick up again and wonder if our turn would ever come. We shuffled on. Slowly the crowd grew thinner. A growing sense of resignation had calmed us down. I heard Ralph's name being announced, saw his back as he was led away. I wished I hadn't paid any attention to him. What business did I have in a place like this? As if to stave off this mounting sense of disappointment, I addressed myself to my easel even more intently than before.

I must have been concentrating so hard that I didn't recognize my own name. Apparently they had to repeat it three times before they got any response. And then my surprise was such that I threatened to lose all coordination, limbs once again thrashing helplessly about. I walked across the room with my slow-mangled gait, jolted by occasional spasms and borne up on waves of envy. A man in a tweed jacket checked my name off on a list, and indicated that I should follow him.

The studio was in semi-darkness. The man warned me to watch my step. Thick cables had been laid on the floor. You could easily trip up. He explained that someone would be along shortly to apply make-up. After that I would be required to do a test to camera. A woman started dabbing at my face with a powder puff. I could feel the powder caking as soon as it was applied. There was a white circle in front of me marked out with chalk. A voice from behind told me to stand inside the circle. As soon as I was inside lights were turned on. They were much brighter than I had expected. Whenever I blinked spots of dazzle stayed there, imprinted on my eyes. I was told to relax. It was all a matter of obeying a few basic instructions. Did I understand? Above my head a microphone hung suspended on a long pole. The camera was facing away from me. It had a small seat on the back like a saddle and was mounted on fat rubber wheels. Two men were pushing it into position. I could see the lens, hooded and black, swinging round towards me.

'Are you ready?'

Such a narrow aperture, so very small, like a rabbit-hole, or the entrance to a long dark tunnel. I peered into it.

'Is everything all right?' the voice was asking.

'How am I ever going to fit through?'

'Don't you worry about that.'

But I was worried. The closer I looked, the harder it seemed. Practically impossible for someone of my build.

It took me a while to realize that a countdown was underway.

'Twenty seconds,' called the voice.

I would have to shrink myself, slip slowly in, hand over hand.

'Ten seconds.'

'Quiet everybody.'

'Five . . .'

There were fingers extended in front of my face,

disappearing one by one.

'Four. Three. Two.'

'One.'

And then the ground dropped away. I felt as if I were falling. Somersaulting along. Flung feet-first round corners and down subterranean shutes. All the time picking up speed, darkness rushing by. Quite jumbled up now, far worse than before.

There up ahead a patch of brightness. Small at first, yet getting bigger. Bigger as well as brighter. Not round, but flattened. Lipped like a spout. Still I hurtled along, faster and faster, the air stretching and tightening around me.

Then bursting forth . . .

Out into the light.

Chapter Twenty-One

In that light I learned to shine. No longer cowed, no longer irresolute, but blazing away. My touch sure, my manner melted on. My signal threading its way through the elements. These battered arcs across the sky. Electrical storms over the Pennines, ball lightning near Basingstoke . . . But still struggling through whatever the weather; stealing into people's houses at dusk, passing through walls, up braids of wire and into their living-rooms. A popular apparition, welcome wherever I went, leaving no trace behind me, no mess or mark at all.

Driving home at night I would often look up and watch the windows stream past outside. Some dark, others curtained with bulbs burning dimly away. Shadows glimpsed within; standing, sitting, shifting about, lost in their own half worlds, bringing their lives to the close of another day. And as I did so, I couldn't help but feel faintly proprietorial. Yes, I would think as another window streamed past, I've probably been in there. And there. There too. All of them, in fact.

I don't think that any of us who went into television in the late-fifties – I'm talking now of men such as Bruce Belfrage, Hugh Greathead, Chester Wilmot, Roddy Ottershaw and myself – could escape a sense of being pioneers. Striking deep into uncharted territory, opening up new worlds. And people were only too eager to follow; they couldn't get enough of us. They looked to us to educate them, to entertain them, to broaden their horizons, or simply to make them forget themselves for a while. This last proved to be something of a speciality of mine. While others headed off for politics, current affairs and the like, I found my level at the less demanding end of things.

Making the transition from radio to television entailed a number of changes to my broadcasting technique. The warmth and authority which I had brought to my radio broadcasts failed to come over on television. Instead I was apt to appear stiff and unyielding – at least to begin with, until I learned to lower my guard and loosen up. Whatever gravity I'd been able to summon before also disappeared. Unable to match itself to my appearance, it simply flew away. But in its place came something else: a lightness and fluency of presentation, an engaging sort of guilelessness, not so removed from my old loose nonchalance, but now fixed securely in place. My voice too changed, apparently of its own accord. It began to veer up slightly at the end of lines, giving me an air of imparting confidences and offering the possibility of instruction.

My new career unrolled before me. I adapted myself accordingly. In doing so I found that I fulfilled a need, that I struck some instinctive chord in people. They looked to me to tell them unimportant things. As such, of course, I was more in demand than ever.

The success of *Down on the Riverbank* had done much to establish me as a friend to country dwellers, a ruralist of renown. This put me at an unexpected advantage. One morning I was asked if I might be free to go upstairs for a meeting with the Programme Supervisor. He greeted me, bade me sit down and proceeded to run through a brief inventory of my qualities; how he saw me as a link with the past – a reassuring presence who could convince those more timid viewers that there was still a place for traditionalism, for the simpler pleasures of life in our bright new technological age. I had grown used to hearing people extol my virtues, and had grown adept, so I thought, at concealing my astonishment at their impressions of me. But on this occasion there must have been something in my face that gave away my surprise. 'Oh yes,' he said, leaning excitedly across the desk, 'I don't think I've ever come across anyone quite like you before.'

'You haven't?'

He shook his head.

'Never?'

'Not as far as I can recall. It's this effortless quality you bring to everything. I don't know how you do it. But then I imagine you don't fully know yourself. It doesn't do to examine these things too closely.'

'No,' I said, 'I suppose not.'

'I thought it would be useful to have a chat and see if I could get some idea of your special areas of interest. To find out what sort of subjects particularly engage you. That you feel passionately about. Is there anything that springs to mind? Anything at all?'

I cleared my throat and gave a hesitant little move. 'This and that.'

'This and . . . ? How right you are, Dickie. How right you are. Adaptability is so important.' And then he began to outline his plans for me.

So it was that I passed from imparting knowledge to testing it in others. Out of the shallows I came, and climbed up into my quizmaster's chair. There to watch and preside as the customary scenes of triumph and confusion were played out below me. Answers hovering above the tips of tongues, brows knotted, heads shaking. And all the while the search for truth got gently teased along.

'No, I'm going to have to stop you there, Dr Cowell. The woodland sprite with coat of yellow-buff and white underside which likes to make its nest in honeysuckle bark is the dormouse. So nothing for you, sadly. Now, Mr Dunford, how would you recognize the leaves of a hazel?'

'The surfaces are very rough and hairy. And, if I'm

not mistaken, the margins are toothed.'

'Absolutely right. Well done. A point to you. Mr Fellows, where would you expect to find a grasshopper's ears?'

'Not on its head?'

'Oh, no. Certainly not on its head.'

'Lower down?'

'Yes, but you'll have to be more specific.'

'On its feet?'

'Oh dear, I'm afraid you've gone down too far. On either side of the base of its abdomen. Mrs Stevens, let's see how you get on with this one, What is a singing hinny?'

'Is it a type of wild cat?'

'A cat? Oh dear, that's nowhere near. Yes, Mr Dunford.'

'They're little black cakes baked on a griddle and they get their name because there is so much butter in them that they hiss while they're being baked.'

'That's a wonderfully comprehensive answer. I couldn't have put it better myself. A more geographical question now for Dr Cowell: the inhabitants of Finland belong to two entirely different peoples; what are they?'

'The Finns?'

'Yes.'

'And the Swedes?'

'Absolutely right. The Finns and the Swedes. With a small Lappish minority. So a point for you. Mr Dunford again, what sort of bird would you hear making this cry, 'a little bit of bread and no che-e-se?'

'Would that be the yellowhammer?'

'It would, it would. Mr Fellows, what wild flower is popularly known as "the sunflower of the Spring"?'

'The dandelion.'

'Well done. Now Mrs Stevens, what nocturnal practice were hedgehogs once thought to be guilty of? . . . I'm going to have to hurry you.'

'Is it . . . dancing?'

'Dancing? My goodness, what can you be thinking of?

Hares possibly. No, hedgehogs were, in fact, believed to seek out cows as they lay slumbering in the meadow and to rob them of their milk. So nothing for you again. But don't you worry, Mrs Stevens. You'll soon get the hang of it as we go along.

'Dr Cowell, in olden days how would innkeepers advertise the fact that they sold wine?'

'They'd hang out a sign?'

'Yes, but what sort of sign?'

'A sign saying that they sold wine?'

'Ha Ha Ha. No, not quite I'm afraid. Yes, Mr Dunford?'

'They would put out a pole and this pole would have a bush attached to the end of it.'

'You've done it again. Quite right. And for a bonus point, can you tell me what proverb owes its origin to this practice?'

'A good wine needs no bush.'

'"A good wine needs no bush" – still in common use to this day, of course. Dr Cowell, geography again. Can you name one European country where there is still a sizeable nomadic population, not counting gypsies.'

'Well . . . the Lapps are nomadic.'

'Yes, the Lapps, so Finland again. At this stage in the game Mr Dunford is out in front with five points, Dr Cowell is not that far behind with three. Mr Fellows has two, while Mrs Stevens, I'm afraid, has yet to score.'

As I grew, so I spread myself in ever-widening circles. It can only have been a matter of months after I made my television debut that I was asked to present a programme called 'Tonight in Town'. The programme was made up of interviews, conducted by me, with various personalities – men and women who had distinguished themselves in their own chosen field, be it music, showbusiness or sport.

The idea seems obvious enough today, back then though it was a considerable innovation. Nothing of the kind had ever been tried before. A great many misgivings were expressed beforehand. There were fears that guests might be ill-at-ease, perhaps made to look half-witted or subjected to lines of questioning they did not care for. I sought to allay any such doubts: no-one need have anything to fear from me.

These days, of course, such a style of interviewing can appear over-deferential, unctuous – even servile. We live in harsher, more confrontational times. Back then though a greater decorum prevailed. Together my guests and I trod our way delicately around any possible areas of embarrassment or dissent. I was as loathe to penetrate their carefully erected exteriors as I was to be penetrated myself. We were in the same business, after the same things. Bear in mind, too, that any obvious manifestations of character in the interviewer were frowned upon. You were simply there to pose a series of painless, easily understood questions to your guests, thereby allowing their natural charm to shine through. It was like a form of conversational handball in which set topics were patted lightly about.

Thus I might pose a question such as, 'I can't tell you what a pleasure it is to have you on the show, Mr –. I understand this is your first time in England. Are you enjoying your stay here?'

And after a few moments to think it over, back would come the desired response: 'I love this wonderful country of yours, Dickie, and everyone in it, from the humblest chimney-sweep, right up to that great lady in Buckingham Palace.'

Again, of course, things have changed. Interviewers now are so eager to make a spectacle of themselves that they barely listen to what their guests are saying. People are insulted and ridiculed, treated without any respect. You wonder why they agree to do it. But with me no-one was caught unawares, no-one had their composure ruffled. And how eagerly they took the opportunities I presented. How they relished the chance to talk about themselves. I grew to recognize that peculiar doggy look that would come over them as they waited to be spurred on to further anecdotal feats, the flicker of gratitude as I obliged. We were like old chums; the one gently prompting the other to give of their best. I suppose I grew to believe in it, too, to see this as friendship of a sort, one that I seemed particularly well cut out for.

At the end of the interview – they only ever lasted five minutes each so as not to put too much of a strain on this instant rapport – both parties would go away happy in the knowledge that they had performed a mutual service. The viewers were happy too. Every week more and more of them tuned in, hundreds of thousands watching as another set of guests were buffed and lustred.

They came and went, a blur of faces in which few, if any, stand out. More and more of them, all waiting patiently, all blossoming under the lights. We made scarcely any impression on one another, a brief touching of self-interests and that was it. But now I knew that I could hold up my head in this sort of company – in any sort of company – and be sure that I no longer had anything to fear. Any little chinks in my armour had been plugged, all my old doubts had gone. Those feelings of disbelief that threatened to rush in and pull me apart soon disappeared; they quite passed from memory.

My life expanded. It grew bigger and bigger, and I swelled to match it. I filled out, assumed bulk – and in the process came not only to believe in myself, but also to take it all as nothing less than my due: the result of considerable effort and shrewdly applied talent. There was a poise, a splendour about me now, a brisk purposefulness as I marched along my intended path. Everything was fixed in place.

Chapter Twenty-Two

At home, of course, I wanted for nothing. Helen made sure of that. Every evening when I returned, there she'd be, waiting with her familiar air of bruised willingness. She was tender, concerned, so eager to please. But all this compliance could prove wearing. It disturbed me to have awakened such outsize feelings in anyone. I didn't know what to do with them; the responsibility got me down. Slowly I moved from being appreciative to something more sinister. I began to take advantage.

'Is there anything you'd like to eat tonight?' she would ask each morning. I don't know where she found the time to go shopping; how she divided herself up astonished me. At first this could scarcely have been more straightforward. As time went on though there were a number of experiments.

'Now, let me see. No . . . I'm sure it would be too much trouble.'

'Do tell,' said Helen.

'Well, I wonder if you could manage Cold Chicken Isabelle?'

Her voice tended to get lower at moments of crisis, as if she had to reach right into herself to stay calm. 'Cold Chicken Isabelle? What is that?'

'Pieces of chicken cooked in a veal stock, left to cool and then coated with a thin layer of almost colourless jelly.'

Her mouth dropped slightly. 'I could try.'

'But where would you get the truffles? The sweet pimentos?'

'I could try,' she said again, doggedly.

There had to be a limit to this, I would think to myself, a point beyond which she refused to go. I struggled to find it. The most I could get out of her was an extended sulk. If I had been particularly unpleasant she would mope about in a wounded way, not saying much, but never raising her voice. At times she seemed on the verge of tears. Then she'd pull herself back again and life would carry on as before. Nothing could dampen her enthusiasm for long. I found she loved nature – flowers, sunsets, birds would all set her off on long heartfelt appreciations of the beauties of the world. The smallest sparrow moved Helen, sent her hand fluttering responsively over her chest. She was brimming over with benevolence.

Yet, despite all this, in our way we were happy. Just occasionally I couldn't get over how inappropriate it all felt; as if I might almost have been tricked into it. But these jitters came and went. Even the dog and I had come to an accommodation of sorts.

'Rags has taken to you,' noted Helen contentedly. 'He needs a master.'

True, at night, there was a price to pay for this contentment. But here too there had been changes. That glimpse of boldness, the directness of gaze I'd once found so disconcerting, had faded away. Somehow Helen had come to see that this satisfying of private desires was a shameful business, best conducted with eyes downcast. She dropped back into herself with a bigger bump every time.

Afterwards we'd lie there in bed, packed together like pressed dates.

'We should invite Ralph over one evening,' she said.

'Should we? Why is that?'

'We haven't seen him in ages. I wonder how he's getting along.'

'I'm sure radio is where he naturally belongs. It's what he's best cut out for.'

'Do you really think so?' asked Helen.

'Oh, I don't have any doubt.'

Ralph's television career had never got off the ground. His skin, already unusually pale, turned out not to take at all well to light. The brighter the illumination, the more absorbent it became. When the film was developed after his audition there was nothing there – he'd hardly even registered.

'I hope he's all right,' she said.

'I'm sure there's no need to fuss.'

'Do you want to read?'

'No thank you.'

And with a click we were in darkness.

There was no reason to imagine that any of this would change. We could have gone on this way for ever.

But then things did change. Although I now spent much of my time at Helen's, I'd kept on my old flat. I was there so seldom that I paid little attention to how much the place had deteriorated. But just occasionally I'd go back, either to pick up any post or to collect some clothes. On this occasion I had gone there to change into my dinner jacket. That night there was to be a special dinner to honour those men and women who had played their parts in shaping British broadcasting. While our industry was still in a state of comparative infancy, no-one could deny that a remarkable amount had been accomplished in a very short time. Within a few years watching television had become an integral part of people's lives. A good many, it seemed, did little else. There was ample cause for celebration.

Helen was to come and collect me later and drive me to the hotel where the dinner was being held – that was all arranged. But when I got back and started running a bath, I found there was no hot water, only an ice-cold stream from both taps.

Cursing away, I set off down the stairs to the

basement. A door in the hallway led to another narrower staircase. At the bottom there was a passageway. Pipes ran overhead mounted on metal brackets. A string of lightbulbs was suspended alongside. There was a strong smell of soot. The lagging had come away from the pipes, it hung down from the ceiling in long quilted strips. At the end of the passage was the boiler room. I walked down the passage, and pushed open the boiler room door.

My first reaction was one of surprise. The boiler had not gone out. It was still alight. I could see the orange glow spreading out across the floor and hear the hushed roar of the flames. The temperature was a good deal hotter than it had been outside. Already I had begun to sweat. If the boiler was still alight and the hot water wasn't working, then what did that mean? Presumably that something was interfering with the heating process – I never claimed to be an expert on any of this.

I went over to the boiler, squatted down and looked in through the glass pane set into the metal casing. At first I could see nothing as the pane was misted over. But then the mist started to clear and white clouds melted away to reveal what lay behind. Even then, I saw nothing amiss. Nothing that struck me as especially odd. Only flames, twisting and twining, knotting together. But the more I looked, the more I thought I saw something hidden, half-concealed in the blaze.

It must have been at this point that I fell backwards and reached out to steady myself. There in front of me, rising out of the flames, thrusting forward, was a face. Features melting in and out of focus. Hair flaring up like a brush. Cracking teeth. Eyes, childlike and lost. Crusted with heat. Beseeching, yet at the same time accusing.

When I tried to pull my hands away they were stuck to the sides of the boiler. Sealed to the metal. It was as if I were being forced to stare inside. His lips were already moving, starting to cry out, though no sound emerged. His eyes still locked on mine, an expression of terrible reproach, as if all this was somehow my fault. A memory rose, unbidden, inside me. I remembered my father, spinning around on the kitchen floor, shredding away before my eyes. This wasn't my father, I was sure of that. But as we stared at one another through the furnace's roar, I thought I could see something familiar about the rise of his forehead, the tilt of his chin, as his flesh seemed to fly off the bone. Some flickering family resemblance that passed between us, hardened for a moment, then was gone.

I fell back onto the floor, my hands tearing away. I got to my feet and ran from the boiler room, along the passageway, into the hallway, scrambling up the stairs. As usual there were men hanging about on the first floor landing. Louche, unhurried types, lounging in the shadows. For the first and only time they drew back, flattened themselves against the walls. Their eyes, normally speckled with indifference, bulged in surprise as I staggered past.

What happened next is unclear. I don't know how I managed to get changed. All the time my hands were swelling, growing redder. When Helen rang the bell a few minutes later I could hardly make it back downstairs to answer the door.

'What's the matter?' she asked. 'Your hands? Your face? You look like you've seen . . .'

'Drive on!' I cried. 'Drive on!'

All through the journey Helen kept bombarding me with questions. Did I want to turn around? See a doctor? But I said nothing. Just sat there, cradling myself, lost in disbelief. All the time trying to push this face away, as it swam up before me. We drove on, inching along in the evening traffic. At last we drew up outside a tall brown building with diamond-pane windows and low, overhanging eaves.

'What gingerbread hell is this?' I demanded. 'Are you sure this is the right place?'

But several of my colleagues were already milling about by the front door. I could see Ted Teagle, Owen Roxborough and Brian Allgood standing in a cluster booming with laughter, clapping one another round the shoulders like oarsmen. Getting out of the car proved more difficult than I had anticipated. I had to lever my way out with my elbows. Helen stood over me fussing away. Various people greeted me as we made our way in. One or two advanced with hands outstretched. But I barged past, leaving them thoroughly confused, wondering what had got into me.

Inside a waiter stood by the door holding out a tray of glasses. 'Would we care for some champagne?' he murmured.

'No, I would not,' I said. 'Fetch me a whisky.'

Clearly taken aback, he recovered quickly enough and sent someone off to the bar. I found that I could open my fingers just far enough to fit the tumbler inside. As I lifted it to my lips and tasted the whisky on my tongue another of my colleagues, a dauntingly jovial man called Ollie Cutts said, 'My goodness, Dickie, what have you done to your hands?'

'Nothing.' And I made to turn away.

'Nothing? But they're all . . .'

'Just an accident.'

'I'll say. Whatever were you doing?'

He had his head tilted to one side, clearly expecting an explanation. Helen was standing alongside looking even more concerned than usual.

'I was gardening,' I improvised gruffly.

'Gardening? Looks as if you caught them in the mower. Are you sure you shouldn't see a doctor?'

But again I wouldn't hear of it.

There was a seating plan pinned to a blackboard just by where we were standing. Cutts went over to have a look at it. 'What a stroke of luck,' he said. 'We're all sitting together.'

Shortly afterwards a man dressed in livery banged a gong and announced that dinner was served. We made our way through into a large room with a stage at one end. On the stage were two microphones, a lectern and a small curtained-off area to one side. The tables were ranged out below, covered in white tablecloths that reached down to the floor. Grace was said in a low, almost inaudible mumble. We sat down. Wine was poured. Waitresses began to bring round the first course.

'Ah, good,' said Cutts, 'Russian eggs.'

Throughout the meal various attempts were made to engage me in conversation, none of them successful. I was hard work. Much of my concentration went on trying to eat. A number of times I loaded up my fork successfully enough and got it up to my mouth, only to let the food drop off at the last moment.

'These eggs are slippery, aren't they?' said Cutts.

Our plates were collected up, to be replaced by others. I wasn't hungry anyway. My meal went untouched. I noticed a number of people glancing in my direction. The woman on my left asked nervously if she might help herself to my carrots. Helen too was staring across the table at me, frowning. Eventually the food stopped coming. Brandy was served, along with cigars. A long blue cloud of smoke settled over the room. The same man who had bidden us into dinner got up on stage and called for silence. He wished, he said, to introduce our host for the evening. Would we please put our hands together for Roger Trimble.

Everyone duly clapped. Everyone, that is, apart from me. Trimble bounded up to the microphone. I knew him slightly, a tall, sandy-haired man unable to stop himself from smirking at his own remarks. The curtain to the side of the stage was pulled back. A line of glass goblets was revealed, each one standing on a plinth. These too were applauded. Then Trimble began to speak. He talked of how we lived in a hugely exciting new era – in communication, in education, in entertainment. How in a few short years television had enriched people's lives, broadening their horizons, rounding them off, instilling tolerance and understanding. And every so often he would stop to allow yet another burst of applause to lend substance to his words.

The first of the night's prizewinners was called to the stage. He made a speech thanking everyone he'd ever worked with for their support and forebearance. I didn't take a lot of notice, being more preoccupied with the state of my hands. They were oddly numb and, at the same time, still throbbing with pain. Each of my fingers now looked to have a little white pillow stuck on the end of it. When I touched one to another, they felt spongy, detached, like bubbles. The light seemed to spread around each one in a pale pink glow. I kept turning them over in my lap, trying to work out what had happened.

Meanwhile Trimble kept talking. Everyone downed their drinks, banged their cutlery and rocked back and forth. The procession of prizewinners marched up to collect their awards. They made their speeches and returned, grinning delightedly, to their seats. On and on they went, with neither the audience nor Trimble showing any signs of wearying. And while I was not above gibbering inanities myself – might indeed be said to have built my career on them – I didn't think I could stand Trimble's wittering for a moment longer. I longed to get away, to stumble out into the night air, to feel it soothing my poor blistered hands. Alone with my confusion and my fears.

As unobtrusively as possible then – hoping even Helen might not notice – I pushed my chair back and half got to my feet. Trimble, of course, kept droning on, smirking away. His words, audible enough but hardly digested, came to me in short isolated bursts: '. . . for his fluency, his self-possession, his remarkable unflappability . . .'

I crept off towards the door where the waiters stood in line, shoulder to shoulder in their white linen jackets, hands by their sides. Back bent as low as I dared, one foot before the other, each step barely brushing the floor.

And still Trimble kept going '. . . his ease with strangers, his tact, his common touch. His absolute integrity of manner . . .'

Almost there now. A clear view through the door, the chequerboard tiles beyond. One or two colleagues staring in surprise as I slunk by.

'Also for making it all look so damnably easy when we know just how hard it really is. But perhaps above all for allowing those of us here and so many others to share in the special allure of what I can only call his personality, it gives me enormous pleasure to present this special award to . . .'

There was a pause. For a moment, I imagined myself slipping through this chink of silence that seemed to open in front of me like the doorway and making my escape.

Then I heard my name being read out. All around people began to applaud. Even the waiters were clapping. The lights which had been dimmed during Trimble's speech, brightened again. 'Well done, Dickie,' said a man's voice from close at hand. 'Yes, indeed,' said another, 'many congratulations.'

People were patting my back. Slowly, I straightened up and made my way back between the tables. I caught a glimpse of Helen, her eyebrows up around her hairline. Trimble was waiting by the steps that led up to the stage. He was holding out the one remaining goblet. I climbed the steps and took the goblet as best as I could, cupped it in my blistered fingers. Trimble moved away from the microphone and gave a small sweep of his hand to beckon me forward.

The applause died away. The room was quite silent. Everyone sat there, waiting for me to begin. Trimble smiled encouragingly. A smile that grew steadily more fixed as time went by and nothing was forthcoming. 'Perhaps you'd like to say something, Dickie,' he said without moving his lips.

I nodded, swallowed and waited for some suitable sentiments to make their way up my throat. Still nothing came. I looked out at the clusters of upturned faces, and it seemed to me that everyone I'd ever met was there, all waiting expectantly. I tried to dig deep into myself, hoping that if I reached down far enough I might come up with something to bridge this dreadful gap. But all I could find – all there was to see – was this face that swam back into my mind's eye. Creased in pain. Twisting and writhing in the heat. Only for an instant – then it was gone. But it was still enough to loosen my sinews, however briefly.

As I looked down, the goblet seemed to slide from my hands, falling through them as if they were coated in oil. The light caught the curve of the rim as it dropped. Sharp, brilliant crescents spun out over the front few tables. The goblet hit the floor and shattered. There was a bang like a grenade going off. Glass flew up all round. Fragments hung suspended in the air, rocking lazily back and forth. A low gasp filled the room.

'Oh my word,' said Trimble quietly.

Several people had jumped to their feet. They were brushing broken glass from their clothes. I heard someone asking if I was all right. But I said nothing. Did nothing either, except hold out my hands, scarlet and swollen, towards the audience by way of explanation. I stayed that way for some time. Just standing there, arms extended like a supplicant, as if I might beg their forgiveness, throw myself on their mercy.

I felt someone touch my arm. Trimble was behind me. With him too, I was surprised to see, was Helen.

'Would you like to come and sit down?'

'. . . I don't know.'

'Why don't you come with us.'

The two of them steered me round and towards the back of the stage. Everyone was chattering away now. I could hear the hubbub stretching out behind me. I was led out into what appeared to be some sort of storeroom. There were chairs stacked on top of one another, tables tilted up and a chaise longue pushed against one wall. Someone was despatched to stand by the door and make sure no-one else got in. The nurse was being summoned, they said. In the meantime, they tried to get me to lie down on the chaise longue, to put my feet up. I'd only agree to sit, the backs of my hands resting on my knees.

We waited there in silence until the nurse came. She prised open my fingers to examine my palms. 'How did you do this?' she asked.

'He wouldn't say,' said Helen.

The three of them went into a huddle. I couldn't hear what they were talking about. After a while the nurse came back and told me that I should go to hospital and have my hands bandaged.

There was hardly anyone left in the dining-room when I was led back in. Those few that were there stopped talking immediately they saw us. Helen was walking anxiously on one side of me and Trimble on the other, each of them cupping an elbow. Together we made our way slowly to the front door. I kept my head down. I didn't want to catch anyone's eye.

Helen left me by the main entrance while she went to fetch the car. She wasn't gone long. With help, I was lowered into the passenger seat. Helen stayed outside for another couple of minutes talking. Several more guests had gathered and were trying to peer in through the car windows without being noticed. I could hear someone telling Helen not to worry. She was doing her best to be businesslike, but I could tell she was finding it a strain. Her voice had slipped down further than ever.

Then she got into the driver's seat, pulled the door shut and started the engine. As we pulled away I could see something glinting on my lapel, lying there like a long glycerine teardrop. I lifted my hand to brush it away. It was a piece of glass.

Chapter Twenty-Three

My hands took a long time to heal. Wrapped in bandages, they hung like clubs from the ends of my sleeves. Of course, I'd been here before – that only made it worse. At least the service was better this time round. Without the use of my hands there was a strict limit to what I could do. Helen had to cut up my food and feed it to me. Dressing myself was also out of the question. I would stand there docilely while Helen buttoned me into some chosen outfit. 'What sort of mood are you in today?' she would ask, standing by the wardrobe. But no colour had been invented that could match my mood. My old peacock feathers had fallen clean away.

I had hopes that my injuries might signal some respite in our sexual relations. But I was wrong. She clung to me even more keenly than before, took advantage of my enforced inactivity. Yet there was a gulf between us now. Helen sought to stretch herself across it, becoming jollier, more solicitous, but I kept pulling back. And after a while she withdrew into a puzzled isolation of her own, circling me warily, not wanting to get in the way. It wasn't easy. Her house was far too small. We were practically living on top of each other. Helen wouldn't hear of me going to my flat. For obvious reasons I wasn't keen to go there either. So I sat and moped, while Helen cooked, provided and nursed me slowly back to health.

I was to stay away from work until I had fully

recovered. Everyone had been very understanding. But I made slow progress. Try as I might I couldn't help thinking about what had happened. My composure could never be the same; it now had blackened footprints across the middle of it. Who did they belong to? What were they doing there? Helen's composure was suffering too. I noticed that she'd started to get clumsy again. Her gestures were all over the place. There had been a number of breakages. In one sense, I suppose, she was trying to re-erect her defences, take shelter behind this flurry of activity. But it was too late. The weight of sadness saw to that. It affected her balance.

I left the house as often as I could. In the evenings I would take Rags for his walk while Helen prepared our evening meal. Always the same route: across the common, past the parade of shops, and back through an avenue of dripping sycamores. Rags tugging away, his lead wrapped round my bandaged hand. And as I walked I pondered, both on my immediate future and my long-term prospects. To be the instrument of unhappiness was a new experience for me. The idea that my own behaviour might have a direct bearing on anyone else took a lot of getting used to. But the evidence was all there. Helen had taken to gauging her own mood by mine; she matched herself to my humours.

The more I thought about it, the more I realized that something would have to be done. We couldn't go on like this. But the search for a solution eluded me. Nothing came to mind. It was all a matter of trying to light on the decent thing.

Always I opened the door to be greeted by new and hopeful smells. Helen would be in the kitchen leaning over saucepans. When everything was ready I sat down, hands propped uselessly in front of me, and had my napkin fastened around my neck.

'What's this?' I asked as she brought a large plate to the table.

'What do you think it is?'

'I have no idea.'

'Guess.'

I sniffed. 'Rabbit?'

'Rabbit? No. It's Sole Cardinal. A whole sole stuffed with pike forcemeat and lobster butter, lightly poached in a white wine sauce and garnished with chopped mushrooms. Now, how much would you like to start with?' She was already holding the fish slice, poised to serve.

'Actually,' I said, 'I'm not that hungry.'

'What do you mean?'

'Well, I don't feel much like eating.'

'But I can cut it up for you.'

'I can cut up my own food now,' I said.

'Can you?' said Helen doubtfully.

'Why don't you serve yourself first. Maybe I'll have some in a minute.'

'Don't you want any?'

'Not for the time being.'

'Are you feeling all right?'

'Yes, thank you, perfectly all right. Do carry on.'

Slowly Helen began to serve herself. She cut herself a small portion and spooned up some sauce to go with it. Then she picked up her fork and took a mouthful.

'You don't seem very hungry either,' I said.

'I find it hard to enjoy food when you're not eating.'

'But your enjoyment gives me pleasure.'

'Does it?'

'Oh yes.'

When she had finished eating she put her knife and fork together on the plate.

'Is everything all right?'

'What do you mean?'

'I wondered if something had upset you.'

'I don't think so,' I said. 'What sort of thing did you have in mind?'

She shook her head.

'It doesn't matter.'

'But it does. I would hate for there to be any misunderstanding between us.'

'I just thought . . . you're not your normal self.'

'What normal self would that be?'

Helen shook her head again. It was almost a shudder.

'I can't think of anything offhand,' I said.

'I said it doesn't matter.'

'Although now that you come to mention it, there is something I've been thinking about. As a matter of fact, it's about us.'

'Us? What about us?'

'You know how close I feel to you.'

'Do you?'

'Of course I do. You know that.'

'You've never said so before.'

'Well I'm saying it now. You've done so much. You've brought me out of myself.'

'Yes,' said Helen smiling. 'And you've done the same for me.'

'I do think though that we've reached a stage when we should be thinking ahead.'

'Thinking ahead,' she repeated.

'That's right. I hope what I say won't come as too big a shock.'

'Oh,' she said. 'Oh. Are you . . . ?'

'What?'

'Are you going to ask me . . . ?'

'Ask you what?'

She was smiling broadly now and her face had turned very red.

'I never thought . . . Oh Dickie.'

'I'm not sure if you understand me.'

'Well, you say . . .'

'It's just that I can't help feeling it would be better if we were to see less of one another.'

Helen picked up her knife and fork again. Then she set them back down.

'How much less?'

'I think it would be better if I didn't come here any

more. I think perhaps we shouldn't see one another again. At least not for a while.'

'Is that what you want?'

'I think it would be for the best.'

'Why?'

'It's hard to explain. I just think it's for the best.'

'There must be something more than that,' said Helen.

'No . . . I don't think so. Not really . . .'

'But there must be.'

'Perhaps I ought to leave,' I said, and got to my feet.

'Where are you going to go?'

'I thought I would go to my flat.'

'To your flat? How are you going to get there?'

'I can drive.'

'Are you sure?'

'It's all right,' I said. 'I'll manage.'

Now that I was going, it suddenly seemed important that I should try to fix things in my mind. The lay-out of the house, the furniture, the ornaments. But it was all going too fast. I went upstairs, collected my clothes from the wardrobe, draped them over my arm and came back down into the kitchen.

Helen was sitting quite still at the table.

'Goodbye then.'

She didn't look up.

I opened the front door. There was the path, the wicker fence. As I stepped out I could feel a cold breeze around my shoulders. The car sprang to life more eagerly than ever. I must have gone several miles before I took any notice of my surroundings. I stared out, beyond the pale mounds of my hands, through the windscreen, looking for familiar landmarks. And there they were, one after another. The junctions, the bridges, the signposts, just the same as always. I found it all oddly reassuring.

The lights grew brighter, the buildings bigger. Soon I was driving down a wide road between rows of large white houses. Some looked to be freshly painted. Others were crumbling away. Plaster showed through, brown and cracked. But as I looked something happened. I glanced up to check in the mirror – and there was nothing there. The streetlamps had gone out. No orange lines thinning and merging behind me. Nothing.

Ahead, the streetlamps burned as bright as ever. They flashed by on either side. I slowed down, took my eyes off the road. Checked once more in the mirror. All black. The lights were being extinguished as I went by, snuffed out as I passed. I knew that the sensible thing would be to pull over, to turn round and see for myself. Not to trust the mirror. But I was beyond the sensible thing. I didn't dare. Instead, I drove on, eyes fixed ahead, as the darkness funnelled out behind me.

PART THREE

Chapter Twenty-Four

On the surface at least little changed in the next few years. My career continued to prosper. I remained just as fluent, as assured as ever. There was nothing to suggest anything was amiss. But somewhere inside me now was this sliver of doubt. I tried to bury it, to ignore it altogether. For long periods I'd think I'd been successful. Then there it would be, stretching and flexing itself once more.

With these doubts came other things. Almost without realizing it, I began to be troubled by premonitions. At first I couldn't work out what was going on. Occasionally pictures swam in and out of my mind. They seemed on the verge of becoming clear, and then disappeared off again. There were voices too, but they were just as indistinct; it was as if people were shouting at me from underwater. All I had were these intimations of disaster, a fear that something dreadful was about to happen. I did my best to pretend there was nothing, hope that they would simply go away.

Instead the premonitions became worse. A pair of doors would spring open, as if on a giant advent calendar, and there, however briefly, would be a glimpse of some misfortune waiting to befall me. I saw myself ruined, brought low by disgrace, barely able to recognize myself. The voices too got more distinct. But it was impossible to work out if they were trying to protect me from this fate or hasten me towards it. I would be about to do something, often something very minor – it could be as simple as crossing the road – when a warning would resound in my ear like a thunderclap. There was nothing for it but to wait while others cast themselves in front of the traffic, until the moment was right for me to cross. I felt as if I was under instruction, responding to signals that passed through me like radio waves. Except that the messages were never that clear and I could only hazard a guess at what I was meant to be doing.

What made it worse was that I couldn't bring myself to believe that these premonitions were really mine. They offered glimpses of a future I had no desire to see. I wondered if I hadn't accidentally picked up someone else's – someone very bad by the look of it – with one calamity after another lying in store for them. There was no telling whose they might be. Any little hatchway that popped open on my own future would, I felt sure, reveal something far more serene.

Hopes that these premonitions might not be my own seemed to be confirmed by their inaccuracy. Having geared myself up for disaster, I found that nothing ever materialized. For a while I was prepared to give them the benefit of the doubt. But then resentment set in. I didn't so much mind being used – that came naturally enough. But to be the vehicle for such falsehoods, to be taken in by these mirages, it left me more brittle, less trusting than ever.

And meanwhile I kept on reciting my scripts, never faltering. But each broadcast came to bring its own fears of dominance and disintegration. I saw myself being swept up in this great electrical cradle; skimming along, light as thistledown, across arterial roads and through darkened estates, the streets below fanning out like veins on a leaf. Higher and higher, until there was nothing left but the shimmer of lights in the distance. Then higher still – up beyond the world. Through the clouds and the vapour trails and into the heavens, to where the satellites drifted round in orbit, all pulsing away, sending out their invisible signals. There to be shattered into tiny pieces, blasted apart, swept about this way and that. Weightless and powerless. Buffeted by these stray impulses. Then hurled down to earth and beamed out across the nation.

It took it out of me. I struggled to put myself back together. It even affected my balance; at times my whole world seemed in danger of tilting, falling out of the frame. The mechanics were far from clear, but it was as if everything were united by this tangle of different strands that somehow joined up in me. I had to keep a very careful grip to make sure they didn't get out of alignment. Buildings would lurch to one side as I walked by, as if they were suddenly being undermined. On pavements I had to pay particular attention to my footing in case I no longer found myself walking on fixed concrete with everyone else, but making my way instead down a strip of flapping, untethered carpet.

To make sure my world stayed on the level, I did my best to compensate for any slippage that had taken place. I made the necessary adjustments.

'Are you limping, Dickie?' inquired one of the floor managers as we walked out to our cars one evening. He was a shy, perfectly pleasant man called Purdy who was always showing me photographs of his children. Slowly I straightened up, expecting the worst. All around shapes flattened out, lost their bulk and started to sway. Everything – trees, houses, a few already sloping pedestrians – teetered, listed, yet managed to stay upright.

There were other, more apparent, effects. I could be testy, get easily upset. Little things set me off. The first time this happened it took me as much by surprise as everyone else. I was hosting a new quiz show in which each of the mystery guests had the same name as a well-known place or object. All the contestants had to do was work out who they were. We were halfway through the first show. Everything was going quite smoothly – Victoria Falls and Morris Minor had both been correctly identified and our third guest, a Mr Albert Hall, was sitting in his booth, blinking uncertainly.

'Are you a thing of some sort?'

No reply.

Again, louder, 'Are you a thing?'

'I suppose I am. In a way.'

'Are you a concrete thing?'

'I . . . I don't know.'

At this point I broke in. 'I think it's reasonable to assume that our guest is at least partly made of concrete. You're getting warm. Let's see how you get on, Mr Loman.'

In front of me, set into the desk where I was sitting, was a small screen showing each of the contestant's scores. I'd noticed earlier that this appeared to be playing up. The numbers were oddly squashed, not properly illuminated. They rippled and swayed before me. It was getting hard to tell which was which. As inconspicuously as possible, I hit it sharply with the flat of my hand.

'Are you a building used for utilitarian purposes?'

'Ah, now, I'm going to have to stop you again if you don't mind, just to check with our guest. You do know what utilitarian means, don't you?'

'Yes I do.'

'Excellent. Do please continue.'

'Are you very tall?'

'Not especially.'

'Are you a very efficient timekeeper?'

'How do you mean?'

'Is your name Ben?'

'No, it isn't.'

If anything, hitting the screen had made it worse. The numbers appeared flatter, even more indistinct. It began to play on my nerves. There seemed something almost mocking about the way these squat, fraying numerals would race across the foot of the screen every time the scores changed, so fast that I could hardly read them. The more I brooded on this, the more disturbing it became.

I looked across at Mr Hall, at the vast, bell-like circularity of him, as he sat peaceably enough in his chair. And I looked back at the screen where these electronic gnats scuttled back and forth. I couldn't help thinking of the other contestants, their identities set in stone and steel and reinforced on the map. It struck me that I was such an insubstantial thing in comparison, all blown up and full of air. Little more than an electronic gnat myself, buzzing around these people of substance, dutifully performing to order. I realized how much I wanted to join their number, to feel the ground solid and unshifting beneath my feet. But all the time I felt myself being borne upwards, lighter and lighter, hoisted aloft by these gusts of static and swept away.

I jumped to my feet, threw down my earpiece – it skittered away across the floor – and cried out, 'I cannot work with defective equipment.'

Everyone sat quite still, frozen in surprise. The panellists behind their desks, Mr Hall in his booth, the studio audience dimly visible in their rows of seats. From the shadows behind me I heard Purdy's voice say, 'Steady on, Dickie.'

'No,' I said loudly. 'No.' And my head shook and my lips puckered up. It was too late for me to steady on. The strangest part was that even as I leaped up, my voice cracking and peevish, I couldn't believe what I was doing. It was like a parody of petulance, the sort of thing I had seen people do back in the theatre, overreacting to some imagined slight. And yet everyone took it quite seriously. Including me. Especially me.

'It's not good enough,' I went on. 'No. Really it isn't.'

Having cast away everything to hand, I found myself at rather a loss as to what to do next. In the end I went over and stood facing the black drapes at the back of the studio, my shoulders heaving up and down. Out of the corner of my eye I could see Purdy coming towards me.

He looked terribly worried. 'It won't take long to sort out the problem, Dickie. You were just picking up some outside interference. We're working on it right now. How would you feel about starting again in a minute?'

I nodded as curtly as I could and my tantrum flew abruptly away, left me there feeling crumpled and ashamed, eager to foster some sort of bond.

'Little Emma is ten, you say?'

'Em . . . ? She's nine and a half, Dickie.'

'I should very much like to meet her one day.'

'I know she'd like that.'

I made my way across the studio, straight-backed, hands jutting out slightly as I walked, and allowed myself to be coaxed back into my chair. Clear, crisp numbers shone back at me from the screen.

'Is that better, Dickie?'

I indicated that it did appear to be.

'Why don't we have another go.'

Everything settled back down. The scores were checked, the panellists composed themselves and Mr Hall prepared once more to be unmasked.

'Do people stand inside you and sing "Land of Hope and Glory"?'

In any other profession there might have been repercussions after an outburst like this. Here, of course, quite the reverse was true. Far from being frowned upon, this sort of behaviour was considered perfectly normal. Everyone was at it; all quivering away, sensitive as racehorses. If anything, it ensured that I was treated with even more deference than usual. People tiptoed around me, making sure everything was to my liking. After all, I was volatile. I could go off at any moment.

Chapter Twenty-Five

However unwelcome these intrusions were, I was determined not to allow them to affect me. My manner may have become a little stiffer, my poise held more fiercely in place; elsewhere though nothing much changed. Still there was that familiar swirl of bustle and intent to me, still that corresponding swirl of excitement as I passed. And just as I showed little sign of any passing time – physically, I remained astonishingly youthful – so everything around me stayed the same. The same narrow numbered doorways; the same corridors smelling of floor polish and disinfectant where I once wandered, lost and stricken.

There, for instance, is the lavatory where I used to sit for hours, struggling to match myself to my outer life. There, on the left, with the door starting to swing open. As I stride on, I'm aware of a voice calling after me. And despite having an enormous amount on my mind, I still take the time to glance round and see who is hoping for a word.

'Dickie. I thought you hadn't heard me.'

'Ah.' Pace slowing, coming to a halt. 'Hello.'

'I haven't seen you in ages. Too busy, I suppose.'

A hand raised, then let fall, in silent acknowledgement.

'You're looking well though.'

I only wished I could say the same for Ralph. But he was paler than ever. His skin had an odd translucence to it, like rice paper. Not for the first time I found myself wondering about his health. I noticed too that he was looking rather shabby. His jacket didn't fit him properly. It sat bunched over his shoulders, the sleeves shiny with wear.

As I was reflecting on the state of Ralph's jacket, I saw to my surprise that he had taken hold of a thread that was hanging out of my own. I made to pull my arm away, but he didn't let go.

'You're coming undone, Dickie.'

He snapped the thread with his thumbnail.

'It's only a piece of cotton,' I said. 'Nothing to worry about.'

'Best to catch these things. I wouldn't want you laddering.'

'A ladder is something ladies are troubled by,' I corrected him. 'In their stockings.'

'I can see you're in a hurry. Please don't let me keep you. I just hoped you might be free sometime for a drink.'

'A drink? Let me see . . . Did you have any particular time in mind?'

'How about this lunchtime?'

'Oh no,' I said, 'I couldn't possibly.'

'What a shame. I used to enjoy our get-togethers so much. Wouldn't you be able to slip out, just for a while? We could just go round the corner to the hotel. It's quieter there.'

Again I made it clear that this was out of the question.

Ralph was looking at me. He had an entreating sort of expression I hadn't seen before. 'Not even for a quick one?'

I tried to explain how he shouldn't take it personally; how my burden of work might prove too much for a lesser man.

'It's a shame to neglect friendships though, isn't it?'

'Yes, I suppose it is.'

'Well then, why don't we say one o'clock, by the entrance?'

'But you don't understand . . .' I was about to say, and the scale of his incomprehension required me to take an especially deep breath.

'Good,' said Ralph. 'Then I'll see you later.'

I waited by the main doors. Ralph was late, although he didn't say what had kept him. We went outside. The traffic was heavy, stacked up nose to tail, inching forwards. I was all for walking up to the lights and crossing once they'd turned red, but Ralph plunged out between the cars. After a moment or two's indecision on the edge of the pavement I followed him.

On the hotel steps I saw Alasdair McNeame. He was standing looking out for a taxi, a small ruddy Scotsman possessed of such consuming eagerness that he had a habit of reacting to remarks that had not yet been made. While this was not unusual among television presenters – especially those of us who had to deal with members of the public – I had never come across such a pronounced case before. During conversation, a torrent of emotions would race constantly over his face as he tried to anticipate an appropriate response to whatever was being said.

He bounded down the steps towards us. 'Dickie, I don't normally see you here.'

'Hello, Alasdair. How are you?'

'Couldn't be better, Dickie. Could not be better. We're just finishing off the Christmas special. Oh, what fun we've had. I tell you, it simply hasn't let up.'

'I don't know if you've met Ralph Harding before.'

He turned to Ralph and grasped him by the hand. 'I don't believe I've had the pleasure before. Delighted to meet any friend of Dickie's. Are you in our line of work?'

'In a way,' said Ralph.

'Really? What is it you do?'

'I read the shipping forecast.'

'The shipping forecast!' exclaimed McNeame. 'What a vital public service!'

'Thank you.'

'So many people relying on your every word. Old salts and weekend sailors. Waves breaking over the wheelhouse. The inky black sea heaving all around.'

Ralph gave a fractional tip of his head by way of further acknowledgement.

McNeame, however, wasn't finished yet. 'Our great fishing fleets setting sail. Casting their nets, trawling the deep. All of them at the mercy of the elements. The crew crowded round their radio sets. And only your voice to guide them, to steer them away from the rocks.'

'Away, you say?' said Ralph.

McNeame sounded momentarily put out. His features rapidly regrouped. 'Away, yes. Isn't that the whole point? Safely through the tempest. Land ho! Then into harbour, anxious faces lining the quaysides . . .'

'Thank you, yes. I get the picture.' The skin seemed to have tightened over Ralph's cheekbones. He shifted his gaze back and forth from one of us to the other.

There was a pause broken by McNeame saying, 'Do you know, I think that must be my taxi.' He checked with the doorman who confirmed it. 'What a shame I have to rush like this. I hope to see you again soon, Dickie.' He turned to Ralph. 'And I am so pleased to have made your acquaintance. I shall look forward to your broadcasts now even more keenly than before. Keep up the good work.'

'I shall do my very best,' Ralph promised.

He shook our hands once more and hurried off to where a cab stood waiting by the kerb.

Ralph and I made our way through to the lounge. Chairs and sofas covered in various floral fabrics were dotted about in clusters. A clock ticked away in the corner. There were only two other people there. Both were asleep. We took off our coats and sat down. The waiter came to take our order.

'Yes. I'd like a barley water, please.'

Ralph asked for a whisky.

'Tell me, Dickie,' he said, 'what do you call that thing you've got on?'

'This? It's a polo-necked sweater.'

'Of course it is. But worn under the jacket – how interesting. Isn't white a very difficult colour to keep clean?'

Having dispensed with my period details we fell into one of our characteristic lulls, broken only by the arrival of the drinks and the sudden waking of one of the other guests. He came to just like my father used to do, with a sudden gasp, staring around in panic, trying to work out where he was.

'Here we are then,' said Ralph, raising his glass to his lips. 'It's hard to keep up with you these days, Dickie. You're everywhere I turn, and in the most unlikely places. Such versatility. It's a real gift.'

'It is a gift,' I agreed. 'And all the more important therefore that I shouldn't squander it on anything unworthy.'

'Come now,' said Ralph, and I had the impression that he was using the rim of his glass to hide a smile, 'I don't think there's any danger of that. No, if I may say so, you've turned out just the way I hoped.'

'That is kind.'

'And how are things at home?'

'Do you know,' I said, 'I'm hardly ever there.'

'Still living alone?'

'Yes,' I confirmed. 'Still alone.'

Ralph shifted himself in his chair. I saw a flash of ankle, as white as bone. He folded his hands.

'I wonder if it's not about time for you to get married, Dickie.'

'Married?' I cried, and my yelp of astonishment resounded round the room. The other sleeping man woke with a start.

'It's a big move, I know,' said Ralph. 'There's a great deal to be said for it though. A settled domestic life. Support and sharing. The companionship of one you love. And, of course, the opportunity to have children – to continue your line.'

'I can't say I've ever really considered it,' I said.

'You should. One can't ignore these things. The years fly by, and before you know where you are it might be too late.'

'I hope there's no danger of that with me. Not for some time, at least,' and I laughed as best I could.

'You must have faith, Dickie. Don't hold back, or cut yourself off from new experiences.'

'Now, it's very kind of you to offer me this advice,' I said. 'And you must not imagine that I don't appreciate it. But I do feel that our paths have diversified somewhat. My life is my own, to do with as I wish.'

'Oh, I wouldn't want to intrude, or anything.'

'I'm sure you wouldn't. Besides, and I think it's pertinent to point this out, I can't help noticing that you are not yourself a married man.'

'No, that's true, I'm not.'

'Why would that be?'

'I don't really think I'm the marrying kind,' said Ralph.

'You don't?'

He shook his head.

'Is there . . . a reason for that?'

But Ralph didn't answer. He just gave his little smile and shook his head again.

'If I may say so,' I continued, 'I would have thought you would be better advised to pay more attention to your own welfare than to mine, however hard that might be. All this selflessness can wear a person down. And anyway, what makes you so sure that I am the marrying kind?'

His smile broadened. 'I've told you before. Sometimes a friend can see these things more clearly, can recognize things that you haven't seen in yourself. Don't you agree?'

'No,' I said, 'I don't think I do.'

'How long have we known one another now? It must be quite a while. Long enough for me to have a pretty good idea of what makes you tick.'

'If that is your belief, then you're perfectly entitled to it. But I find your concern to be misplaced. There's nothing about my life I want to change. As a matter of fact, it's turned out even better than I could have predicted.'

'It's only natural to want the best for people one cares about.'

'That's as may be. I have no doubt though that you can find many more needy cases than myself. The world is full of unhappiness.'

'How right you are.'

'Well then . . . go out and find some.'

In the pause that followed I felt a pain in my chest like heartburn while Ralph continued to regard me in that half-scrutinizing, half-mocking way of his.

'Goodness me,' I said. 'Is that the time? I really must be going.'

I stood up and signalled to the waiter. He took no notice at first and I had to wave my arms to get his attention. Eventually he came over, wrote out the bill and set it down on a plate between us.

'Here, Dickie,' said Ralph. 'Let me. After all, it was my idea.'

He started to dig into his pocket for change. In the process several coins dropped out and rolled across the floor. Ralph set off after them with me following in his wake. I gathered up the ones I saw, and spotted one rolling off in the direction of the sofa where the first sleeping man – now gone – had been sitting. There was a standard lamp to one side of the sofa, and beside it a table with a vase of flowers. I thought I saw the coin rolling around the base of the lamp, wobbling unsteadily but still upright.

In order to look more closely I had to get down on all-fours. I was so preoccupied with searching on the floor that I didn't notice Ralph coming towards me from the other end of the sofa. By the time I looked up our faces were only a few inches apart. Close up,

I could almost see through Ralph's skin, through the pale screen of his cheek to the arch of bone behind.

I gave him the coins I had collected. They lay there in the palm of his hand. 'That's all I found,' I said. 'There may be another one around here somewhere.'

'Oh, don't worry about that. I'm sure it will turn up.'

We were both on all-fours, crouched between the arm of the sofa and the underside of the table top. There was no room to turn around. One of us was going to have to reverse out. Ralph, however, showed no sign of doing so. Indeed he showed no inclination to move at all. In the end I had to crawl backwards as best I could, carefully extending each leg to make sure I didn't knock anything over.

Once I was out I dusted myself off, just as Ralph emerged and got to his feet. Together we made our way back through into the hallway.

'I hope I haven't been selfish and kept you, Dickie.'

'It's not that you've been selfish,' I informed him, putting on my coat. 'Please don't worry on that score. But you have rather kept me.'

Chapter Twenty-Six

I stood upon the deck, looked out across the marina. Saw the masts swaying around, some of them almost scraping the roof. Boats rocking gently back and forth, hawsers twanging, water lapping at their sides. The cries of recorded gulls resounding around the exhibition hall. Beside me a man in a blazer with brass buttons trying to explain just what gave this boat – this one that we were on – the edge over its rivals, while I endeavoured to show an interest.

'How clever to get the flag sticking out like that.'

'I beg your pardon?'

'Up there on top of the mast. Look, it makes it appear as if there's a breeze blowing.'

The man was confused. 'It's only a piece of wire inside the pennant,' he said.

'Is it really? I see, threaded through the material, I imagine?'

'Yes . . . I believe so.'

'Ingenious.'

And on he went, about the craftsmanship, the fittings, the buoyancy, as the water gurgled around us and the invisible gulls screeched overhead. No-one else was due to turn up until after lunch – the camera crew and producer, the usual paraphernalia that accompanied me on these occasions. In the meantime, as befitted my station, I'd been invited to have lunch on the biggest boat in the show, a vast gleaming white ship of state that rose up out of the water and dwarfed all those around it.

I was escorted through a tented archway and down a gangplank, to be greeted by my host. Several girls stood about holding trays. They were wearing little flat sailors' hats and dressed in identical navy uniforms. Food was laid out on long trestle tables. A number of other guests were already there. Introductions were made, I was offered a drink – my hand wavered; all right, but just the one – after which I stood off to one side, half-listening to talk of an uneasily nautical nature.

After a while I walked over to the side of the deck and rested my hands on the rail. The water was only a few feet deep. I could see the bottom quite clearly, the rippled folds in the black tarpaulin. I became aware of somebody standing next to me. One of the waitresses was there holding out a tray. Would I care for an hors-d'oeuvre? she asked.

I looked down: criss-crosses of anchovies on little roundels of toast. Thank you, I said, but no. The waitress went away. I turned back to gaze out over the water. As I did so I saw that things had changed, or were in the process of changing. The wind seemed to have got up. I could feel it blowing against my face and see small waves breaking below. The sky too had darkened. Except I had to remind myself that I couldn't see the sky. We were indoors.

None the less, the air had taken on that bruised, thundery feel. And all the time the wind seemed to be growing stronger. Boats were starting to pitch about. Their decks tipped up, their masts swung around. They banged against each other and dragged at their moorings. Lines of white spume raced across the surface. Waves swelled then crashed, sending up clouds of spray. The water rose and fell, spinning into eddies, then turning itself into lumps that dashed themselves against the sides of the boats.

I could only hold onto the rail and watch in disbelief.

At the same time I felt my own insides start to slew about. It was as if I too were capsizing, taking in water, no longer able to control myself, but tossed about from peak to trough. Just as the moon held sway over the tides, drawing them up or letting them fall back, so I seemed subject to more artificial forces that plucked at me, tugging me about then setting me down, acting on me from I knew not where. Pounded about this way and that; at the mercy of the elements, an abandoned vessel without power or direction. Lost, emptied out, any volition gone. This broken-sparred hulk, drifting the seas like a ghost ship, a thin trail of grey smoke hanging on the water behind. All the time slowly sinking; holed and helpless, filling up from outside. These currents rushing in and pulling me under.

I fought for breath, closing my eyes as tightly as I could, clenching them shut. As if I might push the water level down the more tightly they were closed; force it back to my ankles. And when I opened them again it took me several moments to adjust: the boats had righted themselves, the storm had blown over, the water looked as if it had been freshly ironed. And there at my elbow was the same waitress holding out the same tray, asking me if I might change my mind.

She must have thought my lack of response signalled another no because she had already started to turn away. But I was simply confused, still putting myself back together. Deciding as I did so that, yes, I should have something to eat, that it was vital I shouldn't behave as if anything untoward had happened.

My hand caught the edge of the tray. It flipped up and tipped out of her hands. The hors-d'oeuvre fell to the floor. The tray clattered round and round, the roundels of toast ran off across the deck. Immediately the girl began to apologize. I waved her apologies away, grateful for the distraction, insisting that I was the one to blame. My host looked on unhappily. He didn't like to see me scurrying about like this, demeaning myself. But I was already picking up the escaped discs, hunting down those ones that were still trundling away. As I did so, I had only the briefest recollection of being back at the hotel with Ralph, setting off in pursuit of his coins. Down on my knees, following some other wobbling trail. The memory flitted across my mind, and then it was gone.

'I think that's the lot,' I said. 'There may be one or two left behind the lifebelts.'

I could see that underneath her make-up the waitress was blushing furiously. Her ears had turned red.

'No need for you to bother,' insisted my host. He was trying to prise away the tray from my grasp, but to no avail. I kept hold of it and together the waitress and I made our way through a hatch and down a narrow set of steps into a galley kitchen. I set the tray down and went over to the basin to wash the stray anchovies from my hands. There was some polite to-ing and fro-ing under the tap. She said I should be first. I wouldn't hear of it. Eventually she washed while I waited. And as she lent over the basin, I found myself noticing for the first time what she looked like.

Up until this point I believed I'd been governed more by natural good manners than anything else. Now I was able to see where this common courtesy had got me. My first impression was that I'd been here before. There was something familiar about her, although it took me a while to work out what it was. She reminded me of the girl who had helped turn Mrs Montague over in the hallway all those years before. She had the same pointed features, the same china blue eyes and froth of fair hair. I found myself waiting for her dry cough, but it never came. And slowly, almost reluctantly, I realized that it wasn't the same girl; they only bore a passing resemblance to one another. This one was less soiled; less bold and more awkward.

As I looked, I noticed her ears, now returning to their normal colour – they crinkled attractively, like the hearts of little lettuces. Also I noticed one of her eyebrows which seemed to be pointing upwards. There

252

was, I told myself, a fundamental honesty to her face, a lack of guile. The other waitresses looked steely-eyed beneath their layers of powder and paint; their wiles were written all over them. For some reason I wanted to believe this one was different.

It wasn't as if I was bowled over, or anything like that. Far from it. But then most people hardly made any impression on me at all. I couldn't tell them apart – and, as such, they were treated to my usual all-purpose condescension. For anyone to get beyond that was almost unheard of. It baffled me – when all my instincts were to stay quite stationary, or shoot into reverse. I can only say that I found myself being somehow drawn to this girl, without having any idea why.

There wasn't much room in the galley. When I had finished washing my hands, I turned off the tap and took the tea-towel that was being held out.

'Thank you for helping me,' said the girl.

This too got waved away, but all at once I was nearly overcome with my own generosity of spirit. Suffused with a sense of goodness. Was it not the case that somewhere inside me there lay great reserves of affection? Banked up, accruing away. Had they not been crying out, almost inaudibly, for a home? Had they? I couldn't be sure. It was the first time I had thought of such things in a long while. But somehow these two things – my new-found goodness, along with this dim, leftover yearning for warmth and companionship – knotted together and pulled me on.

'I mustn't keep you,' she said.

'No, no,' I said, looking round the galley – everything had been cleverly miniaturized to fit. 'I'm quite happy down here. As a matter of fact, I prefer it to being up on deck.'

'Do you?' She laughed disbelievingly. 'They'll be wondering what happened to us.' She patted her hair and looked uneasy. I thought it might have been nerves – people often get flustered in my presence. But then I realized she was expected back at work.

253

'What's your name?' I asked.

'My name is Minnie,' said the girl, and she nodded as if to confirm it.

I started to introduce myself, but she broke in. 'Yes. I know who you are.'

There were more trays of food laid out along a counter. Sandwiches cut into little triangles, rows of vols-au-vent, pieces of cheese on sticks. She reached out for one of the trays, picked it up in both hands and turned to me. 'Do I look all right? They're really fussy about appearance here.'

'You look very neat. It's just . . .'

'Yes?'

'It's just that I couldn't help noticing one of your eyebrows appears to be pointing upwards.'

She put down the tray, took a mirror out of her pocket and gave a gasp. 'I had them plucked. Only they didn't look right, so I painted some on instead.'

'Ah. I thought it might have been an anchovy.'

She licked her finger, rubbed out the line and drew another across her brow. 'Is that better?'

'Much better.'

I stood aside to let her go first, then followed her up the stairs towards the open hatch.

At the top there was a square of blue, like the sky in a picture book. The sun had come out, or something like it. Voices chattered away. I came up the steps, got to the top and took a deep breath of imaginary sea air.

Chapter Twenty-Seven

Our wedding four weeks later was a quiet affair. Fortunately, my wife-to-be's parents had emigrated to Canada several years earlier. She was all for inviting them. But I persuaded her that it was best to do these things discreetly – that it would be so much more fun to go and visit them at some later date and give them a delightful surprise. She was upset, even appeared on the verge of protest. In the end though she said nothing, not being sufficiently sure of herself to stand her ground.

With no family or friends to invite, that only left the question of whether or not I needed a best man. It so happened I was sitting in my office mulling over this point when there was a knock at the door. In answer to my abstracted call to enter – it was a difficult question and I kept going round in circles – Ralph walked in. It hadn't been long since our last meeting, but so much had happened in the meantime that it was hard to keep track. However, I noted he was looking better. His clothes were smarter and his skin a much healthier colour. There were little spots of red on the top of each of his cheeks. He looked around him and whistled silently.

'This is quite a place you've got, Dickie.'

'Haven't you been here before? Possibly not. It's where I do most of my thinking.'

He sat down in the chair opposite mine. One leg went over the other in the usual way.

'Was there anything you wished to see me about?' I asked. 'Or is this in the nature of a social call?'

He shrugged. 'I was passing, so thought I might drop in.'

'I see. As it happens, it's a stroke of luck you coming by. There's something I wanted to tell you.'

Ralph said nothing, merely listened attentively.

'Yes,' I went on. 'Something I felt you should know. I'm getting married.'

He didn't react at first. Then he came to slowly, as if he were stretching himself in the sun.

'Married,' he chuckled. 'Well, well, well.'

'I thought you'd like to know.'

'Many congratulations, Dickie. This is marvellous news. So welcome. And unexpected.'

'It is unexpected. But then one never knows what fate has in store. At least, that would seem to be my experience.'

'I'm very pleased for you. May I know the name of your fiancée?'

'Her name? Yes, her name is Minnie.'

'And what does she do?'

'She is in marine catering.'

'How fascinating. Tell me, how did you meet?'

And so I told him, changing the odd detail here and there, trying to make it sound more plausible than it felt.

Ralph nodded along. 'It sounds as if you were made for each other.'

'I wouldn't go that far.'

'Oh yes,' he said, nodding more emphatically than ever. 'These things are intended.'

'Intended? Is that what you think?'

'I don't have the slightest doubt. You two meeting up like this, in such unusual circumstances. It can hardly be anything else.'

'I suppose so.'

'There is a divinity that shapes our ends.'

'Are you sure?'

256

'Well, something like that.'

'We thought we might have a quiet wedding,' I said.

'Much the best idea.'

'My wife-to-be's parents live abroad. There won't be any family to invite. And as for anyone else . . . we haven't quite decided yet.'

'May I offer some advice?'

'By all means.'

'If I were you, I'd do it all as quietly as possible. Why don't just the two of you go off? No guests, no-one else to get in the way.'

'No-one?'

'Not a soul. Only yourselves.'

'That's certainly an interesting idea.'

'What about a honeymoon?'

'We thought Switzerland.'

'Switzerland. Charming. What made you choose it?'

I didn't like to tell Ralph that it was the only country I'd been able to think of with an unreality to match my own. Instead, I mumbled something about mountain air.

'Think over my idea,' he said.

'I will.'

'Discuss it with . . . Forgive me.'

'With Minnie?'

'That's right. Why make life more complicated than it is already?'

'I couldn't disagree with that.'

'And apart from anything else, Dickie, you're going to have quite enough on your plate as it is.'

In the end, we did as Ralph suggested. I booked into the registry office under a false name, and only owned up to who I was when we arrived. In the absence of any guests we needed witnesses. Two men were fetched from the betting shop next door. Thin, suspicious looking characters, they stood silent and bowed as the registrar ran through the vows. Throughout the ceremony Minnie clung to my arm, her voice quavering whenever she had to speak. My own voice rang out, steady and doubt-free. We emerged into the late afternoon sunshine. There was confetti on the steps from the couple who had gone before. A rubbish lorry was passing by and the men riding in the cab shouted out words of encouragement.

We caught a taxi to the hotel where we were to spend the night. Two porters in long double-breasted coats rushed out and collected our bags. We were shown up to our room. It was the size of a tennis court, the bed the largest I had ever seen. On each of the pillows was a single rose, the stems wrapped in tissue paper. We sat and read magazines for a while and then went downstairs for dinner. When our food arrived I found I could hardly eat. Minnie, however, was ravenous. At one point she was about to take a mouthful when our eyes met. She put her knife and fork back down and smiled.

'We're married,' she said.

'I know.'

'Are you happy?'

'Oh yes. I'm as happy as can be.'

Already I had started to notice a pattern to my wife's behaviour: she tended to go in fits and starts; sometimes she would lower her head at a particular goal and pursue it with great single-mindedness. At other times she appeared knocked off balance, and would be almost incapable of following the thread of a conversation, sitting blinking and with her forehead furrowed, as if waiting to be prompted. In whatever mood she was in, however, she remained more fragile than I had expected. She was often jumpy and needed reassurance. Little things set her off – she found it hard to take them all in her stride.

'Yes, I'm happy too,' she said.

We stayed in the dining-room until all the other guests had gone. And then we made our way back upstairs. By now it was getting late, time to turn in, but I showed no inclination to get undressed. Quite the reverse. We sat, either side of an unlit fireplace, talking through the events of the day as I waited for Minnie to show signs of tiredness. But she seemed, if anything, more lively than she'd been earlier. There was a shine to her eyes I hadn't noticed before. The shine grew more intense as our conversation faltered.

We reached the point where there was nothing more to say. I walked over to the window. The street outside was empty; the lights shone down on the deserted pavements. Everyone had gone home. I thought how all I had to do was stay here, just where I was, waiting for the world to turn and a new day to begin. In the meantime, I was quite alone. Except, of course, for my new wife. I walked back to her chair and put my hands on her shoulders. She got to her feet, stood very close to me, chin to my chest. I bent forward and kissed her on the top of the head.

'That's the third time you've kissed me today,' she said.

'Is it?'

'Once in the registry office, once before dinner, and now here.'

'I think you must have missed one out.'

'No.'

'Never mind. We have the rest of our lives before us.'

Minnie went into the bathroom first. She came out sooner than I had expected. She was wearing a white nightdress embroidered with small yellow flowers. Her feet were bare. There was something about her naked toes that unsettled me more than anything else. I looked at them, poking out below the hem of her nightdress, and knew for certain that all this was beyond me.

Then it was my turn in the bathroom. I got changed into my pyjamas. I'd bought them specially: Prussian blue with a fake collegiate crest sewn over my heart. There were mirrors on each of the bathroom walls. Every movement I made rippled out through different planes of glass. I raised my arm to smooth down my hair and a hundred elbows crooked all round me. My stomach felt blown up, full of air. I sat down on the edge of the bath.

After a while I heard Minnie's voice from outside. 'Are you all right?'

'Yes,' I called back. 'Why do you ask?'

'I thought you might have got stuck.'

Minnie was already in bed by the time I got out, the bedside light on beside her. I climbed in on the other side. The bedclothes stretched flat and unrumpled between us. I lay there, knowing what I was meant to do next, equally sure that it was out of the question. Why should things have been any different than they had been before, with Helen? Then I had reached out of myself. Cast aside my clothes and emerged in something different. Another layer of behaviour. Not necessarily my own, but quite serviceable – appropriate too. But now it was different. Whatever set of responses I had been able to engage then was gone. Lost to me. The things I relied upon to sustain me, to bear me up, had all fallen away. Now I was as barren within as I was almost naked without.

Such were the thoughts that passed through my mind as I lay in our marriage bed, and my wife waited for me to broach the divide between us. My behaviour in the few weeks leading up to our wedding had, I think, been taken by her as evidence of an otherwise extinct form of courtliness, the behaviour of one governed by decorum to an unnatural, but strangely endearing degree. However, there was a limit to how long one could keep this up. That limit had now been reached.

The sheet still lay crisp and white down the centre of the bed. There were two small mounds at the end of the bed where our feet stuck up, like pets' graves. I was aware that every tiny movement on my part seemed to provoke an answering quiver from her. I tried to lie as still as possible. Part of me couldn't stop wondering what she was thinking. The greater part of me though would have done anything – anything at all – not to have been so aware of her mounting bewilderment.

'It's been a long day,' I said, in what was supposed to be a warm, pillow-talking kind of way. But even this sounded wrong, almost peevish.

'We've done a lot,' said Minnie from her side of the bed. 'We got married.'

'That's bound to take it out of you. How are you feeling?'

'I feel fine.'

'Do you? Good.'

'Are you feeling all right?'

'Why shouldn't I be?'

'I don't know,' said Minnie.

'There's nothing wrong with me.'

'Would you like some water?'

'No thank you.'

And then I yawned. But it was a shallow, airless sort of yawn, as if I were trying to twist the lid off something with my teeth.

'Shall I turn the light out?' asked Minnie after a while.

'What do you think?'

'If you want me to?'

I turned and scanned her face for signs of disappointment. She was frowning certainly, but it might have been concern.

The switch was on my side of the bed. I turned it off. We lay there in darkness.

'I'll be better in the morning,' I said.

The train skirted the edge of the lake. There were houses on the shore, scarcely visible behind screens of trees. Rows of vines were crammed into little triangular pockets between the track and the side of the mountain where the rock had been blasted away. The lake glinted, turquoise in the sun, swept by the trees as we sped past. Minnie sat opposite, looking out of the window. We hadn't said much since we'd

261

arrived in Switzerland. But then we hadn't said much on the way to the airport either. The mountains rose above us. When the train went round a bend they came into view, standing out in a line, the peaks covered in snow, shelving off into grey lower down. A boat was making its way across the lake. All these things I noted as possible topics to be discussed, then thought better of it and kept quiet.

When we arrived at the station our cases were loaded onto a trolley and taken outside to the taxi rank. It was colder than I had expected. Our breath clouded into long silvery streams, my cheeks stung. I asked Minnie if she was warm enough. She nodded. I put my arm around her shoulders and left it there for the remainder of the journey.

The hotel was only a short ride away. We checked in. I wrote our names in the register, Minnie watching as I did so. The lift was just big enough to hold the two of us and swung from side to side, cables twanging. A porter was waiting outside our room. He showed us the view over the lake, the balcony – a concrete trench with two chairs wedged into it – the drawstring for the curtains and then asked if there was anything else we needed to know.

'The bed,' I said. 'I can't seem to see the bed.'

He walked over to the wall, reached above his head and pulled down a double bed. The pillows were kept separately, on a shelf in the wardrobe.

When he'd gone I said, 'Well, what do you think?'

Minnie looked around her. 'It's nice,' she said.

Soon afterwards we went back downstairs for a late lunch. Minnie's appetite had shrunk from the day before; it was no bigger than mine. She cut her food up into unnecessarily small pieces, her eyes flickering to left and right. It was the first time she'd been abroad, she didn't want to do anything wrong.

I suggested we might take a walk around the lake. Minnie went upstairs to put on more practical shoes. When she came down I saw that she had changed completely. I was already wearing appropriate clothing.

'Those are very baggy shorts you've got on,' said Minnie as we set off along the promenade. This was true enough. I'd bought them thinking they were the height of fashion. But they were, I realized suddenly, almost identical to the shorts my father had worn which had so embarrassed me when I was a child: those great billowing folds that reached almost to his knees.

'They are a form of *pantalon*,' I said as I flapped along beside her.

Elderly ladies in raincoats passed by walking their dogs. The dogs pulled at their leads, claws scratching on the tarmac. The mountains were all covered by clouds. The lake was very still. Water lapped at the shore in long slow ripples. We stopped to feed a swan. Minnie had saved one of her rolls from lunch. She broke it up and threw the bits out onto the water. The swan swam towards us to retrieve the bread. It scooped up what was there and circled about waiting for more.

'I'm sorry,' Minnie called out, 'I don't have any more.' But still the swan swam about by the water's edge, making little runs towards us, dipping its neck and hanging its head out expectantly. She turned to me, a look of real distress on her face. 'It doesn't understand,' she said.

When we got back to our room the bed had been pushed up into the wall. Rather than take it back down, we sat in the easy chairs until it was time for Minnie to change again. For some reason – unknown, to me, at least – the mood lightened over dinner. Something of that old fluency crept back into my voice. I drank, not excessively, but enough to ensure my words kept flowing. It was hard work getting Minnie to open up. I couldn't work out if this was shyness, embarrassment or something else. A natural disinclination to set the details of her life alongside mine perhaps? True, it wouldn't have been much of a contest, but I was keen to find out what I could.

I was hampered though by her almost total lack of curiosity. She operated within set, familiar limits. Outside those she wasn't so much lost as disinterested. Her past was one of those areas that failed to engage her to any degree. In this sense, of course, we were strangely well suited. She wasn't one to look back. Or forward either – at least not to the extent of formulating anything. But then this, as I saw it, was all to do with her admirable lack of guile.

I swirled some local liqueur around in my glass, gazed as it clung to the sides. I had to do it a few times before Minnie asked me what I was thinking about.

'Oh,' I said, coming to slowly, 'I was just thinking how many unhappy people there are in the world. But here we are with so much to be thankful for, and to look forward to.'

If Minnie was taken aback by this she didn't show it. Instead she said, 'I never dreamed I'd be married to someone like you.'

'Didn't you? Who did you dream of being married to?'

'I don't know. Not you though. It still doesn't feel—'

'Feel what?'

She gave a thin, nervous laugh. 'I still can't quite believe it.'

In the dimness of the light a cast of fondness passed over each of our faces.

'Shall we go upstairs?' I said.

The bed had been taken down again, the pillows laid out. Minnie took herself off to the bathroom and came back in a new nightdress, the hem trimmed with lace. I followed her, buoyant at first, changing into my pyjamas with something like excitement, then filling up with misgivings once again as my feet slapped down on the tiled floor.

A few minutes later we lay apart in bed. My face was turned towards the wall. I could feel the sheets rise and fall with Minnie's breathing.

264

'I'm sorry.'

There was no reply.

'I don't know what it is . . .'

'What do you think it is?'

'I don't know.'

'Do you think it's me?'

'No,' I said. 'Not necessarily.'

'We're on our honeymoon,' said Minnie – and this time there could be no mistaking the note of despair in her voice.

When I next turned over I saw that Minnie had got out of bed. She had pulled the curtain back and was sitting on one of the chairs, staring out over the darkness of the lake.

The following morning I rose early and went to the front desk to make some inquiries. The woman there told me that a boat left the nearby pier every half hour. When I suggested to Minnie that we might take a boat trip she hardly made any response, neither saying yes or no. I had to cajole her into it.

We waited at the end of the pier. The boat chugged towards us. The rails were of polished brass, the top of the funnel cut into long serrated teeth. When it docked, a ramp was extended from the deck. There were benches on deck with lifebelts mounted on the rails. We were the only passengers. The boat steamed out into the middle of the lake. One of the crew lowered the Swiss flag and raised the French one instead. It was attached by toggles to the rope and hoisted up the flagpole. The sound of the engine seemed to die away until it was just a rhythmic hum under our feet. The water was like stretched pigskin. I could hear the clang of cow-bells as they carried across the water. The peaks were still in cloud; although the sun shone brightly enough on the lower slopes. The grass was emerald green. There were meadows covered with Alpine flowers, low wooden houses with roofs reaching down to the ground, pine trees that looked like clumps of moss from this distance.

'It's like a postcard, isn't it?' I said.

'What sort of postcard?'

'Why, a picture postcard, my dear. Look at the meadow flowers. They're like the ones you've got embroidered on your nightdress.'

But Minnie said nothing. She just shivered and pulled her coat around her.

The far bank was coming into view. There was another pier, a narrow street, several more women walking their dogs. We docked. A number of people were waiting to get on. They were all elderly and in a group. As they got on, one of the men shouted out instructions at the others. They came and sat on the benches around us, chattering away. After a few minutes we cast off and steamed back out into the lake. When we reached the middle the French flag was taken down and the Swiss one hoisted again.

And all the time I could only reflect how the beauties of the world meant nothing to me, nothing at all. They crowded in on every side, beating against me. But I felt like some slack drum, unable to summon any note of response, however hard I tried.

'Look at the view,' I said desperately to my wife.

'What about it?'

'Do you think it's beautiful?'

She shrugged. 'In a way.'

'But what is it exactly that makes it beautiful?'

'What do you mean?'

'Well, for instance, if you were to take away the mountains, would you still think it was as beautiful?'

'Take them away? You can't take them away.'

'No, but if you could.'

'It would depend what was in their place,' said Minnie.

'I don't know what would be in their place. I haven't really thought about that.'

'There'd have to be something.'

'I suppose there would.'

'You couldn't just have a hole.'

'That's true.'

'They belong here, the mountains. You can't change them.'

'No.'

'You can't change anything.'

We were nearing the shore now. Our hotel was already visible, a dark grey smudge that steadily sharpened into focus. There was the pier, the promenade, the long sweep of the railway track above the town. A number of other people were standing at the rail, taking in the view as the boat slipped through the water, hardly making a sound.

That night I thought I might be coming down with a stomach bug and took to bed immediately after dinner. It had gone by the morning. But by the following evening I was once again feeling under the weather. The dampness in the air appeared to have brought on a mild form of lumbago. There was no sign of it on our fourth night together, although my health remained delicate. Without wishing to alarm Minnie I told her that I thought I might have contracted pellagra.

Fortunately this fear too proved groundless. However, on the fifth night I was experiencing balancing problems — a possible middle ear infection. To be succeeded by the stirring of an abcess on the sixth. And so it went on. A long litany of excuses behind which my worries bubbled away like stomach acid – the seventh. The night after, I was taken aback to see that Minnie was entering into the spirit of the thing and claimed to have caught a touch of flu. Before long we had settled into something of a routine. By the time our honeymoon was over we might have been married for years.

Chapter Twenty-Eight

For the past few years, ever since my old flat had finally become uninhabitable, I'd been living in a serviced apartment near the Regent's canal. It was adequate for me, but nowhere near large enough for a married couple. By now I was of an age where living in the city had lost much of its allure. I wanted quiet, privacy, a high wall of my own. Every weekend then we would drive out in a long loop just beyond the outskirts of London, to be shown houses in all manner of styles by various fawning estate agents. However, none of them raised Minnie's spirits which seemed to be sagging inwardly, a little lower each day. We went further afield, our car piled high with particulars.

One Saturday, in our now customary silence, we followed the river west. Not with any goal in mind. I meandered, all volition gone, searching only for outside forces to surrender to. I'd begun to wonder if we weren't going round in circles. There was something vaguely familiar about the stretch of road we were on; the lie of the land on one side, the way it sloped down to the water on the other. I almost brought the subject up with Minnie, but these pretexts for conversation took it out of both of us. I drove on. It was one of those typical English winter afternoons, the sun barely visible behind a wash of grey, that sense of night waiting to close in. Another futile trip. I decided to continue for another couple of miles, not in any mood of expectation, just to save myself from charges of giving up too easily.

Ahead of us were two lines of trees bending towards one another across the road, the bare branches almost meeting. We swept through, dark columns flashing by on either side. A sound, too, an irregular swoosh against the windows as the air crinkled around us. I began to feel breathless, wanted to tug my collar open. I looked across to see how Minnie was faring. No sign of anything amiss. She sat there, eyes wide, hands folded. The trees stretched away. Some had white hoops painted round the trunks to make them show up at night. Not all though – only occasional ones – so it was hard to shake this sense of being buffeted about from one side to the other. I hunched forward, gripped the wheel and aimed us at the pale gap up ahead where the trees gave out.

When we emerged the light had faded. I needed to blink to let things settle back into shape. As I did so, I was aware of Minnie, now also craning forward, staring out through the windscreen.

'What's that?' she asked.

'What's what?'

'Up ahead. Slow down, can't you.'

I did so, bringing the car down to little more than walking pace.

'There,' said Minnie.

'I'm afraid you're going to have to be a little more specific.'

'*There.*'

She pointed. I followed the invisible line from the end of her finger, across the road to the verge where a 'For Sale' board poked out from a tangle of bare branches. I stopped the car and hauled exaggeratedly on the handbrake.

'Do you want to go and have a look?' But Minnie was already scrambling out of the passenger door.

There was a gate topped with rusting coils of barbed wire. The wood felt soft, even sticky. Minnie was pushing it open, despite its having fallen on its hinges and gouging out a deep muddy crescent on the ground. I wasn't happy about this. Alert to any risk of my own defences being broached, I tended to feel protective towards anyone else's. 'I say, do you think we should . . .'

Again, Minnie took no notice. She had started up the drive which veered to the left of a large clump of rhododendrons and then disappeared out of sight. There were patches of ice on the ground where the sun hadn't reached all day. I hurried after her. When I got alongside, I realized I had never seen Minnie look so determined before, so inquisitive. She had her chin jutting forwards in a way that lent a surprising amount of definition to her face. When she spoke it was as if she could hardly be bothered to pay me any attention.

'It's for sale, isn't it? No-one's going to mind if we have a look around.'

At that point we rounded another bend in the drive and came upon the house. For some reason I knew straight away that there was no-one living there. It wasn't boarded up, or shuttered. There were no obvious signs of it being uninhabited, but none the less I knew; the absence of any human presence struck an immediate chord.

It was not a building that conformed to any obvious, or known, style. Naturally one's eyes were drawn first to the turret. As for the rest, apart from the peculiarly steep pitch to the gables, it wasn't that unusual. The brick was a deep, almost russet colour, the windows divided into long rectangular panes. The house was big certainly, but then this was an area noted for both the size and grandeur of its residences. What it did have though was an air of enormous weight, as if it had dropped out of the sky like a meteorite and embedded itself in the earth.

We walked up to the front door, looked through slips of glass on either side. The hallway was empty, the stairs uncarpeted.

'It doesn't look as if there is anyone here,' said Minnie.

She started to circle the outside of the house, stepping across flower beds, peering in, pulling herself up on the sill when the window was too high. I followed unhappily, concerned about the state of my shoes. At last she stopped by a pair of french windows, felt about in her bag and took out a little pocket knife.

'Minnie. What on earth?'

With an expertise that astonished me she inserted the blade in the crack where the door met the jamb and flicked it sharply upwards. She folded the knife and pushed open the door.

'You're not—?'

But she was. I stood outside after she had gone in, head twisting this way and that, running through explanations in case we were discovered. After a few minutes I decided to follow her. The solitude had begun to get to me. I was alone in a large bare room, the living-room, presumably. It smelt, a strange mix of damp and freshly sawn timber. I went through into the hallway, up the stairs. The light was dimmer here. I had to feel my way up the bannisters. Every few steps I called out, my voice echoey, untethered.

At the top of the stairs a corridor led down to the left. Straight ahead there was a door and beyond it a bedroom. Minnie was pacing from one end of the room to the other, counting to herself as she went. I waited until she had reached the far wall before interrupting.

'I really don't think we ought to be in here.'

When she turned to me, I was aware of a light in her eye. It reminded me of the glint of expectation she'd had on our wedding night, now adapted and shifted onto something else.

'What do you think of it?' she asked.

'Of this place? Oh, interesting enough, architecturally speaking. But far too big for the two of us. We could rattle round in here for weeks and never see each other.'

'I like it,' she said, and twisted slightly on one heel.

'For us? But we couldn't possibly . . .'

'I like it,' she repeated, more firmly.

Even then, shame already had the edge over prudence with me. I may have baulked, but I still knew that I couldn't afford to be anything other than a soft touch. What my wife wanted, she would get – in so far as I was able to provide it.

We went round the rest of the first floor, Minnie marvelling over the space, the possibilities for redecoration, while I brought up the rear. Back downstairs we refastened the french windows – there was a knack to it I didn't wish to see – and wandered across the garden to where the lawn sloped down to the water.

A procession of boats was making its way home in the semi-darkness. Glowing lanterns hung from short squat masts. On an impulse I put my arm around Minnie. She didn't react, neither stiffened up nor melted. But I wasn't really thinking about her. I was thinking how we must have looked from the river. What a tender sight we must have presented; such warmth amid the chill. Such eventide devotion.

I bought the house. The estate agent was thrilled, he'd had it on the market for well over a year. What I hadn't realized when we'd come driving aimlessly past, was just how suitable the area was for us – and us for it. The place was crammed with television people, some of them personalities like myself, others less publicly prominent, but still notable in their way. Few, if any, of us had started life there. We'd moved in when our reputations had reached a certain level; when the yearning for privacy and the desire for ostentation came into proper alignment. This went some way to explaining the 'extraordinary flamboyance of architectural styles' – I'm quoting from something – and also the walls, the hedges, the fences to keep the outside world at bay. We were too popular to risk the careless attentions of the public.

My memories of this period are of a stream of delivery vans unloading more furniture than I had ever seen. Minnie, growing in authority daily, looked like a woman who'd at last found herself, ordering around the workmen, changing her mind about colour schemes, leafing through great piles of home improvement manuals. All the time I sat around getting in the way and fielding questions from men in brown coats. I had no idea how long my finances would hold out – in a way I didn't care. I was inviting trouble, extending it the same sort of free hand as I was giving Minnie.

Eventually the day came when the vans stopped arriving and we found ourselves alone again in our new house. I remember Minnie taking me on a tour to point out the rooms of particular interest. My eyes shrank to behold the mess she had made – it was far worse than anything my mother and Tom had come up with. But under the remarkable collisions of style, I could detect some doomed attempt to find herself through exercising choice – and what was left of my heart softened while my head ached. In her way, I thought, she had as few fixed points to her as I did.

So we sat back amid the technicolour glare and wondered what happened next. I'd imagined that we might get a few neighbours dropping in to wish us well. But I was forgetting where we were. They wished us well by staying away, respecting our privacy. No-one came. That depressed Minnie, I could tell. She wanted someone to show off to. All the confidence, the assertiveness she'd shown when the work was being done gradually deserted her.

Each morning I would brush my wife's cheeks with my bunched white lips on my way out of the house. And each evening I would come back to find her alone, just sitting there as if she'd spent the whole day hardly moving, like a bird edging back and forth along its perch. I used to wonder what she got up to when I was away. I tried not to, but I couldn't help it. I did

273

my best to keep her happy, treating her with such consideration that there wasn't much else she could do but respond in kind. We inquired after each other's welfare, we did each other little favours. All the right mannerisms were there, unencumbered by anything else.

And every night we would take ourselves up to bed. We now had individual bathrooms opening off the bedroom suite, so our staggered undressing of old had gone, replaced by something a good deal more synchronized and modern. Every night too I would find myself affected more deeply than I could understand by the sight of my wife's toes. It was their nakedness, I suppose, their pinkness, the way they jutted out from under her dressing-gown. I felt I had been given some unwelcome glimpse into her inner world; the toes told their own story of confusion and neglect. Whatever slender thread Helen had managed to extract from me had long since run out. We seldom bothered now with specifying what particular impediment lay between us, having moved on to a form of sign language that did the job just as well. I had only to lift my hand towards that day's trouble spot to prompt an answering nod from Minnie. Heartburn, nephritis, rinderpest – it hardly mattered. Her own attempts to match me had soon petered out.

Almost imperceptibly I was getting older. There were small giveaway signs. The flesh around my waist had become soft; when I squeezed it the imprint of my fingers stayed there as if they'd been pressed into dough. My hair too was getting lighter, reverting back to the same flaxen colour that had excited such admiration when I was a child. I even got twinges, nothing serious, but reminders just the same that I was not as young as I had been – that I would never be young again. I could hardly believe it. I didn't feel I had started out properly, let alone begun to wind down.

I suppose I had a choice; I could simply have

accepted the fact that my life was more than half over and twisted my airs and umpteen graces into something more appropriate. Or I could have done my best to ignore it altogether, to push it away and pretend that nothing had changed. That by standing apart from life, letting it pass by, I was not subject to the usual laws of ageing, or anything else. I was immune. And put like that it didn't seem much of a choice at all.

But the strain of sustaining our home life started to get me down. I couldn't sleep. Yet, like Minnie, I was overcome by this terrible sloth. I took to going home later and later. I couldn't bear what I would find when I got there – Minnie still sitting where I had left her that morning, our doomed attempts at conversation, the long climb up to bed. Instead, I wandered the streets alone, aimless and disconsolate. Often I'd walk for hours, with little or no idea where I was – sometimes I'd have to catch a taxi back to my car. Even then, I would put off actually going anywhere and sit for a while longer, staring out as the world went by.

One night I walked further than usual. By the time I drove back, the houses beside the road were edged with frost. Through the top of the windscreen I could see stars shining in the night sky. I was only a few miles from home when I stopped at a set of temporary traffic lights. One side of the road had been cordoned off with cones and a makeshift fence. Beyond was a mound of rubble and broken tarmac. The mist had settled on the river like a long grey cloche. There were no other cars about. After a while, with the light apparently stuck on red, I wondered if I might drive on. But up ahead the road bent sharply round to the left. It was impossible to tell if another car was coming. In the end I decided to wait.

The longer I was there, the more uneasy I became. It was as if the weight of the world pressed down upon me as I sat, waiting for the lights to change; these atmospheric pressures, this tangled net of radio waves drawing tighter and tighter all round. And I had nothing inside me to withstand them, to hold them at bay. I remembered how as a child, after the death of my father, I had been discovered in the hotel games room by myself, throwing the table tennis ball against the wall, the broken tock as it went back and forth, unravelling these patterns of noise, criss-crossing and filling the room. How I had felt cradled by them, corsetted. Back then I'd found some comfort in it, some sense that I was being looked after. Now here I was, trussed up again. This time though there was nothing left, nothing I could control anyway. I was more lost than ever. A plaything, swung about at will on this enormous filigree mesh that bent around the circumference of the earth.

The lights changed. I jabbed my foot on the accelerator. The car leaped forward. I got back to find Minnie already asleep. She'd given up on me. The bedside light was still on. I sat down on the edge of the bed and noted how her hair was spread out around her and her face mashed into the pillow. I felt her arm, it was warm. I turned it towards, me underside up, so that I could see the blue streaks of vein bunching at her wrist. I could hear her heart thumping away, so loudly I was surprised it didn't stir the bedclothes. Such vigour. Then I leaned over so that my ear was resting on top of her chest. Really, it was as intimate as we'd ever been. At the same time I reached under my jacket, slid my hand across and felt for my own heart. I found nothing to begin with – I had to grope about until I found an answering thump of my own. Except it wasn't a thump at all, there was hardly anything there. It was like the feeblest of tremors, just about pulsing through to my fingers.

After that I left it as late as I could, hoping that Minnie would have taken herself off to bed by the time I got back. I'd muffle the light switches with my sleeve, doing everything I could not to disturb her. Once or twice though she did wake up. I heard her,

alert to some presence, call out, 'Who's there?' But I
said nothing. And eventually she went back to sleep,
no doubt thinking she'd imagined it. If indeed it had
registered at all, this spectral figure creeping up the
stairs.

Chapter Twenty-Nine

Gradually I began to fall apart. I can see that clearly enough now. At the time though I had no idea what was happening to me. I felt as if I were running dry, as if I were all cracked and withered inside. Others began to notice it too. They wondered what was wrong. My usual ersatz liveliness had quite drained away. Instead, I sounded dulled, unsure of myself. Suffused with weariness. I moved like a sleepwalker, as if I were making my way through thicker, less certain gravity. When I sat and watched myself in a viewing theatre I seemed to be slowing down in front of my eyes.

There I stood, in the middle of a wood beside a large tree, shifting to keep my footing on a layer of wet leaves. Once again I gave the side of the tree a desultory slap, the bark rough and damp against my hand. 'English oak,' I announced to the camera. 'There is none finer in all the world. Our hearts are fashioned from it, of course. And so too our past. Those mighty timbers that made the *Victory*, hewn from the ancient hunting forests of—'

And again the director butted in, his voice clearly audible on the soundtrack. 'Can't you put a little more into it, Dickie.' He sounded exasperated. 'Try to sound proud of your heritage, of who you are.'

But it was hopeless. The harder I tried, the gloomier, the more lifeless, I became. It upset me more than I can say. What made it all the more obvious was that a new generation of presenters was coming forward – younger, fresher types, brimming with the sort of effusiveness I could no longer muster. They were consumed by it, breaking into vast inane grins at the slightest pretext, all filled with the same coercive jollity. Those of us who came from an older, more reserved school were like slow bovine creatures in comparison, leftovers from another age.

In the end, I went to a doctor to see if he could find anything wrong with me. He asked various questions about my health, about my general state of mind, my domestic arrangements. Also about my sex life. Caught off-guard, I struggled to reassure him that everything was as it should be. He did various tests, including a prostate examination. I bent over while he put on a rubber glove and stuck his hand up my behind. It took a long time. I began to get uncomfortable. My back was hurting, also I was getting cramp in my calves. I half-straightened up and moved my legs around to try and get the circulation going, forgetting that the doctor's hand was still inside me.

He called out in alarm, 'Mr Chambers, we are still joined,' and for a few moments we were stuck together, as I hopped about on the end of his arm and he was pulled along behind. We came to a halt. His hand was withdrawn, the glove snapped off and thrown into a bin.

When we sat down again he asked me about my dreams. He sounded surprised when I told him that they were populated almost entirely by animals. Not by fearsome untamed beasts, I hastened to assure him, but harmless farmyard animals that looked as if they had been given some stuttering approximation to life. Around the farmyard they stumped and whirred, and then high up in the meadows where the grass was sweetest.

A few days later the results came through. My prostate was in perfectly good order. Nor was I anaemic or undernourished, as he had thought might be the case. My heart, however, was not beating as regularly as it should. It never actually skipped a beat, but it was apt to lag behind itself, like a slipping spring on a clock. The doctor said I shouldn't worry. He insisted it wasn't that serious. None the less, he prescribed pills to steady me up. I was to take them three times a day and avoid any undue strain. Apart from that, there was nothing he could find.

But there were further lapses. I was no longer able to trust myself. All those elements that had given me my particular appeal were ebbing away, leaving me as pale and colourless on the outside as I was within. In their place came things I couldn't control. When I opened my mouth I couldn't be sure what might emerge – the neatly anodyne sentiments that littered my scripts, or something else entirely: other, quite unsuitable thoughts that blew into me and were inadvertently given expression.

It was around this time that a most unusual request came through. While I had interviewed a great many public figures over the course of my career, particularly when I was presenting 'Tonight in Town', I'd never had much to do with politicians. On the few occasions when I'd been called upon to interview anyone in politics I proved to be way out of my depth. Even today, my opening question to the-then Foreign Secretary remains the source of much derision. I can only say that, as always, I would do anything to avoid an argument. So when I asked, 'Foreign Secretary, your enemies have accused you of being a heartless warmonger. Tell me, is there one iota of truth in these allegations?' I was merely allowing someone who was under a great deal of pressure to put his case without fear of interruption or contradiction.

It therefore came as a considerable surprise, both to me and to my colleagues, when I was asked to interview the Prime Minister. It was explained to the Prime Minister's office that my lack of any political sophistication rendered me unfit for such a task, that there were plenty of other, more suitable candidates only too eager to interview him. However, back came a message saying that far from this being a disqualification, it was exactly what they were looking for. In fact, the Prime Minister, they maintained, had asked for me specially; he wouldn't talk to anyone else.

What's more, the parameters of the interview were quite clear. There were to be no questions on issues such as economic or social policy. Instead, the Prime Minister wanted the opportunity to put forward a more human face to the electorate, to let viewers see those sides of his character that were seldom explored elsewhere. There was a further delay while final, frantic efforts were made to persuade him to change both the interviewer and the nature of the questions, but in the face of his refusal to budge, they had little choice but to give in.

A list of topics on which he was prepared to speak was sent through in advance: childhood recollections, household hints, his love of the hedgerows and the countryside in general . . . These, at least, were the sort of headings I was used to. I duly prepared my questions and was there waiting, a little anxiously, in the studio when the Prime Minister arrived. Although we had never met before, he greeted me like an old friend. 'How are you, Dickie?' he asked, not only shaking my hand, but gripping my forearm as well. 'I am looking forward to this.' And while I hadn't really been in the best of spirits for some time – had been increasingly worried by my susceptibility to these outside forces – I replied that I was in fine shape and also greatly looking forward to our interview.

We sat down, each in our own easy chair, while the make-up girls darted about with their powder puffs and microphones were attached to our lapels. The Prime Minister, a curiously rectangular figure in his double-breasted suit, made several small adjustments to his posture and pointed his chin expectantly towards me.

Before we began, the sound man asked if he could say something, just two or three sentences would do, in order to check the level in his microphone. The Prime Minister obliged, and in doing so set the tone of much of what was to follow.

He tilted his head and said in a wistful sort of way. 'My Auntie Bee baked the most delicious apple turnover.' There was a tiny pause, and then he lowered his voice fractionally, 'Of course, she's dead now. Bless her.'

An unmistakable ripple of sympathy ran around the studio. It was a subject I thought it prudent to pursue once we had actually started the interview. And, indeed, the Prime Minister proved to be the most obliging of guests, responding to my questions in an expansive, at times even lyrical fashion.

'I don't know, Dickie, if you've ever had the experience of walking at night down a cart track cut in the chalk. It's quite magical. You can see this dim white line unfolding in front of you, stretching off into the distance. I used to go out in the school holidays collecting snails.'

'What a lovely image. And then back to Auntie Bee's, I suppose?'

'Then back to Auntie Bee's,' he confirmed.

'For some of her delicious apple turnover.'

'Well, yes,' said the Prime Minister. 'She did used to cook other things.'

On we went, through coppice and clump, off into household hints, passing slyly on to recipes, and then back once more to another series of juvenile exploits. But as the Prime Minister carried on talking, I became aware of an increasing impatience that took root inside me, a desire to counter with some early recollections of my own. To prove, both to myself and everyone else, that I had my own stock of antique memories to dip into. Once or twice the opportunity seemed to have presented itself, but each time the Prime Minister swept on and I could do nothing except nod encouragingly and try to control this urge for expression that ripened and swelled within.

'The trick,' he was saying, 'is to pack the hay bales together as tightly as possible. Because you're going to have to ride on top of them back to the farmyard and if they're not packed tightly they might all fall down.' He smiled, satisfied by the memory, and prepared to resume.

'I was young once,' I said.

The Prime Minister looked at me blankly. His face was devoid of any expression.

'Yes,' I said, 'I was. It seems so long ago now, so far away, that I can hardly believe it—'

'The bales,' he began again.

'I remember being by the beach,' I said. 'I don't know how old I was. But I remember the box kites in the air. The way the narrow brown waves raced into the shore. The boats splicing through the water. Fat terriers playing in the surf.'

For the first time the Prime Minister began to look agitated. I could see his eyes bulging in surprise. He twisted round in his chair, turning to his aides, apparently seeking an explanation.

'Perhaps it was the day my father drowned,' I was saying. 'I can't be sure. Then I can't be sure of anything. Not anymore. I used to think there must be a point at which everything started to go wrong. If I could only find it then I'd know what the matter was. But I don't know. It's all this terrible mystery to me. Everything seems such a sham.'

At this point the Prime Minister tried to interrupt once again. First he held up his hand. When that had no effect, he began trying to butt in with further memories of his own. For a while each of us struggled to put our human face before the other. After years of dealing with hecklers and all manner of rudeness you might think that the Prime Minister would have been at an obvious advantage here. But when the flurry of raised voices had at last subsided, I was the only one left talking.

The Prime Minister had given up in exasperation. His mouth was hanging open while his shoulders rose and fell in an enormous shrug.

'Everytime I go to sleep I see this face rising before me,' I continued. 'I don't know whose it is. I don't dare to shut my eyes. But I get so terribly tired. I've found these last few weeks especially difficult. One thing piles on top of another, you see. Higher and higher. I feel they're all crushing me, forcing all the air out, until there's nothing left. Nothing at all. I don't know what to do.'

And I started to cry. Except that there were no tears, just these dry pockets of dust that burst upon my cheeks.

'Can you hear me?' asked a voice in my ear.

I lifted my head. 'I think it would be better if you left the studio,' said the voice. 'That's right, Dickie. Now, immediately. No, just leave everything where it is.'

It can only have been an hour or so later that I was summoned upstairs to where my superiors sat in a line behind a long table. There was no preamble. What was I thinking of? they demanded.

I sat bowed and contrite. I didn't know, I said.

They all exhaled sharply. It was like a collective sigh of disappointment. I did try to explain. I told them how I hadn't been feeling myself lately. How I'd been buffeted about by all sorts of things; they gusted through me, stirring my tongue, leading me on. How it was far harder for me to work out than it was for them. But all the time I felt as if I were withdrawing behind my words, falling further and further away, until there was nothing left of me except this huddled shade at the end of a long, dark tunnel.

After a while they fell to whispering among themselves. One of the women spoke. She had glasses hung around her neck and one of those tolerant half-smiles that only served to highlight the distaste that lay behind. They found themselves in a very difficult position, she said. Of course they didn't wish to be unsympathetic. None the less there was the public's welfare to be considered, as well as that of the Corporation. Great store was placed on my reliability; for whatever reason, I had abused that trust. No-one could be allowed to get away with such behaviour, however grand they might once have been. In the circumstances they felt it was best if I took a six month sabbatical – and, while it wasn't their place to make such recommendations, they all felt I should use that time to seek professional treatment.

I looked up. 'But what will I do?'

'Rest. Take it easy. Enjoy your home life.'

'Home life?' I echoed. 'I don't have any life except for here.'

No-one spoke. A few of them coughed in embarrassment.

'You want me to go?' My voice sounded more hollow and faint than ever.

There was a moment when everyone behind the table turned to one another for confirmation. 'That's right,' they chorused, 'go.'

Chapter Thirty

That night I wandered further than I had ever done before. I had no idea where I was going. I didn't care. It began to rain, spattering against walls, drumming on awnings, blowing in flurries between the buildings. It bounced off the pavements, cascaded out of gutters, spread across the roads in broad, overlapping ripples and ran in rivulets down the drains. Passing cars threw up steep arcs of spray. There was no-one about – they'd all run for shelter. But I walked on, head sunk, splashing my way through the wet. I didn't stop for hours.

And still the rain came down. It swung about in the air above, billowing out like sailcloth. Great white drifts, colliding and merging. I had never felt so alone. More than anything else, I longed for someone I could confide in, who would help take the weight of this loneliness. Someone whose loyalty I could depend on, whose advice I could trust. Although I had no capacity for human warmth, I longed for it now with an intensity that was so strong it almost brought me to my knees. I wanted to cry out, to send this appeal flailing out across the rooftops.

At last the rain began to ease up. I was walking down a long, wide crescent lined with trees. It curved round to the left and began to climb a hill. Although there were houses on either side, most of them were set back from the road, half-hidden in the shadows. Everything gleamed as if it had been hosed down with oil. I stopped to see if I could work out where I was. The only street sign I could see was mounted high up on a building opposite. I crossed the road. Even then, it was difficult to read. I stood there, head back, water trickling into my eyes.

As I did so, I became aware of footsteps coming towards me. In the damp air they sounded unusually loud, each heel click ringing out down the street. I paid no attention at first. Then as they got closer, I turned to see a figure approaching. Not hurrying, but strolling along, apparently undaunted by the weather. I turned back, thinking that perhaps I should take this opportunity to ask for directions, then decided it would sound too foolish to explain I was lost. The footsteps came to a halt. I paid no attention – my resolve to work things out for myself had hardened. Besides, I'd almost deciphered the sign.

'Hello, Dickie.'

The figure was standing just behind me in a large puddle of orange light. The light spread around the base of the sodium lamp and seeped into the darkness beyond. I could see the outline of his head edged with orange and the slope of his shoulders, although his face remained in shadow.

'Is everything all right, Dickie? You look rather shocked.'

'What are you doing here?'

'I live just around the corner. I might ask the same question of you.'

'I've been out walking,' I said. 'I . . . I've had a lot on my mind.'

'Poor Dickie,' said Ralph. 'You are in a state. Look at you. You're wet through.' He reached out to squeeze some water out of my sleeve. Until then I hadn't realized how wet I was. But my coat was sodden and my trousers clung round my calves. 'You can't walk the streets like that. You'll catch pneumonia. Why don't you come back to my place for a while and dry off?'

'I wouldn't want to be a nuisance.'

'For goodness sake, Dickie, what are friends for?'

We began walking along together. This time every step I took felt like more of an effort than ever; it was as if I were weighed down by my clothes. I wasn't sure that I was going to be able to make it. Fortunately, Ralph's flat wasn't far away. We stopped outside a modern block with a large silver intercom beside the front door and a row of bells below. There was a smell of boiled vegetables in the lobby. We climbed the stairs to the first floor. Three doors opened off the landing. Ralph turned his key in the lock of the middle door, pushed it open and reached for the light.

'Go through into the sitting room, Dickie. I'll see if I can find something for you to change into.' He came in a few minutes later with a dressing-gown over his arm. 'Why don't you put this on for the time being. I'll hang up your clothes.'

'Where shall I change?' I asked.

'Wherever you like. In here, or the bedroom if you want to be more private.'

I went through into the bedroom. The dressing-gown was made out of some sort of synthetic fabric. It stuck to my skin. I took my clothes back into the living-room and saw that Ralph had also changed. He was wearing an identical dressing-gown. Whenever either of us moved ripples of soft green light seemed to hug the folds of the material.

'I found I was rather wet too,' explained Ralph. He held out his hands to take my clothes.

'I see that you've gone for a tufted carpet,' I said.

'It's not easy to keep clean, as you can see. But I do like the feel of it underfoot. Now can I get you a drink, Dickie? Something to warm you up. A whisky perhaps?'

He went through into the kitchen. I could hear the sound of ice cubes being pressed out of their trays and splintering as the whisky was poured over them. He came back with two glasses and we sat down on the sofa. Ralph crossed his legs; I saw the long shank of his ankle sticking out of the bottom of his dressing gown, as thin and white as a conductor's baton.

'I know that we don't see much of each other anymore, Dickie. But speaking for myself, I can only say that it's always a pleasure, however unexpected.'

'I do keep pretty busy.'

'Of course.'

'And you, Ralph,' I said, 'how have you been keeping?'

'Like yourself, extremely busy. As you probably know, I've been doing quite a bit of television lately.'

'Television? You?'

'Surely it isn't that much of a surprise, Dickie?'

'No, but . . . Never mind.'

'People seemed to feel that I was rather well suited to this more relaxed, less pompous style of presentation that's becoming so popular these days.'

'Well,' I said, 'congratulations.'

'Thank you, Dickie. And tell me, how is Minnie?'

'She's fine. Fine. Couldn't be better . . . Actually,' I said after a pause, 'I don't know how she is.'

'Oh dear. Are you two going through a difficult patch? I am sorry to hear that. Is there anything I can do to help?'

I felt just like I'd done before with Ralph – as if this giant magnet was being trained on me, tugging away, pulling everything to the surface. I started telling him about how our marriage was a hopeless charade. How I was running dry, powdering away inside; how these unseen forces pressed against me and steered me about and did with me what they wished. All this and anything else I could come up with. But far from bringing relief or reassurance, I found that telling Ralph my troubles only left me feeling emptier than ever.

'Poor Dickie,' said Ralph for the second time. 'Voices, you say?'

'Not for a while.'

'Even so . . .'

'I was so pleased with my life,' I said. 'I thought it had worked out splendidly, all neat and tidy. Far better than I could ever have expected. I even came to believe in myself. Now it's falling apart, I don't know what to do.'

'You really have been having quite a time of it.'

'Yes,' I said. 'Yes, I have.'

He shook his head sadly.

'I . . . I don't know what to do, Dickie,' I said again.

'What do you want to do?' asked Ralph.

'I don't know that either.'

'May I offer some advice?'

'Please do.'

'Give up completely.'

'I beg your pardon?'

'Surrender yourself.'

'I thought I'd done that already.'

'Not entirely. You still want to retain some control over your life.'

'Well,' I said, 'that's only natural, surely.'

'But Dickie, there's no point pretending anymore.'

'Isn't there?'

'You're all run down, you said so yourself. What have you got left inside? Anything at all?'

'I've got a few bits and pieces.'

'Anything else?'

'No, not really.'

'You can't carry on like this, can you? All on your own?'

'I don't think I can.'

'Isn't it time to let others have a go?'

'Others? Who do you mean?'

'Others more . . . more potent than yourself, let's say,' said Ralph. 'Able to invest you with some of their pluck. Let them stoke you up, revive you, set you back on the right course.'

'Steered protectively by the hand of friendship?'

'Yes,' said Ralph, 'that sort of thing.'

'But where would I find these people?'

'It's principally a matter of attitude, as I understand it. A matter of laying yourself open, as wide as can be.'

He was leaning over, staring intently.

'You're shivering, Dickie. Are you warm enough? I could put the fire on.'

'I can't see a fire,' I said.

'Not in here, no. But there's one next door.'

'I don't think that would be much help. Anyway, I'm quite warm enough.'

In truth, though, I could hardly stop my teeth from chattering. I pulled my dressing gown around me, but there was hardly any warmth in the material. Ralph reached over and put his hand on my knee. At first I thought that he must have made a mistake and put his hand on the wrong knee. I sat and looked at it resting there, so light that I could barely feel anything.

We stayed that way for a while, both of us quite still. The folds of green light ran across from one dressing-gown to the other. Then I started to cry again.

'Poor Dickie.'

'Please help me,' I said.

Ralph pulled me towards him. I offered no resistance. I would have done anything for comfort, or just some semblance of it. All the stuffing had gone out of me. I remembered how, all those years before, I had been piloted around the dance floor by my tongue-tied partners. Clasped to their chests, going through their paces, as limp and compliant as a rag doll.

'What are you doing?'

Ralph didn't say anything.

'What are you doing?' I asked again.

'Trust me, Dickie.'

'Oh.'

'Trust me.'

'I don't know if I like this.'

But Ralph took no notice.

He just carried on.

He just carried on, his hands roaming, probing, pulling me apart.

The green ripples slid to the carpet, lay there in a pool.

'This is the end for me,' I said.

'Oh no, Dickie,' said Ralph. 'There's still a way to go yet.'

How I shrieked to suffer such intrusion. To be pierced and penetrated, possessed in this way. Except that I didn't say anything. I never even uttered. I just knelt there motionless, bent over the sofa, as Ralph thrust and grunted and pushed his way inside me. Not that it mattered. No response was called for, or expected. And when he was through, when he had quite finished, I stayed where I was, steeped in my shame.

A little later Ralph came back in. He was holding something in his arms.

'I think your clothes are almost dry by now, Dickie,' he said.

When I got home that night the house was as blank and unrevealing as always. I parked the car and let myself in, with that familiar sense of being an interloper in my own home. I climbed the stairs, careful not to wake Minnie. But when I got to our bedroom I saw that she was still up. At least there was no sign of her in bed. I looked in her bathroom. She wasn't there either.

I went back downstairs and into the kitchen. There was no-one about. This was strange, but not unheard of. She might have gone out with a friend. I couldn't recall her having any friends – we were as bad as one another in this respect. Still, it was possible that she had met someone, that they had gone out together. It was possible. At this point though I realized that her bathroom upstairs had seemed peculiarly empty. Reluctant to climb the stairs once more, I tried to work out what it could be. And soon enough, the answer came through: the bottles, tubes, oils, ointments, all those things that, in the early stages of our marriage, at least, Minnie had spent so much time applying to her face and body to make herself as appealing as possible, had gone.

I turned on the living-room light. The furniture was all there. Minnie's chair was where she liked it best, turned towards the window, a footstool within easy reach. But there was no sign of the cushion that Minnie kept on her chair. A small, embroidered thing, she was much attached to it and never sat down without wedging it in against her thigh. That had gone — nothing else. More mystified than ever, I wandered back to the kitchen. And it was only then that I saw the note on the table in front of me, my name written clearly on one half of a folded piece of paper. I opened it and glanced down at the signature. It was from Minnie. I'd hardly ever seen her writing before. It was like a child's — the looped 'l's and squat 'm's. But neat enough for all that, a precise, rounded hand that ran straight down invisible margins.

—I cannot stay here anymore. I am wasting away. Each night I cry myself to sleep. I don't know where you are. I don't know what is happening. I don't know why you married me in the first place . . . Please do not try and get in touch. I don't know what I am going to do, or where I am going, or how things will work out. But I managed before on my own and anything would be better than this.

I have taken this month's housekeeping money which you gave me. But no more. I do not wish you harm. I mean this.

I put the note back down on the table. How odd to see it fluttering between my fingers.

Chapter Thirty-One

There were no depths to which I did not sink over the next few weeks. I was hardly aware if it was dark or light. I ate when I was hungry, slept when I was tired. I stumbled about lost to the world. No-one took any notice of me; no-one made conversation, or even came close. Perhaps they didn't believe their eyes and assumed that this couldn't possibly be me, but some stricken lookalike.

I sought out low company, the lowest I could find. It proved far easier than I had ever imagined. There was a language here, not so different from the faint semaphore I had once employed with Minnie. Another network of shrugs and tics that signalled my intent and got my message across – always to the same sly, disengaged types. They lounged in doorways, listened impassive while I blurted out my requirements, then took my money and set to in the same dulled, stupefied way.

I bade them do their worst, trying to fill myself with whatever was to hand. Hoping that some of their, admittedly diminished, life force might find its way inside me; that they might inseminate me, get me going once more. And just occasionally I thought it had worked, that I had been roused and rekindled. Restored to life. But it never lasted long. It all soon drained away. Then back I'd go and try once more.

I grew used to the smell of these places. Sweat and

cologne; always those same mingled odours of vanity and decay. I grew used to the decor; the same compacted pile of bedding, the stained sheets and blankets like boards. The bedside tables pitted with cigarette burns, the piles of crinkled magazines, the strewn towels and twists of tissue that littered the floor. And most of all I grew used to the look in their eyes; contempt, but with some trace of pleasure at the full extent of human failings. They stood and watched and waited as my fingers twitched over my belt buckle.

On one occasion I was down in a basement somewhere soaking up my punishment, when I became aware of something moving above my head. Nothing specific, just these dim black and white shapes shifting about. Being otherwise engaged – another hired brute bent over my back, rutting me – I paid little attention at first. But a little later I looked again, and saw in the polished headboard the reflection of the television that was playing away at the foot of the bed. There was nothing unusual about this; the hired brutes liked some sort of distraction while they worked. But as I looked I saw something familiar scudding across the headboard. A shape like all the others, but one that seemed to strike a distant chord.

I struggled up and twisted round. There, staring back at me, was my younger self. Disinterred and dusted off for some late night compilation; holding a microphone as if it might topple over at any moment and asking a Mr Waverly from Chester how many of his sons were in the armed forces. Two, he said proudly, plus one at catering college.

Part of me wanted to look away, but I couldn't. I just kept staring back, lost in disbelief. There I was, so sleek and apparently assured, puffed up and full of myself, turning to catch the light. Yet I felt no more affinity with my younger self than I did with any of the other figures looming out of this monochrome haze. How could I believe in my past when I'd never acknowledged it as my present? It couldn't be done. All this time I'd been

295

waiting for my life to get underway, and all the time it had been disappearing, powdering off in these public guises.

And here I was now, puddled and forlorn, altogether wretched. The more I looked, the more the gap between us widened – and the more I shrank to see both what I had been and what I had become.

Meanwhile my younger self had moved on to another contestant. 'Can you tell us a little about branding?'

'Branding,' replied my new guest, a short bespectacled man brimming with information, 'is now mainly practised on animals. But in the Middle Ages it was quite common for humans to be branded. Either convicted criminals, or those who had offended against the moral proprieties of the time. They would be ostracized as a result, excluded from normal society. Forced to shut themselves away and live like hermits, the hallmark of their disgrace etched upon their faces until they went to their graves. And possibly beyond,' he added, 'since it was generally believed that we kept the same physical appearance in the afterlife. Doomed then to walk eternity, forever bearing the mark of their shame.'

There was a short pause after he had finished. Either disturbed by some early precognitive trembling, or else simply taken aback by the comprehensiveness of his answer, I seemed lost for words. Momentarily dumbstruck; left stranded in this flickering time tunnel.

At this point the picture changed. My black and white self was swept away and there instead was a face so bright, so highly coloured, that I was almost dazzled. It hung there in front of me like some piece of burnished fruit, pouring scorn on my clothes, my hair, my antediluvian manner and ludicrous diction. Such stiffness, such self-importance. Was this really what people had once marvelled at? Could we have come so far in so short a time? It seemed scarcely credible.

I knew the voice, of course. Even in the state, the circumstances I was in, I knew the voice. But still it took me some time to recognize Ralph as he stood there, crowing over my shortcomings. The audience rocked with laughter; they couldn't believe it either. People were doubled up, barely able to contain themselves.

Ralph too had grown so red, so engorged with mirth, that his face almost filled the screen. And as I looked, it seemed to grow brighter and brighter. Ballooning all the while, pushing up against the glass and gazing out across the tangle of bedding to where I lay.

Chapter Thirty-Two

Broadly speaking, my humiliation came in two parts. First were the revelations of my private life. I came downstairs one Sunday morning a little later than usual – there was nothing for me to get up for – to find the papers had already been delivered. They'd been forced through the letter flap and had burst open on the mat. I bent to pick them up, more preoccupied with the twinge in my back than anything else. It wasn't until I was almost down at floor level that I saw what was in front of me.

There I was again. Everywhere I looked. My shame writ large, and in such detail. They had it all. Just where the story had come from was never properly established. Obviously I hadn't been as invisible as I thought. Someone must have recognized me; this was far too good an opportunity to be missed. But while the predominant tone was one of disgust – inured to most forms of human depravity, they'd never come across anything quite like this before – a good deal of amazement was also expressed. How could I have been so blatant? Why had I made no effort to cover my tracks? I'd even written out cheques in payment for services rendered, signed them with my own name.

Various psychologists, amateur and otherwise, deduced that, deep down, I must surely have wanted to be caught all along; that my vile behaviour constituted one long warbling cry for help. If so, it was not a cry anyone felt like heeding. The following day I received a letter briefly informing me that my employment was at an end, with immediate effect. I should not bother to return after my six months' sabbatical, it said. In fact, I should never attempt to return.

Next came the news that Minnie planned to divorce me on the grounds of non-consummation. Those sentiments she'd expressed in her note hadn't lasted long; now she'd taken advice and wanted retribution. This news caught everyone offguard. They didn't know what to think. Least of all my lawyer, who questioned me closely on our marriage.

'Had we never attained any form of intercourse?' he wanted to know, 'not even on our wedding night?'

I tried to explain how the conjunction of two people was a complicated business, by no means natural. One moreover subject to almost infinite mishaps.

'So nothing then?'

'No,' I said. 'Nothing.'

It was at this point that I retreated to my riverside estate and shut myself away. The press camped by the gate, hoping for a comment, trying to persuade me to show myself. But I stayed put indoors. Days went by, one after the other. Nothing to mark them out except the volume of hate-mail which rose and fell on unseen gusts. I was hardly aware of the passage of time. The only signs of life were in the garden which, left to itself, soon grew wild and, in places, impassable. In this insulated world little escaped and nothing got in. I thought that no-one else could touch me. In this I was more or less correct. But not quite.

I still took the papers; not to find out what was going on anywhere else, simply to see if they had turned their attention away from me. They might have done so more quickly had not my mother chosen this moment to come forward and announce what sort of a son I had been. Not once had I attempted to contact her in all these years, she said. Nor had she ever wanted to embarrass me by complaining or making a fuss.

This despite enduring terrible financial hardship and personal tragedy – her second husband had apparently lost a hand in a lathe accident.

After running through my deficiencies, my cruelties and childhood quirks, she ended with a plea. It wasn't too late for us to be a family again. All she had ever wanted was to be close to her son. Now she was near the end of her life, would I repulse her, with death so close at hand? Even now, if I could see myself to helping her out in any way, she was prepared to forgive me everything.

This was accompanied by a photograph of her looking remarkably well. I thought at first that the pictures must be old but, according to the captions, they had been taken only the day before 'in the small but immaculately kept mobile home she shares with her second husband'. He too was photographed, grimly clasping my mother with his one good arm. She leant back against his shoulder, contriving at once to look proud and hard done by. Maybe it was the angle of the photograph, but her neck looked shorter than I remembered it. Either that or she'd retracted it specially.

None the less, there was still something faintly amphibian about her, as if she weren't altogether at ease on dry land. Behind the two of them was a window, and through the window a view. It meant nothing to me at first. But then I looked more closely. Light glinted off the surface of a river. It bent round out of the window and then reappeared near the top of the photo. Other mobile homes were dotted about beyond. In the distance the ground rose and was crowned with a line of straggling, unkempt trees. On one side was the half-hidden outline of a house.

It was mine. I knew it. It had to be. My mother was camped less than a mile away. Among the vulgar intruders, where she could monitor my movements and keep me under siege. I crumpled up the paper and threw it away. It was a long time before I went outside again.

300

Months passed. All but the most persistent of my poison-pen letter writers finally gave up. No-one called. Meanwhile I'd let myself go. My hair grew down over my collar, my shirts frayed, my sweaters unravelled and fell apart. Occasionally people on passing river craft would point me out as I wandered around my garden. A stooped figure, alone with his thoughts. They'd come in closer for a better look and I'd wave my arms to try and make them go away and roar and throw leaves, while they laughed and clicked their cameras.

It was over a year before I ventured out. I thought that I would be unrecognizable by now, that I would be able to make my way back quite unobtrusively into the world. First I went to the bathroom and inspected myself in the mirror. I hadn't done so in months. My eyes seemed to have retreated into my head, my beard was streaked with grey, my hair had twisted itself into knots like ivy. I looked like Ben Gunn. Not only that, my face seemed to have developed a character of its own: grave, sad, almost dignified. Melancholy suited me.

I got dressed, trousers gathered loosely round my waist, shirt crumpled, and went outside to the garage. Getting the doors open proved more difficult than I had imagined. They'd rusted on their hinges. The car was covered in dust. It took several attempts before the engine caught. The pedals were stiff, the steering was much heavier than I remembered. The leather on the seats had started to crack. I swung the car round and set off up the drive. The gates swung open to let me through. One smooth and vigorous as always, the other fitful and slow. I stopped at the main road and looked to left and right. The road was clear. I indicated left and pulled away.

I drove for an hour, then two, until I was in a part of the country I'd never been to before. The scenery flattened out, the trees disappeared. On either side of the road were wide green verges. The fields beyond looked as if they'd been combed clean. Cows fed in neatly drilled lines. There were no buildings, no cars either. I'd begun to feel hungry and thought I might stop for lunch. But the chances of finding anywhere looked increasingly remote.

Then up ahead I saw a sign. It had been fixed to a post and hammered into the ground. The name of a pub. Home cooked meals and friendly service. Only a mile to go. I drove on. And there it was, set back from the road but impossible to miss. I didn't think I'd ever seen anywhere so idyllic in my life. It was everything a country pub should be, right down to the hollyhocks around the door.

There was a car park for patrons. I parked and went inside. The bar was empty apart from the landlord who was drying some plates with a tea towel. He had an enormous pair of sideburns sprouting from his cheeks.

'Good day to you, sir,' he said, putting down the towel.

'Good day to you,' I answered.

'What can I be getting you?'

'A pint of your best bitter, I think.'

He pulled the pump and handed me a glass. It was only half-full. 'Excuse me,' I said, 'but I wonder if you might fill it up to the top.'

'I do apologize, sir,' he said taking it back. 'My eyesight is not what it was.'

'Delicious,' I said, sipping from the now-filled glass. 'You can't beat a good English ale.'

'Indeed you can't.'

'You're very quiet today.'

'There isn't much passing traffic in these parts. I daresay it will fill up later. You're not a local man yourself, sir?'

'No, no. Just out for a drive.'

'A lovely day for it.'

'I hope you don't mind my saying so, but those are the most magnificent pair of mutton chops.'

'Sir?'

'Your sideburns.'

'Very kind of you. Bugger's grips they used to be called in the Navy.'

'Did they really?'

'Of course that was a long time ago now. Will you be wanting food?'

'Food? Well, what do you have?'

'I could do you a nice ham sandwich. Nice and lean.'

'That sounds perfect.'

'Where would you be liking it, sir? In here, or outside in the garden?'

'I'm not sure.'

'I'd advise the garden. Especially on a day like this.'

'The garden it is then.' I went outside and sat down. There was a child's swing at the end of the garden and several tables and chairs laid out alongside. It was a lovely day. But I hadn't been sitting there long when I noticed that there were clouds of what appeared to be very fine grit blowing through the air. It got into my beer and stung my cheeks.

'Here we are, sir.' The landlord put my sandwich on the table. 'Wind's got up, I see.'

'Yes it has.' I was about to tell him that I thought I might eat inside after all. But he'd already turned round and was halfway back to the door. The ham sandwich was full of fat. There were a few pink shreds of meat, but the rest was fat, great white wedges of it. The grit was getting everywhere too, into the sandwich, my eyes, my shoes. It came in thick brown gusts. I didn't see how I could stay. After a few more minutes I gathered up my plate and glass and walked back into the bar.

There was no sign of the landlord. I called out a few times, but got no response. In the end I put the plate and glass on the bar and went out to the car park.

The landlord was standing by the door of my car. 'Did you enjoy your sandwich, sir?'

'I did, yes. Thank you.'

He patted the chassis. 'Lovely workmanship. You don't see many of these anymore.'

'No,' I agreed. 'You don't.'

'Not stripped back to the metal like this. Very unusual. May I?'

'Please.'

He stepped onto the running board and looked inside. 'Had it long, have you?'

'Several years.'

He was trying to see the mileometer. 'Must be my eyesight playing up again. That figure can't be right.'

'As a matter of fact, it is,' I said.

'But that's nothing. No mileage at all. Keep it for special occasions, do you?'

'Well,' I said, 'in a manner of speaking. I don't go out much. At least, not lately.'

He was looking at me with the same intensity as he'd been staring at the mileometer. 'I could see that from your clothes. Do I know you?' he asked.

'I don't believe so.'

'Yes,' he said. 'I'm sure of it. I know your face.'

'I think you've made a mistake.'

'No, not me.'

'Actually,' I said. 'I must be going. I never intended to come this far.' And I made to get into my car. But the landlord was in the way.

'May I ask a favour?' he said.

'You can ask.'

'Will you take me for a drive?'

'You? A drive? Where to?'

'Nowhere in particular.'

'I'm afraid that's quite impossible. You see—'

'Just a spin. We'll be back before you can turn around.'

'I don't want to turn around,' I said. 'I want to go home.'

The landlord shrugged. He had his top lip tucked inside his bottom one. 'In that case I shall have to ask you to pay for your lunch, sir.'

'But I've already paid.'

'Oh no.'

'Yes I have. In the bar.'

He shook his head. His hand was stretched out.

'Anyway, my sandwich was horrible. It was full of fat.'

'You said you enjoyed it.'

'I was only being polite.'

Still he stood there with his hand extended.

I dug in my pocket for some more change. 'Here then, that should cover it. You have a charming place here. I only wish the service matched the surroundings.'

'I don't know how you can live with yourself,' he said.

'I beg your pardon.'

'The things you got up to. Ooh, it turns my stomach just to think of them.'

'I must say I find your attitude extremely offensive.'

'Will you be coming back this way again?'

'I very much doubt it,' I said.

'You won't be recommending us to your friends then?'

'I don't have any friends, so your point is hardly relevant.'

'Oh dear. All alone, are you?'

I started the engine and put the car into gear.

'Have a safe journey back, sir. And don't you go worrying about what I said. It's just that . . . well, we all have our scruples.'

He stood aside to let me past. Everything shone in the afternoon light; it looked as if it were illuminated from within. I drove past the cows I'd seen earlier. They were still stretched out across the field, equally spaced, advancing in step through the gleaming grass.

After that I stayed inside for several more months. But almost without my knowing it, a precedent had been set. The next time, I reasoned, couldn't be as difficult. One morning I decided to go up to London.

Instead of driving this time, I ordered a taxi to take me to the station. On the way there, I sat back and looked out at the birds stirring themselves in the trees, spreading their wings, flying heavily over the fields. So this is nature, I thought, as we drove past. Somehow it seemed quite different to anything I was used to. The great currents of life crackled all round me.

At the station I attracted a few strange looks. You don't get many people on public transport in my sort of condition – not in these parts, anyway. My hair and clothes signalled me out as someone to avoid. I could see the other passengers shifting back, fearful at my approach lest I ask them for money. The suspicious glances they gave me when I kept away, as if I were working up to some sudden rush, the surprise when I produced a ticket for the inspector to punch a hole in.

At the other end I joined the flow of pedestrians, streaming from the station and out into that greater throng. My shoes had split, the soles were barely attached to the uppers. The only way to stop them coming off completely was to keep my feet on the ground at all times, shuffling along as if I were on skis. With no purpose in mind, I found myself making my way slowly up Regent Street. Nothing seemed to have changed. The buildings were the same – so were the people; as hard-faced and indifferent as one another. I was buffeted about, spun round and elbowed as everyone rushed by, hurrying to get to places where they felt they might belong. Not that I minded. I felt oddly peaceful, detached, as though there was no longer any possibility of my ever being a part of anything.

Ahead of me I saw the tall grey prow of Broadcasting House, the mast on top jutting up into the sky. The doors were opening and closing, people making their way in and out. There were faces I recognized going by. My old colleagues. And although I was pretty sure that I was now unrecognizable, I stayed half turned away at first – just in case – only facing the tide as my confidence grew. Still they came, marching by, those great disseminators and household names. How brim-full of themselves they seemed, how very much at home.

I stood there as the crowd swept past, half in dread, half in expectation, trying to tell myself that I wasn't looking for anyone in particular. But all the while increasingly aware that despite everything I'd been through and the misuse that had been made of me, nothing had changed: I still sought substance elsewhere, sought to bestow myself upon another. Someone who might plug these gaps and render me whole. I couldn't help it. So I watched and waited and yearned for a faint tug of affinity. But everybody rushed by, taking no notice, looking straight through me. In all these familiar faces, there wasn't one I could batten on to. And it was as if this absence outside struck an answering gulf within and sent it spreading into my furthest corners.

At last I stepped back into a shop doorway where one of the mannequins was being lifted up and carried out from the window display.

A woman was standing nearby. She wore glasses and a hat pulled down over her forehead. She held herself awkwardly, a handbag clasped to her chest. My first impression was that she was in almost as bad a state as I was. To my alarm, I saw that she was smiling, presumably acknowledging a fellow misfit.

'Hello,' she said. She was twisting the strap of the bag between her hands.

'Do I know you?' I asked.

She started trying to push back some strands of hair that were sticking out from under her hat. But the manoeuvre wasn't as straightforward as it should have been. She put too much into it; her hair stayed where it was while the hat got knocked to one side.

'Helen?'

'Hello, Dickie.'

It was hard to tell which of us was more shocked. Although I wasn't in any position to be judgemental, I couldn't get over how Helen looked. Physically, she wasn't so very different, more lined certainly, greyer. But she seemed to have fallen in on herself, to have lost all her old vigour. Everything had retreated inwards. In her way she, too, had let herself go.

'You didn't recognize me, did you?'

'No,' I said. 'Not immediately.'

'I was sure it was you. I knew right away. We've both changed though, haven't we?'

'Yes, I suppose we have.'

She gave a little shrug and smiled again, sadly.

'And are you still living in the same house?' I asked.

'It suits us.'

'How is Rags?'

'Poor Rags can hardly walk,' said Helen.

'I am sorry.'

She told me what she'd been up to. There wasn't much to tell. Seeking a change of atmosphere, she'd left her job. But her fresh start hadn't worked out as she had hoped. A spell proof-reading knitting patterns had brought on migraine attacks. Now she was back doing the same thing as before.

'I'm sure everyone was very pleased to see you back,' I said.

'I don't know if they noticed I'd ever been away. It's funny, isn't it,' she said, 'the tricks that fate can play.'

'Yes. Yes it is.'

'I must be going.'

'Must you? Perhaps we could walk together.'

'Which way are you going?'

'Well, I was going down there,' and I pointed back the way I'd come.

'Unfortunately I have to go in the opposite direction.'

'Ah.'

She turned, put her bag over her shoulder. 'Goodbye then.'

'Don't go . . .'

'Goodbye, Dickie,' she said, and turned away.

Chapter Thirty-three

I thought that my end had come. And at any other period in history it probably would have done. I'd have been left alone with my ignominy, stuck with it for ever. But we live in forgetful times. I hadn't realized what short memories people have – especially with television. Nothing sticks; it all goes straight through them.

I served my time in the wilderness. Then, little by little, I began to get offers of work. I refused them at first, didn't want to know. But after a while I began to think, what harm could it do? How else was I to occupy my time? And so I bought some new clothes, shaved off my beard and prepared to rejoin the world. My face reverted to type. Any character I'd put on vanished with a few strokes of the razor.

I emerged to find that things had changed in my absence. Although none of the big networks wanted anything to do with me, a number of new outlets had appeared. Small, local stations whose signals withered in the air within a few miles of their transmitters. Someone of my experience represented quite a catch. I did whatever I was asked to do – I read out the traffic reports, the sports results, the lunchtime weather and the early evening schedules. I played record requests and fielded late night calls from jabbering maniacs. It might not have been what I'd been used to – it wasn't anywhere near it – but I couldn't afford to be too grand. It was an opportunity, a platform to build on.

And I built. Up and up, another edifice took shape beneath me. I won't pretend it was easy, perseverance was required. Slowly though I settled and prospered. I'd gained a certain notoriety, it was true, but the reasons for this soon became as blurred as everything else. People proved surprisingly tactful. Either that, or the stories they heard about me proved so at odds with the way I came across that they couldn't match them up. After a while they stopped trying.

Amends had been made, dues paid. I'd been away. Now I had returned. All my old difficulties had been forgotten. All my troubles were over. Smooth and untroubled, free from any outside interference, my new life unrolled before me.

Chapter Thirty-four

Polished and pomaded then, ready to go. My lapels have been brushed down, my tie hoisted into place. Trica is busy checking some timings. She sits jotting them down, her writing arm cupped around the top of the paper like someone guarding against cheats in an exam. Cameras are being pushed into position, microphones swung about. Behind me I can hear anxious voices, occasional shouts. Amid all this activity one face alone remains composed, calmly waiting for the countdown to transmission to begin – and that face is mine.

At the corner of my vision I can see Tony, the floor manager, wandering about with his habitually worried air. He has already come to check that I have everything I need. After our exchange on the control room steps the previous night he is even less sure how to deal with me than usual. Any embarrassment should, of course, be on my side, but experience has taught me that discomfiture bounces back off a smooth surface, leaving me untouched and him all over the place.

The lights dim. A hush descends. Tony stands in front of the camera, the fingers of his right hand outstretched, then disappearing as the final seconds tick away. Trisha begins this evening's round-up – we alternate. She smiles in her winsome way as the green light comes on, and I look up from some intense paper-squaring to give my own special variant. First the headlines: the standard recital of robberies, redundancies and road repairs. Then it's my turn to lighten the mood and reassure viewers that good deeds can still shine through in our tarnished world.

'A tremendous response to our appeal for volunteers to help drive local waterskiing champion Dawn/ Doreen's boat as she trains in search of national honours . . .'

Forty-five minutes later, with one last look at snowflakes stuck like targets on the weather chart, and we're through. We wish everyone a good evening and make our pretend small talk as the playout music fades away. I mouth my mute set phrases at Trisha and she mouths hers back at me. Trisha then hurries home to poach some more hake for another bunch of unsuspecting dinner guests, while I am left wondering how to fill the time until the end of another day.

Everyone disperses quickly – they all have places to go. All except Tony and myself who find ourselves thrown together on account of our both being alone, shunned and friendless. I like to believe that I am shunned for different reasons – to do with awe and intimidation, whereas people avoid Tony simply because he's so dull. Still, the end result is the same: two middle-aged men hanging about wasting time, drawing things out for as long as possible before they have to leave.

One of these days I suspect we will have to go for a drink together – I've already sensed him inching towards the suggestion, trying to gauge my likely reaction. Perhaps this is to be our night. Oddly enough, I would almost welcome it. I can't shake off this constant feeling of foreboding. In the past I might have summoned up a presentiment around this point. But all that had gone. I am on my own now. I only know that I would do almost anything not to have to go home.

Tony, however, shows no inclination to suggest a drink – too nervous presumably – and I can hardly make the suggestion myself. Finally, the cleaners arrive with their buckets and mops and our departure can't be put off any longer.

Together we walk out to the car park. The air has turned colder; it vaporizes in front of my face. I can feel the pinpricks of moisture as I walk through each cloud of breath. Showers of snow that fell earlier in the day are still lying on the flowerbeds. We wish one another good night. I go to my car; Tony, muffled up in scarves and a specially quilted suit, trudges off to his moped. At the car park gates the attendant emerges from his cabin, slapping his arms, to lift the barrier. The gritting lorries have been out earlier. In the headlights there's what looks to be an orange stain stretching ahead of me all down the road. Few cars go by.

After I've gone a few miles it starts to snow again, much more heavily this time; swirling about, buffeting the side of the car. Almost immediately the snow starts to settle on the trees, piling along the branches. Everything seems suddenly very quiet. By the time I get to the river it's hard to work out where the road has gone. There are no tyre tracks to point the way, only a level space between the verges.

To begin with the snow had picked out the shape of things, outlining them against the dark of the sky. Now it's just burying them under great white heaps that rear up on either side. The flakes dance above the water, disappearing as they hit the surface. There's a creaking sound from under the wheels as the car rolls across the fresh snow. We might be moving through pack ice. And all the while this sense of dread seems to thicken around me. I don't want to carry on. But if I don't I will be buried in the blizzard, dug out when the thaw comes, still hunched solid over the steering wheel. So I keep going as the snow closes in and the wipers squeak drily on the windscreen.

The road straightens, the trees thin out. Almost home. I turn into the driveway. At the gateposts I wind down the window to shout out my name. A curtain of snowflakes is falling in front of me. No

313

reaction from the gates. They don't want to know. I try again, louder. Nothing. I get out of the car and press my lips up close to the grill. Snow falls on my shoulders. It gets in my mouth when I speak, making my voice sound slack-lipped and blubbery. This time there's a pause, as if news of my arrival is being digested elsewhere, and then the gates start to swing open.

The house looks as unwelcoming as always, the windows dark, the porch unlit. I feel as much of a stranger as I did on the day I first saw the place. I park the car, step out and leave a trail of giant footprints up to the front door. The key slides into the lock. I turn on the light. The post has blown off the bannisters. Several envelopes are lying at the foot of the stairs. I don't bother to pick them up. Instead I go from room to room, checking to see that I am alone. Normally at this point I would draw the curtains in the main rooms. Tonight though I leave the curtains open and turn the garden lights on too.

The wind has died. The snow drifts slowly downwards, rocking away from side to side. It's hard to imagine anything more peaceful, more soothing. But I am beyond all that. Brilliantly illuminated, exposed on every side, I can only sit waiting, staring out into the night.

I must have dropped off. I awake to hear a tapping sound. A light tapping, more apologetic than insistent. It appears to be coming from out in the hall. But when I get to the hall there is nothing there. I look through the window. The snow has almost stopped, a few stray flakes still spiralling down. It has obscured the line of the steps and covered the boot scraper. I peer through the glass. After a while I go back into the drawing room.

I am about to sit back down when I see a line of footprints in the snow outside. At first I think they must be mine. But out where the light shelves off into the darkness I can see my car, heaped high with snow.

Leading from it are my footprints, by now almost filled, grey dips against the white. The other footprints are new. Deep dark holes that cut across mine, as if circling the house.

Leaning forward, I try to see where the footprints go. It is impossible to tell. As I stand there, I hear the tapping start again. Not from the hall this time. From further away. I walk down the corridor and stop outside the dining room door.

After a few seconds, the tapping dies away to be replaced by something else – a thin, sandy sort of scratching. I unlock the door. The room is empty. A table, some straight-backed chairs. A sideboard. Curtains frame the window. They hang down in thick brocaded folds. When I brush against them clouds of dust fall in front of my eyes.

As the dust clears I see a figure standing outside. I rear back, almost lose my footing. A hand is pressed against the glass, the fingers tapered, blackened at the tips. The other hand held across his face. We stare at one another. He takes his hand away. His mouth opens. I see the skin stretch over his collapsed cheeks. The lips, folded back already, can go no further. Still they gape and I have this sense that he is trying to smile. The eyes, locked on mine, light up with recognition, imploring. We see each other quite clearly. I see his clothes, hanging down in ragged strips. His scorched hair, his flesh barely clinging to the bone. This look of terrible pity and sadness. I can see the dry leatheriness of his skin. Almost feel the withered lightness of him.

And we know. We both know. Despite everything, we recognize each other. We note the same features. Eyes, noses, mouths – both gaping now. We both know. He seems about to fall, his knees sag. I start forward, as if to catch him, but he holds onto the window sill. We straighten up again awkwardly. He beckons me closer. His hand comes up and my hand goes to meet it. Together they move across the glass.

We are one. He tries to say something. His lips move.

No clouds of breath, no condensation on the window pane. He gives up and beckons once more. His arm swings back and forward. The blackened fingers curl round, scooping away. He wants me to go outside.

When I open the front door, cold air rushes in, fastening onto my shoulders. I step out into the snow. My feet sink through the thin crust. Nothing stirs. No wind. No lapping water from the river. I make my way around the house, snow gripping my ankles. By the time I reach the dining room window, there is no-one there. I see another set of footprints, disappearing off beyond the car. But whereas the earlier prints were crisp black holes, this is more like a long, continuous trench. The sort a stricken animal might make dragging itself along.

I follow the trail across the lawn, skirting the remains of the box hedging, and round towards the spinney. Ahead the wall of vegetation rises up like a mass of interlocking pipes, each traced with white. I can hear gasping in front of me, short breaths wrenched from the air. Branches scratch my face. The path snakes around, a twisting dark tunnel. Just when I think I must be heading back the way I came, it opens into a small clearing.

The clearing is overhung with trees. At the far end is a bench. And there on the ground, slumped against the bench, lies a dark shape. I run through the snow – how it drags at my feet – and kneel down by the bench. Catch him in my arms. He is so light. Nothing but a bag of bones. His face is turned towards mine. Once more he smiles up at me and tries to speak, to work some moisture into his mouth.

'Don't,' I say. 'Not now. Later.'

He shakes his head and whispers. 'Too late.'

'No,' I say. 'No.'

He puts his hand over mine. I don't think I've ever seen anyone look so sad, so compassionate. The lips seem to pull back still further from the pale gums. And again he whispers, 'Too late.'

'No.' But even as he says it I know that he is right. Already his breathing is getting more forced, his grip slackening. I clasp him to me as tightly as I can.

Too late.

In that moment everything I have lost rises up before me. I have emptied myself out. Let my life be governed by contrivance. For so long I felt that there wasn't enough of me to go round. That I would have to look to others to round me off and bulk me out. And so I tried to reinforce myself from the outside. Cloaking myself with quirks, piling up affectations, one on top of another.

I spoke with a voice that wasn't my own, that had never felt as if it belonged to me. I answered to urges that were not my own. Always dissembling, never knowing what I meant. And all the time this voice, this lost self inside me had been trying to get through. But I'd pushed it away. Let it starve. Banished it to some cold barren world while I dwelt in another barren and brittle world of my own. Instead, I'd opened myself up to all manner of intrusions, to stray imagined currents. To the attentions of other, unscrupulous parties. Had looked to them to take my life and run with it as they wished. How much easier it was to believe in signals from outside, steering me about, bending me to their will, rather than heeding a voice from within.

I'd scooped myself clean, made myself an empty vessel. Let others swarm in and take advantage, hoping that some of their substance, their spark might find its way into me. So much time spent cut off from the greater part of myself. A life unacknowledged, shaped only by humbug. Other people felt pain, joy, grief, were subject to all life's swings. But I'd cut myself off from all that. Bundled it up and cast it aside. All the while the affectations piled up higher, crushing the life out of me, pushing it further and further away.

Look. Just look what I have become. I go through the motions, that is all. Inside, there is nothing to me. Nothing left. An empty husk, a pathetic teetering creature. And at last I see. See that this ghost, this poor sad creature dying in my arms, is more real than I have ever been.

I want to press him back into me, to fill this emptiness inside. But it is too late. Too late to reclaim myself. I hold this frail balsa body against mine, the breaths coming now in shudders through the loose cheeks. Stroke the side of his head – the sharp hair, the papery ears – trying to summon words of comfort, while he tries to do the same for me. But there is no comfort to be had. Not anymore.

His eyelids begin to quiver. His breathing grows slower and slower, like a train fighting its way up a steep slope, and finally stops.

Still I hold him against me, tighter than ever. He is so light, so fragile. I feel his bones start to crack. He is crumbling away in my arms, disappearing into dust. At last there is nothing left. Nothing but this sad, reproachful stain that seems to sit upon the snow for a while, then fades away.

I am lost. Lost to myself. This soul within me had cried out, struggling to make itself be heard. But I had ignored it. I'd turned away and let it wither and die from neglect. Now there is no reclaiming it. No filling this emptiness that rolls and echoes inside me. It is too late. And I see that I will stay this way for as long as I live. Alone, separated from everything that might have let me join the great mass of humankind. A pale wraith, having no self or substance of my own, drifting through the remainder of my days in this barren, purposeless haze.

The snow is falling. I lie there as it heaps itself on my shoulders. Hoping that if I stay for long enough the snow might bind us together again. And all the while knowing that it cannot. Nothing can do that now. It is too late. At last, when the cold has quite entered my bones, I rise to my feet and begin to walk back towards the house.

THE END

BEHIND THE SCENES AT THE MUSEUM
Kate Atkinson

WINNER OF THE WHITBREAD BOOK OF THE YEAR AWARD

'WITHOUT DOUBT ONE OF THE FINEST NOVELS
I HAVE READ FOR YEARS'
Mary Loudon, *The Times*

Ruby Lennox was conceived grudgingly by Bunty and born
while her father, George, was in the Dog and Hare in
Doncaster telling a woman in an emerald dress and a D-cup
that he wasn't married. Bunty had never wanted to marry
George, but he was all that was left. She really wanted to be
Vivien Leigh or Celia Johnson, swept off to America by a
romantic hero. But here she was, stuck in a flat above the pet
shop in an ancient street beneath York Minster, with
sensible and sardonic Patricia aged five, greedy cross-patch
Gillian who refused to be ignored, and Ruby . . .

Ruby tells the story of The Family, from the day at the
end of the nineteenth century when a travelling French
photographer catches frail beautiful Alice and her children,
like flowers in amber, to the startling, witty, and memorable
events of Ruby's own life.

'WRITTEN WITH AN EXTRAORDINARY PASSION . . . PACKED
WITH IMAGES OF BEWITCHING POTENCY, THIS IS AN
ASTOUNDING BOOK'
The Times

'WITTY AND ORIGINAL . . . A REMARKABLE DEBUT NOVEL'
Daily Mirror

'ENCHANTING. IT HOPS WITH SPRIGHTLY OMNISCIENCE FROM
PAST TO FUTURE AND BACK AGAIN'
Sunday Times

'A FIRST NOVEL WRITTEN SO FLUENTLY AND WITTILY
THAT I SAILED THROUGH IT AS THOUGH BLOWN BY AN
EXHILARATING WIND. I LOVED IT'
Margaret Forster

0 552 996181

BLACK SWAN

A SELECTED LIST OF FINE WRITING
AVAILABLE FROM BLACK SWAN

THE PRICES SHOWN BELOW WERE CORRECT AT THE TIME OF GOING TO PRESS. HOWEVER TRANSWORLD PUBLISHERS RESERVE THE RIGHT TO SHOW NEW RETAIL PRICES ON COVERS WHICH MAY DIFFER FROM THOSE PREVIOUSLY ADVERTISED IN THE TEXT OR ELSEWHERE.

99618 1	BEHIND THE SCENES AT THE MUSEUM	Kate Atkinson	£6.99
99532 0	SOPHIE	Guy Burt	£5.99
99568 1	DEMOLISHING BABEL	Michael Carson	£5.99
99692 0	THE PRINCE OF TIDES	Pat Conroy	£6.99
99602 5	THE LAST GIRL	Penelope Evans	£5.99
99589 4	RIVER OF HIDDEN DREAMS	Connie May Fowler	£5.99
99599 1	SEPARATION	Dan Franck	£5.99
99616 5	SIMPLE PRAYERS	Michael Golding	£5.99
99609 2	FORREST GUMP	Winston Groom	£5.99
99538 X	GOOD AS GOLD	Joseph Heller	£6.99
99605 X	A SON OF THE CIRCUS	John Irving	£7.99
99567 3	SAILOR SONG	Ken Kesey	£6.99
99542 8	SWEET THAMES	Matthew Kneale	£6.99
99037 X	BEING THERE	Jerzy Kosinski	£4.99
99595 9	LITTLE FOLLIES	Eric Kraft	£5.99
99580 0	CAIRO TRILOGY 1: PALACE WALK	Naguib Mahfouz	£7.99
99569 X	MAYBE THE MOON	Armistead Maupin	£5.99
99649 1	WAITING TO EXHALE	Terry McMillan	£5.99
99603 3	ADAM'S WISH	Paul Micou	£5.99
99597 5	COYOTE BLUE	Christopher Moore	£5.99
99536 3	IN THE PLACE OF FALLEN LEAVES	Tim Pears	£5.99
99664 5	YELLOWHEART	Tracy Reed	£5.99
99130 9	NOAH'S ARK	Barbara Trapido	£6.99
99647 5	LAPSING	Jill Paton Walsh	£5.99
99673 4	DINA'S BOOK	Herbjørg Wassmo	£6.99
99500 2	THE RUINS OF TIME	Ben Woolfenden	£4.99

All Transworld titles are available by post from:

Book Service By Post, PO Box 29, Douglas, Isle of Man IM99 1BQ

Credit cards accepted. Please telephone 01624 675137, Fax 01624 670923 or Internet http://www. bookpost.co.uk for details.

Please allow £0.75 per book for post and packing UK.
Overseas customers allow £1 per book for post and packing.